First Impressions

DEBRA WHITE SMITH

HARVEST HOUSE PUBLISHERS

EUGENE, OREGON

Pride and Prejudice quotes are taken from Jane Austen, *Pride and Prejudice* in *The Complete Novels of Jane Austen,* vol. 1 (New York: Modern Library, 1992).

Cover by Koechel Peterson & Associates, Inc., Minneapolis, Minnesota

Published in association with the literary agency of Alive Communications, Inc., 7680 Goddard Street, Suite 200, Colorado Springs, CO 80920

FIRST IMPRESSIONS
Copyright © 2004 by Debra White Smith
Published by Harvest House Publishers
Eugene, Oregon 97402

ISBN 0-7394-4031-4

Printed in the United States of America

For Dr. Michael Murphy, the professor who first introduced me to Jane Austen.

Cast

Calvin Barclay: Based on Charles Bingley from *Pride and Prejudice*. Dave Davidson's good friend and a veterinarian in London, Texas.

Carissa Barclay: Based on Caroline Bingley from *Pride and Prejudice*. Like most of the single women in London, Texas, Carissa would be thrilled to marry Dave Davidson.

Cheri Locaste: Based on Charlotte Lucas from *Pride and Prejudice*. Eddi Boswick's friend, Cheri is a no-nonsense pragmatic who has never been accused of being a romantic, or being spontaneous. She teaches English at London High School.

Conner Boswick: Based on Mr. Collins from *Pride and Prejudice*. Conner is an eligible bachelor and vice president of Boswick Oil in Houston, Texas.

Dave Davidson: Based on Mr. Darcy from *Pride and Prejudice*. Dave owns a ranch outside of London, Texas. Handsome and untamed, he fends off the numerous women eager to make his acquaintance…and so much more.

Eddi Boswick: Based on Elizabeth Bennet from *Pride and Prejudice*. The middle Boswick daughter, Eddi moves to London, Texas, to start her new law practice. Brillant yet practical, she isn't expecting to have her world shaken by love.

Edward Boswick: Based on Mr. Bennet from *Pride and Prejudice*. The Boswick patriarch, Edward chose his own career over a life in high society as a family employee of Boswick Oil. Edward lives in Houston with his wife, Mary.

George Wallace: Based on Georgianna Darcy from *Pride and Prejudice*. George is Dave Davidson's younger brother.

Jenny Boswick: Based on Jane Bennet from *Pride and Prejudice*. The eldest Boswick daughter, Jenny is a community college coach who lives north of Houston in The Woods, Texas.

Linda Boswick: Based on Lydia Bennet from *Pride and Prejudice*. The youngest Boswick daughter, Linda's goal in life is to be the life of the party.

Madelynne DeBloom: Based on Lady Catherine de Bourgh from *Pride and Prejudice*. Dave Davidson's aunt, Mrs. DeBloom is the owner of the community theater, which is operated in her mansion named Huntington House. Mrs. DeBloom stepped in as Dave's mother when his parents were killed.

Mary Boswick: Based on Mrs. Bennet from *Pride and Prejudice*. The Boswick matriarch, Mary is a high-strung woman who majors in complaining about her nerves and trying to manipulate her daughters' love lives. She lives in Houston with her husband, Edward.

Rick Wallace: Based on Mr. Wickham from *Pride and Prejudice*. Rick enjoys making himself look much better than he is. The woman he's interested in is usually the one who is closest. He is a policeman in Houston, Texas, and a foster "cousin" to Dave Davidson.

One

⁓⁓

"'It is a truth universally acknowledged, that a single man in possession of a good fortune must be in want of a wife.'" Madelynne DeBloom looked up from reading her cherished copy of *Pride and Prejudice*. She glanced around the Victorian mansion's parlor.

Eddi Boswick languidly shifted in the velvet-covered settee and followed the aging woman's gaze. It fell smack on her nephew, Dave Davidson. He owned a 400-acre ranch outside London, Texas, and just happened to be single. By the resigned looks of the dark-haired, boot-clad cowboy, he was not thrilled to be cooped up half the day with a bunch of literary types. He narrowed his right eye and smirked as if the *last* thing he wanted was a wife—despite Jane Austen and any female in town.

Mrs. DeBloom, tall and thin and aristocratic, continued reading as if her nephew agreed. "'However little known the feelings or views of such a man may be on his first entering a neighborhood, this truth is so well fixed in the minds of the surrounding families, that he is considered as the rightful property of some one or other of their daughters.'"

Mrs. DeBloom laid her book on the Queen Anne tea table by which she stood. The smell of her ever-present Tea Rose perfume commanded the air around her just as the lady commanded the group. This time her haughty blue gaze fell upon Eddi like a vulture pinpointing her prey.

"Miss Boswick," she began in a shrill voice, "from what I understand, you constructed a Master's thesis on Jane Austen. Would you care to expound on Austen's opening lines from *Pride and Prejudice?*"

"Well..." Eddi coughed and glanced around the room.

All twenty people observed her as if she were the small town's literary guru—everyone except Dave Davidson. That gentleman had apparently endured enough bookish musings this lazy Saturday morning. He'd pulled out his Palm Pilot and was examining the screen as if reviewing a schedule.

Eddi tried to dismiss Mrs. DeBloom's sullen nephew. But *he* was the one who seized her attention. The irony was that Eddi had never been arrested by the cowboy type. Rumor had it, his wealthy aunt even purchased his ranch for him.

She pinched the seam in the settee and tried to concentrate on the question before her. "Well..." she repeated. "Of course, Austen created the epitome of romantic comedies. Her commentary on society was not only subtle, it was brilliant." Eddi waved her hand, "Her opening lines are a clear example of her subtle humor."

She cut a glance back to Dave. His indolent yawning reminded her of a long-maned, sepia-eyed lion who ruled his den—except this lion wore blue jeans with a hole in one knee and a faded denim shirt that had suffered hundreds of washes. Dave's face scrunched as he rubbed work-worn fingers along his shadowed jaw. He shook his head and pressed a button on the Palm Pilot.

The lion needs a haircut...and a shave...and some lessons in being more polite, Eddi thought. In the times she had seen Dave around town and at church, she deduced much the same about him. He never looked or acted much differently, even at Sunday morning services.

She glanced back to Mrs. DeBloom. The lady's right eye twitched. Eddi figured she was ready for the complete answer.

"What Jane Austen is saying," Eddi rushed and forced her attention to the issue at hand, "is that when a single man of large fortune moves to a neighborhood, the women in the community will assume he is looking for or in need of a wife—whether he really is or not."

An unceremonious comment spewed from the jeans-clad lion, "You can say *that* again!"

Caution suggested Eddi shouldn't look at Dave. She joined the room's occupants and looked anyway. His cynical appraisal rested upon Eddi.

"Whatsa matter, Dave?" a masculine voice called from across the parlor. "The ladies been husslin' ya lately?"

Eddi tried to follow the voice to a man who sounded like the new church youth director. Her perusal was interrupted when a nearby college man said, "Poor baby."

In the seat next to Dave, Calvin Barclay erupted into good-natured guffaws. The fair-haired veterinarian whacked his friend on the back. "Would that we were all so tormented."

Dave's face settled into a hard-lipped scowl. He shoved the Palm Pilot into his shirt pocket, rose from the straight-backed chair, and marched from the room. His snake-skin boots clipped against the polished wooden floor with the rhythm of a horse's canter. Head high, he looked as if he belonged in a royal procession, with himself in the lead, naturally.

You don't have to worry about me, Mister, Eddi thought as Mrs. DeBloom cleared her throat. *I'm not in the market for the arrogant, untamed type—no matter how much money he has...or how nice his hair is...or his eyes...or his build.* Eddi frowned at the last glimpse of his broad shoulders. Dave Davidson was *not* her type—not even a little.

"As you were saying, Eddi?" The town's self-appointed cultural guardian shoved a pointed look at her nephew's retreating back.

"Actually, I…I was pretty much through, so I guess I'll just rest my case," she said with a faint smile and a demure downward glance at the oriental rug.

Calvin's chuckle escalated into outright laughter. "Oh, I get it!" he said. "I rest my case…and you're a lawyer! Ha! What a hoot!"

Eddi appraised Calvin and wondered how the easy-going veterinarian could be such good friends with someone as sullen and proud as Dave Davidson.

A round of chortles scurried across a room that was replete with a marble fireplace and French antiques. Eddi picked up her cup of cinnamon tea, rested her lips against the china rim, and sipped the inviting liquid. As the sweet warmth slipped down her throat, she basked in the general acceptance from the surrounding participants. After six months of hard labor, London, Texas, was finally acknowledging Eddi as part of the community.

The first few weeks after she opened her law practice, she had wondered whether or not she could succeed in such a town. More than once, a good ol' boy from the neighborhood traipsed into her office, took one look at the young, blonde female behind the desk, and asked to see the lawyer. When Eddi informed them that *she* was the lawyer—not the secretary—several of them banged out of the office. In this part of the woods, nineteenth-century attitudes thrived unchecked.

Maybe Jane Austen won't be too much of a stretch for them, Eddi thought.

Surprisingly, Mrs. DeBloom had procured a solid crowd this June morning to discuss the new community play based on *Pride and Prejudice.* The town had been buzzing all week about who would be cast in the different roles. Madelynne DeBloom, the theater's sponsor, would announce her cast choices at the first practice in two weeks.

Eddi was hoping to play the part of Jane Bennet, the supporting role and sister of the book's heroine, Elizabeth Bennet. But Eddi would be happy for whatever part might befall her. Any hobby would help ease the boredom after she closed her office every day. While Eddi had managed to solicit some clients, business was still far from booming.

A rumble of thunder rolled across the mansion as rain pelted the roof.

"Aunt Maddy," Dave's call floated from the entryway, "Tammy says the brunch is ready."

Eddi glimpsed Dave at the parlor's opening before he removed his broad-shouldered self back to the dining room.

"Well, that would be good timing." Mrs. DeBloom nodded and shifted the lace collar on her straight floral dress. "I can't talk over this rain anyway." She looked past the top of her reading glasses and peered out the window behind Eddi's head.

"We've been under a tornado watch all morning," she continued. "Let's hope it's not upgraded to a warning."

The group collectively scrutinized the gray pall shrouding the classic neighborhood. Eddi had learned last fall that tornadoes were a common threat in east Texas. Few residents took tornado watches lightly.

"Let's adjourn to the dining room, shall we?" Mrs. DeBloom suggested, her troubled gaze never leaving the window.

The room's occupants shuffled to their feet as Eddi settled her cup back into its saucer, set it on the coffee table, and stood.

She wasted no time joining the crowd and filling her plate in the buffet line. She caught a glimpse of Dave and Calvin heading through the kitchen toward the back door. A porch that wrapped around the back and side of the house waited on the other side. Eddi looked out one of the floor-to-ceiling windows to note that the rain had stopped as quickly as it started. Only a fine mist now caressed the yard full of lush oaks. The air took on a surreal pink glow that hinted of another storm brewing. Her plate of finger foods in hand, she decided that accessing the porch's side through the parlor's French doors would provide a safe distance from the two men.

Her grumbling stomach dictated haste, so Eddi hurried through the parlor and opened the French doors. Ensconced in the scent of fresh honeysuckle, she stepped onto the porch and gingerly dodged puddles along the floor. Several wicker chairs and snack tables lined the porch. Eddi settled into the seat nearest the door because the chair cushion was dry.

Mrs. DeBloom's home sat atop a small hill, just inside the city limits. Her peach orchard was situated just outside the city limits. The mansion—traditionally dubbed Huntington House—overlooked London and served as a regal focal point for the citizenry.

Eddi took a bite of one of the finger sandwiches. Enjoying the delightful taste of chicken mixed with pineapple and pecans, she eyed the weather. In the distance, twin gigantic thunderheads sent towering plumes into the sky. They resembled two boxers squared off for a fight. Eddi squinted and strained to listen for any thunder. A curtain that looked like fog hung between rows of peach trees a quarter mile away.

"Must be more rain," Eddi mumbled between bites of crisp broccoli coated in ranch dip.

The air was as still as Sam Houston's statue on the town square and held so much moisture it could be squeezed out by hand. Eddi eyed the distant rolling hills, covered in pine trees and ample grass. The emerald carpet attested to the frequent rains that had characterized late May and early June.

"This looks like a good spot," a deep voice drawled from around the corner. "At least the cushions are dry."

The voice belonged to the exact man she wanted to avoid. Eddi cringed and glanced over her left shoulder. While her chair hugged the wall, the dining set around the corner sat closer to the bannister. She caught intermittent glimpses of masculine legs as two men settled into side-by-side chairs.

"Yes, dry cushions. What a concept!" Calvin Barclay agreed. "I'm going straight home as soon as I can get outta here and change pants. Why didn't you *tell* me I was going to sit in a puddle of water?"

"I tried, you idiot!" Dave chided. "You were too busy looking at the clouds to listen to me." A scrape and thud suggested one of the men had scooted a wicker chair after sitting in it.

"I'm telling you, man, those clouds look evil. There is a tornado watch on. I don't like this pink business either. Have you forgotten? Last time the air looked like this, we wound up with a tornado. Even though the thing skipped over London, a tornado is a tornado. And I think I smell one!"

Two pairs of legs remained visible around the corner. At the end of one pair Eddi observed cowboy boots sticking out of jeans frayed at the hem. The other pair of legs ended with a brown leather loafer on the right foot. The left foot rested on the table's lower rail and sported a tan sock with a large hole at the toe. The missing shoe lay on the floor beneath Calvin's foot.

"I thought Aunt Maddy was going to have some real food," Dave complained. "I could go for some barbeque and potato salad."

"When have you ever known any meeting like this to have real food?" Calvin answered. "It's the stuff artsy chick parties are made of, man."

A companionable silence settled upon the men, and Eddi imagined they were devouring the very eats they'd just complained of. She debated whether to ease into the parlor or stay put. Eddi's attention was teased back to the men. Her stomach fluttered.

Better go back inside, she thought and wished for her elder sister, Jenny. A good dose of Jenny's common sense would end

Eddi's distraction for a man as suited for her as hay string for lilies. Besides, Eddi doubted Dave even knew her name. The times she encountered him, he acted as if Eddi were a local farmer in overalls, rather than a tall blonde female dressed in her finest city gear.

Eddi screwed the lid off her bottled water and downed a swallow of the cool liquid. A faint trace of ozone mingled with the smell of honeysuckle and fresh rain. Eddi observed the approaching storm with new interest. The curtain of rain neared. The sound of rushing droplets promised the thunderhead, now inky and swirling, was leveling a path toward London. Her hand paused on the edge of her plate as she reflected upon Calvin's tornado worries.

With a wrinkle of her nose, she shook her head. *It's just more rain,* she insisted and stood up to go back into the mansion. But Calvin's humor-filled jibe halted Eddi's progress.

"So, are you going to sign up for the play?"

"Remember, I just came to watch you make a fool of yourself," Dave said in a flat tone that brooked no argument.

"Yep—and because your aunt would have *killed* you if you didn't show."

"Gotta keep my main lady happy," Dave acquiesced. "But it only goes so far."

"I hear she wants you to play Darcy."

"Who's Darcy?" Dave asked.

Eddi rolled her eyes. "He just happens to be one of the most famous heroes of all classic literature," she mouthed.

"You slay me, man," Calvin said through a chortle. "Darcy is the hero of *Pride and Prejudice*—uh, you know, the play your aunt's putting together. I'm sure Mrs. DeBloom thinks you're hopeless."

"Pretty much—and proud of it," he affirmed. "Last thing I need is more culture. I've had my fill of it."

"Ah, come on," Calvin urged. "You need to be in this play. The exposure will do you good. I promise, when you enter that first scene as Darcy, every single woman in the audience will want your autograph after opening night."

"Oh, brother," Eddi murmured.

"That's the last thing I need right now," Dave retorted.

"Ah, yes, I remember. You're the guy with all the ladies chasing you."

"I've learned it's smart to lie low in this town, that's all I'm saying. These local women must not get out much. They act like I must be dying to get married next weekend. To put it bluntly, I haven't seen one around here who's caught my eye enough to let her put a matrimonial noose around *my* neck."

"Whoa, now!" Calvin's foot found its loafer. "What about the new lady lawyer? What's her name…Eddi, Eddi Boswick. That woman is class personified."

Warmth rushed over Eddi as she anticipated Dave's response. She sat back down, forgot all about her sister Jenny, and negated every scrap of common sense. Her sole concern became whether or not the attractive rancher found her worth pursuing.

If he does… she thought with a sly grin, *maybe I won't be so hard to catch.* Eddi scooted back in her chair.

"So, aren't you going to say anything?" Calvin prodded.

"I hadn't planned on it," Dave retorted.

A cautious precognition suggested Eddi should stop eavesdropping. She rubbed her fingertips along the buttons on her linen jacket. A daredevil streak challenged her to ignore caution just this once.

What has caution gotten me so far? she asked. *An empty townhouse with a dog pound refugee and two resentful felines to keep me warm at night.* She crossed her legs and gazed past the honeysuckle-laden trellis to a woodpecker that was determined to pound his beak into the oak at the porch's corner. All the while she pined for any signal of interest from the renegade rancher.

"Oh, so we're not commenting on the lawyer?" Calvin teased. "Why not?"

Dave remained silent. Eddi looked down and pulled at the top of a piece of broccoli.

"Whatsa matter?" Calvin blurted. "Are you afraid of her?"

A caustic laugh bounced around the porch. "Yeah, right," Dave retorted.

"Or maybe you're worried she's too smart for you! Ha!" Calvin laughed. "That's a good one."

Eddi snapped her attention from the broccoli to the porch's corner. Calvin slid his chair back and his legs disappeared.

"Oh, shut up," Dave groused. "If you must know, Eddi Boswick would have to be way more classy to keep my attention for long. In the first place, she's too short."

Eddi's mouth fell open. *Short!* she thought, *I'm nearly five foot nine.*

Calvin snorted. "She's as tall as I am."

"You're too short, too," Dave shot back.

"It's a good thing, 'cause I'm not going out with you!"

"And she's too prissy for my taste," Dave added as if his friend had never cracked the joke.

Prissy! Eddi's warmth from Calvin's praise escalated into heat. Her curiosity ignited in ire. Her rebel interest in Dave plummeted to a crashing death.

"Yep, too prissy," Dave added more firmly. "And—and since she's a lawyer…you know the type…she probably runs off at the mouth day and night and likes to pick fights wherever she can find them."

Eddi clenched her fists in her lap. The corners of her mouth turned down. Her eyes narrowed.

"I bet she even wears combat boots to bed!" Dave complained.

"Combat boots!" she hissed. Eddi stood and stepped toward the men.

A gust of humid wind whipped around the porch and swept her plastic fork across the wicker table. Mrs. DeBloom's empty garbage can crashed into the street and rolled to the hill's precipice. Eddi's concern for the weather postponed her spontaneous urge to defend herself.

She glanced skyward. A mile away, curling patches of clouds jabbed at each other, and the pink hue phased into gray-green. The neighbor's basset hound started a mournful howl an acre away.

"So, I guess you're waiting on one of those long-legged city women who stands six feet tall and looks like she stepped off the pages of *Mademoiselle*." Calvin's latest claim diverted Eddi back to the insufferable conversation around the corner.

Eddie inspected her slender legs that protruded from the tailored city shorts just above her knees. A pair of high-heeled sandals wrapped her narrow feet. She thought the outfit was classy, even if the high and mighty Dave Davidson did not.

Okay, so these legs aren't going to get me on the cover of Mademoiselle, she had to admit. *But they were good enough for a regional championship in cross country…and third place in state.*

"I'm not so picky that I want a supermodel sort," Dave remarked after a pause. "But the ladies are going to have to get better than London's selection before I think of settling down. If I ever *do* decide to spend my time with a lady, she's going to have to like me for who I am, *not* what I own. And she'll have to be interested in more than keeping up with her friends' weddings or who's going to be football sweetheart this year."

"Why don't you just marry your Aunt Maddy, then?" Calvin asked. "She seems really broad-minded, and I think she'd love you if you were broke and starving."

Eddi chuckled. *I like you, Calvin Barclay,* she thought.

"Oh, get outta here, will ya?" Dave barked. "Give it a rest. What's gotten into you anyway? You're starting to sound like Aunt Maddy. She's always trying to get me married off—but she's determined it should be to an aristocratic sort who will understand my 'position' in life." His voice took on a falsetto mockery then turned to a low growl. "Namely, her best friend's daughter."

"I really wish you'd give the attorney a chance. I bet she'd give you a run for your money on anything you want to discuss and turn your cowboy brain inside out before you knew what hit ya."

How about an internship with a leading barrister in the real *London, buddy?* Eddi placed a hand on her hip. *Or six weeks in the Amazon jungle helping a Bible translator? I bet there's nothing in your cow pastures that can match that!* She sat back down and decided not to waste her time confronting Dave Davidson. He wasn't worth the energy.

"If you're so impressed with the attorney, Calvin, why don't *you* ask her out," Dave challenged, "and leave me in peace?"

Eddi's eyes rounded. She scrutinized a puddle of water on the porch's slick, gray surface. She and Calvin had shared several pleasant conversations around town, but she never considered him more than a friend. Interestingly enough, Eddi suspected Calvin sensed the lack of chemistry as well. She had even wondered if her sister Jenny might like to meet him, but Jenny had been seeing Hal Gomez for months now.

"Ah, I don't know," Calvin hedged. "I don't think I'm her type."

"Oh, and you think *I* am? Please, don't flatter me!" Dave added with a sarcastic twist. "Besides all that, why don't *you* try out for the part of Darby?"

"That's *Darcy,*" Calvin said, his words thick with laughter.

"Whatever," Dave drawled.

"Really, if you don't think you're going to try out, I believe I will."

"Be my guest," Dave agreed. "Maybe you'll get lucky and the lawyer will play the leading lady."

"One day, you're going to regret this attitude," Calvin prophesied. "Mark my word, before the summer's over, I predict you'll be on your knees begging her—"

Dave's scornful jeer hurled Eddi into action. *Enough is enough!* she thought. *Even though I'm not going to confront the jerk, I don't have to sit here and listen to this a minute longer!* She snatched up her plate and bottled water, stood, and cast a final glance toward the approaching storm.

She had been so focused on the conversation she failed to realize the wind had stopped blowing and an eerie silence permeated the countryside—a silence, broken only by the basset hound's worried whines. The thunderhead, once safely in the distance, now bore down upon the outskirts of London like a blackish-green omen of doom.

The curtain of rain in the peach orchard oscillated as a snake-like tail, white as cotton, dipped from the sky, stirred up a cloud of debris, and hurled peach trees into the air.

Eddi dropped her plate and water bottle. A gurgled exclamation parted her lips as the funnel zipped back into the clouds.

A hard-line wind swooshed into the deathly silence with a gust that whipped at Eddi's French braid and shoved her linen jacket away from her body. The snaky tail dipped to earth again. A trainlike roar testified to the beast's evil intent as it tore a jagged path toward the mansion.

Two

Dave shared a wide-eyed stare with Calvin. He looked back toward the peach orchard to make sure he wasn't hallucinating. Sure enough, the white-tailed monster dropped into the orchard and cut a zigzag trail toward the house.

A hot wave sent a flash of perspiration across Dave's forehead. He sprang up and stepped forward. Out of the corner of his eye, he caught sight of Eddi Boswick standing on the porch's west wing—her face ashen, her eyes wide.

Whirling on Calvin, Dave said, "Get inside and tell Aunt Maddy and the others to get into the storm cellar."

Calvin knocked over the wicker chair as he scrambled toward the back door.

With each second the wind's velocity increased. What once seemed a distant train's rhythm now crashed against Dave's ears like the roar of a demonic dragon. By the time he took another glance at the funnel, the beast had skipped within three hundred yards of the city limit sign. The snowy tornado ripped leaves off trees and bushes and crushed them into its unforgiving vortex.

Dave pivoted toward Eddi. She covered her mouth with her hand and backed against the house. "Tornado!" As she turned for the French doors, her hoarse bellow was barely discernible.

Again Dave observed the tornado and debated the best route of escape. The devil snaked across the landscape, dipping and weaving like a cobra ready to strike.

Dave hurled himself toward Eddi and glanced at the cyclone every other second. The beast sucked up the roof of a storage building on the edge of the orchard. A klatch of birds struggled to escape the maelstrom only to disappear into the pale interior. Dave's gut twisted with a nauseous quake.

By the time he got to Eddi, she was clawing at the doorknob. Her contorted face accompanied her screaming "Tornado!" as a warning to the mansion's occupants. But her shrieks were lost in the gyrating monster's hiss and boom.

Dave grabbed her arm and screamed "No!" into her ear. "Calvin's already warning them. There's a storm cellar on the east side of the house. We've got to get in it!"

"Mrs. DeBloom!" Eddi shrieked and tried to force the door open. But the vacuumous spiral insisted the door remain closed.

Dave cupped his hands around her ear and screamed, "Calvin has warned them." He cast a final glance toward the serpent, which was a mere hundred yards away. Grinding his teeth, he decided this was no place or time for an argument.

He grabbed her arm and pulled, leaving Eddi no choice but to follow. The wind became less chaotic and more directive. The relentless suction urged Dave to release his will to the inevitable, to allow the tornado to gobble him and Eddi as it had the birds. The warrior within refused that option. Dave ducked his head and marched toward the back porch. His grip on Eddi tightened, and a primeval force urged him to wrap his arm around her. She didn't resist, but rather clung to his side and joined him in trudging toward the steps. They inched past overturned furniture as the wind-driven rain blurred their path.

Out of nowhere a mammoth limb crashed onto the porch. Its wiry arms shoved the pair against the wall. Clutching Eddi, Dave's knees hit the floor. He covered his eyes with his free arm and tumbled onto the porch's gritty surface. Pain, like shards of glass, pierced his knees and elbows and chin. Eddi toppled beside him. Her French braid slapped him in the mouth. The taste of hairspray mingled with the feel of grit between his teeth. The funnel's suction yanked them from the limb's grasp and tugged them toward the storm like a seductive lover. As they slipped toward the demon's clutches, a planter filled with shredded elephant ears banged into them.

Dave instinctively covered Eddi and took the brunt of the clay pot that pummeled the small of his back. He winced and bit the end of his tongue, tasting blood. When the darts of pain subsided, Dave realized Eddi was sobbing. Her body's quivering vibrated against his chest. Dave responded with trembling of his own. He buried his face in her floral-scented hair, closed his eyes, and released a heavenward plea for a miracle.

The air hurled tiny debris bullets into Dave's skin like cactus thorns. As the roar became a defeaning death call, Dave dared to open his eyes but a centimeter. Less than seventy-five yards away, the funnel twisted and waved on the hillside as if debating what to destroy next. For several seconds, the ghastly specter appeared to remain in one spot. Then, as if yielding to the beckoning of a thousand demons, it veered north and headed down the hill, toward the town square. The crash and thunder of uprooting trees and smashed buildings mingled with the roar.

As the noise subsided, Eddi nudged Dave's chest. Coughing against the thick air, he raised enough for her to peer at the receding storm. Near the town square, the tornado ripped at houses and businesses and hurtled toward the old Lone Star Theater. The theater's roof exploded as if it were flimsy straw. The next target in the twister's path was the county courthouse, a hundred-year-old remnant of the past.

"Oh, no," Dave groaned.

"Oh, no, not the town square," Eddi rasped. "My office is there."

Like a capricious adolescent, the funnel rose to the sky as quickly as it had dropped. When the white vortex disappeared, Dave relaxed and sank back to the floor. He stared straight up at the porch's fractured ceiling. The sound of dripping rain punctuated the silence—a silence that screamed of a contest with death.

Soon, Dave realized his arms were still wrapped around Eddi. She opened her eyes again. The two stared at each other while a deceptively gentle breezed rustled the invasive branch's leaves. A stray raindrop plopped onto the end of Eddi's nose. With a wobbly smile, Dave whisked aside the moisture and trailed his finger to the puddle of tears beneath her eyes, the color of a gray kitten's down. For just an instant, admiration, gratitude, and a hint of fire sharpened her gaze.

Dave marveled that any attraction Eddi felt for him was most likely genuine. He had spent too many years with women throwing themselves at him because of what he owned, not because they really cared for him. Now, nobody in London knew the extent of his possessions, his legal name, or that the name he'd assumed was his childhood nickname. Therefore, her response could only be linked to her appreciation of him as a man—period.

When he left Dallas three years ago, Dave had purposefully chosen a tiny, secluded town in which to settle. He'd checked into a hotel and roamed the streets and stores for a month before deciding London, Texas, population 6,352, was a safe place for him and his Aunt Maddy to move to. No one had recognized him. No one—not even Calvin Barclay. Most of the residents could trace their roots back three or four generations—families who were born and raised in London and didn't travel or read enough to discover Dave's identity.

When Eddi Boswick moved in from Houston, Dave cringed the first few times she looked him square in the eyes. Finally, he understood she possessed no idea who he really was, despite the fact that she arrived from the "outside world."

Now with her in his arms Dave tried to deny what he wouldn't have ever admitted to Calvin Barclay. She wasn't the only one experiencing the fire. Dave had had his eye on Eddi Boswick for months. The first Sunday she sashayed down the church aisle dressed in a stylish red suit, Dave possessed no idea what songs were sung or the sermon subject. In a church with four hundred attendees, he had easily escaped before someone introduced them. He'd spent the last six months "escaping."

Truth was, Calvin was right. The woman scared his boots off. For the first time in years, Dave was beginning to think he might have met up with a lady who had the character to look past his money and appreciate him for who he was. Instead of being elated by the possibility, Dave was terrified. He'd been on his own thirty-five years. The prospect of matrimony brought images of his parents' marriage—of lost harmony and bitter battles.

His gaze slid to Eddi's lips, and he figured he'd better put some space between them before he did something rash.

Eddi stirred in his arms and wiped strings of wet hair from her cheeks. "Would you mind letting go of me?" she growled. Her lips protruded in a stubborn line he'd seen on a few barracudas.

"Uh, sure," Dave mumbled. He released her and missed her warmth the second she rolled away. An impish urge prompted his next suggestion. "The tornado might come back, you know," Dave uttered before he considered the implications.

She leveled him a doubtful scowl that suggested he curb his tongue *for good.*

A flash of understanding pierced his conscience. Dave recalled every syllable of the conversation with Calvin. When he spotted Eddi, she had been standing just around the porch corner. *No telling how long she'd been there,* he thought, and he wondered if she overheard his negative comments.

Guilt stabbed his gut. Dave had been scrambling like a trapped calf to come up with a list of reasons why he shouldn't ask out Eddi Boswick. He'd been shocked that Calvin hadn't laughed him to scorn when he said she was too short, too prissy, and classless.

She struggled to her knees and attempted to stand. Dave grabbed the side of an overturned table and gained his footing, even though his aching back suggested he not stand straight. He rubbed at his stinging arms and face, and his palms came away lined with grit.

"I guess I'm covered in dirt," he said, his voice unsteady.

Eddi staggered across the porch like a one-legged sailor and stopped beside a high-heeled sandal, imbedded in the edge of the limb. Dave glanced down at her feet; one was without its shoe.

"Yes, you're covered," she said. Her lips tight, she struggled into the other shoe and stared at him as if he were about as interesting as a fence post. "You look like you've been slimed or something, actually," she added, no smile in sight.

"Oh, wow, thanks," Dave said with a grin as wobbly as his legs. "You do know how to flatter, don't you?"

"You should feel like you're in good company, then." She marched toward the parlor door.

Dave winced and stopped wondering if she'd heard what he said to Calvin. *Oh well,* he thought, *might be for the best.* He rubbed his gritty neck and relished the fact that no woman's noose rested there. Dave Davidson was still a free man.

"I'm going in to see if anybody was hurt," Eddi said and snapped open the parlor door.

"My guess is if we weren't, they couldn't have been. We came close to kissing that baby."

Rapid footsteps from the backyard preceded Calvin's voice. "Dave?" he bellowed.

"We're right here," Dave responded and attempted to peer through the branch that had ruptured the porch railing. He caught glimpses of his friend's blue shirt through the leaves as Calvin rounded the porch.

"Oh, my dear!" Mrs. DeBloom's aghast exclamation floated from the parlor. "You look absolutely wretched."

"I feel it," Eddi said as she slumped against the doorjamb.

Dave stifled the urge to rush to Eddi's side and hold her up. Despite his calm façade, his legs were weakening. He began doubting his ability to hold himself up—let alone her.

"And what about Dave?" Mrs. DeBloom's urgent inquiry brought on Dave's response. "I'm fine, Aunt Maddy," he called.

She appeared in the doorway, next to Eddi, her hair like tufts of cotton candy around her smudged cheeks. Her moist eyes brightened like bits of blue sky in a lined face drawn with anxiety.

"I am so relieved." She covered her lips with her fingertips. Mrs. DeBloom stepped toward Dave and then turned to Eddi. She looked back at Dave and posed a silent question.

"I'll be okay," he said. "Calvin's coming for me."

His aunt grasped Eddi's arm and walked into the parlor.

Calvin took the porch steps two at a time, all the while watching Dave as if he were a space alien. "Are you okay, man?" Calvin asked and gripped Dave's shoulder.

"Yeah," Dave grunted. He noticed a nasty gash along Calvin's jaw that oozed beads of blood. "Yow!" Dave winced. "Looks like you didn't come out without a fight."

His friend ran a finger along his injury and flinched. "We left the storm cellar door open as long as we could waiting on you two. But when we finally decided we had to shut the door, I jumped to it. I'd love to say this was some sort of hero's wound, but I actually tripped and scraped my chin on the steps. Really, I was so worried about you and Eddi, I was hardly thinking." Calvin's ginger-brown eyes rounded in candid certainty.

"We survived okay, I guess," Dave said. He glanced toward the parlor and noticed Eddi slumped on the sofa near the doorway. Dave's legs wobbled, and he decided he'd better join her. He rubbed the small of his back where that planter had landed and stumbled forward. "Sounds like everybody made it in the cellar okay."

"Yep, everybody but you two." Calvin moved closer and placed an arm around Dave's body.

The increasing tremors suggested he not reject his friend's assistance.

"What happened?" Calvin asked.

"Eddi was trying to get into the house to warn Aunt Maddy and the rest. I wound up dragging her away from the door. We were trying to make it off the porch and around to the storm cellar. But by that time, the tornado was nearly on top of us."

"You saw it?"

"Yeah," Dave said. Closing his eyes, he leaned against Calvin and reflected upon his own mortality. Raw horror blazed through him as if he were seeing the tornado all over again. "We watched it go down the hill. It took the roof off the theater and tore up some housetops. I hope nobody was killed."

"Let's just get you inside," Calvin urged. "You're going pale on me. I don't want you to go into shock or anything."

Dave attempted to wave aside his friend. "I'm going to be okay," he protested with a gruff edge. "You've seen one tornado, you've seen 'em all."

"Not when they're sucking at your collar," Calvin said.

Dave stumbled into the parlor, and glass crunched under his boots. Nearing the sofa, he perused the shattered row of windows at the front of the parlor and frowned. Not only were the windows sucked out, the large mirror on the south wall was shattered across the floor.

"Everybody okay in here?" Cheri Locaste, a high school English teacher, stepped into the parlor as the rest of the group tumbled out the front door.

"Yes, I believe so," Madelynne DeBloom said. "You people go on and make sure none of your houses were damaged. Tell everyone I'll be in touch."

"Okay, I will." Cheri eyed Eddi and Dave while attempting to untangle her waist-length ponytail. "Someone said they think the theater took a hit."

Mrs. DeBloom's eyes rounded, and she pivoted to face Cheri. "Oh, no."

"Yes, it did," Dave affirmed. "Eddi and I saw it take the roof off."

"Oh, no," Mrs. DeBloom repeated. "Whatever will we do about the play?" She waved her hand and shook her head. "Oh well, we'll worry about that tomorrow. Right now..." She turned back toward her nephew. "Here, Calvin," Mrs. DeBloom adjusted a pillow, "let him sit by Eddi," she suggested as if Dave were a five-year-old.

Dave lowered himself onto the couch near Eddi and rested his head on the back. His ears ached, and the tornado's roar echoed in his memory. He closed his eyes, but all he could see was a white-tailed demon dancing a hundred yards away. All he could feel was the funnel's suction and the panic that he and Eddi were history. Dave covered his gritty face with both hands and commanded himself to get a grip. He pressed his fingers against his eyes and shook his head.

"Okay, that's it," he mumbled and made a determined effort to clear his mind. The time had come to start acting like a man. "I need to get out to the ranch and see if there was any damage there." He opened his eyes and stared through the glassless windows.

"I wonder if my truck is okay," he added and couldn't stop the tremors that assaulted his hands, no matter how much mind control he asserted.

"Oh, and my car," Eddi groaned and struggled against the sofa's cozy folds. "I just got it out of the body shop last week after a drunk woman ran into it in the Wal-Mart parking lot." She stood and wobbled in her high heels.

Dave glowered at her feet. "Why don't you take those heels off, woman?" he growled and stood.

"For the same reason you aren't taking off your boots," she snapped. "There's glass all over the floor. Or haven't you noticed?"

Calvin chuckled, and Dave issued him a silent dare.

"I'm not so sure you two need to be walking around right now," Mrs. DeBloom fussed as she flitted from Dave to Eddi and back again.

"I'm going to be fine," Dave asserted. "I'm just a little shook up. That's all. We just got the living daylights scared out of us."

"We all did," Madelynne agreed as Eddi moved toward the entryway. "I was scared to death the tornado got you." Her voice wavered, and she released a garbled hiccough.

Dave turned toward the woman who had been a mother to him for the last sixteen years. "I'm not going to check out on you, Aunt Maddy," he said with a weak smile. He hugged his aunt and held her for a tight squeeze. Her ever-present Tea Rose perfume convinced him that nothing had really changed. "Don't you know I'm too ornery for any tornado?"

She clung to him and trembled. A decisive sniffle attested to her gaining control of her emotions. "I guess I need to go outside with everybody and see what's happened to the house."

"Yes. Let's go," Dave said.

"Oh, dear," Madelynne fussed, "if the theater roof is gone, where will we have the first practice?"

"We can have it at my house as long as you need to," Dave said before he thought through his offer. That would mean he'd be forced to put up with these literary types for weeks—including Eddi Boswick. And he'd be giving his aunt ample opportunity to squeeze him into the part as Darby or Darcy or whatever that guy's name was.

Eddi steadied herself against the side of the arched doorway that led into the entry. Calvin neared from behind and placed a hand along her waist. He spoke something that resembled an inquiry about her equilibrium. Eddi shook her head and moved from his clasp. As Calvin trailed her into the entryway, Dave recalled the feel of Eddi in his arms. He clenched his teeth and wondered how long it would take him to forget her crying against him.

"I guess what I need to do now," he said, "is see if my truck is okay and then head on home. Here I am offering my house as a place to practice, and for all I know the whole thing might be blown away." His sprawling ranch house and 400 acres rested just on the other side of the peach orchard. There were no guarantees that the twister hadn't bounced around awhile before they spotted it.

"I pray it's not." Mrs. DeBloom eyed her shattered windows. "Have you noticed the dining room?" She pointed to the place where they all had filled their plates minutes before. Like the parlor, the windows had been sucked out. The carpet was soggy. And the chicken sandwiches along with the rest of brunch were plastered against the north wall like a mixed-up smorgasbord. A sweet and sour odor testified to the wide array of cuisine.

"Holy toledo," Dave mumbled.

"I know," Madelynne agreed. "I'm going to need a place to stay until I can get the house repaired. "I hope your place wasn't hit. What will we do if we don't have a place to go?"

Dave rested an arm around his aunt's rigid shoulders and leaned toward her ear. "Aunt Maddy, don't worry," he whispered. "You know I'll cover it. Either you can stay at my house or I'll put you up in a hotel." With every minute that passed, Dave's heart pumped new strength into his body. He gave his aunt's shoulders a squeeze. The regal woman felt small and frail in his grasp, even though she nearly matched his six-foot frame.

Mrs. DeBloom gripped Dave's free hand and nodded. "I know, but sometimes I forget. I guess I just needed to be reminded." She smiled into her nephew's eyes. "You've been better to me than a dozen sons."

"And you deserve it all and more," Dave affirmed, glad to be the one who kept his aunt in the lifestyle she enjoyed her entire married life. No shock had been greater for her than examining her late husband's portfolio and discovering he had amassed as much debt as he had assets. All Madelynne had left was her air of status—until Dave made his fortune.

In companionable silence, the two followed Eddi and Calvin onto the front porch. The rain had stopped and white tuffs of harmless clouds lazed across the sky. The air smelled as if only the gentlest of spring rains had fallen. At the base of the hill, the whole town milled about the debris-ridden streets and assessed damage. Dave paused long enough to peer toward the theater. A group of men neared a crumble of shingles and wood that blocked Main Street. Nearby, the Lone Star Theater stood decapitated.

Mrs. DeBloom's tremorous sigh preceded her claim. "I can't look at it. I just can't!"

Dave steered her off the porch and picked his way across the front yard cluttered with leaves and shingles. When they rounded the house, they nearly ran into Eddi Boswick and Calvin beside the parked vehicles.

"This is too weird for words," Eddi was saying as she examined her shiny red Mustang. "I don't think there's a scratch on it."

Dave scrutinized his Chevy pickup twenty feet away. "Would that we were all so lucky," he grunted as he took in the monster-of-a-limb embedded in his windshield. He stepped around Eddi's Mustang toward his truck.

"Which one's your vehicle?" Eddi asked.

"The blue Chevy pickup," Dave said grimly. "The one with the limb shoved through the windshield." He looked toward the pine tree about ten feet away. Several low limbs had been twisted off as if the massive trunk were a mere flower stem. A quick survey of the unharmed parked cars revealed that he was the lucky guy who was blessed with one of the limbs.

"Ooo, that looks awful," Eddi said. Her high heels crunched into the gravel as she neared from behind.

Dave placed his hands on his hips and walked the remaining steps toward his beloved vehicle. While he could buy a whole fleet of the things, he liked this truck. It had served him well three years, and he held no plans of replacing it.

"Looks like it's just the windshield," Dave admitted and rounded the cab to the driver's side. He gripped the offending limb with both hands, ground his teeth, and hauled it out. Bits of glass toppled inside the cab and scattered across the hood with a series of clinks. As Dave shoved the sizable limb to the ground, a stab of pain erupted from his spine. He bit back a groan, hung his head, and grabbed the small of his back.

"Are you going to be okay?" Eddi neared and placed her hand on his arm.

Dave stepped away. "I'm fine," he groused.

"Uh, do you…need a ride anywhere?" Eddi asked. "Do you think you ought to go to the doctor?"

The pain subsided, and Dave barely looked at her. He didn't miss the impact of damp hair and gray eyes as large as a traumatized child's. An unexpected masculine instinct urged him nearer to this lovely lady he'd felt such a strong desire to protect.

"No thanks," he bit out and decided his better option was to run in the opposite direction. "No doctor for me—not right now anyway. Aunt Maddy and I are just going to drive out to my ranch to check and see if it was hit. We'll take her Cadillac. It's in the garage."

"Oh, well then, all right," Eddi answered.

Dave busied himself unlocking his door, but noticed that she had yet to leave. Once he opened the truck, he pointed a direct stare at her and raised his brows in silent query.

All traces of resentment had vanished from Eddi Boswick. Only gratitude and a hint of repentance crossed her face. "I just realized I never thanked you for protecting me," she offered. "I'm afraid your back injury was a direct result. Didn't that pot of elephant ears fall on you?"

"I've been hit by worse than a pot of elephant ears. Last week, one of my longhorns gave me a shove. That bull made the pot seem like a flea."

"Okay then," Eddi answered as if she didn't quite know what else to say.

Dave eyed her red toenails, peaking from the ends of those strappy sandals that hugged her arched feet. Right now even her toenails looked good. Everything about her looked good, down to her messy hair and smeared lipstick. All he could think about was the way her hair smelled when he buried his face next to her neck...and her warmth...and the fact that he'd really wanted to kiss her once that tornado disappeared.

Then, he'd acted like a teenager and made that flippant remark about the tornado possibly returning. No telling what impression he'd made. Maybe she thought he was hinting about starting a relationship. His throat tightened, and Dave rubbed the front of his dirt-splattered shirt. He needed to put an end to any hopes Eddi Boswick had about the future.

"Besides," he finally said and kicked at a spattering of glass along the running board, "any decent guy would have protected you." He allowed his gaze to trail up to her mud-streaked face. Dave looked into those gentle gray eyes and forced himself to be tough.

"So don't get your hopes up," he added with cold resolve.

She gasped. Her eyes sparked with mute fury. The results were exactly what Dave hoped for—despite the softness a woman like Eddi Boswick could offer. The tempting thought ushered in Calvin's prediction that Dave would be begging for Eddi's attention by summer's end. Calvin's assertion couldn't be ignored. The last thing Dave needed was allowing this lawyer to make him go soft.

Some men aren't meant to be tamed, he added to himself, *and I'm one of them...no matter how good lookin' the tamer is.* He peered past Eddi to observe the east side of Huntington House, where the chimney top was now a crumpled mass of brick on the ground.

"Have you said all you wanted to say?" Dave looked down at his driver's seat, covered in shards of glass. "I've got a lot to do, and Aunt Maddy is upset."

When he looked up, Eddi was stomping toward her car, her back stiff. By the time he shut his cab door, she was backing out of the driveway. She didn't even look at him when she sped by.

"More power to her," he mumbled and could only imagine what the summer was going to be like, especially if they started play practices at his house.

Was I out of my mind when I offered? he thought.

Dave watched his sixty-five-year-old aunt standing near Calvin. Her fingertips pressed against her lips, she observed the flurry of activity at the bottom of the hill. The community was wasting no time restoring order from chaos. Dave's heart softened. He'd do anything in the world for the woman who took in him and his kid brother when their parents were killed—even if it meant suffering literary torture in his own home...or facing the threat and lure of a sassy lawyer.

Three

~ ~

Two weeks later, Eddi gassed her Mustang along the country lane leading to Dave Davidson's ranch. Her sister Jenny claimed the passenger seat. After a busy Saturday afternoon shopping with their talkative mother and sister, the two had settled into a pleasant silence. Within minutes, they would arrive for the first practice of *Pride and Prejudice*. Actually, the assembly was more in line with an organizational meeting. Mrs. DeBloom would be assigning roles, and they would be reading over some of the early scenes. The town's cultural guardian was also providing finger foods, which seemed to be her forte.

Eddi thought of having to be in the same room with the "great" Dave Davidson and dug her fingernails into the steering wheel. She'd been furious for a week after their last encounter and had dodged him at church several times. Last Saturday, she even scurried into the produce section at the local grocery store to avoid meeting him in the pet food aisle. For a few minutes after that tornado, Eddi had perceived that maybe Dave really was attracted to her—despite his protests to Calvin. But after his arrogantly telling her not to get her hopes up, Eddi decided the only person the man could ever really love was himself.

The longer she pondered his prideful manner, the more her ire rose. The more her ire rose, the more exasperated she became with herself for ever being attracted to him in the first place. Eddi upped the air conditioner blower one notch. She pointed a vent at her face and welcomed the cold air on her cheeks and nose.

Being angry is no way to begin the first practice, she scolded herself.

"Mind if I turn on some music, Jenn?" she asked and eyed her CD player.

"Not in the least," Jenny responded through a yawn. "Are you hot?" she asked as Eddi switched on a classical guitar CD.

"A little," Eddi answered. "You're not?"

"I'm freezing," Jenny said and rubbed her freckled knees.

"That's what you get for wearing that shorts set," Eddi teased.

"You're just jealous because it's a Liz Claiborne, and I got it for ten bucks." Jenny offered a blue-eyed dare. "Admit it! You've been envious ever since we left Foley's."

"I'm not admitting a thing," Eddi purred. She lowered the air conditioner blower and chuckled.

As the guitar music wove its magic, Eddi enjoyed the solace. Not only did the tune soothe her dread of seeing Dave again, it also relaxed her a bit after the taxing day shopping with her mother and two sisters. Their mother had claimed exhaustion and pleaded to stay at Eddi's townhouse with their twenty-year-old sister, Linda.

Eddi hadn't said anything yet to Jenny, but she'd smelled alcohol on Linda's breath when they arrived mid-morning. She decided now was a good time to question Jenny about their rebel sister. Jenny, a college coach, lived just north of Houston in The Woods, and saw their family more often than Eddi.

"So…" Eddi began, "everything the same with Linda?"

"Need you ask?" Jenny questioned. She fumbled through her leather purse until she produced a hair band. Jenny retrieved a brush from her purse and tackled her shoulder-length strawberry blonde hair. Within thirty seconds, she pulled her hair into a ponytail that made her look closer to twenty than thirty. Her sporty shirt and shorts only increased her youthful appearance. When the two sisters were together, most people assumed Eddi was the eldest and would never guess that Jenny was actually two years her senior. Eddi looked down at her ankle-length broom stick skirt, cotton shirt, and wide belt. This morning when she put on the ensemble, she felt stylish. Now, next to Jenny, Eddi felt almost matronly.

Oh well, she thought, *there's nobody at this play practice I'm trying to impress anyway.* Eddi disciplined her thoughts to the subject at hand.

"I don't guess Dad has put his foot down and made Linda get a job yet?" Eddi lifted her hand off the steering wheel and placed it onto the floor gearshift. "Why am I even asking that?" she queried and glanced into the rearview mirror to note there were no vehicles behind her. The view ahead attested that the two-lane highway, surrounded by rolling east Texas hills, was likewise vacant.

"I think Linda's still as content to hang out at home as she was the day she dropped out of college," Jenny said. She deposited her brush back into her purse and rummaged some more. Jenny pulled out a miniature bottle of body spray and spritzed some on her neck. A light citrus smell filled the car.

"Good thing the Boswick inheritance allows us all two grand a month for life," Eddi said and rolled her eyes. "I guess that gives Linda some pocket change." The same inheritance had ensured her father an income of a hundred thousand a year— mere pennies in comparison to the Boswick Oil millions Edward Boswick had rejected in favor of his freedom.

"Oh, yes," Jenny said, "Linda would have fun trying to survive on two thousand a month if Dad made her move out. With her lifestyle, she'd sink. She doesn't seem to have one clue about a budget." Jenny lifted the bottle of body mist. "Want me to give you a spray?" she offered.

"Thought you'd never ask." Eddi held out her arm and awaited the cool mist that settled upon her skin. "That stuff smells great!" she added.

"Yeah, I love it."

"Well, I guess we can look at this Linda business from the bright side," Eddi said and rested her hand back on the gearshift. "Maybe some rich man will fall madly in love with her and not mind keeping up the lifestyle she prefers."

"He better not mind having a booze bill," Jenny grumbled.

"Did I smell alcohol on her breath when you guys arrived this morning, or was I imagining things?" Eddi asked. The vehicle's steady hum seemed to affirm her question.

"I think the Coke she sipped all the way up here was laced with rum," Jenny admitted.

"And then she had three margaritas for lunch," Eddi said and rubbed her thumb across the gearshift. Seeing her sister tipsy while they shopped at the mall had done little to enhance her afternoon. And that was after Linda had winked at three policemen who, in turn, decided to make a pass at her and her sisters at the restaurant. Eddi had resorted to her firm lawyer persona and convinced the men to get lost.

"The thing that really irks me," Eddi continued, "is Mom's attitude toward the whole thing. She seems to be in complete denial that Linda has these problems or that she should have done anything but drop out of college."

"Maybe because she's too much like Linda to see it all."

"Mom never touched a drink in her life," Eddi claimed.

"No, but she and Linda are still a whole lot alike. I mean, Mom dropped out of college too."

Eddi sighed. "You're right. She lasted one semester didn't she?"

"Yep."

"How's Dad these days?" Eddi asked. "I talk to him all the time, but I mean how is he *really?*" She shifted in her seat. "I guess what I'm trying to say is—"

"Why don't you just get it out?" Jenny said with a laugh.

"Okay, I will then!" Eddi smiled. "The last time I was home—two months ago—I tried to talk to Dad about Linda. I told him he needed to do something to make her take some responsibility."

"You did?" Jenny gasped.

"Yes, I did," Eddi affirmed and looked at her sister.

Jenny's carefree application of cosmetics enhanced her natural beauty far beyond any level Eddi could ever hope for herself. She looked back at the road and concentrated on driving. Nevertheless, a bundle of negative memories nagged at her. When she was seventeen, Eddi overheard their mother telling a friend that Jenny was by far her most beautiful daughter and that Linda got all the personality. She made a begrudging comment about Eddi getting nothing but brains, as if a sharp mind were the last thing a woman could possibly want or need. At the time, Eddi had been crushed. But as the years rocked on, she eventually stopped seeking her mother's elusive approval. She possessed her father's doting favor, and somehow that made up for her mother's lack of preference.

"So are you going to tell me what Dad said or not?" Jenny prompted.

"Oh sure…sorry. I guess I drifted, didn't I?" Eddi eased up on her accelerator as an eighteen-wheel truck zoomed around her. "Okay," she said when in the wake of the truck's roar. "Dad told me that Linda was young and fickle like all girls her age—"

"But she's twenty. She's a young woman. She's not a little girl anymore."

"I know. It's like he thinks she's still twelve or something," Eddi said. "Besides all that, by the time you were twenty you were only a year away from graduating with your bachelor's degree and were already looking to grad school."

"Well, I don't think we should expect that out of Linda," Jenny said. "Or that she'd even *think* about going from grad school to law school like you did!" she added. "I was gagging by the time I finished my Master's degree, and you just shoved right through that and into law school." Jenny punched her on the arm as if Eddi were a champion.

"I just hate to see Linda wasting her life," Eddi fretted.

"Look, let's just put it all out of our minds and enjoy the evening, shall we?" Jenny said. "Dad and Mom were talking about coming back up here to spend July Fourth with you. That's under three weeks away now. Maybe it will give you another chance to talk with Dad."

Eddi scrutinized the nearing turnoff that lead to Dave's ranch. "I don't know if he'll listen," Eddi mused. She shoved the disturbing subject from her mind and slowed the vehicle. "Let's talk about something else."

"Well, tell me more about the play," Jenny said with a bright smile.

Eddi squeezed Jenny's hand and said, "You have *no idea* how glad I am you're coming to this practice with me. It's such a relief to have someone there who's on my side."

"Oh, so we're back on the subject of Dave Davidson?" Jenny said with a wink. Her guileless smile enhanced her dimples. "Surely he can't be as big of a monster as you've made him out to be! It's probably just one of those personality conflict things."

"Oh, Jenn," Eddi sighed, "sometimes I think you'd find something good about the devil himself."

"And you'd find something negative about Michael the archangel," Jenny teased.

"Well, now that you mention it, his wings are a little big for his body. Don't you think?" She waved her hand.

Sisterly laughter abounded as Eddi turned on the right blinker. She hung a sharp right and sped onto a narrow, black-topped road. According to Mrs. DeBloom's directions, this road was a private lane that cut across Dave's property and led straight to his home.

"Seriously, Dave Davidson has got to be the rudest, most arrogant, most prideful and critical person I have *ever* met," Eddi asserted. "Trust me, when you meet him, you'll see what I mean."

A sharp whistle erupted from Jenny as they rounded the road's final turn. With but one glimpse of the estate in front of her, Eddi didn't have to ask about the reason for her sister's reaction. She slammed on the brakes. The car jolted, and her seatbelt ate into her shoulder.

Her eyes wide, she drank in the scene before her. A sprawling, southern farmhouse stood in front of a verdant hill covered in pines. The front porch wrapped around the front and sides of the two-story home and was covered in ferns and geraniums. The seven o'clock sun dipped toward the hill and cast a golden glow upon the home—an estate that looked to be five thousand square feet. The roof, a deep shade of reddish brown, enhanced the shutters, the color of ripe cranberries.

A rose garden graced the right side of the massive yard dotted in lush oaks. Toward the east, a pasture filled with Texas longhorns stretched to the base of a pine-covered mountain. A pecan and pear orchard claimed the west. Several of the trees with the tops twisted out of them testified to the recent tornado that caused a million dollars in damage to downtown London but claimed no lives. A Border collie lying near the front door announced another newcomer with a round of barks.

"Oh my word," Jenny mumbled. "It's your dream house, Eddi!"

The mellifluous guitar music lost its calming impact, and Eddi turned up the air conditioner once more.

Last year, the two sisters had acted upon a whim and taken a builder's tour of homes south of Houston. At the end of the day, they each chose the house that was their dream home. Jenny decided upon a Greek revival mansion with pillars and a circular driveway. Eddi fell in love with a home nearly identical to this one—right down to the porch swing that swayed in the June breeze.

"Maybe Dave Davidson won't be quite as awful as you remembered, now. What do you think?" Jenny tapped her sister's arm.

Eddi tried to laugh but couldn't. All she could think about was the warmth of Dave's arms around her and the glimpse of attraction she'd seen in his eyes once the tornado was gone. Eddi would have wagered her life's savings that he'd even been tempted to kiss her. His teasing about the tornado coming back had validated that he'd enjoyed their closeness.

Her final encounter with Dave that day crashed through the warm memories. She had actually felt sorry for the guy when she saw the limb in his windshield. That, plus his being her human shield during the tornado, had dampened Eddi's irritation over what Dave said to Calvin. But his conceited remarks had drowned both pity and gratitude and made her dread the very sight of him.

"No wonder he's such a snob," she mumbled. "He must have money running out his ears." For the first time, she began to understand his reaction to her Jane Austen comments about a single man in possession of a good fortune. She also started doubting the rumor that Mrs. DeBloom was the source of his cash flow.

"Money out his ears," Jenny mused. "Hmmm…that would make him Mom's dream son-in-law."

Eddi rolled her eyes. "Heaven help the woman who marries this guy!" she declared. "There's not enough gold in Fort Knox to make me endure the misery he'd dish out." She took her foot off the brake and encouraged the Mustang with a tap on the accelerator. Just as Eddi pulled into a parking place beside a row of vehicles, the front door opened and the dark-haired renegade himself stepped onto the porch. He bent, scratched the Border collie's ears, straightened, and eyed Eddi's vehicle.

Turning off the ignition, Eddi dared to sneak another peak at him. Dave was dressed exactly as he'd been two weeks ago—the jeans, the boots, the over-washed denim shirt. His hair was a little longer, but for once he was clean shaven. He eyed her vehicle as if he were the marshal of a dusty town and she were a suspicious stranger.

Eddi squirmed in her seat and refused to allow him to intimidate her. She'd faced meaner opponents in court and walked out the victor. She wouldn't flinch from this challenge—not even a little.

Jenny giggled.

Eddi looked at her and frowned. "What's so funny?"

Her eyes dancing, Jenny observed Eddi as if she possessed some guarded secret from the ancients. "If you have to ask, there's no need for me to tell you," she answered with a mystical wink.

"Whatever!" Eddi said. "Let's just go in and get this over with. Don't leave my side all night. Got it?"

"Yes, ma'am," Jenny said with an army salute.

"If it weren't for the fact that I'd promised Mrs. DeBloom I'd be in the play," Eddi mumbled as she undid her seatbelt, "I'd quit tonight!" Eddi got out and slammed her door a second before Jenny shut hers. The two sisters met in front of the car, and the hot evening air only served to up Eddi's agitation.

"Can you believe he actually said I was too short and too prissy?" she whispered. An unexpected chuckle escaped her as his comments took a ridiculous ring.

"You always *did* have a wicked sense of humor," Jenny claimed. "I wondered when it would kick in."

"I think it just did," Eddi whispered back. Their sandals clicked along the massive driveway as they neared the winding walkway leading to the front porch. "I wonder what he'd do if I grabbed him by the front of the shirt as soon as I walked up on the porch and just kissed him smack on the mouth." A chortle burst from her. "I could say something like, 'How's that for too short and prissy' and then, I could just calmly walk into the house like nothing happened."

"You'd probably tilt his world for a week," Jenny said.

Eddi leaned close to her sister and looked her square in the eyes. "Dare me?" she asked. A whippoorwill's whistle floated on the warm breeze as if to answer her question.

Jenny's expressive eyes danced. "You wouldn't really, would you?"

Eddi slowed her pace. The porch steps were only fifty feet away. She offered a discreet look at the renegade, who was playfully batting at the Border collie's mouth. The animal snarled while sporting with his master.

Dave straightened and peered straight at the sisters. Eddi hated that he'd caught her staring and resisted the urge to glance away. Instead, she held his gaze and didn't blink.

"He seems familiar," Jenny hissed under her breath.

Eddi looked at her but didn't reply.

Jenny's eyes narrowed. "This is so odd," she continued as they neared the steps. "I've seen him somewhere before...or maybe I've just seen his picture."

Four

"Aunt Maddy is waiting on you," Dave said the second Eddi stepped onto his porch.

"Oh?" Eddi lifted her brows and silently challenged him. Her fresh citrus scent wafted on the breeze and urged Dave to move closer.

"Yep," Dave answered and put his hands on his hips.

"I understood the practice started at seven," Eddi offered. "Was I wrong?" She secured her purse strap upon her shoulder.

"That's right." Dave glanced at the aging Timex that had once been his father's. "It's five after," he said as if pronouncing a grave sentence. He narrowed his right eye and dared her to refute his claim.

She looked good—really good. As good as she'd looked every other time Dave had seen her. In that long skirt and sandals Eddi Boswick appeared to be more an elegant queen of the castle than a lawyer.

But from what he'd heard around town these last few weeks, Miss Boswick was a formidable foe in court. The whole town was talking about the victory won for the Farmer family. From what Dave could gather, Eddi had filed suit on behalf of the Farmers and saved their family estate from the clutches of a land developer who wanted to gobble up their twenty acres as a part of a new roadway.

Dave couldn't deny that he liked a woman with some grit. The longer he stood here with Eddi, the more he liked what he saw. The more he enjoyed the view, the more Dave lingered over the memory of her in his arms.

He scowled and glanced toward the lady standing next to Eddi. She appeared close to Eddi's age and had the same long nose and pouty lips. He nodded and figured they must be related.

"Welcome," Dave said and barely lifted one corner of his mouth. Her cool, blue-eyed observation left Dave unmoved. Figuring she was safe, he relaxed a bit and increased the smile.

"This is my sister, Jenny Boswick," Eddi's voice was barely civil. "Jenny, Dave Davidson." By the time Eddi got to his name, she sounded as if he were the personification of the bubonic plague.

"Jenny, good to meet you," Dave drawled and didn't resist the impish urge that prompted him to defend himself. "Don't believe anything your sister tells you about me. I'm really a nice guy."

"Oh, I'm sure you are," Jenny agreed and extended her hand.

Dave took it for a brief shake. As their fingers parted, her gaze sharpened to scrutiny. Soon, scrutiny turned to certainty—a certainty that Jenny had seen him before. A trickle of sweat oozed down his chest. With a duck of his head, Dave pretended interest in scratching his collie's ear. Bo leaned against his leg and closed his eyes. A pleasurable grunt rumbled from the dog's chest while a knot of anxiety formed in Dave's.

Whether Jenny knew about Dave or not was anybody's guess. If she was half as tenacious as her sister, she could easily discover his identity. Dave gave Bo's ear a final rub.

He looked up at Eddi. "Are you going to stand here all evening or go on into the practice?" he asked.

"I wondered if you'd forgotten we were here," Eddi answered. "We were waiting on an invitation from the host." She flicked her long French braid over her shoulder. "In the civilized world, it's not considered polite to just march into somebody's home without an invitation."

"Oh, well, let's be civilized by all means." Dave twisted the knob and shoved on the polished maple door. The door only moved a few inches when it hit an obstacle who yelled.

"Yikes!" Calvin exclaimed. "Watch out, will ya? There's a person here!"

"Oops!" Dave reached for the knob, but Calvin whipped open the door. "What's taking you so—" He stopped talking the second he spotted Jenny.

"I was being held hostage," Dave claimed and waited for his friend to laugh.

Calvin remained silently focused upon Eddi's sister. Eddi rolled her eyes as if Dave's comment were ludicrous. Calvin barely acknowledged Eddi and stepped in front of Dave.

"Hi," he said, "my name's veterinarian. I'm the town Calvin Barclay. Are you new in town?"

Dave released a single guffaw that went unnoticed by both Jenny and Calvin. His friend didn't seem to have a clue that he'd jumbled his introduction, and Jenny didn't seem to care. She demurely shook his hand, and Dave half expected harp music to burst from the cloudless sky.

"I'm Jenny Boswick—Eddi's sister," she explained. "We—my sister and mom and I—are just visiting for the weekend."

"So your sister and mom are here, too?" Calvin looked toward the yard. A longhorn's moo floated upon the humid breeze that tossed Jenny's ponytail as if she were a carefree teenager.

"No, we left them at Eddi's place," Jenny explained. "I just came because I was interested in the play." Jenny's attention drifted to her hand, which Calvin still grasped.

Oh no, Dave groaned to himself, *I smell trouble.*

"Well, I'm glad you're here," Calvin said and eyed her left hand, as if in search of a wedding band. He released her fingers, shoved his hands into his slacks pockets, and pulled them back out. He crossed his arms, uncrossed them, and stammered, "Uh...w–would you like to join us?" Calvin stepped aside and offered his arm as if he were a British gentleman.

Dave wrinkled his brow as he witnessed his friend morphing into a cross between Barney Fife and Prince Charming.

"Mrs. DeBloom is threatening to start casting within the next few minutes," Calvin continued. "We're all on pins and needles, wondering who is going to get what part."

"Of course. I'd love to," Jenny said. She took Calvin's arm and stepped in front of Dave.

Calvin ushered her through the door. "If you look too interested, you might find yourself with a part." The closing door cut off any more of his teasing remarks.

Dave blinked. "The blockhead just shut the door on us," he said.

Eddi's lips curled as if she'd eaten cactus. "A lot of help *she* is," she spewed. "I brought her to—" She stopped and looked at Dave. With a huff, Eddi brushed past him, opened the front door, and marched inside.

Dave offered a final pat to Bo and a quick perusal of the east pasture. His herd of longhorns languidly grazed the emerald pasture as if they didn't have one concern. Dave had added two new bulls to the group this morning. The other males had been disturbed most of the day, but now they appeared settled.

Satisfied, Dave followed Eddi inside. The smell of brewing coffee and his aunt's cheese dip mingled with Eddi's sweet fragrance. Despite Dave's commitment to self control, his stomach fluttered.

To the left, he offered one hard stare at the portrait hanging over the dining room's fireplace. The images, ensconced in a simple oak frame, jolted Dave back to reality. His late mother and father smiled back at him as if they were the happiest couple who ever lived. Dave knew differently. Despite the surface appearance of matrimonial felicity, the artist hadn't missed the hint of desperate resignation in his parents' eyes. Eyes that were equally as dark as Dave's. Eyes hinting that Jacob and Karen Davidson endured a marriage that resembled a perpetual civil war. Blonde and petite, Karen Davidson seemed the personification of the southern belle. But beneath the gentle façade lay a steel disposition that demanded her husband comply. Jacob Davidson not only refused to comply to any of Karen's wishes, he expected Karen to fold herself into his life and his goals without a question for hers. Together, the two had lived a lie. At the church they pastored, they presented themselves as a blissful married couple. At home, they remained at each other's throats. As a teenager, Dave vowed to *never* marry if his parents' misery was the inevitable result.

Dave moved past the dining room and neared Eddi. Miss Boswick was as blonde as his mother and probably twice as strong willed. Whether she would insist upon battling with her husband was an unknown. *And it will remain that way!* Dave declared. The potential was there enough. Those kitten-soft eyes of hers held a streak of steel smack through the middle. Her growing reputation in court validated that the woman wasn't afraid of the devil himself.

Eddi stood at the base of the curved stairway, looking from left to right, as if she were a little girl lost in a giant department store. The image almost tempted him to take pity upon her. *Looks can be deceiving,* Dave told himself and annihilated all benevolent urges.

"They're all in the back room," he drawled in an emotionless voice and pointed through the formal living room. "This way." He cocked his head to the right toward a room his aunt had insisted on making look like a furniture store.

"Nice place," Eddi commented, as if her admission were a statement of fact and nothing more.

"So I've been told," Dave answered and attempted to hide his surprise. Most women fell into a round of ardent babbling over his home. At that point, the single ones usually decided Dave was prime matrimonial material. "I built it to suit Aunt Maddy. She insisted. And—" Dave stopped himself. No use explaining that the home was the replica of his mother's dream home, right down to the grand piano mere feet away. Even though she and his father didn't get along, Dave still loved her and missed her. Somehow, the house made him feel as if she were with him.

He observed his dusty boots and figured he was leaving a trail across the cream-colored carpet. The housekeeper would not be happy.

"Hope you left at least one room for yourself," Eddi said and whisked past the piano.

"I did." He stepped in beside her and didn't expound on his haven in the backyard. It was none of her business anyway. "The group's at the end of this hallway," he explained as they stepped into a short corridor.

Laughter drifted from the pool room, and Calvin Barclay's voice floated above the mixture of voices. "Go ahead and laugh, then!" he quipped. "But what man doesn't get his tongue tied in the presence of a beautiful woman?"

Dave didn't bother to hide his groan this time. Calvin was clearly smitten with Jenny Boswick. If Jenny discovered who he was and Calvin and she got cozy, then Calvin would eventually find out about Dave. If Calvin found out, he might leak the information to his nosy sister, Carissa Barclay. She would leak the information to their mother, who'd promptly tell the ladies' mission auxiliary. Within twenty-four hours, the facts would be all over town.

He sensed Eddi's critical stare. Her interpretation of his groan was probably not to his advantage. Dave imagined numerous things she must be thinking—all in defense of her sister. Presently, he didn't care.

Dave neared the pool room turned drama chamber and paused for Eddi to enter before him. The smell of cheese dip and coffee originated here, and Dave's stomach rumbled. Before the group arrived, he'd barely had time to shower, much less eat.

"There you are, my dear!" Madelynne DeBloom, dressed in her typical straight dress and flat shoes, stood beside the refreshment bar laden with sandwiches and snacks. The French doors behind her ushered in a shower of evening sunshine that lent a festive glow to the room's activities and highlighted the crackle of excitement in the air.

Mrs. DeBloom removed the narrow glasses from the end of her nose and observed her sister's son. Dave nodded toward the group, all reclining in chairs they'd transported from the theater's basement. Calvin and Jenny stood beside the pool table that had been moved to the corner. A makeshift stage claimed the opposite corner. Dave's hired hand, Francis Schmidt, had spent the weekend building it.

"I guess we can all get started," Aunt Maddy continued.

Dave slipped a hand into his jeans pocket and leaned against the door frame while Eddi sashayed toward her sister. Her elegant skirt swished just above her strappy sandals, and Dave glowered at the thing. He wished she'd have the decency to wear something ugly for once.

"As I was saying…" his aunt rustled a stack of papers lying on the refreshment bar, "after a lot of thought and prayer, I've decided to renovate Huntington House into a dinner theater. So our first performance of *Pride and Prejudice* will be there instead of at the theater, as first planned."

A polite ripple of applause punctuated the lady's speech, and she nodded with a regal air that left Dave smiling. Aunt Maddy always acted as if her every decision *should* be applauded.

"As you all know, the city is debating whether to repair the old theater, construct a new one, or forgo a civic theater altogether. I believe that renovating Huntington House is the perfect answer for our group, so we can stay on track no matter what the city decides. This is a long-time dream of mine. I've wanted to own a dinner theater since my dear husband died, but..." she paused as if the next scrap of honesty was too much a strain to speak. "But I've not had the funds until now." She propped her reading glasses back on her nose. "Thanks to a benevolent donor who has set up the fund to help our city recover, there will be some extra money for me to renovate Huntington House, aside from what the insurance will cover. I'm really excited!" She shook her head and her eyes glistened as if she were a six-year-old on Christmas morning.

Dave shifted his weight and adopted a disinterested persona. No sense in giving anyone a clue that he was the "benevolent donor."

"Now, tonight, I've decided I'm going to start by announcing whom I've chosen for the play's roles," Mrs. DeBloom continued. She picked up a paper from the top of her pile and eyed it with interest.

Dave's attention wandered past his thin aunt, and out the glass doors behind her. His land stretched to the base of an imperial hill and beyond. Fifty yards behind his home stood a small brick building that could easily be turned into a one-room apartment. For now, the necessary structure served as the haven he'd chosen not to discuss with Eddi. Dave hadn't consulted Aunt Maddy about one element of its interior or exterior. He shifted his weight from the doorjamb, and his mind wandered to the reason for the building. If Dave let himself, he would spend every waking moment out there and neglect his ranch and financial management. That would defeat the building's purpose. Presently, he allowed himself two hours a day in his haven, and no more.

"...my nephew, Dave Davidson."

The mention of his name tugged Dave's attention back to his aunt. A murmur rippled across the small audience as if they were stunned. Dave shot a glance toward Calvin.

"You old goat!" Calvin crowed. The sun christened his friend's fair hair and accented the pink scar along his jaw line. "You took the part right out from under me, didn't you?"

A whistle preceded a round of applause, and Dave pieced together the reason. His aunt had just announced that he had agreed to play Darcy. How that happened was anybody's guess. Looking back, Dave realized Aunt Maddy had approached him last night with an agenda. One minute Dave had been stubbornly adhering to his decision to stay out of the play. The next minute, he heard himself say, "Oh, okay, Aunt Maddy. Anything for you." Sometimes Dave wondered if his mother had learned her manipulative skills from a master—her elder sister. Long ago, Dave had determined that his aunt could convince a cat to bark if she so chose.

He lifted his hand. "I figured it was harmless to agree. I'm sure you'll all be begging Aunt Maddy to replace me after the first practice anyway."

New laughter abounded.

Dave glanced back at Calvin. "You'll probably wind up with the part by nine tonight."

"Oh no he won't," Mrs. DeBloom cut in. "He's playing the part of Charles Bingley."

More applause underscored the announcement.

"You people are starting to act like the audience on *The Price Is Right*," Dave groused good-naturedly.

Jenny's burst of laughter opened the door for the whole group's mirth. Dave's attention drifted from Jenny to her sister. Whether Eddi heard his comment or not was anybody's guess. Her focus rested on the French doors and beyond. Dave narrowed his eyes and wondered if she'd spotted his haven.

Cheri Locaste stepped beside Eddi and made a comment. With a pleasant smile, Eddi turned her attention to the high school English teacher, who seemed bent on choosing the plainest attire. Cheri's long, dark hair was pulled into a simple ponytail at the nape of her neck. The style did little to compliment her oval face, void of cosmetics. Aunt Maddy had told Dave last night that Cheri would be playing the part of Elizabeth Bennet, which placed her as his leading lady. That choice suited him fine. Nothing about Cheri Locaste's plain appearance and colorless personality moved him. Dave would have stubbornly refused to play Darcy if the leading lady had been assigned to any woman who might take the role a little too seriously. He glanced across the crowd and counted exactly three women who fell into that category. Four, if you considered Eddi Boswick.

Dave scrutinized the tips of his boots and debated whether or not Eddi would have enjoyed playing opposite him. No doubt the sparks had flown when they were in each other's arms after the tornado. But so had Eddi's disdain—more than once. With a satisfied grunt, Dave decided that Eddi would have been as loath to play his leading lady as he would be to play her hero.

Mrs. DeBloom cut through the group's revelry for her next announcement. "I thought long and hard in assigning the role for Elizabeth Bennet. Last night, I was settled upon one person." She allowed Dave a sheepish grin, and he tensed. "But I lay awake until midnight worrying about my first choice until at last I knew I must change my mind." Her smile increased as she observed Eddi Boswick.

Dave's eyes widened. His palms moistened. His back stiff-ened. "Elizabeth Bennet needs to be played by a strong woman who can command the stage and not shrink from Darcy's imperious ways." Mrs. DeBloom stood on her toes for a second as she waved her arm in theatrical grace. "I firmly believe the best choice for that role lies with Eddi Boswick."

Five

“But I wanted to play the part of Jane,” Eddi squeaked. Her faint claim was lost in the group’s revelry. As Mrs. DeBloom continued to announce her choice for characters, Eddi frantically glanced toward Dave. He stared at the floor, his face as rigid as granite.

A frenzied urge to run nearly proved too strong to ignore. If she played Elizabeth and Dave played Darcy, the two would have to spend hours in each other’s company. A summer full of practices stretched into September. Then, the play would start and run every weekend the whole month of October. By November, she would have spent more time with Dave Davidson than with her own sister. Her legs weakened, and Eddi wondered if this were a twisted nightmare that would soon end.

The pressure of fingers on her palm proved too real to be part of a dream. “What are you going to do?” Jenny whispered.

“I’m thinking of coming down with gangrene of the throat,” Eddi hissed back. The earnest comment took a hilarious resonance the second it left her lips.

A giggle erupted from Eddi, and Jenny covered her mouth with her hand as she smothered a chortle. "You have a sick sense of humor," Jenny whispered as blue fire sparkled in her eyes.

"So do you," Eddi responded and ducked her head in an attempt to control the mirth. "Otherwise, you wouldn't have laughed."

"I might have laughed. But the difference between me and you is that I would have never thought it."

"Or if you had, you'd have never said it."

"Are you two scheming behind my back or what?" Calvin stepped nearer Jenny, his amiable smile ever in place.

"No, it's nothing to do with you," Jenny answered, and Eddi wondered if her sister was still seeing Hal Gomez. Jenny hadn't mentioned him once this trip and didn't seem to have him on her mind. "Just a private sister joke," Jenny added.

"Okay," Calvin said with a nod and a wink. "I won't pry then." He peered toward Mrs. DeBloom who continued assigning roles. Every time a new name was mentioned, the group applauded her choice. "I'm curious about who's going to play Jane," Calvin explained. "She would be *my* leading lady."

"Well, I tried to take that role," Eddi supplied, "but apparently Mrs. DeBloom has decided to cast someone else as Jane."

"So far, she's left that one out. It surprises me, actually, since Jane would be considered Elizabeth's supporting female character." Calvin shrugged. "Charles Bingley, Darcy, Elizabeth, and Jane are the most prominent roles. Since she's already assigned Charles, Darcy, and Elizabeth..."

Eddi rubbed her throat. "I think I feel my neck turning green now," she muttered under her breath.

Jenny burst forth with renewed laughter.

"Okay, okay." Calvin crossed his arms and rocked back on his heels. "You two are gossiping about me right under my nose, aren't you?"

"No—no—for real." Eddi shook her head and giggled. "Scout's honor." She held up her hand to salute. "I was actually once a member of the *Greeeeeen* Berets…a special force of girl scouts."

Jenny groaned and rolled her eyes. "Now, you're getting really corny," she said,

"It's my only means to sanity," Eddi claimed.

"Excuse me," Dave's voice rumbled from behind.

His deep tenor offered the antidote for her wacky humor. Eddi sobered and debated whether to acknowledge the man or drift across the room as if she never heard him. The skin along her shoulders prickled, and she knew escaping was not a possibility. Eddi pivoted to face Dave as if she were a soldier marching into enemy territory.

"Maybe you can make sense of these two," Calvin teased. "I'm afraid they're laughing at me."

"I don't think it's *you* they're laughing to scorn." Dave looked down his prominent nose as if he were royalty and Eddi were a mere peasant. Mrs. DeBloom had looked at her the same way a time or two. Eddi didn't shy from his srutiny any more than she did his aunt's. She stood her full height and stared right back at him.

"I'm assuming one of us will want to decline a role," Dave said with an assured twist of his lips.

"Oh?" Eddi questioned. "Are you going to bow out then?" She smelled a challenge. And challenges were something Eddi Boswick never shrank from—*ever*. At once a new desire, amazing and unexpected, sprouted in her mind; a desire to play Elizabeth Bennet and out act Dave Davidson, even if she *did* develop gangrene of the throat.

"Actually, I was thinking *you* would bow out." Dave crossed his arms as if the decision were settled. The sleeves of his worn denim shirt rustled with his movement.

"Me?" Eddi questioned. "Why not *you?* I didn't think you wanted to play the part of *Darby* anyway."

Dave's right eye narrowed, and a spark of ire flickered midst the inky depths. Eddi hid her smile. If he ever had doubts that she'd overheard his conversation on the porch two weeks ago, they were now officially banished.

"I believe that's Darcy," Dave corrected.

"Whoops." Eddi covered her lips with her fingertips.

"Let's not play games, shall we?" he said as if Eddi were the most boring woman on the planet. "We've got a problem here. Let's deal with it like adults."

A flash of irritation swooped upon Eddi, but she refused to give the man the pleasure of reacting to his barb. Instead, she smiled as if he were the most charming human being and nodded.

"Let's do," she agreed.

"My aunt wants me to play Darcy," he said as if that settled the whole argument. "I believe you're the one who has a freer choice."

"Do you always do everything *exactly* the way your aunt wants?" Eddi raised her hand in a wide sweep that included the spacious room. His house within itself was answer to her question.

"That woman means the world to me," Dave answered. "So yes, I try to please her." He glanced toward the elderly lady who was now handing out scripts to a trio of participants. "I figure she might have a good twenty years left. Maybe twenty-five, if she lives into her nineties. I want to make certain those years are the tops for her. I owe her big—for me and my kid brother."

"Your brother?"

"Yes."

"And he lives…"

"He's outside Dallas." Dave's gaze faltered as if he were declaring the subject closed.

Eddi didn't care to close the subject. "And does *he* always hop when your aunt speaks?"

"No, never," Dave bit out. He bent his head, and Eddi observed his dark curls, damp and inviting. Despite her commitment to dislike Dave, Eddi wondered how his curls would feel under a woman's caresses. Eddi swallowed hard and balled her fists.

"Now," Dave began and crammed a hand into his back pocket, "what about the part? Are you going to tell her you won't play Elizabeth or should I?" He leveled a glare at her that suggested she not argue.

"Who said I wasn't playing Elizabeth?" Eddi lifted her chin and rubbed her toes against her leather sandals.

"*I* did," he answered, his voice a little too quiet for comfort. Dave took a step closer. At the new angle, his nose appeared longer, his gaze keener. The faint scent of something masculine reminded Eddi of those minutes she'd trembled in his arms. A delicious desire uncurled in her midsection, but a primeval urge insisted Dave Davidson was the enemy.

Eddi would never deny that the man was an imperious foe. His sepia eyes suggested there was an undefeated warrior in his lineage. She squirmed inside, but revealed not one hint of fear. Instead, Eddi stiffened her legs and stood her ground. The guy had accused her of wearing combat boots to bed. Now was the time to show him he might have been closer to the truth than not.

"I've been assigned the role of Elizabeth Bennet," she explained in a soft tone, threaded with iron. "I will play the role of Elizabeth Bennet."

Dave's nostrils widened. A crease formed between his brows. He worked his jaw as if he were astounded that anyone would dare cross his wishes. Eddi tilted her head to one side and produced a smile void of warmth.

The scent of roses erupted upon their battle seconds before Mrs. DeBloom appeared. "Here you two are," she said in a breezy voice. "I have your scripts ready." She placed her narrow glasses on the end of her nose, and the pearl chain swayed on either side of her lined face. "I've highlighted your parts," Mrs. DeBloom explained as she flipped past two pages of the top script. "We're going to break for refreshments and then have our first reading tonight." She handed Eddi her script and pointed a red fingernail to her first line, colored in pale blue.

"Mrs. DeBloom?" Calvin called, and Eddi gazed over Dave's shoulder to his friend. For the first time, she realized that Jenny and he were no longer nearby. The two had drifted toward the makeshift stage.

"Yes, I'm coming," Mrs. DeBloom answered. She shoved a second script into Dave's hands and said, "You'll see your part highlighted as well. We'll start the first reading immediately after refreshments. You two be ready, okay?"

With that harried order, Madelynne hurried toward Calvin and Jenny.

"You know," Eddi said as she fumbled with the script, "somehow you don't strike me as the literary type." She ran her finger along the top of her script and couldn't resist the impulse to needle Dave. He'd indicated at their first drama meeting that women were chasing him. Maybe the time had come for him to encounter one who purposefully repelled him.

"Are you sure you're up to the role of Darcy?" she prodded. "He's probably one of the most celebrated heroes of classic literature."

A red tinge crawled beneath Dave's tan. "Don't underestimate me," he snarled.

"Who said I was underestimating you?" Eddi questioned and didn't impede the drive to continue. After all, he hadn't hesitated to take shots at her—no matter how unfair. "I'd just be shocked if you ever even read the book," she continued. "After all, many people don't encounter it until college lit."

"What are you suggesting?" Dave purred.

Eddi shrugged and hid the fact that she was struggling for a clever retort.

"If you must know, I stopped attending college before the end of my freshman year." Dave's blunt statement held no regrets. He dropped his script into an empty chair, calmly rolled up one sleeve, and started on the other. "Most people I meet don't seem to mind—especially around these parts." Satisfied with his sleeves, Dave directed a penetrating glare straight into Eddi's soul. "But once in awhile, I meet up with an intellectual snob who makes a big deal of it," he said as if every insulting word tasted like honey. "For the most part," he lifted a hand to encompass his home just as she had minutes before, "I think you'd have to agree I've managed in life just fine."

Her eyes widening, Eddi lost all ability to hide her growing animosity. "Are you insinuating I'm a snob?" she snapped and flipped her French braid over her shoulder.

"Now, what would make you think that?" he queried with a smirk.

She wadded her skirt in her hand and imagined herself yanking at a clump of his damp hair. Forget loving caresses! This jerk had officially declared war, and Eddi didn't plan to shrink from one battle. A sixth sense suggested that the angrier she got, the better Dave would like it. She told herself the wisest move would be feigning tranquillity; but tranquillity proved beyond her reach.

"You know," she finally choked out, "it's been my experience that those who accuse others are usually guilty of the exact sins they criticize." Her voice grew steadier with each syllable, as if her words were hammering the truth into him.

"Oh?" Dave asked as a sharp ring interrupted their conversation. Without taking his attention from her, Dave reached to his belt loop and whipped out a phone. He flipped open the blue-lighted device and spoke a sharp greeting into the receiver.

Eddi prepared to remove herself from his presence, but Dave's gasp stopped her. "What? You're kidding!" he bellowed.

A knot of three participants a few feet away looked up from perusing their parts. Cheri Locaste stopped speaking with Mrs. DeBloom and observed Dave. Eddi eased away from him, claimed a seat, and pretended interest in her script.

"No way!" Dave continued as if he'd won a million bucks.

Holding up her script, Eddi sneaked a glimpse of Dave.

"This is great!" His eyes sparkled and a chortle filled his corner of the room. "Oh sure! Yes...yes...just as we agreed. I'll take care of it now! No problem! Sure...sure...okay...thanks for calling so soon! Yes, everything's set, just like we agreed. I'll take care of everything," he rushed and ended with an abrupt goodbye. Dave closed the phone and hurried to his aunt. "I'm going out back," he said.

Mrs. DeBloom frowned. "You're going to go into your little house and not come out, aren't you?" she accused.

Eddi forgot to look at her script as she strained to follow the conversation word for word.

Dave grasped his aunt's upper arm. "No, I promise, Aunt Maddy. This time, I'll be back in..." he checked his wristwatch, "...give me twenty minutes. If I'm not back here in twenty minutes, then you come after me."

Mrs. DeBloom glanced at Eddi. She jerked the script toward her face, and pretended deep interest. The next time she looked up, Mrs. DeBloom was whispering something to Dave. He frowned and looked toward Eddi. She feigned nonchalance and allowed her gaze to drift past him. The next glimpse Eddi caught of him, he was dashing up the hallway.

"Okay everybody!" Mrs. DeBloom called emphatically. "Let's go ahead and eat. But make it quick, people! I want to read through the whole script tonight. We won't worry about blocking for awhile. Tonight, we'll just be getting the feel for our parts."

For once, Eddi found herself near the head of the food line. A plethora of finger foods and cheese dip crowned the bar, but this time Eddi wasn't interested in food. Another scene commanded her attention. Dave strode across the back lawn toward the small brick building as if he were a captain about to board his prized ship. He paused near the white-framed doorway, twisted the knob, and stepped inside.

Eddi's mind reeled with what that building must hold and what news could have prompted such enthusiasm from Dave. The possibilities spanned everything from a personal business venture to gambling to money laundering. When she began to wonder about international drug smuggling, Eddi halted her wild imagination.

Whatever Dave's up to, it's got to be legal, she thought. *Doesn't it?* Her forehead wrinkled as her focus roved toward the swimming pool and small pool house to the west of the brick building. *He has made a lot of money somehow,* she reasoned. *Just because he looks honest doesn't mean he is.*

"Hello, up there!" Calvin snapped his fingers. "There's a line waiting. Are you in a trance or what?"

"Oh, sorry," Eddi apologized. She offered a smile and realized Jenny was standing between her and Calvin. "I didn't even know you were there," Eddi mumbled and put a few odds and ends on her plate.

"No joke," Jenny answered. "You were on another planet." She picked up a cherry tomato and popped it into her mouth.

"I just want to know what he's up to out there," Eddi said under her breath.

"Probably smuggling diamonds over the Texas/Oklahoma border," Jenny whispered as if they were FBI agents. "You know how famous that route is for smugglers."

Eddi rolled her eyes. "Mock me if you will," she whispered, "but I wager the man's got something up his sleeve he doesn't want anyone to know about." She grabbed a diet soda from an open cooler on the floor and turned from the bar. After settling into a chair, she looked at her plate, which held exactly three chips and one olive. Eddi possessed no memory of placing the items on her plate.

Jenny claimed the chair next to Eddi's and popped the top on her soda. "I promise, Eddi, I've seen Dave Davidson somewhere before." She pursed her lips and stared at the empty chair in front of her as if the mystery were tearing at her mind. "Maybe if I could figure out where, we could find the answer to what's in the building."

"We're starting to sound like Nancy Drew here," Eddi said with a wry smile.

"That's always the effect you have on me, woman," Jenny quipped. "I show up a normal person and go home a suspicious, clue-sleuthing maniac who suspects every person I meet of foul play."

"I guess it just goes with my territory." Eddi munched a salty chip and peered out the French doors.

"What territory?" Calvin asked and plopped into the chair in front of Jenny.

"Oh, being curious goes along with being a lawyer, I guess," Eddi said and searched for a means to change the subject. The last thing she needed was Calvin telling Dave she and Jenny had been discussing him.

"Actually, I was just telling Eddi that Dave really looks familiar to me," Jenny said.

So much for Calvin not finding out we were discussing Dave, Eddi thought.

"Do you have any idea where I might have seen him before?" Jenny continued.

"You mean like on a wanted poster or something?" Calvin asked with a ridiculous light in his brown eyes.

For starters, Eddi thought. She unscrewed the lid on her Diet Dr Pepper and didn't voice her mental comments.

"Oh, get serious," Jenny said as if she and Calvin were life-long friends. She tapped his arm, and Eddi made a mental note to ask Jenny about Hal Gomez. A few weeks ago, Jenny had even mentioned that Hal was hinting about marriage. Right now, he seemed like the *last* thing on Jenny's mind. And Jenny seemed like the *first* thing on Calvin's mind.

"Okay, seriously," Calvin said, "I can't imagine why you think Dave looks familiar."

"Well, how long have you known him?" Jenny queried.

"About three years. That's when he moved to London."

"Where'd he move from?"

"Dallas." Calvin crammed a cheese-laden cracker into his mouth.

While Calvin crunched, Eddi watched the small brick building. Still no sign of Dave. She checked her watch and noted ten minutes had elapsed. He promised his aunt he'd be back in twenty minutes.

"Do you know what he did in Dallas?" Jenny asked.

"He owned a ranch there as well I think," Calvin said before guzzling his soda. "You know," he finally said, "I'm beginning to think you're more interested in him than me." Calvin winked. He seemed fond of winking tonight.

Eddi toyed with a chip and silently watched as her sister turned into a demure sixteen-year-old. Jenny tugged on the end of her ponytail and looked down. A tinge of pink touched her cheeks, and Eddi wondered what poor Hal would think if only he knew.

So she sat for the next fifteen minutes watching Calvin shamelessly flirt with her sister, and Jenny not doing one thing to discourage him. Only when Mrs. DeBloom announced the beginning of practice did Eddi check her watch again. Twenty-five minutes since Dave left the room.

"Oh, and Eddi…" Mrs. DeBloom called and rushed to her side. She knelt beside Eddi's chair as if they were grand conspirators. For once, Mrs. DeBloom seemed to forget her role as "matron superior." "I told Dave that if he wasn't back in here within twenty minutes I'd send you after him."

"You what?" Eddi gasped and recalled Mrs. DeBloom looking right at her while talking to Dave. His face had gone hard as if he detested the very idea of what his aunt suggested. *Makes perfect sense,* she thought, and possessed no doubts that Mrs. DeBloom fully understood the antagonism between them. So much so, she'd used Eddi as a threat to get him back into the house on time.

Eddi prepared to decline the honor of going after Dave, but stopped herself when she thought of that mysterious building. "Sure, I'll go get him," she offered and tried not to sound too curious. She turned to tell Jenny she'd be right back, but Jenny had cruised off with Calvin again. The two sat on the edge of the stage, sharing Calvin's script.

Standing, Eddi found the nearest trash can and discarded her plate and soda. By the time she turned from her task, Dave was slipping through one of the French doors behind the refreshment bar. With a confident swagger and a jubilant glow he meandered toward his aunt. After placing an arm on the small of her back, he spoke into her ear and offered the thumbs-up sign. Mrs. DeBloom patted his face as if he were a favored son.

Eddi eyed that small brick building. One day she would discover what lay between those walls—even if it took two years.

Six

Later that night, Eddi lay across the middle of her brass bed while Jenny claimed the floor. Her back propped against the bed, Jenny stretched her legs upon the area rug. Eyes bleary, Eddi observed the digital clock on her night stand. Midnight was nearly upon them, and Eddi had promised her mother and sisters she'd take them to her church in the morning.

After arriving home from play practice two hours ago, Eddi coerced Jenny into reading some of the play with her. During practice, Dave had spoken most of his lines with precision and far more finesse than Eddi ever imagined—and that after merely glancing at his script. She, on the other hand, had been tied to her manuscript, even though she had recently read the book.

The gloating triumph that Dave didn't attempt to hide drove Eddi to have all of Act One memorized by the next practice, a mere seven days away. Presently, Jenny was reading every line but Eddi's.

"Let's finish this scene," Eddi said and shifted her weight to her right elbow. "I think it's a good stopping point."

"Great." Jenny yawned and flipped her ponytail onto the mattress. She closed her script, dropped it, and propped the back of her head against the bed's edge. "You're about to wear me out. I came up here this weekend to relax. I didn't know I was going to encounter a slave driver."

"Oh, give it a break!" Eddi grumbled and tugged her sister's ponytail. "This isn't so bad, and you know it. Besides all that, you never gave Mrs. DeBloom a final answer about whether or not you'd play Jane. If you accept the role, you'll need all the practice you can get."

"She *said* Carissa Barclay was her first choice," Jenny said. "Remember?"

"Yes, but Calvin wasn't so hot on the idea of his sister playing the leading lady." Eddi rested her chin in her hand.

"I know."

"And, Mrs. DeBloom seemed to think Carissa might not be that dependable. She even missed the first practice."

"Yeah, and like I'm going to be more dependable! I'd be driving from The Woods for every weekend practice, and there's no guarantee I wouldn't miss a performance this fall after I start teaching again." Jenny repeated the yawn.

"Well, maybe you and Carissa could strike a bargain. You could both play Jane. You could play her the weekends you could get free from work, and she could perform the other weekends. That way, neither of you is so tied down."

"Oh, I don't know," Jenny flexed her neck. "I'd still have to memorize my part. I'm not really sure I'm committed enough to memorize all these lines. I've never been a bookworm like you, you know." She lifted her arms and stretched them to the ceiling.

"I'm beginning to wish Mom and Linda had been awake when we got home. Maybe you would have roped one of them into this contest of wills between you and this Dave character." She rubbed the back of her neck. "The way things look, you're going to *kill* yourself trying to outdo him before this play is over."

"I think the jerk has a photographic memory." Eddi rested her forehead in her palm and enjoyed the faint scent of citrus body spray that lingered on her skin.

"So, let him 'win'!" Jenny waved her hand.

"If only I could," Eddi said, "but it's just not that easy."

"I don't understand why you even accepted the role of Elizabeth, considering how you feel about him. Or maybe you don't really dislike—"

"I couldn't *not* accept it—not after the way he acted."

Jenny sighed and lifted her head. "Nothing like a little cooperation among the cast."

Eddi flopped onto her back and held her script inches from her face. "Would that we were all so agreeable as you, Jenny," she drawled. "At least Calvin seems to think so anyway." Eddi looked at her sister out of the corner of her eye.

"Where *were* we anyway," Jenny asked and rustled her script. "I've lost my place."

"Okay…" Eddi examined her lines and smiled. That was the third time Jenny had sidestepped a reference to Calvin. "We're to the part where Elizabeth, Jane, and their mother are discussing Darcy with Charlotte Lucas and her family." Eddi placed her finger on the text and found the last line they'd read. "Okay, you're supposed to start with Charlotte where she says, 'Darcy's pride does not offend *me* so much.'"

"Oh, sure, okay," Jenny agreed. "Here we go. 'Darcy's pride does not offend *me* so much as pride often does, because there is an excuse for it. One cannot wonder that so very fine a young man, with family, fortune, everything in his favor, should think highly of himself. If I may so express it, he has a *right* to be proud.'"

"'That is very true,'" Eddi read and tried to commit Elizabeth's lines to memory, "'and I could easily forgive *his* pride, if he had not mortified *mine.*'"

Jenny's unrestrained giggles tottered around the room.

"What?" Eddi asked and lowered her manuscript. She stretched her legs and looked at the ceiling fan's brass-trimmed blades lazing through rotation after rotation.

"Oh, nothing," Jenny said. Her giggles escalated to hilarity.

After a sigh, Eddi rubbed her sagging eyes and began to think she may have truly driven Jenny too hard. Her sister was developing a serious case of the Boswick midnight goofies.

"This is all just too funny for words," Jenny finally said.

"What?" Eddi demanded again and sat up. She swung her legs off the side of the bed, and her bare feet brushed the thick-piled rug.

"If you have to ask, there's no sense in my telling you," Jenny said. She looked up at Eddi as if she were the possessor of some mystical secret, just as she had in the car before play practice.

"Okay, the time has come to spill it, sister dear," Eddi challenged. "We've never beaten around the bush with each other. No sense starting now."

"I think the person who's pride has been hurt is *yours,*" she blurted. "And you and Dave Davidson are *both* protesting too much about your dislike for the other."

"What's *that* supposed to mean?"

"It means that he seemed to be using his photographic memory to memorize every detail of *you* tonight as much as his lines and that you—"

"Are you saying you think he's attracted to me or something?" Eddi croaked.

"Well, it would appear—"

Eddi grabbed a pillow and crashed it against Jenny's head.

"Hey, you!" Jenny swiveled to look up at her sister.

"Don't you ever say anything like that to me again. If you do I'll make you *eat* this pillow."

Jenny snatched the pillow from Eddi and bounded to her feet. She whacked Eddi in the face, and Eddi toppled backward. She reached for the head of the bed and grabbed more ammunition. By the time Jenny was posing for another blow, Eddi smacked her midsection and then dragged her onto the bed. Both sisters collapsed into a tangle of arms and legs and dissolved into a chorus of laughter.

"Oh my word," Jenny said, "I think I landed on your script." She rolled to her side and extracted the text. "Here, take it, and go torment somebody else with it." She dropped the play on Eddi's face.

Eddi snatched it off and started to close the pages for the night, but a section of dialogue grabbed her attention. "Okay, Miss Smarty Pants, here's one for you—straight from Charlotte Lucas," she accused and began reading a few more lines. "'Happiness in marriage is entirely a matter of chance. If the dispositions of the parties are ever so well known to each other or ever so similar beforehand, it does not advance their felicity in the least. They always continue to grow sufficiently unlike afterwards to have their share of vexation; and it is better to know as little as possible of the defects of the person with whom you are to pass your life.'"

"That's about the dumbest thing I've ever heard," Jenny said.

"Elizabeth Bennet would agree with you. But..." Eddi propped herself up on her elbow and gazed down at her sister, "I'm wondering if Calvin Barclay wouldn't agree with Charlotte Lucas. He seemed ready to trot down the aisle tonight with somebody we won't mention after knowing her only a few hours."

"I thought you said we didn't beat around the bush, sister dear," Jenny said and confronted her with frank appraisal.

"You've done nothing but beat around the bush about Calvin ever since we left the play practice."

"And you've done nothing but sidestep my hints," Eddi admonished.

"Well…"

"Whatever happened to poor Hal Gomez?" Eddi asked.

"Poor Hal Gomez?" Jenny echoed. "Since when are you on *his* side?"

"*His* side?" Eddi repeated. "Since when are the two of you divided into sides? I thought you were talking marriage. Now the next thing I know you're blushing and falling into Calvin Barclay's lap!"

"What?" Jenny erupted. "I did no such thing!"

"Yeah, and you didn't discourage the guy, either."

"Well," Jenny rested her arm against her forehead and gazed at the ceiling, "I've just been wondering lately if Hal is the right one, you know? Marriage is such a big, big step. I don't know…" She shrugged.

"Well, Hal certainly does seem to care about you. And in my opinion he's better looking than Calvin any day. I guess it's just the Latin appeal or something, I don't know."

"Good looks aren't everything. If they were, you'd be after Dave Davidson."

"Oh pulllleeeezzzze!" Eddi howled.

"Besides all that, Calvin isn't half bad, if you ask me. Your problem is you've always preferred tall and dark over blond. You know, the Dave Davidson variety," Jenny added with a mischievous smile.

Eddi feigned a bear growl before Jenny continued, "In my opinion, Calvin's every bit as good looking as Hal."

"So I gathered," Eddi drawled. "And I'd hazard to guess Calvin didn't think you were half bad either. I'm not kidding, he seemed ready to pop the question after one meeting."

"Oh, Eddi, don't be so melodramatic," Jenny said. "Calvin and I just met, and Hal and I aren't even engaged. You're acting like we're already married, and I'm some sort of polygamist."

"I guess I just thought the two of you had an understanding."

Jenny remained silent. Tense and silent.

The sound of canine toenails clicked on the hallway tile, and Eddi sat up. "Hey, Roddy!" she called. "I'm in here, baby."

A pug bulldog trotted into the room and wagged his way toward Eddi's bed. She bent to pick up her prized friend. Someone had actually turned him in at the dog pound a few months back. Eddi had arrived within two hours of his incarceration and immediately adopted him.

Roddy grunted and licked her face.

"I just *know* I've seen Dave Davidson before," Jenny mused, her gaze still upon the ceiling.

"Yes, we've all heard that rumor," Eddi quipped. "He's probably just a movie star look alike or something," she added and wondered at Jenny's fixation over the subject.

"He's got the looks," Jenny admitted.

"If you like a cross between Clint Eastwood, Sylvester Stallone, and Count Dracula."

"Oooo, you're cold, Edwardia," Jenny said.

Eddi shot her an if-you-ever-call-me-that-again-I'll-kill-you look.

"Oops!" Jenny covered her lips. "Sorry."

"You look really sorry, Jenni*fer!*"

"I think it's time for me to go to bed." Jenny sat up. "Otherwise we might not ever speak to each other again."

"Sweet dreams," Eddi said and slapped Jenny on her rear.

"Keep your hands off me," Jenny hissed and wrinkled her nose at her sister. "I'm not that kind of woman!"

"How well I know," Eddi said. "If anybody out there will be a virgin on her wedding night, it will be you, sister."

"I hazard to guess we won't be able to say the same thing about Linda," Jenny mused, and her eyes clouded. "She's probably already blown that option for all we know."

"If she hasn't," Eddi said, "she will at the rate she's going. Can you believe she actually *winked* at those policemen at lunch?"

Jenny touched her forehead. "I *nearly died!*"

Roddy snuffled at Eddi's neck and yawned. "Are you ready to go night-night, boy?" Eddi crooned and picked up the scent of cat food on Roddy's breath. While her two felines resented the dog for his canine dispositon, they despised him when he stole their food.

"Most husbands don't have it as good as that mutt," Jenny grumbled on her way out.

Eddi snatched a throw pillow and hurled it at Jenny. The missile hit her head, crashed into the oak dresser, and toppled to the floor.

"I'm going to pretend that didn't happen," Jenny said without ever turning around. "I'm too tired to retaliate." She paused in the doorway and faced her sister. "But don't think I'll forget it." Jenny shook her finger at Eddi and disappeared down the hall.

With a satisfied chuckle, Eddi scratched her dog's ears. She stood, shoved back the covers, and deposited Roddy on the bed. The pug walked to his side and plopped down. After crossing his paws, he propped his head on them and looked up at Eddi.

Soon, Eddi had prepared for bed. She clicked off the lamp, slid under the covers, and relaxed against the pillow. Observing her pet snuggled in the shadows, Eddi wondered if she'd be the one Boswick sister left sleeping with her dog until she retired. She stroked the dog's ears. He licked her fingers, and Eddi rested her hand on his back.

She closed her eyes and allowed her muscles to relax, her mind to unwind. Soon, she drifted into a light sleep, harassed by erratic dreams that escalated into nightmares. Eddi was dressed in a wedding gown, walking down the aisle. The groom, his back to her, faced the minister. The organ music bellowed across the sanctuary and sounded more like a horror movie theme than a day of celebration. Eddi strained to identify the groom, who remained an enigma...until he turned to take Eddi's hand.

The evil groom with glowing red eyes was none other than Dave Davidson. She tried to scream, but only produced a pathetic garble. Dave's black goatee proved the perfect companion for a sinister smile that resembled the devil himself. He enveloped her hands with his even though Eddi fought against his grasp. She tried to pull away, but he held on to her so hard her arm tingled up to her shoulder. Her heart pounding, Eddi released a stifled cry for help.

Another hand gripped her from behind. Eddi strained against the threat, but her feet refused to move. Jenny's voice floated from a distant land, and Eddi screamed for her sister's help. Eddi's struggles heightened Dave's resolve. His eyes glowed redder as he wrapped his arms around her and lowered his face. A demonic roar hovered over the chapel, and the rafters collapsed to the floor with the boom of shattering wood.

Dave's arms grew tighter. He threw her to the floor and shielded her with his body. As the roar diminished, his face hovered over Eddi's. His eyes changed from devilish red to an inviting pool of inky resolve. The goatee vanished. Eddi's pulse, once pounding in dread, now hammered in anticipation. She reached to tangle her willing fingers into his unruly hair.

But Jenny's urgent voice began jarring Eddi's mind as profusely as the hand that shook her shoulder. Eddi tried to knock the hand aside as she strained to press her lips against Dave's, but her left arm was tingling instead of moving.

Finally, she crashed to consciousness and realized she wasn't in Dave's arms, nor was she wearing a wedding gown. Instead, Eddi was tangled in suffocating sheets, her pulse hammering at the base of her throat. Drenched in sweat, Eddi rolled onto her back and opened her eyes a centimeter. Jenny's pale face hovered inches over hers, and the hallway light offered a dim illumination of her animated features.

"What do you want?" Eddi slurred, her mouth dry.

"I couldn't go to sleep. I've been on the internet with my laptop," Jenny claimed while Eddi tried to organize her disoriented thoughts.

"It's taken me two hours," Jenny continued, "but I found out who Dave Davidson *really* is!" Her eyes wide, she tugged on Eddi's arm. "Come on! You're not going to believe it!"

Seven

~ ~

Jenny's words worked like a double jolt of caffeine. "What?" Eddi demanded. She tossed aside the covers and lowered her feet to the floor. "Did you say he's *on the internet?*"

"In living color." Jenny crossed her arms and shook her head as if she'd solved the case of the century.

Roddy's offended woof underscored Jenny's claim. Eddi reached for the pug and offered a reassuring pat. "It's okay, baby," she soothed and flexed her left hand as the tingles gradually decreased. "I'll be back."

Yawning, Eddi padded after Jenny to one of the guest rooms down the hallway. Her perspiration chilled as she reveled in the cool air conditioning. The wild dream still nagged her mind, and Eddi recalled the urgency with which she wanted Dave to kiss her. A warm veil crept under the perspiration and heated her face.

As she entered the room, Eddi vowed to never tell a living soul about her secret desires—not even Jenny. Whatever attraction

Eddi held for the guy, it was nothing more than the natural chemistry between two people of opposite sex.

I would never fall in love with the likes of him, she claimed. *Never!*

Jenny rushed to the antique bed. Her laptop lay amid a tangle of covers. A telephone line connected the computer to the phone jack near the glass-top lamp table.

Jenny plopped onto the poster bed and patted the spot next to her. Eddi hurried to comply. As the smell of clean sheets enveloped her, she scanned the computer screen.

"You're looking at an article featured in *People* magazine three years ago," Jenny said as she picked up the laptop and cradled it in the center of her crossed legs.

"*People?*" Eddi croaked. "Three years ago, and you remembered it?"

"I couldn't remember *where* I'd seen him or why," Jenny explained. "I just knew I had. It took me a couple of hours to track him down."

"You mean, Dave Davidson was in *People?*" Eddi blurted.

"The one and only. Except his name *isn't* Dave Davidson."

"I knew it! It's an alias, isn't it?" She wadded the sheet and skimmed the multicolored web page. "Is he a wanted criminal or something? Believe it or not, I just had a dream about him!" Eddi continued. "He looked like the devil—red eyes, goatee, the whole nine yards!"

Balancing the computer on her lap, Jenny covered her mouth and fell back onto a pile of covers. Her face reddened. Her eyes bugged. Her shoulders shook.

"What?" Eddi demanded. "It's not *that* funny, is it?"

"I am going *to die!*" Jenny wheezed past her fingers. "Your imagination has gone crazy."

Eddi snatched the computer from Jenny. If the dream hadn't also included Eddi's attempt to press her lips against his, she would probably have joined Jenny in revelry. But as things stood, there were too many things about her dream that weren't funny for her to laugh at the ridiculous parts.

"Are you on the right website?" she asked and settled the computer on her lap.

"Start reading here," Jenny said through diminishing mirth. She pointed toward the bottom of the screen. "Here, let me hit the page down button for you." Jenny pressed the appropriate button, and Dave's face scrolled to the top of the screen. He was standing beside a drop-dead gorgeous blonde, and Eddi wondered how much *she'd* wanted Dave's kiss.

"You need to start reading here." Jenny touched the screen near a long section of text. "His real name is William Fitzgerald Davidson. And he was featured among *People's* 'Top Twenty Most Eligible Bachelors' three years ago."

"Oh, so *that's* the reason you remembered the article!" Eddi nodded.

"Ha, ha, ha," Jenny drawled. "Actually, when you get a look at these guys, you won't forget them either. There's a *reason* they're the most eligible bachelors in the U.S." She leaned away from the computer. "Put on your seat belt and read."

Eager for every detail, Eddi gripped the sides of the computer and prepared to devour the words. But the photo continued to command her attention and stopped her from absorbing the information. Dave was dressed in a tuxedo and standing near a limo's open door. The blonde clung to him as if he were her rightful property. On closer inspection, Eddi realized she'd frequently seen the woman on the big screen. Her pale pink evening gown, covered in sequins, sparkled beneath the theater's glistening lights. The caption beneath the photo read, "William F. Davidson, founder of USA Online, with his latest heartthrob, Laura Schock." The theater's marquee read, "Now Playing, Laura Schock in *For Your Heart Only.*"

Eddi absorbed the implications. All she could do was stare at the photo. Dave looked like he belonged to a completely different world. His hair, neatly trimmed, was styled to perfection. His clean-shaven face offered a sculpted canvas for a million-dollar grin that flashed white teeth. The man looked like he had the world by the tail—and well he did.

She scanned the words that provided all the pertinent facts about Dave's life, including his mansion in Dallas, his ranch in Waco, his horse-breeding hobby, and the fact that he was listed among Forbes 500.

"Oh my word, he's in the top 500 richest men in America!" Eddi looked at Jenny who nodded without so much as a blink.

"Yep. He founded USA Online," Jenny answered. "That company virtually *owns* cyberspace."

Eddi gaped. She felt as if the rafters from her dream were crashing into her thoughts. "We—we use that server—both of us," she stammered.

"I know. Isn't this all just too weird?" Jenny shook her head and laughed. "I can't believe you're crossing swords with one of the richest men in America. It's too funny for words." She covered her mouth and stifled another round of laughter.

"*Now* who has a sick sense of humor?" Eddi asked. Her challenge was dashed aside by the memory of her recent conversation with Dave. Before play practice, she hinted that he didn't have the intellectual ability to read and comprehend Jane Austen. He'd wasted no time implying that she was a snob. Eddi groaned. She placed her elbow on her knee and covered her eyes with her fingers.

"What?" Jenny asked.

"I guess I stuck my foot in my mouth at play practice." She lowered her hand and raised her gaze to Jenny.

"You? No way!" Jenny's guileless expression punctuated her sarcasm.

Eddi glared at her.

"What did you say *this* time?" Jenny asked.

"It doesn't matter," she snapped and decided it really didn't.

"So…" Jenny leaned closer and fluttered her eyelashes, "I'm assuming Dave Davidson is getting more attractive by the moment?"

"No way. The guy's a jerk," Eddi said and lifted her chin. "A jerk is a jerk is a jerk! I don't care how much money he has. I wouldn't go out with him if he were the last man on the planet—let alone marry him. Even if he weren't a jerk, we still have nothing in common. He doesn't know good literature from a phone book."

"Probably because he got kicked out of college toward the end of his freshman year," Jenny continued as if she were a TV hostess spieling details for the latest documentary.

"What? He told me he quit. No, wait!" Eddi touched her temple. "He told me he *stopped attending* the end of his freshman year."

"There's an article on the Forbes website that says he got kicked out." Jenny snuggled her feet under the covers.

"What for?"

"He was in the computer science program at Baylor University. He and the head of that department didn't get along. As in, this guy was his *main* professor. Anyway, Dave tells in the article about how he reprogrammed all the computers and refused to give the professor the new operating codes." Jenny tugged her knees to her chest and rested her chin on them.

"Sounds about right," Eddi mumbled. She stared at the window trimmed in forest green blinds and relived the ease with which Dave stated his lines from memory. "The moron has a photographic memory and the disposition of a rabid mountain lion."

"Einstein got kicked out of college, too," Jenny mused. "So did some of the most famous poets. And Thomas Edison's teacher finally told his mother he was incorrigible and that she refused to teach him."

"So!" Eddi blurted. "None of his genius absolves rudeness and arrogance and…and…being a general jerk!"

"You've mentioned the jerk diagnosis several times now."

A lock of hair fell across Eddi's eyes, and she flopped it back. "Yeah, but did I mention that he's a *jerk!*" she added.

"Sheesh!" Jenny said and stretched her legs. "I really thought when you found out all this info you'd change your attitude about him a little."

Eddi didn't comment. After finishing the details regarding just how eligible a bachelor William Fitzgerald Davidson was, Eddi scrolled up and glared at the photo of him with Laura Schock. During their first meeting about the play, Dave had erupted with a diatribe about women chasing him.

"No doubt he's had women throwing themselves at him for years," she mumbled and decided to never again watch a Laura Schock movie *or* dream that she was about to kiss Dave.

"Yeah, everybody but *you.*" Jenny patted her sister on the back as if she were issuing an award.

Eddi passed the computer back to her. Jenny accepted the laptop and eyed the screen.

"If and when I *ever* get married," Eddi claimed, "it will be because I'm madly in love with the man—not what the man owns." She pulled the end of her French braid over her shoulder and tugged the hair band from its end. Her waist-length hair relaxed. The braid began to unravel, and the smell of her floral shampoo enveloped her.

"I know," Jenny said with a resigned sigh. "I'm in the same boat."

"So, that's why you're hedging on a commitment to a real-estate tycoon and flirting with a small-town veterinarian."

"Yes." Jenny looked at her sister. "If the truth was known, though, Calvin's probably better off than Hal. Hal doesn't mind taking financial risks and losing money. He came within a hair-breadth of filing bankruptcy a few months ago." The smudges of mascara under Jenny's eyes made her look like a raccoon. The undaunted honesty oozing from her soul lent her a wisdom beyond her thirty years. "That's neither here nor there, though," Jenny continued. "I can support myself, for that matter. The problem is, I'm really doubting whether I'm truly in love with Hal—or if I've ever been in love at all."

She observed the computer, clicked a series of buttons, and set the instrument on the glass-topped nightstand.

"I don't think I ever have been," Eddi admitted. "Sometimes I wonder if I ever *will* be." Her mutinous mind replayed those minutes after the tornado. She would never admit it, but Dave Davidson had stirred her in ways she had never experienced.

Eddi frowned. "I never have liked Laura Schock that much. Have you?"

Jenny punched her pillows. "I don't care one way or the other," she said and plopped back on the pillows. "Why should you?"

"I have no idea," Eddi admitted. A lazy yawn overtook her. She rubbed her eyes. They felt as if the stale mascara were matting them together. She further deduced that she probably had the raccoon look like Jenny. Eddi extended her legs and rested her hands on her thighs.

"I think if one of us doesn't get married soon, Mom's going to have a stroke," Jenny observed. "All she talked about all the way up here was how their home goes back into the Boswick Oil estate when father dies. I don't think she'll ever forgive him for bowing out of the Boswick millions."

"I think he did the right thing," Eddi said. "Horticulture suits him. High society and oil don't...me neither, for that matter." She released a chuckle. "Imagine what Mom would think if she found out how rich Dave is. He could probably buy a dozen houses like Mom and Dad's with his pocket change."

"If she ever finds out he's so rich, she'll never speak to you again if you let him get away."

"Humph! And Dad would never speak to me if I *did* marry him." Eddi stretched.

"At least Dave doesn't seem to be affected by all the money. He's not putting on airs, that's for sure," Jenny said. "What you see is what you get."

"Ha!" Eddi mocked. "Your memory is shot, if you believe that! Hello?" She snapped her fingers. "Remember? The man is using a pseudonym and has hornswaggled a whole community into believing he's something he's not!"

"Hornswaggled?" Jenny exclaimed. "Aren't we using big words these days?"

"Oh good grief!" Eddi rolled her eyes. "Everybody around here says that. I guess they're rubbing off on me."

The sound of canine toenails clicking down the hallway signaled Roddy's nearing. The pug's face soon appeared in the doorway.

"There's my main man," Eddi crooned.

"Just your type, too." Jenny eyed the pet. "Short, pudgy, and *broke.*"

"Yeah, but with a heart full of love that's worth all the diamonds in Africa." Eddi softly whistled, and Roddy grunted his way toward her. She leaned off the side of the bed and scooped the dog into her arms.

After settling against the pile of pillows, Eddi rubbed the bulldog's velvet ears. She kissed his head, and his hair prickled her lips.

"I guess I'll mosey on back to bed," she drawled in an affected accent, "unless you have some other amazing discovery to unveil. Did you also find out Mrs. DeBloom is really from Saturn?"

"Very funny," Jenny said and scratched Roddy's neck. The dog offered a friendly lick.

Eddi slipped from the bed. "You know," she mused and eyed the silk ficus tree in the corner, "that article didn't say anything about Dave moving here."

"No, it didn't," Jenny agreed. "It was probably written before he moved."

"Does he still own USA Online?"

"I don't think so," Jenny said. "Remember when we got the server message that USA Online had been bought out by Alltel?"

"When was that?"

"A few years ago," Jenny said.

"As in three?" Eddi dug her toes into the cotton-soft carpet. Jenny shrugged. "Maybe."

"Did I hear Calvin tell you Dave has lived here nearly three years?" Eddi asked. She stroked Roddy's feet and ran her thumb along his tender paw pads.

"Yes." Jenny tugged the band from her hair and it fell around her shoulders.

"So, I wonder what happened? I wonder why he moved here—to this isolated little town where nothing much happens."

"Why did *you* move here?" Jenny asked and tossed the hair band on the night stand.

"To get away from…" Eddi trailed off and mentally finished the thought, *all the family stress Mom was putting me through.*

"So, maybe Dave was trying to get away too," Jenny offered.

"From what?" Eddi asked. "He brought his aunt with him, so it couldn't have been the family thing, could it?"

"Who knows?" Jenny said.

"And if looks are anything to go by, he's totally changed. After seeing him in jeans and boots all this time, it's hard to imagine him *ever* wearing a tux."

"And after seeing him in that tux, it's hard to imagine him chasing longhorns, for that matter." Jenny stood and rummaged through her overnight bag.

"Humph." Eddi meandered toward the doorway and side-stepped a piece of Jenny's luggage. "All this makes me wonder what he's up to in that little building behind his house."

"Maybe it takes a whole building for him to file the marriage offers that come down the tubes." Jenny pulled an oversized nightshirt from her bag.

"That's probably truer than we know." Eddi stepped into the hallway. "Good night," she softly called and debated about ways to sneak into the brick building.

⸎ ⸎

Linda Boswick opened the door to the guest bedroom. Her vision bleary, she observed Eddi slip into her bedroom. The light went out in Jenny's room.

As usual, she thought and grimaced. *Those two are connected at the hip, even at two in the morning.* Linda couldn't remember a time growing up when she ever felt as if she were part of their "party." Living with them was as bad as having elder twin sisters.

The spaghetti strap on her gown slipped down her arm. She tugged it back up, stepped into the shadowed hallway, and headed toward the bathroom. She couldn't sleep. That was nothing new. She flipped on the bathroom light and squinted against the glare. As usual, Eddi's house was immaculate, right down to the freshly scrubbed basin and the new hand soaps, shaped like roses, no less.

Linda grabbed her toiletry bag from the sink side. The smell of baby powder emanated from the bag as she fumbled across shampoo, facial cream, and two hair brushes. At last, she wrapped her fingers around a cylindrical bottle. The label featured her name and said the contents were Seldane, a common prescription for allergies. The pills were not Seldane. They were valium. She'd filched them from her mother's endless supply. Mary Boswick had been taking them for her nerves as long as Linda could remember. They proved the remedy the days Linda was too wired up to sleep…or too uptight to relax…or just because she liked the mellow feel the pills evoked.

Linda unscrewed the lid and popped one of the pills onto her tongue. She grabbed a disposable cup, filled it with water, and tossed the liquid into her mouth. The valium slipped down. After dropping the bottle back into the bag, she examined her appearance in the mirror. A rumpled bush of strawberry blonde hair surrounded pale blue eyes. Unlike Jenny, Linda possessed no freckles—only a dark mole at the left corner of her mouth. "The perfect beauty mark," her mother proclaimed when Linda was twelve. But Linda was no fool. Jenny was the beauty of the family. Eddi got all the brains. *That leaves me with nothing,* Linda thought.

She scowled and rubbed at the dark circles under her eyes. Eddi had threatened to take her mom and sisters to church in the morning. Linda had no desire to attend church these days, and she'd lain awake the last hour trying to figure how to get out of the dreaded event. The problem still stumped her…until she reconsidered the valium.

Linda's lips turned upward, and she reopened her bag. The last time she took two valium, she'd been so knocked out she hadn't been able to get up until one o'clock. All she had to do to get out of church was take a second valium. When everyone got up to go to church, she would awaken enough to explain to her mother that she didn't feel well. Linda would then sleep through lunch. That would convince them all that she'd been telling the truth.

She reached for the prescription bottle, only to discover it lying atop another prescription—a flat container of pills that ensured Linda wouldn't get pregnant. But that was only as long as she took them. Linda gasped. She'd placed the oral contraceptives in this toiletry bag three days ago. She hadn't taken one since before stepping into Larry's arms.

Or was his name Barry? she thought and pursed her lips.

"Oh, who cares?" Linda growled and snatched up the birth control pills. She slid out the tray and counted the missed pills.

"Exactly three," she breathed. Shock started at her feet and rushed to her hairline.

"How could I have been so bone-headed?" The gynecologist had firmly warned her that the pills only worked if she took them every day at the same time. Even one missed pill could result in a pregnancy.

"Oh, God, don't let me be pregnant," she prayed and pushed out three tablets. Linda threw them into her mouth and downed another cup of water.

Her fingers shaking, she dropped the rest of the birth control pills back into the bag and retrieved the valium. She unscrewed the lid and poured out another tablet. Two fell out, and Linda nearly popped them both into her mouth. It might take three valium to get her to sleep, now that she was worried about a pregnancy. Linda hesitated. She'd never taken three before. But then she'd never skipped three birth control pills, either.

"Better not," she mumbled and tipped the extra valium back into the bottle. *I don't want to take so many that Mom starts missing them,* she thought before swallowing the second valium.

Eight

Three weeks later, the London Community Church's July Fourth picnic proved just like every other picnic they'd enjoyed the last twenty years, at least according to Cheri Locaste. Since this was Eddi's first picnic, she had no previous experiences with which to compare it.

She stood in the church's massive yard at the end of a picnic table laden with watermelons. Cheri loaded slice upon slice of fragrant, red watermelon onto paper plates and handed them to Eddi. Her job was to pass the plates to those standing in the line that stretched past the homemade ice cream table.

"These people just don't quit, do they?" Eddi mumbled under her breath.

"Every year, there's a hot item," Cheri explained. "Last year, it was the ice cream. This year, it's the watermelon. I think it's just so hot this year that the ice cream is too heavy." She sighed, picked up a paper napkin, and swiped at her damp forehead. Cheri had wisely refrained from cosmetics, as usual. Eddi figured by now every scrap of her makeup was slipping to her chin.

Cheri's simple blue T-shirt clung to her torso as damply as Eddi's decorated cotton blouse cleaved to her.

Eddi lifted her braid off her neck and let it flop back in place. A trickle of sweat ran down her temple. Perhaps the year had finally come to get rid of her mile-long hair. Thoughts of a cute wedge cut were swiftly proving too tempting to resist.

"Miss," a tiny voice said near her elbow, "may I please have some watermelon?" Eddi looked down. A dark-skinned boy stood with one hand on his hip. He held a worn ball glove under his other arm. The lad couldn't have been a day over five. He wore a Texas Rangers ball cap, and his shirt read Tommy.

A rush of pleasure warmed Eddi, and she squatted to get on eye level with the child. The smell of little boy sweat and dust heightened her delight. "Well, we'll get you the biggest, juiciest piece of watermelon we have." Eddi tugged on his ball cap. His bottom lip protruding, Tommy nudged his hat back up. Eddi's smile only increased.

A man walked up and laid his tanned hand on Tommy's shoulder. "We've been playing catch. Give this guy the biggest piece you have," a familiar voice proclaimed.

Eddi's grin stiffened. The watermelon's once inviting smell now turned her stomach. She recognized that voice all too well. When she arrived at the picnic an hour ago, Eddi had spotted Dave in the church ball field behind the brick church. A group of men had been playing catch with several boys. They were all warming up for the peewee baseball game that would occur that evening. Eddi had wasted no time volunteering on the other side of the churchyard and hoped to avoid speaking even one word to Dave Davidson. Her growing dislike of the man was nearly enough to make her want to attend another church. If not for her blossoming friendship with Cheri Locaste, Eddi would have seriously considered changing churches. The only thing she and Cheri had in common was their long hair. Otherwise,

Cheri was as introspective as Eddi was outspoken. But Eddi had grown to thoroughly enjoy Cheri's company.

"I'm sure you'll be the best baseball player out there tonight," Eddi continued as if Dave had never spoken. She stood and took the watermelon-laden plate Cheri offered. Eddi presented the treat to the little boy and kept her gaze lowered. She decided that if she pretended Dave wasn't present, he'd just go away.

"Thank you, ma'am," Tommy said as he accepted the watermelon. He devoured a giant bite of the red meat before taking one step. Red juice dripping from his chin, he sank his teeth into the melon again.

"Hey, you little piranha," Dave teased. "At the rate you're going, there won't be any for the rest of us."

"Oh, there's plenty," Cheri said. "Here's a big piece just for you."

Eddi accepted the plate.

"You're looking fresh as ever this evening, Mizz Boswick," Dave drawled.

The very fact that Dave had paid her some form of compliment took her so off guard Eddi forgot her vow not to look at him. Her gaze flicked up to his face. He wore a baseball cap that read USA Online, and Eddi nearly blurted something about his once owning the billion dollar company.

Dave observed her with one eye slightly narrowed. Eddi couldn't decide if the guy really meant the compliment or if he were mocking her. In her estimation, there was no way she looked fresh—not by a long shot. Presently, she was just hoping her antiperspirant didn't fail. Eddi shifted the watermelon and plate to one hand. A fly buzzed by her ear, and she swatted at it. She looked toward the western horizon to note the unforgiving sun was still about three hours from setting. She couldn't remember a day in her life when she'd been so hot.

No way do I look fresh, she thought. *Dave is mocking me.* Which was exactly what he'd somehow managed to do the last three play practices. Last night, he'd even corrected one of her lines. And his aunt had added insult to injury when she told Dave he shouldn't expect his level of memory from the rest of the cast.

"If you think I look fresh, you need glasses," she snapped and shoved a hefty slice of watermelon into his hands.

Dave juggled the paper plate and his ball glove before the giant slice of melon toppled to the grass.

"Oh great," Eddi mumbled, exasperated that anything would keep Dave in line one more second than necessary. "I'll get it," she offered.

"No, I will," Dave said.

The two bent and both reached for the melon. Dave attempted to pick it up at the same time Eddi did. The result was a five-second battle over the slice—a battle that ended when Mary Boswick's squeal echoed from the parking lot.

"There's Eddi beside the watermelon table!" Eddi's mom continued, "Eddi! Over here!"

Eddi dropped the watermelon and welcomed the distraction of her family. She straightened and waved toward her plump mother and angular father as they walked across the parking lot with Jenny in their wake. Her mom returned the wave as if Eddi were sailing into harbor from a decade journey at sea. More than once Eddi had been embarrassed by her mother's robust manner. Today, she welcomed Mary Boswick's yelling across the yard the minute she spotted her daughter. Jenny, Linda, and her folks had all promised Eddi they'd come to the picnic. She'd been watching for them the last hour.

Eddi pivoted to face Cheri and turned her back on Dave. "I'm going to take a break, okay? My family just arrived."

"Oh, sure." Cheri nodded. "Go on." She nodded and focused upon Dave. "Here, I'll take that watermelon and give you a fresh piece."

Standing, Dave extended the soiled watermelon to Cheri. "Thanks," he said.

Their conversation faded as Eddi stepped across the lush grass and neared the parking lot. She had kicked her gold thongs off near the watermelon table and didn't consider that she was barefoot until her toes contacted the baking pavement.

"Ouch!" she exclaimed and scooted back onto the St. Augustine grass.

Mary Boswick rushed toward her daughter. "Look at you without your shoes!" she admonished. She shook her finger at Eddi's nose as if she were eight. "I thought when you finished law school you'd start acting more civilized."

"Not a chance, Mom," Eddi said with a half grin. She exchanged a hug with her wiry-haired mother and was genuinely glad to see her. When Eddi moved from Houston, she'd been so relieved to be out of her mother's sphere of control, she didn't think she'd ever miss her. Today, Eddi welcomed her mom's presence—mainly because she and the rest of the family offered a buffer between her and Dave.

"Hi, Eddi." Edward Boswick stepped forward and enveloped his daughter in a bear hug. He finished with a kiss in the middle of her forehead. "Let me look at you," he said and backed away.

"Ah, Dad," Eddi complained, "you act like I'm ten and you haven't seen me for a year."

"You mean you aren't still ten?" the gentleman asked and shoved back his golf hat. His gray eyes were round in mock disillusionment.

Eddi chuckled and shook her head. "Not on your life," she said.

Jenny neared from the side, and Eddi exchanged a quick hug with her sister. When they parted Eddi noticed Jenny's hair. Her mouth dropped open. "Oh my word! You got a new haircut!" She touched her sister's neck. "It's so short...and so cute! You look like...like Meg Ryan!" Eddi exclaimed.

"That's what Mom said when she saw me this morning," Jenny said. She ran her fingers through the top of her hair. "I don't care if it makes me look like Minnie Mouse, it's cool and easy to take care of."

"I'm going to do it, too," Eddi said with a firm nod. "I've been threatening to do it. I think now's the time to follow through. I need a more professional look around here anyway. Maybe it will help some people take me more seriously."

"Speaking of the local yokels, look who's coming now," Jenny mumbled.

"Excuse me," Dave's voice floated from behind.

Eddi stiffened and swallowed a groan. "Thanks for the warning," she mumbled.

"Cheri asked me to bring your shoes to you." Dave stepped beside Eddi, and she offered a rigid grin.

"Thanks." She accepted the gold-toned thongs, dropped them to the ground, and scooted her feet into them.

Dave glanced at her family and then nodded toward Jenny. "How are you, Jenny?" he asked.

"Fine," Jenny responded with a warm smile.

Eddi scowled at her sister and wished she wouldn't encourage him to stand around and talk. Besides all that, he'd abandoned the standard jeans and boots and was wearing shorts and a T-shirt. Despite Eddi's resolve to disdain him, she couldn't deny that Dave offered a nice view.

"Are these your parents, Eddi?" Dave asked.

"Yes. This is my mom and dad, Mary and Edward Boswick."

A tense pause followed. "Nice to meet you," Dave said and shook hands with Eddi's folks.

Jenny cast a pointed look at Eddi, and she couldn't figure out what her sister was trying to imply. Finally, Jenny said, "Mom, Dad, this is William Davidson."

"Oh!" Eddi said. "I guess I forgot to tell you Dave's name."

"Is it Dave or William, then?" When Mrs. Boswick offered her inquiry, Eddi's eyes widened and she focused upon Jenny, whose color was fading fast.

A cautious glimpse of Dave proved his face a rigid mask of disapproval. "Around these parts, I'm just known as Dave," he uttered as if he were choking. "If you'll excuse me, I think I'm needed on the ball field." Dave stalked toward the baseball diamond, his shoulders hunched.

"Well, he wasn't exactly friendly, was he?" Mary glared after Dave as if he were the big bad wolf. "Some people!" she huffed.

"He might have his moments," Jenny said, "but he's filthy rich. I guess when you've got as much money as he does, you can afford to be brusque when it pleases you."

"Not with me." Mary squared her pudgy shoulders and made a face at Dave's back.

A horn's raucous honk and the rev of an engine cut off any new speculation. A silver PT Cruiser wheeled into the parking place beside the Boswick's minivan.

"I guess we failed to tell you that Linda has purchased a new vehicle." Edward crossed his arms, and his shoulders stiffened. "Nothing would do but for her to follow us up here instead of riding with us. And it looks like she's got a couple of friends with her this time, whether any of us likes it or not," he added as if she were in the company of skunks.

Eddi grinned at her younger sister, who hopped out of the Cruiser and vigorously waved. "Hi, Eddi! I've got some people for you to meet!" she exclaimed.

"Great!" Eddi posed a silent question to Jenny who shrugged.

"I've not met them," Jenny said.

Two men crawled out of the vehicle's passenger side. Both were tall and lean. One had dark, well-groomed hair, a heavy brow line and straight nose. The other sported a white-blond flat top and looked like he belonged to a Beach Boys club. As they neared, the men stood on either side of Linda, and Eddi couldn't determine which one would be considered her current boyfriend. The dark-headed man looked to be closer to Eddi's age than Linda's. His kind brown eyes and pleasant expression suggested that for once Linda had attracted somebody who was both good looking *and* decent.

Linda and her friends stopped near the Boswicks, and Linda didn't hesitate to make introductions. "This is Rick Wallace," she said, placing her hand on the arm of the kind-eyed man. "And this is André Owens," she continued and smiled toward the blond.

"Nice to meet you." André nodded.

Rick extended his hand toward Edward Boswick, who returned the handshake with a relieved light in his eyes. "Glad to meet you," Edward said as he also shook hands with André.

Linda continued to make introductions. Eddi examined the whites of Linda's eyes. They were clear. Her speech was precise, and she didn't seem overly giggly. For once her younger sister wasn't tipsy.

Jenny offered a discreet thumbs-up, and Eddi responded in like manner.

"Now, what do you wonderful young men do for a living?" Mary Boswick asked.

"They're on the Houston police force," Linda oozed and grabbed both their hands. "Isn't that just the coolest?"

Mary nudged Linda aside and stepped between the two gentlemen. "Policemen!" she exclaimed. "Oh, how exciting. I remember once, long before I got married, I dated a policeman. He was *sooo* nice." Her full cotton dress swishing with every step, Mary walked along the sidewalk, her arms looped in each of the men's. Linda followed close behind.

Jenny, Eddi, and her father fell in after them. "Some days I wonder who's more silly—your mother or her youngest daughter," Edward whispered.

"Oh, Daddy," Eddi admonished.

"Tell me you weren't thinking the same thing...or that you didn't move to the backside of nowhere just to get away from them both." Edward lifted the front of his golfer's shirt away from his neck and glanced toward the blazing orange ball nearing the horizon. "Would that we were all so fortunate."

Eddi examined her father's profile. A few times in recent years, he had forgotten to pretend with Eddi. Only in the last five years had Eddi suspected that her father had stayed in his marriage because of his dedication to his wedding vows and his love for his daughters. Eddi had finally come to the conclusion that if her father weren't a God-fearing man, he would have long ago left her mother. Eddi thought of all the friends she had known growing up whose homes were broken. Of their splintered lives. Of the times she had complained about her family, and they told her she didn't know just how fortunate she was. A rush of love and appreciation welled up within Eddi, and she spontaneously kissed her father on his cheek.

"Hey! What's this all about?" Edward asked and acted as if he were pushing her away. His pleasurable smile belied his actions.

"Just because I love you, and I appreciate you," she said.

Edward kissed her hand while Eddi gazed after her mother and Linda. Between the two of them, they were entertaining the policemen in the highest of spirits.

As the four headed toward the ice cream table, Eddi said, "Let's just hope that these new friends of Linda's will be a turning point for her." She scrutinized her father for any sign that he was taking Linda's exploits seriously. If not, Eddi wondered how she could convince him that Linda's problems ran much deeper than a case of the sillies.

"Well, we'll see." Edward yawned. "We will indeed see."

Jenny stepped beside Eddi and whispered, "I can't believe I let that slip about Dave's real name. I *nearly died!*"

"I think he did, too," Eddi agreed and released her father's arm. The two sisters stepped ahead of him and delved into a private chat session.

"If you ask me, the more I think of it, the funnier it gets." Eddi chuckled like a panther who's cornered a jack rabbit. "Here he is, thinking he's duped a whole community full of country bumpkins. He's so cockeyed sure he's fooled them all he's even wearing a USA Online cap! He's convinced nobody will even make the connection. It serves him right that somebody was sharp enough to blow his cover."

With a satisfied smirk, Eddi skimmed the churchyard to discover Dave in the distance, back on the ball field. He stood on the pitcher's mound, drinking a bottle of water. A tyke ran up to him from across the field, and Dave set the water on the ground. Behind the little guy, Calvin Barclay trotted toward the pitcher's mound.

"There's Calvin," Eddi said. She nodded toward the field, and Jenny followed her lead.

"Yes, I see him," Jenny said as Edward caught up with his daughters.

"Is he the young man you mentioned meeting the last time you were here?" Edward asked.

"In the flesh," Jenny admitted.

"And he's a veterinarian?" Edward quizzed.

"Yes."

"You could do worse, my dear," he said with a shrewd stare at his eldest daughter. "Much, much worse."

"I know, Dad," Jenny said with a lift of her hand. "You don't have to remind me that you don't like Hal."

"I never said I don't like the fellow," Edward claimed. "Now listen to you. You're starting to blame me for things I've never even said." He tugged on the back of Jenny's hair. "You get your hair all cut off and then go sassy on me." His eyes dancing in revelry, he looked at Eddi. "Why don't you get a haircut like this and the two of you can just take over the world together."

"I just might!" Eddi proclaimed.

"I'm going to go over to the ice cream table and see if I can keep Linda and your mother out of trouble." An eruption of shrill laughter floated from across the yard.

Eddi observed her sister and mother, bent in hilarity as they each clung to their policeman of choice.

"See what I mean?" Edward asked before walking toward them.

"Has Calvin…uh…mentioned me at all?" Jenny asked the second her dad was out of ear shot.

"Oh yes," Eddi answered and offered only a sly smile.

"Well, are you going to tell me what he said or not?" Jenny demanded.

"Oh? You want to know?" Eddi asked.

Jenny narrowed her eyes.

"Okay, I'll tell you then." She examined her polished nails. "Every time I saw him he double-checked to make sure you were still coming up this weekend. As interested as he is, I'm amazed that he hasn't called and asked you himself." Eddi scrutinized her sister.

"He doesn't have my number," Jenny explained.

"You mean he didn't ask for it when you were here last?"

"Of course, I just conveniently forgot to give it to him. All I gave him was my e-mail address."

"Ah, playing hard to get?"

"No…not necessarily," Jenny said and tilted her head. "Just not overly easy. I want to keep him interested, you know. I *have* responded to all his e-mails the last few weeks."

"Well, he's interested, and that's for sure." Eddi slipped her hands into the pockets of her capri pants. "As a matter of fact, Mrs. DeBloom has asked the whole cast of *Pride and Prejudice* over for tea tomorrow evening at six. She wants us to see how the remodeling on Huntington House is going. I think she's going to want us to run through the first act on the stage to see how the blocking will go." Eddi swiped at a trickle of sweat along her temple. "Anyway, Calvin asked me when I got here if you were still coming to the picnic and if you were going to be at Huntington House tomorrow night. I think he's still wanting you to play his leading lady."

"Well, I guess if he insists, then I will." Jenny ducked her head and smiled.

"You will?" Eddi blurted and paused near a massive oak tree.

"I guess. I just can't seem to get Calvin off my mind these last few weeks," Jenny admitted, her blue eyes revealing candid validation of her words. "I know it's way too early to make any kind of commitment, but I'm beginning to wonder if he's the one I've waited for all these years."

"What about Hal?" Eddi asked.

Jenny's brow wrinkled. "Oh…" she fretted and nipped at the end of her pinky, "why did you have to bring him up?"

"I don't know." Eddi shrugged and kicked a loose pebble along the sidewalk. "Maybe because this could all start becoming a problem for you if you aren't careful."

"It's not like Hal and I are engaged, for pity's sake." Jenny pulled a tissue from her pocket and pressed it against her upper lip, beaded in sweat.

"But isn't that what he wants?" Eddi asked and wondered how her sister could look so cool, even while blotting sweat.

"He keeps hinting about getting a ring." Jenny slipped the tissue back into her pocket.

"And you aren't discouraging him?" The smell of the first smoke from an outdoor grill attested that someone had begun the hamburger and hot dog cooking.

"I'm not exactly discouraging him," Jenny said. "But I'm not *encouraging* him, either. I'm just so confused and uncertain right now—especially with all these unexpected feelings about Calvin thrown into the mix."

"Well, here comes somebody who looks like he's wanting to *un*confuse you," Eddi said.

Calvin strode toward them from the field. He waved his ball glove and shouted, "Jenny!"

When Jenny waved back, he upped his pace to a trot. "Great to see you!" he puffed the second he stopped beside her. His full blond hair peeked from beneath his ball cap. And Eddi couldn't determine whether Calvin was glowing with the radiance of heat or the excitement of seeing Jenny.

They were within a few feet of an oak tree beneath which sat several empty chairs. By silent consent, the three meandered toward the chairs. A light breeze tickled the oak, and its leaves shimmied in the promise of approaching evening.

"This has been a hot day." Calvin's attention riveted upon Jenny, and he rubbed his hand across his flat abdomen. "But you don't look the least bit bothered by all the heat."

Calvin seemed oblivious to his tank top damply clinging to his midsection. Eddi decided the guy was glowing with excitement, not heat.

"Why should I?" With a demure smile, Jenny looked down. A tinge of pink pleasure touched her cheeks. "I've been driving in an air-conditioned vehicle all the way from Houston."

Jenny was wearing that same linen shorts set she got for ten bucks the last time she and Eddi went shopping. As they all sat down, Eddi eyed her own rumpled, white capri pants and sleeveless blouse. The outfit had promised to be appropriate for the event. As usual, Eddi felt faded in comparison to Jenny.

"You got your hair cut didn't you?" Calvin asked.

"Yes," Jenny answered. "It's shorter than it's ever been. I'm still trying to get used to it." She stroked her neckline.

"I love it!" Calvin claimed with so much enthusiasm Eddi figured he would love it if Jenny got a Mohawk.

Eddi crossed her legs and looked toward the rolling horizon, covered in east Texas pine trees. *I might as well not be here*, she thought and wondered how Cheri was faring at the watermelon table. She peered in her direction to note that the line had finally diminished.

"Excuse me, Eddi?" Dave's voice startled Eddi, and she hid the tiny jump.

She gradually shifted her attention from Cheri to him. The last thing she would ever do is let the man know he flustered her...or that if he had ever been nice to her she probably would have fallen at his feet. But he had destroyed that option. Whether she wanted to admit it or not, William Fitzgerald Davidson did what few people could ever claim: He intimidated Eddi with the sheer force of his personality and masculinity.

But only a tiny bit, she hedged. Eddi lifted her chin and gazed up at him.

Dave tugged at the bill of his cap and said, "I need to talk to you," in a blunt voice that demanded no opposition.

"Oh, really?" Eddi asked and crossed her legs as if she planned to move nowhere. "Well, go ahead then."

"Not *here,*" he said and darted a glance toward Jenny and Calvin.

"Those two don't even have a clue you're here," Eddi said.

"Whatever," Dave said, his lips stiff, "I still want our chat to happen where no one can hear." His eye twitched. "And I think you know why."

When Eddi refused to stand, he reached for her arm and tugged her to her feet. Before she could protest, Dave was dragging her toward the ball field.

Nine

⁓ ⁓

Dave wasted no time marching toward one of few isolated spots in the vicinity. The dugout offered the perfect place for this necessary conversation.

Eddi twisted her wrist in his hard grasp. "Has anyone ever told you you're nothing but a big bully!" she huffed.

Keeping his gaze fixed upon the dugout, Dave refused to respond or to release her. The woman was an idiot if she thought for one second he would allow Jenny's slip to go by without an interrogation. Nobody in London knew who he was—not even Calvin Barclay. The last thing he needed was for a smart alec newcomer to blow his cover.

When his sneakers crunched across the dugout's sandy con-crete, Dave nudged Eddi before him, stopped, and slammed the dugout's gate. The fencing rattled as he shoved the sliding lock into place.

Eddi turned on him, her fists balled at her side. Dave stepped into her space and expected her to back away. She didn't budge.

A rash of perspiration covered her forehead. Her blonde hair looked nearly white against her flushed face. Dave would have presumed her overheated if her pointed gaze hadn't insisted she was incensed.

"How long have you known?" he barked.

She poised to answer, but Dave held up his hand.

"And don't act like you don't know what I'm talking about."

Eddi crossed her arms. "Jenny found out when she was here last," she explained, her voice steadier than Dave expected.

Her ability to keep her voice calm irritated him. "How?" he demanded.

"The internet." Eddi offered a sarcastic smile and eyed his cap. "It's a new invention. Haven't you heard?"

Dave yanked off his hat and slammed it onto the bench atop a scattering of ball gloves. "Blast you, Eddi Boswick!" he yelled. "Why did you have to move here?"

"This is a free country," she purred. "You're perfectly free to leave if you don't think we can coexist." She extended her hand toward the dugout gate.

"Oh, we can coexist," he snarled, "but only if you'll keep your mouth shut."

Her eyes narrowed, and Dave expected her next statement to hold some irritation. "I haven't mentioned a word to anyone for three weeks," she said, her tones as cool as ever.

Dave propped his hands on his hips and stretched for every nuance of her meaning. "So?" he began and waited for her to finish.

"What makes you think I care enough to have a conversation about you with anyone?" she asked.

He remained silent and searched her soul for any hint of duplicity. All Dave detected was brutal sincerity laden with stony resolve. He stepped back and grappled for a hot retort. None came. Instead, he tried to decide if he were relieved that she hadn't revealed his identity or disappointed that she didn't care enough to talk about him.

"I thought by now your opinion of me would have changed," Dave finally said.

"What's that supposed to mean?" Eddi asked.

A wisp of a hot breeze stirred up red dust on the ball field and floated into the dugout. Dave detected the faint floral scent he recalled so well the day he'd buried his head in her hair and prayed the tornado wouldn't eat them alive.

"Most women decide they really like me once they find out about my money." Dave didn't mention how much he hoped Eddi's opinion of him hadn't been affected by her knowledge of his fortune.

"Humph." Eddi gazed toward the sizeable church. "I don't base my opinion of people on how wealthy they are. I value people because they are created in the image of God. That means I'll value and respect my garbage collector as much as the bank president. As for you…" Eddi turned her attention back to Dave, "it doesn't matter to me if you own the whole internet."

"Oh, so you haven't suddenly decided I'm a prime matrimonial prospect?" Dave didn't question why the answer to his verbal jab was so important. Or why he'd begun to look forward to play practice with more warmth than he'd admit. Or why he'd been disappointed when there wasn't at least one kiss scene in the whole play.

Eddi brushed past him and unlocked and opened the squeaky gate. "When I get married, it will be for love," she growled. "So don't get your hopes up." She stomped out of the dugout.

Dave winced at her using his own words against him, but he wasted no time following her. "Eddi!" he called and rushed through the squawking gate. "Eddi!" he hollered again.

He spotted her twenty feet away, storming past the portable bleachers as if she were a charging warrior. Dave ran to her side and placed his hand on her shoulder.

"What?" she snapped and turned on him. She glowered at Dave as if she were seriously thinking of snatching him bald.

At last, Dave had rattled her composure. He repressed the satisfied smile that begged to be expressed. Dave needed a promise. He wasn't in the position to gloat. He hated having to plead for her cooperation, but the necessity couldn't be denied.

"Would you and Jenny please promise not to tell anyone?" he asked. "I've built a new life here. I like my privacy."

"What exactly are you trying to hide, William Fitzgerald Davidson?" Her head bobbed from side to side as she spoke his name.

"Hide?" Dave prompted. For a wrinkle in time he wondered if she had somehow discovered his secret in the building behind his house.

"Yes." She crossed her arms and observed him as if he were a wicked pirate. "Or might I better ask, *who* are you trying to hide from?"

A stream of stinging sweat seeped to the corner of his eye. *No way does she know,* he thought as he peered into her accusing eyes. *No way.*

"I'm trying to preserve my privacy," he enunciated each word as if she were a daft three-year-old.

"You have a flamboyant way of doing that, don't you?" she prompted.

"Meaning?"

"Anybody with half a brain can tell the person who owns *your* ranch has to have plenty of dough." Eddi flipped her braid over her shoulder, and Dave wondered what her hair looked like hanging freely down her back. He'd only seen it braided or in a chignon.

"That place is modest compared to what I could afford," he said. "And besides…" Dave paused and eyed a thunderhead towering in the distance, "local rumor has it all my money comes from Aunt Maddy." He offered a mild grin. "Haven't you heard?"

"Yes, I've heard, but I stopped believing that the minute I saw your ranch."

Dave imagined her in court saying, "Let the record show," or whatever it was lawyers were supposed to always be crowing. "You might have stopped believing," he said and faced her, "but the rest of the town hasn't."

"Okay," she acquiesced. "I won't tell anybody."

"And Jenny? Will you ask Jenny to do the same?" He gazed past Eddi, to the oak tree where Calvin sat, enthralled with Eddi's sister.

"I'll make sure she doesn't tell anyone." Eddi crossed her arms. "Happy now?"

"Delighted!" Dave was so relieved he was tempted to kiss her whole face. Even though the prospect heated his veins, his imagination insisted on another reaction for her. Dave pictured Eddi hacking and gagging and on the verge of regurgitation. The refreshing part of that scene was that no amount of money he owned would sway Eddi to make a play for him. None. Dave laughed out loud.

"What?" Eddi asked.

He observed a trio of tykes scrambling for the baseball field. The smell of charcoal promised a rewarding meal after the game. "Oh, nothing," Dave mumbled and trudged past her. "Nothing that would interest you."

He felt her watching him, but kept a steady gait toward the three boys. His humor diminished as he recalled those minutes after the tornado when Eddi had been in his arms. She'd been a long way from gagging—a long way indeed.

A warning jolt reminded Dave he was flirting with his own destiny. From the first time he met Eddi Boswick, Dave suspected she would never base her value for him on his wealth. This evening proved his assumption. But the fact that Eddi had a good heart and Dave found her increasingly attractive didn't void his fear of falling into the same kind of matrimonial patterns his parents exhibited.

The young ball players ran for Dave and wrapped themselves around his legs. Dave bent and attempted to tickle all three of them at once. They clamored for more, so Dave grabbed the shortest, turned him upside down, and jiggled his tummy. He screamed with laughter while his two friends hollered, "Me next, Coach Dave! Me next!"

As Dave obliged each of them, he wondered what it would be like to one day have his own son. His attention was tugged back to Eddi as she walked across the church grounds, past a group of elderly men playing horseshoes.

If I don't get married, I'll never know what it's like to have my own son, he thought and began to speculate if Eddi Boswick would make every effort to live at peace with her husband. *She's so tangled up in her own career, she probably wouldn't waste her time on perpetual conflict,* he thought as he tickled the final boy. Dave smiled and decided that when he ever *did* get married, he wanted a woman like Eddi. A woman secure in who she was and what she was about.

Dave deposited the last boy onto the ball field and made his announcement. "Okay, it's time to get warmed up! You guys get your gloves and head to the outfield. We'll practice catching!"

The boys dashed to the dugout for their gloves, and Dave used the lull to steal another glimpse of Eddi. She paused by the ice cream table and stood beside her parents. A younger woman who favored Eddi was also in the circle, along with two men. Dave figured the gal was Eddi's younger sister.

Shrill laughter erupted as the young woman ran from the circle and the dark-haired man chased her. She pitched a bottle of Coke into the air, and the man attempted to catch it. But the gal was too quick. She raced toward the ball field with the man in merry pursuit. As they neared, Dave realized the man resembled a person he'd known some years before. A person he hoped to forever forget. A scoundrel named Rick Wallace.

The name echoed through Dave's mind like a haunted mantra of pain. The years swept away, and Dave recalled standing in his house, sobbing like a shattered child.

Dave's throat tightened. He leaned forward and scrutinized the dark-haired man. Like Rick, he looked to be the most respectable man on the planet. Like Rick, he chose decent clothing and portrayed a trustworthy image. Like Rick, he displayed a charming smile that duped more people than not.

Before Eddi's sister reached the bleachers, she took a sharp right and ran back toward Eddi. The man, completely focused upon her, never looked Dave's way.

Dave's whole body went rigid. The man bore more than a resemblance to Rick Wallace. He *was* Rick Wallace!

His first instinct was to warn Eddi and her family, to tell them the truth, to dismantle whatever lies Rick must already be offering. He took three hurried steps toward Eddi and stopped.

If I tell her about Rick, he thought, *I'll have to tell her everything. Everything!* Dave stood on the precipice of indecision. On one hand, he reasoned that the Boswicks needed to know. On the other hand, he argued that none of his family's upheaval was any of their business.

As if his paternal grandfather had arisen from the grave, his voice filled Dave's mind. *Always remember to preserve your pride no matter what. Take pride in yourself and our family name. Never show weakness. Never admit failure.*

His grandfather's voice settled Dave's internal debate. He had no idea why Rick Wallace was with Eddi's family or how long he would associate with them. All he could do was silently hope that Rick's effect on the Boswicks was less devastating than it had been on the Davidsons. He forced the final shreds of doubt from his mind and convinced himself he was making the right choice. His self-respect would never allow him to divulge his error in judgment or his family's shame.

Besides, he thought and studied Eddi from afar, *Eddi Boswick has a good head on her shoulders. If ever a person could see past Rick's lies, it will be her.*

Ten

The next evening Eddi pulled her Mustang into the driveway of Huntington House. She looked in her rearview mirror to see Linda's PT Cruiser close behind. "I hope she hasn't been drinking," Eddi mumbled and cast a dubious glance to Jenny.

"She's been out all day with André and Rick," Jenny said with a certain nod. "I'll be surprised if she hasn't imbibed at least a little. This *is* July Fourth weekend."

"But they're policemen," Eddi countered as she applied the brakes. "Besides, I really thought Rick seemed like the decent, responsible sort. He and I talked quite a bit last night. I really liked him." Eddi didn't expound on exactly how *much* she liked him. She was beginning to think Linda's tastes were running along her preferences now.

"Actually, I think Rick's decent, too. I was hoping that maybe he would be a good influence on her. I'm just not so certain about André. Just because they're policemen doesn't mean they don't drink. There have been policemen who were arrested for driving while intoxicated, you know."

"I know," Eddi agreed. "And André seemed nearly as immature as Linda. I'm just glad Linda stayed at my place. I was afraid she was going to stay at the hotel last night." Eddi put the car into park and turned off the ignition. "Probably in André's room."

"I don't think she'd do that with Mom and Dad on the scene," Jenny claimed and released her seat belt with a click and slide. "She still seems to have some respect for their morals."

"So you *do* think she'd have gone to the hotel if Mom and Dad weren't here?"

"Unfortunately, yes." Jenny held Eddi's gaze for a candid moment.

"Is she using something for birth control or is she just taking chances?" Eddi asked as she removed her keys from the ignition. They clinked together as if clamoring for a response. She stared at the keys and debated whether she really wanted the answer. "Or do you even know?" she added and peered at Jenny.

"I found some birth control pills in her toiletry bag the last time we were here," Jenny answered without a blink. "That's the reason I'm thinking she's started sleeping around."

Eddi examined her sister and tried to piece together the facts. "Have you finally seen the light and started snooping or what?" she asked. Jenny had spent most of her teen years trying to convince Eddi not to be so nosy. Eventually, Eddi's perpetual nosiness had proven the winning edge in numerous cases.

"No, I'm not snooping." Jenny raised her chin. "I accidentally knocked her toiletry bag off the counter after church, and the pills fell out."

"Well, I guess the evidence is too incriminating not to assume the obvious," Eddi mused and didn't attempt to hide the heartsick thread in her voice.

Jenny touched her hand. "We really need to pray for her," she said.

"Yes," Eddi agreed. She tried to flip her braid over her shoulder, but found nothing to flip. Eddi touched the base of her hairline and fingered the short bob. That morning, she had walked into her hair dresser's with Jenny at her side and asked for a new look. The results were strikingly attractive and professional.

With a sigh, Eddi remained silent and eyed the mansion. In the midst of her remodeling schemes, Mrs. DeBloom had changed the paint color. The house was now a rich taupe with white trim. The ample foliage and azure sky completed the unspoken invitation for all to enter. The house seemed to be calling "welcome" from its captivating porch to the matching sign that read, "Huntington House Dinner Theater."

Everything about the place spoke class and underscored Mrs. DeBloom's desire to preserve the small community's cultural tastes. Eddi would have staked her life's savings that Mrs. DeBloom's dreams were being assisted by her nephew's massive wealth. While Dave seemed to be more interested in himself than not, Eddi deduced he'd do anything for his aunt.

She relived last night's heated conversation in the dugout when Dave had questioned her about wanting to marry him for his money. By the time Eddi rejoined her family, she'd been so angry she would have gone home were it not for her relatives. The man's arrogance was insufferable, and his unfounded assumptions inequitable. Eddi wrapped her fingers around the floor gearshift and squeezed. She could hardly wait until November, when the play would be over. After that Eddi planned to find some other interest. The theater was apparently not her calling—not as long as Dave participated anyway.

Eddi rested her head on the steering wheel and contemplated the coming evening. Last night, Mrs. DeBloom had insisted upon not only inviting Jenny on stage at tonight's practice, but she welcomed Eddi's parents, Linda, and her two friends as observers. She was thrilled with her dinner theater and wanted to show it off to anyone who'd come. Eddi sensed the matron wasn't guiltless of gloating. The more guests, the greater her glory. Mrs. DeBloom seemed oblivious that Dave glowered at Rick and Linda every time he neared them or that he seemed to watch Eddi's mom with a hint of disdained amazement. She imagined her younger sister tottering from room to room tonight, hanging onto one or both of her male companions, her laughter shrill, her breath reeking of rum.

No telling what he was thinking about Linda and Mom last night, Eddi mused and wondered why she cared so much. The man obviously thought he was better than the whole town, including her.

"Are we going in now?" Jenny asked and opened the door. "Or are you just going to sit here and stare at your speedometer all night?"

A waft of hot air invaded the vehicle's cool interior, and Eddi raised her head. She glanced out the passenger window. Linda, Rick, and André were walking across the manicured yard. Eddi popped open her door.

"Que sera sera," she mumbled as Jenny tumbled from the car.

Her sister didn't reply because Calvin appeared on the porch. Jenny closed the car door and sauntered toward the mansion. Her wide-legged linen slacks billowed in the evening breeze as if Jenny were strolling along the sea with no purpose in her direction. But Eddi knew better. Jenny had talked of nothing but Calvin since the picnic last night. Eddi presumed Calvin had talked of nothing but Jenny. Her sister needed to have a little chat with Hal Gomez—and soon.

By the time Eddi neared the open doorway, Calvin stood just inside the foyer with Jenny now at his side. "I'm the appointed doorman tonight," he claimed. "Mrs. DeBloom asked me to direct everyone inside. Fortunately, Jenny arrived in the nick of time. The job was getting to be such a bore." He looped his fingers through Jenny's in a familiar gesture, and Eddi marveled at how sedate Jenny appeared. Her impassioned comments about Calvin certainly contradicted her composure.

But then, Jenny has always guarded herself with the opposite sex, Eddi recalled. One day her husband would be grateful the restraint had stopped her from any rash choices. *If only Linda would watch and learn.*

Worriedly, Eddi searched the foyer for her younger sister and found her exactly as she'd imagined. Linda stood at the base of the curved stairway, clinging to both Rick and André so tightly Eddi still couldn't determine which was her favorite. The scent of Giorgio perfume reached Eddi even from fifteen feet away. Linda always had liked to make a statement and usually chose the strongest scents.

Rick noticed Eddi's arrival, even though André and Linda were oblivious to everyone but themselves. He nodded toward Eddi, who wiggled her fingers and proffered a welcoming grin. His dark eyes were as sincere as ever, his appearance clean-cut, right down to his Docker slacks and leather loafers. If Linda continued to favor André, Eddi considered the possibility of enjoying more of Rick's company. She sensed his attention following her into the parlor and wondered if perhaps Rick shared her interest.

The second she stepped into the room that had been the parlor, Eddi skimmed the growing crowd for any sign of Dave. She told herself it was imperative to ascertain the position of her enemy. When she didn't spot him, Eddi relaxed and took in the mansion's renovations.

As she moved through the play's cast, Eddi picked up on their delighted exclamations that spanned a host of compliments: "delightful"…"classic"…"dazzling"…"No wonder Mrs. DeBloom is so excited."

Eddi deposited her handbag upon a shelf near the door and agreed with every comment she heard. Even though the renovations weren't complete, the wall between the parlor and the back den had been removed to create one massive room. A sizable stage, still lacking varnish, claimed the den's south wall. A variety of small antique dinner tables stood in the room that once housed Mrs. DeBloom's heirloom furnishings. Someone had shoved most of the tables toward the front windows, now sparkling new. The section below the stage was crowded with props, costumes, and cardboard boxes.

Mrs. DeBloom stood upon the stage, fumbling with the great blue velvet curtain. "Carissa," she called, "try it now." When the curtain didn't move, Mrs. DeBloom fretfully marched past several cast members who sat on the stage's edge, reading their lines aloud. "I'm going to look for Dave, Carissa," she called backstage. "Maybe he can help us."

Eddi watched for the regal redhead to appear from behind the curtain, but she never showed. Calvin's sister had been absent from the church picnic last night, and Eddi had begun to wonder if she was ever going to attend play practice. Now that Carissa had decided to arrive, Eddi wondered who would play Jane, Calvin's leading lady. Calvin seemed more determined than ever to insist upon Jenny rather than his sister.

She dismissed thoughts of Calvin's sister and pivoted to absorb the complete ambiance of Mrs. DeBloom's dream. Two ornate chandeliers hung from the ceiling. They emitted a welcoming glow that christened the whole creation. Eddi crossed her arms and couldn't deny the approving smile as she meandered toward a nearby wall.

She touched the exquisite wallpaper that featured a baroque relief pattern in shades of bronze and cream. The wallpaper only covered half the room so far, but the effect was breathtaking. Someone mentioned that this was an exact replica of the original design and that Mrs. DeBloom had found a company who was able to duplicate the house's nineteenth-century coverings.

A massive marble fireplace occupied the middle of the west wall. A play of lights flashed beneath a collection of stone logs and created the impression of flames dancing around wood. Above the polished marble mantle a life-size portrait gazed down on her. The man's stern face, angular and tawny, was softened by a mysterious smile that hinted both good humor and intelligence. Eddi had seen Dave with the same expression.

She perused the painting with more interest as she caught a decided family resemblance between the patriarch and the ranch owner who gave her so much grief. In a fit of fancy, Eddi imagined the man's eyes glowing red and thought she detected the faintest trace of a goatee. She released a rebellious chuckle and understood why Jenny had laughed so hard when Eddi told her about the crazy dream.

Before the familiar image proved too inviting, Eddi chose another focal point. The urge to touch one of the antique dining tables overwhelmed her and she allowed a few discreet caresses. A feeling of oneness with the room overcame her, and she was transported to the time someone first stood where she was and felt the same awe she sensed. Breaking her reverie, she observed her fellow cast members equally entranced. Eddi suspected the impression was universal—which was exactly what Mrs. DeBloom must have envisioned.

"Brilliant," Eddi pronounced and decided the singular word best summed up the whole effect.

"Are you commenting on the painting over the fireplace or the room as a whole?" Dave's question floated from behind.

Eddi tensed and prepared herself for the magnetism and repulsion. Never had she met a man whose very voice evoked fantasies as well as fears.

She turned to face him, fully expecting the shaggy-haired, jeans-clad cowboy with whom she'd grown accustomed to sparring. Instead, she faced a clean shaven gentleman whose freshly cut hair suggested a recent trip to the barber. The frayed jeans and denim shirt were replaced with a crisp white shirt, new jeans, and a pair of polished boots. When he flashed her a white-toothed grin, Eddi felt as if she were looking at the picture from *People* all over again. The effect was as magnetizing as the end of her nightmare had proven. And Eddi wished she'd worn a classy skirt and heels instead of the nondescript pantsuit and sandals she'd found at the back of a discount rack.

She held her breath and reminded herself that the man had said she was too classless for his tastes. As if that weren't enough, he'd suggested Eddi would pursue him for his money alone. All admiration vanished. Last night's aggravation reigned.

"So are you going to answer me?" Dave prompted.

"Answer you?" Eddi crossed her arms and tried to recall his question. While preparing for battle, she determined to keep her tone void of emotion.

"I asked you if you were saying the effect of the room is brilliant or the image above the fireplace is brilliant. Which would it be Mizz Boswick?" he challenged.

"I presume you'd love me to say the image above the fireplace because he so resembles you," she said with a tilt of her chin.

"Why do you find such joy in purposefully taunting me?" Dave asked. A hint of sarcastic revelry stirred his dark eyes. Eddi suspected the guy was taking some twisted delight in her barbs.

She rubbed her tense toes against her sandals. "And why do you find such joy in purposefully baiting me?"

"Maybe I enjoy making you despise me," he said.

"Or maybe you enjoy despising me for the very sake of creating enemies." A rebel thought nibbled at the edge of her mind. Eddi decided the time had come to let the great William Fitzgerald Davidson know she had at last memorized her every line. Maybe for once, she could even throw him off and come away from tonight's practice with the upper hand.

"So…despise me if you dare." She enunciated the words of Elizabeth Bennet with the British accent Mrs. DeBloom insisted upon for the whole cast.

Eddi rejoiced as Dave's cocky assurance wavered. She read every hint of his expression from recognizing the line from their script to grappling for a response. A surge of adrenaline rushed Eddi as it did every time she closed a victorious argument before a jury. She turned and marched toward the stage. Tonight would be the best practice yet.

But Eddi was too quick in assuming she'd triumphed. A pair of strong hands gripped her arms as Dave's warm words caressed her ear. "Indeed I do not dare," he said, his British accent as exact as her own.

Eddi was plunged into the very situation which she'd hoped to throw Dave. As she fruitlessly searched for a brilliant retort, fragments of memorized lines bombarded her mind. None of them proved a sufficient response. As if her mental wrestling weren't enough to disturb her equilibrium, Dave had yet to loosen his grip. Eddi swallowed and lambasted herself for being so moved by the touch of a man she was supposed to detest.

"There you are, Dave!" Mrs. DeBloom called from across the room.

Eddi stepped from Dave's hold.

"Carissa and I need help with the curtain. We're in a dreadful fix!" Mrs. DeBloom waved her hand in theatrical grander.

"Yes, of course," Dave responded and left Eddi as quickly as he'd swooped upon her.

Eddi ducked toward the foyer. She suspected practice would be delayed for some time, and she desperately needed to regain her composure. Last night Mrs. DeBloom told the cast that the whole mansion was open for them to look through whenever they chose. Eddi decided now was a great time.

She cast a final glance over her shoulder before exiting the parlor. Dave stood on the stage near his aunt, who gesticulated toward the curtain. Eddi's pulse still vibrated in her temples, and she prayed Dave would never suspect her reaction. Right now,

Eddi would have agreed to a tour of a dragon-infested dungeon to get away from him.

"Whoa!" A man gripped Eddi's shoulders.

She halted and focused upon the person in front of her.

"You nearly ran into me," Rick Wallace said, his brown eyes alight with respect and kindness.

"Oh, I'm so sorry. I was distracted," Eddi breathed and resisted the urge to dash another glare toward Dave.

"Yes, I noticed." Rick eyed the stage as if he were observing a nest of vipers.

Eddi witnessed an identical expression last night when Dave spotted Rick. A new realization posed itself upon the horizon of her mind. At some point in their lives, Rick and Dave must have crossed paths, and neither of them enjoyed the encounter.

All Eddi could think of was how much more agreeable Rick was than Dave. Both men had rich brown eyes. Both men were dark complected with hair the color of polished walnut. Both were tall. Admittedly, Dave was by far the best looking.

But looks aren't everything, she thought. *Neither is money.*

While Rick made ends meet on a policeman's salary, Dave probably owned enough loot to buy all of Dallas. Eddi would choose a man of character over a man with money any day. Rick probably possessed more character than Dave ever would.

"Last night Mrs. DeBloom asked everyone to tour the rest of the house if they wanted," Eddi said with an inviting grin. "She's been doing a lot of remodeling and redecorating, and I think she's proud of her work."

"I would be too," Rick agreed and scanned the foyer. "This is a show place. I'd never be able to afford it, that's for sure."

"Really." Eddi motioned toward the curved staircase. "Want to go on the grand tour with me?" she asked.

"I thought you'd never ask," Rick said with a dimpled smile.

Eddi surreptitiously glimpsed her sister talking with André. With his head bent toward Linda, André looked as if he were thinking of kissing her. Linda leaned toward him and didn't attempt to hide her attraction—despite the crowd.

They did make a striking couple with their tans and fair hair. While André still had some maturing to do, he was leagues better than some of the men Linda had dragged home. Eddi could only hope her younger sister was finally beginning to grow up.

When Linda placed a hand on the side of André's face and gurgled with laughter, Eddi dashed aside any reservations about talking to Rick. Hopefully, Rick would enjoy her company tonight as much as Eddi did his.

Linda's attention drifted from André as she noticed Eddi enticing Rick up the stairway. She frowned. Eddi had also monopolized Rick during most of the picnic last night. She was obviously wasting no time continuing the act tonight.

A hard burn erupted in Linda's gut. *Rick is* my *guest, not Eddi's!* she thought. *This is like ninth grade all over again!*

Five years ago, Linda had arrived home from school one Friday, her boyfriend Brian in tow, only to discover Eddi home from college. Linda and Brian had planned to attend the high school football game together, but Brian coerced her into hanging out at her house instead. By eight o'clock Brian had spent the majority of the evening flirting with Eddi, and Linda understood the real reason Brian wanted to stay home.

As Eddi and Rick paused halfway up the stairs, Linda gritted her teeth. An insecure urge insisted she go to the bathroom and double-check her appearance. Her mother had always insisted she was much cuter than Eddi, but Linda still worried—especially when, even after hinting that he'd like to spend the night with her, Rick spent most of his time looking at Eddi.

She refocused upon André and tried to shape her stiff lips into a smile. He droned on about some motorcycle he owned back in Houston. Linda attempted to appear interested while keeping tabs on Eddi and Rick from the corner of her eyes. André's angular face, tanned and lean, proved the perfect compliment for his shocking blue eyes. Even though André was better looking than Rick, even though he and Linda had far more in common, as of now she was beginning to prefer Rick.

She allowed her gaze to casually drift past André to the top of the stairs where Eddi and Rick turned a corner and disappeared. The only thing that remained was Eddi's melodious laugh drifting down the stairway.

The burn in Linda's midsection exploded into an inferno. "Excuse me, André," Linda mumbled and shifted her shoulder bag. "I need to go to the restroom."

"Oh, sure," André said and stepped aside.

Linda rushed past him and a knot of visitors gushing over the mansion's beauty. She glowered straight ahead, beginning to hate this place.

She entered the bathroom left of the stairway and snapped the door shut. The smell of the peach candle flickering on the cabinet reminded her of the candles Eddi always burned in her room before she left home. Linda blew out the candle and stuck it inside a door under the sink.

She gazed into the oval mirror. Her strawberry-blonde hair, usually straight and lifeless, now hung around her face in golden ringlets. Given the salon finish of her recent permanent, the curls appeared natural, not frizzy. The perfect finish of designer cosmetics enhanced her faint tan and made her nearly as pretty as Jenny—and definitely more attractive than Eddi. Her cosmetician suggested that Linda dot the mole at the corner of her mouth with some black eye pencil, which added a seductive touch to her whole look.

Linda dug through her purse and pulled out her cosmetic pouch. She extracted a red lip gloss and slathered on a thick layer. The gloss proved the perfect match for her buttoned-front T-shirt and enhanced the full curve of her lips. She dropped the lip color back into her purse and retrieved a tiny bottle of Giorgio. Linda added one light mist to her neck and welcomed the scent over the peach candle's odor.

She deposited the perfume in her purse and removed one more item from the inside pocket—her flask of courage. Linda unscrewed the lid and poured a generous dose of the whiskey into her mouth. She swallowed hard and winced. The wad of liquid slipped down her throat like a hot coal, warming her stomach with a daring boost.

Linda set the whiskey aside and eyed the buttons on the front of her snug shirt. With a calculating smile, she unfastened the top three. The material slid away to reveal a hint of cleavage.

"Rick Wallace," she whispered. "I'm coming upstairs for you *now*. By the time we get back to Houston, you won't even remember Eddi's name."

Eleven

❦ ❦

As Eddi and Rick ascended the second floor, his admiring smile and unaffected air nearly made her forget Dave's rude behavior. The tension began to ease from Eddi, and she didn't protest when Rick placed his hand in the small of her back.

"Let's go into this room," he said and nudged her through an ajar door.

They stepped into a sizable bedroom, filled with exquisite antiques and scented with a spicy aroma that reminded Eddi of a forest dripping rain. The room stretched as far as a sitting area near a pair of French doors that opened onto a balcony. The final rays of evening sunlight caressed the decor schemes of rust and emerald and black. A leopard-print comforter hugged the queen-sized poster bed that featured rich brown gauze instead of a canopy.

"This is gorgeous," Eddi breathed and pivoted to examine the room.

"Yes, lovely," Rick mumbled with a lusty undertone.

At first, Eddi suspected Rick wasn't talking about the room at all, but about *her*. Such a come-on would be in line with the men Linda normally brought home, but Eddi had begun to expect more of Rick. The hair on her arms prickled, and she doubted the wisdom of entering a bedroom with her new acquaintance. Eddi darted him a keen glance. Rick's attention was riveted to the French windows. He walked across the area rug toward the doors, seemingly unaware of Eddi's presence.

Finally, Rick motioned to her and pointed toward the windows. "Did you notice this view?" he asked.

Eddi moved toward him and dismissed her moment of caution. Rick was beyond doubt every bit as honorable as she had assumed him to be. The lusty undercurrent must have been the sole product of her imagination. Eddi had always gone with her gut instincts when it came to men. While she didn't consider herself infallible, her first impressions were often the most accurate.

That certainly had been the case with Dave Davidson. From their first meeting, Eddi had tagged him as someone who perhaps thought more highly of himself than he ought. While her initial judgment had wavered in the face of her attraction for him, it had proven to be the correct assumption.

Rick, on the other hand, seemed to be everything Dave could never be—kind, courteous, a true gentleman who'd never bait a woman to appease some twisted need for verbal fighting.

Eddi paused beside Rick and gazed upon a sky too spectacular for any artist's brush. The indigo sky stretched toward a fiery ball dipping toward the east Texas hills. Pink clouds, sprinkled in gold dust, floated against a teal canvas that dazzled the mind and captured the soul.

"Get a load of *that!*" Rick exclaimed.

"Wow!" Eddi breathed. "The mansion is great, but—"

"No decorator could ever match what God can do with the sky," Rick finished.

Surprised at his reference to the holy, Eddi examined Rick's profile.

He faced her and tilted his head as if posing a silent question. "Did something I say bother you?"

"No," Eddi said. "I was just…uh…" she slipped her hands into her pants pockets, "…impressed, I guess, that you mentioned God."

"Oh?"

"Yes, you see, He's very important to me, and I—"

"And well He should be." Rick nodded and crossed his arms. "He's always been important to me. Since childhood. I've longed to be in the ministry, even."

"Oh?" Eddi asked. "But you became a policeman instead?"

"Well, yes." Rick's shoulders sagged, and he nudged at the thick piled rug with his loafer.

A heavy silence settled upon the room—a silence that wrapped Eddi in a pall of repression. "So that wasn't your first choice?" Eddi observed.

"No." The gloomy slant of Rick's features hinted at years of disillusionment.

Eddi debated whether or not to prime Rick for more information. She certainly didn't want to come across like an interrogating lawyer, yet her curiosity proved nearly too intense for silence.

"How long have you known Dave Davidson?" Rick asked.

"What?" Eddi tried to make sense of the rapid change of subject.

"Dave Davidson—" Rick repeated. "How long have you known him?"

"Not long," Eddi admitted. "About six months. I met him when I moved to London. Why?"

"He's my cousin—or rather, my *foster* cousin, I guess you could say."

"What?" Eddi blurted.

Rick nodded. "Amazing, isn't it, how paths can cross in our lives."

"No kidding!" Eddi glanced toward the sky once more. The clouds, once pink, were taking on a purple hue. Instead of again falling into rapt admiration, Eddi's mind raced with the bits of news Rick was supplying. She finally came to the conclusion that Rick's not going into the ministry must somehow be related to Dave's being his cousin.

"Actually, Dave is the reason I didn't go into the ministry," Rick said.

Eddi narrowed her eyes and examined Rick. "I was beginning to wonder if that was coming next."

"You've got a sharp mind," Rick said. "It's no wonder you're a successful lawyer." His studied Eddi's face in a way that made her feel as if he were looking beyond her femininity to honestly admire her mental capabilities. Few people had offered such unbiased accolades of late.

Frowning, Eddi moved past the French windows toward a wide window ledge, suited for sitting. She nudged aside a trio of teak colored pillows and sat down. "I've noticed that you and Dave don't seem to be members of the mutual admiration society," she observed.

"No, we aren't." Rick turned toward the window. The sun cast a radiance upon him that seemed supernatural and lent a glow of truth to Rick's every word. "Do you know his real name is William Davidson?"

"Yes."

"Doesn't surprise me that you found out," Rick said without ever taking his attention from the sky. "And you probably already know he developed the internet company USA Online?"

"Yes, and that he's one of the richest men in America." Eddi observed a mantel clock perched atop the center of the baroque maple dresser. The second hand ticked around as if it were counting the facts concerning Dave.

Rick chuckled and faced Eddi. "He couldn't hide anything from *you* for very long, could he?"

Eddi tried to flip her braid over her shoulder. Instead, she touched the base of her bobbed hair. "I wish I could claim credit for all this information, but my sister Jenny was the one who found it."

"Ah, yes, Jenny. She favors Linda quite a bit, doesn't she?"

"Yes, I took after my father more, I guess. Linda and Jenny look more like Mom."

"Well, you *all* are lovely ladies," Rick said as if he were the finest of well-bred gentlemen.

"And you are very gracious," Eddi replied and decided Dave could learn a thing or two from his foster cousin.

"He was always jealous of me, you know."

"Who, Dave?"

"Yes. He seemed to think our grandparents favored me over him and his younger brother."

"And you don't think so?"

Rick shrugged. "No. I really don't. I think Grandfather and Grandmother cared for me as *much* as they cared for them. And, I think Dave couldn't stand that because I wasn't a *real* relative." He neared Eddi and sat next to her. Rick propped his elbows on his knees and leaned forward. He stared at the carpet as if he were watching the replay of an old movie.

"My foster father was Dave's uncle, by the way—his dad's brother," he added. "I was their only child. They couldn't have kids, and they couldn't adopt me because my parents wouldn't release their rights. So I wound up living with them from the time I was ten until I left home. They were good to me—really good. Almost everyone in the family accepted me."

"Except Dave?" Eddi asked.

"Well," Rick hesitated, "yeah. Everyone except Dave."

"Humph," Eddi grunted. "That figures."

Rick straightened and picked up one of the teak-colored pillows. "It's hard to believe he's got so many wrong attitudes when his parents were in the ministry," he said.

"Were they missionaries or—"

"No, his parents copastored a church east of Dallas, not far from where I lived, but they really loved missions. That's how they got killed. They'd gone on a missions trip to Mexico with a church group." He sat up and leaned against the window frame behind them. "The traffic down there is horrific, and well, they wound up in an awful accident. Neither of them made it out alive."

Eddi toyed with a pillow tassel and wondered about the circumstances that placed Rick in a foster home. She rested her hand on Rick's arm, and he covered her hand with his.

"That was terrible," she said.

"Yes, it was terrible. Dave was nineteen and his brother was only fifteen. Mrs. DeBloom took them in as her own. This is only the second time I've even seen her. The other time was at my aunt's funeral."

"Oh, really?" Eddi queried.

"Yeah. Mrs. DeBloom was Dave's *mom's* sister. She lived west of Fort Worth, and we were on the east side of Dallas. I don't think she even recognized me last night when she invited us all to the practice tonight." Rick waved his hand. "Anyway, shortly before I got out of high school, our grandfather passed away. This was actually a year before Dave's parents were killed. Believe it or not, Grandfather left a sizable sum for me to go to seminary on—and that was the stipulation, that the money be spent on seminary and no other college. If I didn't want to go to seminary, I was granted ten thousand cash and that's all. That was fine with me because I sensed God was calling me to the ministry. I was ready for seminary. Grandfather knew that, but..." He rubbed his face and shook his head.

"What happened?" Eddi prompted and could only guess where this was leading. Somehow, Dave had been a hindrance to Rick's calling.

"When Dave learned of the will's specifications, he was determined to stop me. I was so naïve that when he called and asked about the seminaries where I'd applied, I told him. Little did I know he would convince his father to call the seminaries and essentially ruin my reputation." His face drooped into a melancholic mask. "None of the seminaries would admit me after that. I was so disheartened, I wound up taking the money and going to the police academy." He gazed across the room as if he were trapped in a painful past.

"But that's slander!" Eddi burst. "You could have filed a lawsuit and—"

"I would *never* do that," Rick said and shook his head. *"Never!* It would have created a huge family stink. One thing our grandfather insisted upon was that we keep our family pride. A lawsuit would have been like dragging my grandfather's name through mud. If he'd been alive, he would have been mortified. I just couldn't do it."

"But," Eddi prompted and squeezed his arm, "Dave cost you your calling and your reputation."

Rick pulled her hand between his and stroked the inside of her palm with his index finger. While the gentle gesture warmed her regard for Rick, it in no way evoked the volatile reaction she knew from Dave's touch. Eddi slipped her hand from Rick's.

She stood, paced toward the bed, pivoted, and approached Rick. Dave's every haughty expression floated through Eddi's mind. Each point of Rick's story confirmed what she already knew. Dave Davidson was a cad who'd take the last dime from his own grandmother if that meant increasing his fortune.

A deep well of animosity erupted from the bottom of her soul. "I know this isn't the most Christian thing to say, but I really can't stand William Fitzgerald Davidson," she enunciated the name as if it were covered in thorns.

"It would appear that you have learned quickly what I learned the hard way," Rick said, his eyes troubled. But soon his features softened. Rick stood and reached for Eddi's hand. He moved closer and smiled into her eyes.

"Let's forget about him, okay?" he said. "We've got many more pleasant things to discuss. I still don't know what your favorite color is, or if you've ever been to New York, or if you like cats better than dogs, or—"

"Hello in here!" Linda's voice accompanied a battery of knocks.

Eddi turned toward the door. Her younger sister marched into the room as if she owned the place. Her T-shirt was daringly gaping in the front. Her perfume was stronger than ever.

"I wondered what happened to you two," Linda said as she traipsed into the room. "Mrs. DeBloom is calling for the cast, Eddi." She tossed a sweetly stiff smile toward her sister before sidling up to Rick. "And you somehow got away from me, you naughty boy," she teased. Linda stroked his jaw with her index finger and tucked her free hand beneath his arm.

A hint of irritation troubled Rick's features before he relaxed and shrugged. "Eddi and I were just taking a tour of the mansion. Heaven forbid that I should escape you," he said as if he were a doting elder brother.

"Well," Eddi said, "if Mrs. DeBloom is calling for the cast, I guess I better go back downstairs."

"That's fine, Edwardia," Linda said. "I'll finish the tour with Rick." With a saucy smile, she rested her head on Rick's shoulder and then lifted it again.

Eddi's shoulders stiffened, and she scrutinized Linda for any signs of bitterness. Linda knew as well as Jenny how much Eddi hated her full name—despite the fact that it was a derivative of her father's. The only times Linda ever used the name against Eddi was when she was irritated.

"Well, okay then," Eddi agreed and tried to keep her voice even, although she detected a hint of jealousy in the lift of her sister's chin. Eddi glanced back at Rick.

With another good-natured shrug, he waved goodbye.

"I think there's supposed to be a library up here," Linda said and pulled Rick toward the doorway.

"Yes, there is." Eddi walked into the hallway and pointed to the right. "I believe it's at the end of the hall that way." She glanced down the wide corridor lined with oriental runners. Along the walls hung more portraits similar to the one downstairs. Eddi made a mental note to one day peruse the paintings. But for now, she was forced to face the most disagreeable man on the planet.

Twelve

"If the cast will please move near the stage," Mrs. DeBloom called, "we'll begin our practice."

Backstage, Dave glanced toward his aunt. She stood on the stage's edge and motioned toward the cast. He had known she loved theater before, but the light in her eyes tonight went unmatched. Dave paused for a moment to bask in the warmth of her joy—a joy that Dave's money helped incur. He pressed a switch on the wall, and the velvet curtains hummed open.

Mrs. DeBloom turned and gave Dave a thumbs-up coupled with an exaggerated wink.

"Finally," Carissa Barclay said from behind. A chorus of discreet clapping erupted from the cast.

"Believe it or not, Carissa, somebody just got a wire crossed." Dave gave the theater wire box's screws a final turn. He dropped the screwdriver back into the tool caddie with a clink. The smell of unfinished lumber and scattered sawdust attested to the remodeler's presence earlier that day.

Dave looked at Carissa. Her approving beam reminded him of the redhead's goals. Dave groaned. Carissa usually interpreted every hint of a smile, every benign kindness, every utterance of her name as a sign that he might be interested in a relationship. Ever since she moved back home a year ago, the green-eyed lady had been friendly—really friendly. Carissa didn't seem the least bit interested in whether or not Dave had a good heart or how committed he was to his Lord or his church. Like a dozen other London ladies, Dave figured she wouldn't take a second look at him if he were a man of golden character who was also broke.

Ironically, Carissa was a long way from penniless herself. Dave equated her with the likes of a bloodthirsty hound who smelled more money and wanted it. Since she was Calvin's sister, the situation was particularly sticky. Dave didn't want to hurt her feelings or offend Calvin. But the truth was he'd never be interested in the jeans-clad, rodeo-loving woman. They might both enjoy horses, but that's where their common interests stopped.

Abruptly, he turned and walked across the stage, toward his aunt. Carissa's boot heels clicked on the wooden stage behind him. Dave debated if she'd be on his trail all night. So far, she'd complimented everything from his haircut to his new boots. He wondered if she had convinced herself his efforts were for her.

The second Dave moved onto the open stage, some buffoon released a wolf whistle a mile long. "Oh look, it's Darcy!" Calvin Barclay shouted. A chorus of chuckles followed the eruption.

"Calvin, you idiot," Dave mumbled and scanned the crowd for his friend.

From the back of the small group, Calvin waved and Dave pointed at him as if his days were numbered.

"Well, if we can all get settled down..." Mrs. DeBloom directed her remarks toward Calvin. "This is no time for adults to start acting like adolescents," she continued and sniffed.

Dave descended the stairs along the side of the stage and heard Carissa following. He moved toward the back of the group and studied Cal. His friend draped his arm around Jenny's shoulders and gave her an affectionate squeeze. Dave was surprised Cal had taken his focus off Jenny long enough to even notice he was on stage. If anybody was acting like a love-stricken adolescent, it was Calvin Barclay. He'd talked of nothing but Jenny since he met her three weeks ago.

Dave could only hope that Jenny felt as strongly about Calvin as he did her. Otherwise, his friend was about to get his heart broken. Dave scrutinized Jenny and wondered if her sedate expression was a clear indicator of her heart. If so, she cared precious little for Cal. The bells of caution clamored within Dave. He and Calvin had formed a deep bond in the last few years. He'd hate to see Cal hurt.

Without examining his motives, he skimmed the crowd for another familiar face. This time, he didn't spot Eddi Boswick. Dave figured she'd probably materialize any minute, ready to sling a script line at him like a warrior hurling her dagger. The woman certainly kept him on his toes. Dave had studied his lines until he committed every syllable to memory. He loved watching Eddi matching him word for word, as if they were in some sort of contest.

Maybe we are, he mused and couldn't deny he was enjoying the sport.

For once in his life, he'd met a woman who didn't give one flip about his money. After their dugout encounter, Dave realized that if Eddi ever became interested in him it would be because *he* pursued *her.* She certainly wouldn't pursue him. The thought left him almost heady. The last time he'd really pursued a woman had been his freshman year of college—before he started his own business and met with such startling success.

Maybe Eddi's the reason I got the haircut and pulled out the new jeans and shirt, he thought and looked down at his apparel. This morning when he got up, Dave didn't question the urge for a cleaner image. Instead, he'd driven toward the barbershop and just asked for a haircut. The next thing he knew he was digging to the back of his closet for his new duds.

If I'm not careful, I'll wind up falling in love with her, he thought. The admission caught him so off guard that he stopped. He stared straight ahead, past the entryway, into the old dining room.

As his aunt began her typical short lecture on Jane Austen, Dave decided to find a bottle of water. In his younger days, he would have searched out something stronger, but he had quit drinking alcohol the same year he quit smoking. If he weren't careful, this growing distraction with Eddi Boswick would drive him to resuming both habits. Dave figured his aunt had a whole ice chest full of drinks somewhere near the kitchen. Suddenly, he felt as if he'd been in the desert a week. On top of that, he couldn't remember why he'd been so opposed to marriage for so long.

Dave hurried forward and searched out the cooler. He discovered it beside a stack of boxes in the dining room. After grabbing a bottle of water, he downed half of it. That's when he noticed Eddi's mother enter the front door. Mr. Boswick, close behind, shut the door and the two stood in the vacated foyer as if debating what to do. Dave stepped forward, but stopped when Mrs. Boswick pointed toward the theater room. As the pudgy woman began to speak, Dave was stricken with how much her hair reminded him of an overused Brillo pad.

"Oh, they're all in there, Edward," she exclaimed, her voice shrill. "And look, there's Jenny. Oh good! She's standing with that *wonderful* veterinarian. I'm *so glad* she's interested in him, aren't you? I've been so distraught over that fiancé of hers."

Fiancé? Dave thought and swallowed another gulp of water.

"I just don't believe he can provide for her as well as this Calvin Barclay. Oh! If only all our girls were so lucky!" Mrs. Boswick continued.

Edward removed his golfing hat. "Yes, they could all have a house full of dogs and cats and potbellied pigs," he drawled.

Dave sputtered over a sip of water.

"Oh stop it!" Mrs. Boswick slapped his arm. "You know what I mean. If Jenny gets such a good catch, she might never have to work again in her life. She'd be set financially."

"I guess that would be a real bummer if she actually *wanted* to continue her career, now wouldn't it?" Mr. Boswick placed his cap upon a row of hooks near the front door.

"Oh you! You know as well as I do that she doesn't."

"Really?" he retorted.

"I think this thing with Dr. Barclay is a smart move, if you ask me." She rushed on. "But then, Jenny always has been sensible."

"Unlike others we know, I assure you," he mumbled.

"Now, if we can only find such rich men for our other daughters, dear, we'll all be set!" Mrs. Boswick declared, never once acknowledging one word of her husband's caustic remarks.

"Ah, yes, a veterinarian in a town of six thousand people," Mr. Boswick groused. "He should be rolling in dough—exactly what we need for Jenny. *Exactly.*"

Dave gripped the neck of his water bottle. Beads of cool moisture seeped through his fingers. What Mr. and Mrs. Boswick couldn't know was that Calvin Barclay was indeed rolling in dough—not nearly as much as Dave, by any means, but the vet would be considered a good catch by many fortune-hunting ladies.

A year ago when his father died, Calvin and his sister were left a small fortune. Calvin had been able to pay off all his debts and even enlarge his clinic. After giving a chunk to a deserving charity, he'd set the rest aside for a tidy nest egg. The woman who married Calvin really wouldn't have to work.

Dave recalled Jenny's composed expression. All at once, the memory took on a sinister cast. Perhaps the reason Jenny seemed so unmoved was because her interest was in Calvin's earning potential and not the man. Dave had encountered enough goal-oriented women to suspect any female of ulterior motives—even Eddi Boswick's sister.

As if the mere thought of her made her materialize, Eddi trotted down the stairs. "Oh, hi!" she said to her parents before exchanging a brief hug. "I'd begun to think you two weren't coming."

"No, we came." Edward yawned, and Dave was stricken with how much his daughter favored him—right down to the keen gray eyes that missed nothing.

He looked back up the stairway and saw no signs of Rick Wallace. Dave thought he'd seen Rick and Eddi walk out of the parlor together shortly after Aunt Maddy called him to help on stage. Dave had been glad Eddi was spending time with Rick. The sooner she detected the knave's character, the sooner she would warn her family.

When Eddi stepped away from her parents, she spotted Dave. He lifted his water bottle as if toasting her, and Eddi offered nothing but one of her barracuda glares.

Dave laughed out loud and strode past the Boswicks without acknowledging them.

"…that rude man," Mrs. Boswick's words trailed him.

Dave grimaced. He hadn't intended to be rude; he just had a few things on his mind. He spotted Cal and Jenny again and began to wonder how he could convince his friend to back off.

Maybe telling him she's engaged will be enough, Dave hoped.

Thirteen

~ ~

After Eddi arranged for her parents to sit at one of the small dining tables, she slipped to the back of the group and concentrated on Mrs. DeBloom.

"So, we'll be starting there," she said and Eddi hoped "there" didn't involve a scene which featured her character. She had no idea what Mrs. DeBloom had said before. "I guess all we need at this point is our Darcy and Elizabeth, as well as the Bennet family, Charlotte Lucas, and of course those of you playing the dance line as well as the crowd."

Eddi debated whether or not to raise her hand and admit her lack of knowledge. She imagined Mrs. DeBloom's disapproving sniffle as she reexplained the directions. It was enough to make Eddi feel like an inattentive seventh grader. She chose to move toward the stage and hoped to glean information about the starting point.

"Did you hear what scene we're working on?" Dave's low voice delivered a jolt of aversion that overpowered the man's masculine appeal.

Rick's story, still fresh, had acted like acid upon an open wound. Eddi would rather eat live leeches than interact with Dave. She determined to ignore him just as he had rudely ignored her parents. But his powerful presence evoked an answer. Eddi responded before she could stop herself.

"I have no earthly idea where we're starting." She squeezed her way around the crowd and rushed toward the stage's stairs.

The heavy fall of boots in her wake insisted Dave followed close behind. Ahead of them, Jenny and Calvin ascended the stairs with Cheri. Eddi increased her pace and called for Cheri. The upcoming practice loomed before her, and Eddi wondered how she would survive.

"Cheri!" she called again.

Her friend ended the conversation with Calvin and pivoted to face Eddi. With a friendly wave, Cheri stepped toward Eddi, who was so honed upon escaping Dave, she stumbled over the lowest stage stair. For the first time in her life, Eddi fell *up* a flight of steps. The more she tried to prevent the fall, the harder the stairs' edges banged into her. By the time she rumbled to a stop, her shins ached, her right elbow throbbed, and her hip insisted it had received a whopping bruise.

"Oh…" Eddi moaned and tried to tell herself this was not the time or place to indulge in a cry. Nevertheless, the humiliation coupled with the pain sent a telltale sting to her eyes.

"Are you okay?" Dave's concern intensified Eddi's emotions. He was the last person she ever wanted to witness her weak moment.

"I'm fine," she whimpered and wished she could steady her wobbly tones. Eddi willed away the sting in her eyes as a huddle formed around her. Fellow cast members began a series of concerned exclamations.

"Do you think you can stand?" Dave knelt in front of Eddi. The gaze that often flashed with mockery now caressed her in genuine concern. "Your ankles—do they feel twisted?" Dave's firm fingers probed her bare ankles.

"No, they're fine—really." Eddi brushed aside his hands and wished she didn't revert to delicious tingles with the man's every touch.

"And what about your knees?"

"Knees feel fine," she said and tried to stand.

"Here, let me help."

She attempted to protest, but to no avail. Dave used one arm for support and the other to pull Eddi to her feet. He rested his hands on her shoulders and steadied her. As Eddi gained her equilibrium, she rasped out her thanks. The rest of the cast, convinced of her well-being, bustled up the stairs. Dave ushered Eddi toward the wall.

"Are you going to be okay?" he repeated.

"Yes, I think so," Eddi said and wished he wouldn't stand so close. "Nothing seems broken anyway." She focused on his shirt's top button.

"You got a haircut." A trace of disappointment tainted his words.

"Well, so did you," Eddi defended and found the courage to look into his eyes.

"So I did," he acquiesced and flashed one of his *People* magazine grins.

They hadn't been this close since after the tornado. The scent of subtle masculinity reminded Eddi of her yearning for him to kiss her on the porch—even after he'd insulted her.

Dave's attention lazed toward her lips and ended any doubts that he might likewise be thinking of their porch encounter. He'd even teased her about the tornado coming back that day. Without a hint of warning, her imagination fabricated a scenario that replicated the closing seconds of her crazy dream. Except this time, the fantasy didn't end until Dave actually kissed her.

Despite her commitment to despising the man, an electric ripple tempted her to move closer. Eddi bolted backward and bumped into the wall. Never had she been so simultaneously attracted and repelled by a man. Never. William Fitzgerald Davidson had proven himself an egocentric scoundrel with a deadly tongue—not only to her, but also to Rick Wallace. And only God Himself knew what Dave was up to in that building behind his house. Nevertheless, her knees threatened to collapse again.

"Are you okay?" Cheri called. She waited at the top of the steps with Jenny and Calvin at her side. As the last participants walked onto the stage, they started down the stairs.

"Sure, I'm fine," Eddi answered and trotted up the steps toward them. "See!" She stretched out her arms and stifled a gasp as her elbow protested. "Just a few minor bumps."

"Some people will do anything for a little attention," Jenny teased.

"So, we won't talk about the time you fell down the steps at the state capitol," Eddi chided and gently punched her sister's arm.

"No fair! You're dragging up the past," Jenny complained and looked at Calvin. "I was only twelve!"

"I'm sure it was a graceful fall," Calvin doted.

"Yes, the most." Jenny crossed her arms and directed a pretend glare at her sister.

"If you think a knotty-kneed sixth grader tumbling head over heels down stone steps is graceful, then I guess she was." Eddi stuck her tongue out.

Jenny laughed outright. "You are so mean, Eddi!" she complained. "Come on Calvin, let's take our positions before she tells more of my dark past."

"Hey, maybe I want to know about your past," Calvin teased.

"Don't forget to tell him about the bank robbery, then, Jenny," Eddi called as they walked toward center stage, just behind Dave.

"Oh, get outta here," Jenny returned.

Cheri remained silent during the exchange. When Eddi followed the direction of her gaze, it rested upon Dave, whom she eyed with a hint of speculation. Eddi hoped she'd ask no questions. Yesterday evening Cheri had commented on seeing Eddi and Dave come out of the dugout together. The last thing Eddi needed was for a thread of gossip to link her and Dave in more than just their acting roles.

Dave walked toward his aunt while Cheri stared after him. "You know, Eddi…" She looped her arm through Eddi's as they walked on stage. "Dave watches you a lot. Have you noticed?"

"No—not in the least," Eddi blurted. *Although*, Eddi recalled, *he knew exactly where I was last night when he summoned me to the dugout interrogation. And he found me easy enough tonight when he pestered me about the painting.*

"He's probably the most wealthy man in all of Cherokee County," Cheri continued. "If you played your cards right—"

"A happy marriage is based on more than money, Cheri," Eddi countered.

"Oh, but my mother always said it was as easy to fall in love with a rich man as a poor man." Cheri nodded sagely, and her waist-long ponytail swayed against her cotton dress.

"Apparently, she never met Dave Davidson," Eddi quipped.

"Well, I'd say he liked what he saw when he met you." Cheri leaned toward Eddi as if she were disclosing a national security secret. "He's had a whole town full of single women after him for three years. Not once has he given one of them the attention he's giving you."

Cheri's very suggestion made Eddi feel as if Dave were watching her. She hunched her shoulders, laughed, and hoped her mirth sounded genuine. "If he's giving me attention it's because he wants to harass me," she said. "It's not because he likes what he sees. Mark my word, he's looking for a way to take shots at me." The new stage floor creaked beneath them as if to refute Eddi's claim.

"You Boswick women are certainly an interesting lot, that's all I know," Cheri said as her attention drifted to the back of the set.

"Why do you say that?" Eddi followed her focus.

Jenny and Calvin had settled onto a velvet settee near the faux fireplace. He leaned toward Jenny who sedately lowered her head. Calvin's smile held a hint of uncertainty. While Eddi had seen Jenny's exact moves hundreds of times, she wondered about Calvin's interpretation.

"Does Jenny care much for Cal?" Cheri asked.

"Yes, I believe she likes him a lot," Eddi assured her. "That's all she's talked about since she arrived last night."

"She doesn't show it that much. You know, Eddi, I don't believe Cal is half as rich as Dave, but he does have a solid inheritance from his father. That, plus his practice will make some woman a good catch. If I were your sister I'd make certain he knew I was interested."

"Jenny is interested in marrying for love, not money. I think she's wise to use some caution." Eddi softened her expression and tempered her words so they didn't sound too harsh. Nevertheless, she kept her tones firm. "While you might be able to fall in love with a rich man as easily as a poor man, you can be as miserable with a rich man as a poor man any day. No amount of money can substitute for a heaven-on-earth marriage."

Cheri's hazel eyes took on an obstinate gleam. "Here's hoping you find yours, but there *is* such a thing as setting the stakes too high," she claimed as if she were a renowned consultant on matters of the heart.

I'd rather them be too high than too low, Eddi thought, and for once she chose not to express herself. Last week Cheri had confessed that precious few men had ever admitted an interest in her. Eddi wondered if that was because Cheri seemed determined to purposefully make herself unattractive. Her cotton dress, the color of a dirty camel, drained her complexion and magnified the dark circles under her eyes.

After years of repelling the opposite sex, Cheri may have lost faith in marrying for love. Eddi stubbornly clung to her youthful dreams. She would never compromise her standards for the sake of money—never.

As Cheri drifted toward her position near the fireplace, Dave brooded his way across the set. After a brief hesitation, he approached Calvin and Jenny and sat down in a commanding armchair as if he owned the place.

He might as well, Eddi thought and speculated about how much he must have donated toward his aunt's dream.

"Okay, as I said earlier, we'll be practicing all of Act One, including the famous dance scene between Darcy and Elizabeth," Mrs. DeBloom announced.

Calvin and Jenny picked up the scripts they'd placed on the coffee table. The shuffling of turning pages announced that the rest of the cast would likewise be reading their lines. Dave's gaze, however, remained fixed upon his aunt. He propped his elbows on the armrests and made a tent with his fingers, no script in sight.

"Remember, this nineteenth-century dance scene is a metaphor for the whole book as well as Austen's style of crafting her novels," Mrs. DeBloom continued. "It serves as a model for the way Darcy and Elizabeth move together and pull apart throughout the entire story." She turned toward Eddi. "It's important that you two put everything you've got into it," she said and encompassed Dave with a graceful shift of her hand. "Let's make it sparkle, shall we?"

Eddi realized she was staring at Dave when he looked at her. All traces of the person who kindly assisted her on the steps had vanished. In his place, sat the lazy-eyed lion who offered only a smirk and a silent challenge. Eddi determined she would not miss one letter of her lines that night. She knew the whole scene by heart. Eddi would not only pronounce her part with finesse and precision, she determined to out-act Dave.

Carissa Barclay arrived near Dave, her script in hand. She knelt beside his chair and posed a request. Dave began thumbing through her script. When he stopped, he pointed to a page on the right and said something. Eddi watched the redhead for several seconds as she leaned against the chair's arm and discussed the scene with Dave. Whatever had stopped her from showing up at the previous practices, Eddi sensed she was now here to stay. Carissa's posture and expression assured Dave and anyone else that she was ready and available for him.

More power to her, Eddi thought. *Maybe they'll ride off into the sunset and be miserable together.*

She didn't bother hiding her limp as she walked toward her position at right front. Eddi's shins ached as if they'd been assaulted with a baseball bat. Wondering how she would get through the dance scene without stumbling, Eddi glanced at Jenny. Frowning, her sister thumbed through her script, and she and Calvin stopped at intermittent points for brief discussions.

Mrs. DeBloom approached Carissa. With the cast in a state of continuing conversation, Eddi couldn't detect the gist of Mrs. DeBloom's comments until Carissa looked at Jenny. She rose and followed Mrs. DeBloom toward Jenny and Calvin. Smiling, Jenny stood and the two women shook hands as Mrs. DeBloom made introductions. Carissa seemed perfectly amiable to Jenny, who returned her overtures with a warmth of expression she'd yet to use with Calvin. Eddi speculated that the two must be discussing the possibilities of sharing the role of Bingley's sister, Carolyn.

Soon, Mrs. DeBloom called the group to order and the practice began. Tonight's efforts went more smoothly than any yet. While only Eddi and Dave had their parts completely memorized, many were beginning to feel the rhythm of their characters while connecting with the nuances of the play.

Eddi fulfilled her goal of not missing a line. By the time she found herself in the flow of the famous nineteenth-century dance scene, she detected a trace of respect in Dave's eyes—as if he'd finally realized that she really could act. Furthermore, Eddi couldn't deny that Dave was a natural on stage, despite his initial protests. Clearly, Mrs. DeBloom knew her nephew well.

But none of his talents nullified his flaws. While Dave played the role of an admirable hero, Eddi could never respect his true character. As if the hateful things he'd said to her and about her weren't enough, he'd stopped a commendable young man from going into the ministry because of his own petty jealousy. She could only imagine the number of people Rick Wallace could have impacted were he given the opportunity to work for Christ. The longer she mulled over Rick's story, the more perturbed she became. In that instance, Dave had gone beyond merely expressing his dislike. He had interfered with the work of God, thus putting himself in the place of God.

As the simple flute and guitar music floated across the stage, Eddi concentrated on not limping through the dance that flowed just as Mrs. DeBloom had anticipated. She and Dave participated with a whole line of dancers who schooled their features into a mask of calm contentment. Numerous times she and Dave drew near and parted, all the while exchanging banter with the precision of two skilled actors.

During the dance's halfway mark, Eddi and Dave walked down the middle of the line of couples, as planned. They stopped at the end. Last week, they'd practiced nothing but the dance until the whole group had it down. Now, Eddi found it nearly second nature to keep step with the music while engaging in conversation. Soon, Dave began their final dialogue sequence—a dialogue that took on the undercurrent of Rick's betrayal.

"'Do you and your sisters often walk to Meryton?'" Dave posed the question as if he were the best bred British gentleman.

"'Yes, we do,'" Eddi answered as the flautist and guitarist kept perfect rhythm with a light, simple tune. "'When you met us there the other day we had just been forming a new acquaintance.'"

Dave scowled, exactly on cue, and Eddi noted with what adeptness he expressed disapproval. "'Mr. Wickham is blessed with such happy manners as may ensure his *making* friends—whether he may be equally capable of *retaining* them, is less certain.'"

"'He has been so unlucky as to lose your friendship, and in a manner which he is likely to suffer from all his life,'" Eddi said.

Dave took her hand. They stepped together and then parted as they joined the line again. Eddi went beyond acting and looked into Dave's soul. "'I remember hearing you once say, Mr. Darcy,'" she continued as they grew nearer, "'that you hardly ever forgave, that your resentment once created was unappeasable. You are very cautious, I suppose, as to its *being created.*'"

"'I am,'" he answered with all of Darcy's typical gravity.

"'And never allow yourself to be blinded by prejudice?'" She marveled that a man of his success could have clung to a childhood prejudice enough to actually destroy Rick's chance in the ministry.

"'I hope not,'" Dave answered and responded to her scrutiny by narrowing his right eye.

"'It is particularly incumbent on those who never change their opinion to be secure of judging properly at first,'" she challenged as they moved in cadence with each beat.

"'May I ask to what these questions tend?'" he asked. The shuffle of footsteps mingled with their own.

"'Merely to the illustration of *your* character. I am trying to make it out.'" *Actually, I've already made it out,* Eddi thought with a slight frown that wasn't written in the script.

"'And what is your success?'" Dave asked as if he really cared.

"'I do not get on at all. I hear such different accounts of you as puzzle me exceedingly.'" Eddi produced the arched smile that so characterized Elizabeth Bennet.

"'I can readily believe that reports may vary greatly with respect to me; and I could wish, Miss Bennet, that you were not to sketch my character at the present moment, as there is reason to fear that the performance would reflect no credit on either.'" Dave reached for her hand as the two faced one another before preparing to part.

"'But if I do not take your likeness now, I may never have another opportunity.'" Eddi concentrated on her lines and told herself her palms were clammy because of the effort of acting.

"'I would by no means suspend any pleasure of yours,'" Dave's words took on a personal caress that would have brought color to Eddi's cheeks had she been the blushing variety. Fortunately, she hadn't blushed since grade school, and she didn't intend to start now.

Dave held her hands one measure longer than the script allowed, and Eddi didn't stop him. With a daredevil twist of his lips, he pulled her away from the archaic dance line and flowed into a slow waltz. Eddi, caught by surprise, followed his steps before she realized what she was doing. His dashing smile remained intact as he silently dared her to stop him. Snared by the moment, Eddi felt as if she were under Dave's hypnotic powers. Powers that hinted at more than just a dance. Powers that made her feel like Cinderella in the arms of her prince. He had twirled her across left center stage for six rotations when Mrs. DeBloom's exasperated voice broke the moment.

"Mr. Davidson, what do you think you're doing? None of this is in the script!"

The guitarist and flautist stopped their tune while the rest of the cast broke into laughter.

"Oops!" Dave said. "I must have forgotten my part."

He loosened his hold on Eddi, who was as breathless from shock as from pleasure—a pleasure she would never admit. Dave had proven as graceful a waltzer as he was an actor. She stepped behind a wingbacked chair, gripped the top, and feigned an irritated stance. If the rest of the cast suspected that Eddi hadn't wanted the waltz to end the rumors would fly.

I don't like him, Eddi told herself. *I do not!*

Mrs. DeBloom marched onto the stage. With a condescending huff and a yank on her straight dress, she waved her arms. "Let's just call this practice to an end." She checked her watch. "We've been here nearly two hours anyway. You've been great!"

She glowered at Dave, yet her attempt at disapproval dissolved into a doting smile. "Well, most of you, anyway," she added as if Dave could never hold her disapproval for long.

Fourteen

"Oh, Aunt Maddy, you're such a slave driver," Dave drawled and got the exact result he wished for. The group on stage erupted into another round of mirth, and his aunt continued in her offended pretense. Dave knew better than to believe his aunt could ever be really angry with him—not for very long anyway.

Eddi chose that moment to exit the stage. He wasn't certain *how* she got away. All he knew was that his arms were now empty. The woman who had filled them was sauntering across stage as if she couldn't care less that they'd just shared a special moment or that he would be dancing with her all night…in his dreams.

"Next practice Monday night at Dave's place," Mrs. DeBloom announced. "They'll be painting this stage then. I'll be in touch Monday morning."

Pretending nonchalance, Dave wandered to a safe vantage behind the velvet curtains. He was at an angle where he could watch Eddi but she couldn't see him. He couldn't say what had possessed him to step into that waltz with her—perhaps a wild impulse to sweep her off her feet. Her shocked expression attested that the act had certainly surprised her, so much that she'd failed to resist. Dave wondered if those seconds had left her as eager for more as they had him.

Eddi trotted down the steps and neared her parents. Only when she got within six feet of them did she slow into a slight limp. Dave tilted his head and knitted his brows. He hoped that his spontaneous dance hadn't irritated her wounds from the fall up the stairs.

As soon as Eddi stopped by her parents' table, her father stood and patted her on the back as if he were offering congratulations for a good practice. Dave had to admit Eddi had performed stupendously. Mrs. Boswick was so focused upon Jenny and Calvin that she offered little feedback for Eddi.

Hand in hand Calvin and his lady walked toward the family cluster. Dave grimaced and wondered why Jenny didn't wear an engagement ring. Certainly she must have more in common with her flighty younger sister than with Eddi, who seemed by far the most stable of the three sisters—or their mother, for that matter.

Linda burst upon the scene with Rick on one arm and the blond guy on the other. Dave crossed his arms and watched Eddi as she approached Rick. She smiled up at him as if he were a trusted friend in whom she held the utmost confidence.

Dave's mouth twitched. By now Eddi was supposed to be seeing through the moron's act and taking steps to remove him from her family. But Dave saw no signs that Eddi detected one shred of Rick's Dr. Jekyll–Mr. Hyde personality.

Could it be that Rick has poisoned Eddi with a twisted lie? he thought. *He fooled even you,* Dave reminded himself. *Why shouldn't he be able to fool Eddi?* Dave stepped from behind the curtains and strode toward the short flight of stairs that led offstage. Even if his family pride wouldn't allow him to tell Eddi the whole story, perhaps a well-placed hint would give her enough information to make her question Rick's sincerity.

Before he descended the first step he was halted by Carissa's calling his name. He pivoted to face the eager redhead while keeping Eddi visible from the corner of his eyes.

"Cal and I are inviting a group of people over to his place tonight for dessert and coffee. Want to come?" she asked with a glossy-lipped smile that said she'd *love* to be a part of his world.

"Uh…" Dave tore his attention from Carissa just as Eddi slipped through the parlor door with Rick close behind.

"I guess you're wondering if Eddi Boswick will be there to bother you, but I'm not including her," Carissa offered with haughty assurance. "Mrs. DeBloom says the two of you really can't stand each other."

"Oh, really?" Dave questioned and turned his full attention to the redhead.

"Yes." Carissa nodded.

"When exactly did my aunt say that?"

"Before practice," she explained and hooped her thumb through her jeans belt loop.

"Before the dance?" Dave queried and slyly smiled in a way he hoped suggested that he immensely enjoyed the dance.

"Oh…yes," Carissa replied, "before the dance." She observed the unfinished floor and then looked back at Dave. "I guess that whole scene was some of your best acting."

"Actually," Dave drawled and conjured a section of script that would probably give Carissa a thing or two to think about, "'your conjecture is totally wrong, I assure you. My mind was more agreeably engaged' during that scene. I was too busy 'meditating on the very great pleasure which a pair of fine eyes in the face of a pretty woman can bestow' to be concerned with how well I was acting."

"Oh," Carissa said with a blank stare.

I can tell you haven't read the script at all, Dave thought. He wagered that Eddi Boswick would have recognized those lines for Darcy's and shoved a retort right back at him from her part.

"If you'll excuse me," he said before turning toward the stairs. "I need to speak with someone before she leaves."

"Of course," Carissa responded.

Dave spent five minutes trying to ease away from people congratulating him on a great performance. Finally, he rushed onto the house's front porch, into the humid July evening. Next door, the rev of a lawn mower preceded the smell of freshly mown grass. Calvin stood on the edge of the lawn waving toward a red Mustang as it purred out of the driveway. A silver PT Cruiser zipped up the road. Through the eight-thirty twilight Dave caught a glimpse of Rick Wallace looking at him from the Cruiser's front passenger seat.

He trotted to Calvin's side and nearly pursued the red Mustang. On second consideration, Dave decided to halt beside Cal and wait to warn Eddi. Given that dance sequence, he was starting to act like a compulsive fifteen-year-old. The last thing he wanted Cal or anybody else to witness was his chasing after Eddi's vehicle. The rumors would fly unchecked.

I'll call her later, he thought.

"I finally got her phone number!" Calvin beamed and waved a piece of note paper.

"She wouldn't give it to you before?" Dave asked and suspected the answer. An engaged woman was usually careful about what man she gave her contact information to—especially a man she was flirting with behind her fiancé's back.

"No, nothing like that," Calvin assured. "I asked for it, but somehow we started talking and she forgot to give it to me. I did get her e-mail address, and we've been chatting on the internet since she was here last."

"Oh?" Dave said. He curled down the sides of his mouth and shook his head. "I see. And you didn't think to ask her for her phone number via e-mail?"

"I thought about it," Calvin said, "but I didn't want to be too pushy."

"Right," Dave said, "as cool as she is, it probably wouldn't take much to seem too pushy."

Calvin observed him. "What's *that* supposed to mean?"

Dave inserted his hands into his back pockets and looked at the Saint Augustine grass that stretched across the lush lawn. The crickets shrieked about the approaching night as fireflies blinked near the row of oaks between his aunt's mansion and her neighbor's brick home. No one would guess the neighborhood had survived a near miss with a tornado mere weeks before.

Dave debated how best to tell his friend about Jenny's fiancé. He hated to disappoint the guy. After all, Cal wasn't known for his good experiences with women. A couple of years ago, he'd put his faith in a lady who promised to marry him. Two weeks before the wedding, Calvin found her in the arms of another man. Cal really knew how to pick the ones who would break his heart.

Feeling his friend's scrutiny, Dave finally blurted the truth. "She's engaged, Cal." He lifted his head and didn't flinch.

"What?" Calvin hollered and immediately covered his mouth. He glanced around the yard. The dozen people who lingered on the lawn all turned their attention toward the two men.

Once they resumed their conversations, Dave took the note paper from his friend's hand, tore it in half, and extended it back to him. "Jenny Boswick is already engaged. I don't know what games she's playing, but I don't think she gives a hoot about you."

"How did you find out?" Calvin asked, as if he doubted the veracity of Dave's source.

"I overheard her mother talking to Mr. Boswick before practice. She mentioned Jenny's fiancé and how much better a catch you were because you could make more money."

"Money?" Calvin bleated as if it were a foreign word.

"Haven't you heard? There are actually people in the world who'd marry somebody just because they have money." Dave chose not to mention that Calvin's sister fit that mold herself.

"You think Jenny is one of those?" Calvin rubbed the two pieces of paper together. The scraps created a rasp that took on a forlorn quality.

"Honestly…" Dave wished he could soften the truth, but decided brutal honesty would better serve his friend. "Yes," he said. "I've watched her closely, and well…" He shrugged.

"Yeah, I know." Calvin lowered his head. "I've wondered a time or two if maybe I was a little crazier about her than she was about me—right in the middle of thinking she might be the one," he added under his breath.

Calvin held up the torn note. "Now what'll I do? I promised her I'd call next week. Carissa even agreed to play another part so Jenny could play my leading lady."

"If I were you," Dave said, "I'd bow out as graciously as I could and chalk it all up to experience."

"Right," Calvin agreed and peered toward downtown London.

Dave followed his lead and admired the new roof that now topped the Eat a Bite Cafe. Unfortunately, the theater didn't rank the same repairs. In light of Mrs. DeBloom opening her dinner theater, the city chose to tear down the old theater completely. A gaping hole full of splintered wood and crushed mortar marred the street corner where the theater once proudly stood.

"Did Carissa invite you over?" Calvin finally asked. "We're supposed to be having some friends over for coffee and dessert and maybe a movie."

"Yes, she invited me," Dave said, "but I'm going to pass this time. I've got some loose ends at the ranch to wrap up." Dave's haven was calling his name. He couldn't deny the haunting whispers that urged him into the small building. After last night's church picnic, he'd stayed there until midnight. He would probably repeat the scenario tonight.

"Is Jenny going to be there, by chance?" Dave asked and considered changing his plans if maybe Eddi was joining her sister at the Barclays'.

"Nah." Calvin shook his head. "I asked her and Eddi, but they said they needed to hang out with their family."

"Figures," Dave said.

"Yeah, figures." Calvin wadded the scraps of paper and stuffed them into his pocket.

Fifteen

~ ~

By Thursday night, Dave had spent five evenings straight in his haven. Aunt Maddy had been stricken with a horrible case of summer flu and called off all play practices for a week. That left Dave free to pursue his first love.

At midnight Thursday Dave had exhausted all of his mental stamina. He stepped out of the brick building and clicked the door behind him. A habitual twist of the knob attested that the door was still unlocked. Dave started to reopen the door and lock the knob, but decided he was feeling too lazy to exude the effort. When he first constructed the building, Dave had thought of installing a deadbolt lock. Soon, reason set in and he realized there was nobody way out in the country who would be interested in going inside.

Dave stretched and yawned, the humid night air filling his lungs. His boots swished against the grass as he approached his back porch, alight with the full moon's radiance. A hoot owl's haunting call floated from the pecan orchard and sent a stab of loneliness through him. The bitter smell of Aunt Maddy's geraniums covering the porch heightened his forlorn gloom.

He stopped at the base of the porch steps, placed his hands on his hips, and peered around the estate. For the first time since he'd built his home, he dreaded going in alone. All he could think about was the lady he'd twirled across stage and how he wished she were inside awaiting him. A dull ache gnawed at Dave's gut—an ache that whispered he was not complete. Not without his Eddi.

He rubbed his mouth with callused fingers and traced the line of his jaw. No amount of denial could jar him from this unexpected turn of his heart. For over seven months he'd avoided Eddi because he feared the very thing that had finally overcome him.

"I can't be in love with her," he denied and scowled toward the back pasture. A massive red barn sprawled beneath the moonbeams and seemed to whisper of work that needed to be done. Francis Schmidt and three other hired hands had helped him repair fences most of the day. Another section of fence waited for tomorrow. He looked at his palms, pricked and worn. Not even hard, physical labor had expunged Eddi from his mind.

Dave shifted his attention toward the pool. He'd promised himself while sweating in the unforgiving sun that he'd indulge in a swim. While Francis and the hired men had accepted Dave's invitation for a dip in the pool he had opted for a cool shower. Now, the crystal blue waters glittered in the moonshine and beckoned him into their sweetness.

Dave burst into a hard stride toward the pool's deep end. He stopped on the concrete edge, still emanating warmth from the unforgiving sun. After yanking off his boots and socks, Dave stripped to his boxer shorts. With a light spring, he dove into the pool. The cool water enveloped him like a welcoming friend. He swam down until he reached the bottom. With a flip and kick, Dave shoved off the bottom and shot upward. He broke the surface with a splash and hiss of air entering his lungs. The taste of chlorine on his tongue, Dave struck out across the Olympic-sized pool and swam as if he were dashing for his life. All the while, his mind ticked off the reasons he shouldn't be in love with Eddi Boswick.

She's not the one for me, he argued. *She can't be. I'm not sure she even likes me.*

He thought of those minutes after the tornado...of the close encounter at Saturday's play. Both times, Dave wanted to kiss her—he *really* wanted to kiss her. Both times, he would have vowed he saw the same in her eyes. *So she must feel some attraction for me,* he countered and floundered in a sea of uncertainty.

But her family... he argued with himself. *One sister is a blatant man-chaser. The other one is a subtle man-chaser. And obviously, her mother isn't the most sensible woman in the world.*

Dave pushed off the side of the pool, glided fifteen feet, and attacked the water. It churned around him in white waves as he continued his mental dialogue. *I can't imagine going home to her family every Christmas. Heaven help me,* he thought, *her mother would probably look at me like I'm First National Bank!*

With a gulp of air, he dove beneath the surface. As he descended, Dave released the air from his lungs. Copious bubbles left his nose as he plunged the pool's depth. No matter how deep he swam, Dave couldn't escape what he carried in his heart—the first bloom of love. Real love. The kind that didn't evaporate when infatuation ended.

He swam along the bottom of the pool until he felt as if his chest would burst. With a final desperate push, Dave erupted upon the surface and sucked air into his burning lungs.

Suddenly, none of his arguments mattered. All that mattered was Eddi. *I must be crazy. Yeah, crazy about her,* he countered. *And I've gone crazy all week because I haven't been able to see her at practice.*

She hadn't even responded to his e-mail Tuesday. He fell into a lazy crawl toward the pool's side. After debating a dozen different options for warning her about Rick, Dave had finally scrounged her e-mail address out of the church directory and wrote her a quick message. "Don't believe everything Rick Wallace tells you." Then under that, "Enjoyed practice." For forty-eight hours he hoped for a cyber message, but received none. Whether she took his warning to heart or not was anybody's guess. If she likewise enjoyed practice, Eddi kept the secret to herself.

Dave reached the pool's side, hoisted himself up, settled onto the warm edge, and dangled his feet in the water. A midnight breeze sent a chill along his arms and chest. The smell of freshly cut hay mingled with a whiff of cattle. A longhorn's hollow bellow only intensified Dave's loneliness.

He eyed his empty house and then gazed up at the star-studded sky. A snatch of holy text reverberated through his soul, *It is not good for man to be alone.*

"So God created woman," he mumbled.

A falling star streaked across the velvet canvas, blazing a silver path in its wake. Before the star disappeared over the west pasture, Dave begged God to either deliver him from his torment or make Eddi love him as desperately as he was beginning to love her.

Eddi opened her office Friday morning for the sole purpose of getting her finances in order and answering the phone. So far, she had managed to handle all positions at Boswick Law Firm. She hadn't hired a secretary, receptionist, or accountant. The last few weeks, business had been steadily increasing. On top of winning a significant child-custody case, Eddi had also gleaned the business of London Savings and Loan. She now handled all their real-estate closures. Real estate was by far her least favorite work, but Eddi couldn't specialize in such a small town.

Earlier in the week, she'd threatened to hire a secretary for the first time. But by Thursday evening, Eddi had cleared her desk and taken care of all commitments. Now that the week was coming to a slow close, Eddi was thankful she hadn't placed the help wanted ad in the paper.

Balancing a mug of tea, her purse, and portfolio, she stepped across the area rug, a plaid offering of burgundy and forest green. The rug complemented her wallpaper as if the two were designed by the same hand. Before going back to Houston Sunday, Jenny had insisted that Eddi add the silk ficus tree near the pair of wingbacked leather chairs. As Eddi settled behind her desk, she admitted that the greenery softened the room's professional appearance.

She dropped her purse under her desk and pushed her computer's on button. As the machine booted up, Eddi sipped her lemon tea and relished the herbal liquid, tart and warm. As soon as the computer was ready, she activated her USA Online account and scanned the blue screen that featured her In box. The top e-mail from Dave Davidson bade her read it for the twenty-fifth time.

> Eddi,
>
> Don't believe everything Rick Wallace tells you.
> Enjoyed practice.
>
> Dave

Eddi tapped her blunt fingernails against her desk's polished surface. For three days she'd debated about how to answer Dave's e-mail—or if she should answer at all. The memory of that magical waltz enticed her to tell him how much she likewise enjoyed practice. For the first time, Eddi wondered if perhaps she should look past Dave's shortcomings and give the guy some encouragement. The e-mail blurred. Eddi could no longer deny that there was a special chemistry between them. Neither could she deny that Dave felt it.

She gripped the chair's arms and shook her head. "Wait a minute," Eddi demanded. "This is not a fairy tale and he's not Prince Charming. Just because we've got some sort of surface attraction doesn't make him a man of character." The words extinguished her fantasies.

She reread the e-mail and reminded herself of the irony of his message. While Dave told her not to believe Rick Wallace, he had duped a whole town into believing he was a rancher and nothing more.

"If I'm going to have to choose what man to trust," Eddi mumbled, "I believe it would be Rick. At least he has never stooped to insult me."

From there, Eddi forced herself to relive every nasty thing Dave had ever said to her or about her. *Too short, too prissy... classless. Wears army boots to bed. And if that weren't enough, he insinuated I'd be interested in him for his money!*

"You've not only been rude to me, you've also been rude to my parents! Now, you're sending me this e-mail full of advice like I'm supposed to heed it. I don't think so." Eddi plopped her tea down. After three days of brooding over the message, she hit the delete button.

"No thank you," she said. "And I'm glad you enjoyed practice. At least that makes one of us."

As Eddi checked her e-mail for other messages she relived the waltz yet again. Her casual pantsuit became a ball gown. The office turned into a chandeliered suite. The elevator music trickling from ceiling speakers transformed into a live orchestra. Dave, now dressed in his *People* magazine tuxedo, wrapped his arms around her, and they floated across the floor together.

"Okay, maybe the waltz was nice," she admitted and eyed her clothing. The pantsuit replaced her ball gown. The chandeliers were gone. The orchestra disappeared. Only Dave remained. Dave in his tux.

Lately, she had begun to wonder if the man were purposefully doing things to attract her. *But what if he found out I was enjoying it?* she mused. A potential scenario played through her mind. *Dave would probably take arrogant satisfaction in telling* me *not to get my hopes up and then accusing* me *of chasing him for his money.* Eddi narrowed her eyes. *That was exactly what he'd done in the past. Why would the future be any different?*

"Whatever you're up to, it's not going to work," she decided. "I don't care how many times you help me up when I've fallen or how many times you twirl me around stage, I won't admit to a living soul that I enjoyed one second of it—and especially not to you!"

Eddi disciplined her wayward mind, dismissed Dave, and scrutinized the messages as they popped into the In box. The first message was from Jenny. The subject line read "Huge Disappointment." Eddi picked up her mug and indulged in another mouthful of tea. She opened the e-mail and eagerly scanned the message:

Eddi,

I've never been able to keep secrets from you. So, I guess I'll tell you that I'm crying as I write this e-mail. It's eleven Thursday night or I'd call you. I haven't checked my e-mail for a couple of days— you know me and e-mail. Anyway, I was up late tonight and decided to check my e-mail. Now I wish I'd never checked it. The wild part about all this, Eddi, is that I was beginning to think that maybe Calvin was the man I've been waiting for. Please don't misunderstand me. I'm not suggesting that I'd marry him so soon by any means. But, I still thought I was sensing something special between us.

After coming home Sunday night, I even called Hal and talked to him. Essentially, I called us off—*completely*. I just couldn't keep seeing him with things warming up so with Cal and me. Now, it looks like everything has gone cold. Sniff, sniff. Call me when you get the chance. I'm shamelessly in need of consolation.

Love, Jenny

P.S. I've pasted Calvin's message below.

> Jenny,
>
> As things have turned out, I think it's best for Carissa to play the role of Jane Bennet. Thanks for taking the time to chat with me when you've been in town. I know you mentioned that your coaching position gets hectic and that you have seminars to attend this summer. Please don't alter your schedule for any trips to London on my behalf. Given the play schedule and my professional commitments, I've got a really tight schedule, and there's no guarantee that I'll be able to see you anyway.
>
> Calvin Barclay

Eddi gripped her mug with both hands. The warmth did nothing to ease her mounting tension. *Calvin Barclay must have been playing some sort of sick game when he pursued Jenny.*

In her opinion, there wasn't a woman as pure-hearted as her sister. Eddi, with her quick temper and iron will, had often dreamed of being everything lovely and sweet like Jenny.

"She deserved far better than this!" Eddi declared.

She drained the last trace of tea, placed the mug on the spotless desk, and opened her bottom desk drawer. Eddi pulled out the phone book and dragged her phone closer. Like a warrior defending the queen's honor, she flipped through the phone book until she found Barclay Animal Hospital. Halfway through dialing Calvin's number, her cell phone emitted a series of beeps from her purse.

With a growl, Eddi suspended dialing the final numbers. She lifted the Velcro tab on the side of her purse and pulled out her cell phone. A glance at the screen testified the caller was Jenny.

Eddi pushed the send button on the cell and hung up her office phone. After a swift greeting, Jenny said, "Have you checked your e-mail this morning?"

"Yes, I just did," Eddi said. "And yes, I got what you sent last night. Jenny, I'm so sorry!"

"Oh, I know. So am I!" She sniffed. "I guess I'm acting like a twelve-year-old here, but this has really affected me." Her voice's wobble added to Eddi's irritation.

"And well it should!" Eddi claimed. "This is not high school. We're adults here. Calvin Barclay had no business encouraging you like he did if he was going to just—just—"

"Dump me," Jenny whimpered.

"Well, I wasn't going to—"

"No, it's the truth!" Jenny wailed. "That's exactly what he did. He just dumped me like a bunch of stinky garbage."

Eddi propped her elbow on the desk and placed her forehead in her palm.

"At least when I broke it off with Hal, I had the decency to place a personal phone call and be kind about it," Jenny said.

"I think this e-mail is the rudest thing I've ever read," Eddi blurted. "It made me so mad I was in the middle of calling him when you called me."

"Oh no, Eddi, please," Jenny begged. "If you call Calvin, I will *die!* You can't call him. Promise me you won't call him or—or talk to him or anybody about any of this. Promise me, Eddi!"

"Okay, okay." Eddi shifted the phone. "I promise."

She grabbed her empty mug and walked through a narrow hallway. Eddi passed a larger empty office she planned to use once she hired a secretary. At the end of the hallway, she stepped into a tiny kitchen.

"Would you like some company this weekend?" She set her mug on the counter.

"Who me?"

"You *are* the person I'm talking to, right?" Eddi's words softened with the evidence of her smile.

"I'd love some," Jenny said.

"Okay, good." She peered down the hallway toward her desk void of all paperwork. "My day is pretty much empty. I've just decided I'm going to close the office at noon and head that way. Heaven knows, I need a break from these people in this town as much as you need moral support right now."

"That sounds great," Jenny said. "It might even be a God-thing. Besides my problems, there's something else brewing."

"What?" Eddi asked.

"It's Linda—she's wanting to go to Hawaii with some friends."

"Hawaii?" Eddi squeaked.

"Yes."

"What are Dad and Mom saying?"

"Mom is beside herself wanting Linda to go. Sometimes I wonder if Mom is living vicariously through Linda. She's saying she would have loved to have gone to Hawaii when she was twenty."

"That doesn't surprise me," Eddi said. "And Dad?"

"He's not so sure, but he's not saying no either. He said something yesterday about her being twenty and there wasn't much he could do to stop her if that's what she wants to do."

"Oh, Jenny, we've got to somehow stop her," Eddi said. "I don't trust her flying all the way to Hawaii with a bunch of party animals."

"You just hit the nail on the head," Jenny said. "I'm afraid it's going to turn into a perpetual beer bash and who knows what else."

Images of Jenny finding Linda's birth control pills sent a dark precognition through her spirit. Eddi stood erect and checked her watch. "Mark my word," she vowed, "I'll be there by six tonight. We'll go from there."

Sixteen

~ ~

After his late night in the pool, Dave took Friday off. At nine o'clock that morning, he'd met Francis Schmidt at the door and told him to handle things on his own. By ten, Dave was halfway to Dallas. At eleven, he stood in a country church's cemetery east of the metroplex—a cemetery that seized Dave's past and held it in mute captivity.

Three years had lapsed since Dave visited the cemetery. All the times he thought of going back, the pain had been too great...the memories too overwhelming. So, Dave had put on a tough front with Aunt Maddy every time she asked him to join her in visiting the grave sites. Looking back, he doubted she believed his claims of not needing to visit the lonely, grave-marked yard.

The weather had taken an unusual turn for a Texas July. Instead of yesterday's heat index of 108, the thermometer read only 88. A cool wind whipped up the smell of bitterweeds and dust. A strong blast rushed through the yard full of gravestones and tilted a row of young mesquites on the west edge. A whirlwind of dust erupted near his truck. Dave's shirttail rustled over his jeans. That morning he'd been too grouchy and too distracted to tuck it in.

Dave looked beyond the flat pastureland and eyed the horizon marred by an inky thunderhead. The urge to find a storm cellar proved almost too powerful to ignore. Even though that white-tailed twister had only cost Dave some back pain, it had marred his psyche. He hadn't observed a bank of clouds the same since. Like a soldier about to face an attack, Dave tensed and searched for a place to take cover—just in case.

The backdoor of the abandoned wood-framed church banged shut and then hurled itself open again. Dave nodded as if in answer to the door's suggestion. He found peace in knowing the graying structure possessed a basement. In his youth he had set off a round a firecrackers in the corner of that basement one Sunday during children's church. His parents had not been thrilled with him for a whole week.

The faded sign in front of the church read Lakeland Community Church. His father and mother had felt a call of God to refurbish the old sanctuary and reopen it for services. They'd seen years of success in ministering to the community, and the church thrived. Dave often marveled that God blessed his parents' efforts even though their home life was a battleground. Once his parents died, the church board searched for another minister while attendance steadily dwindled. Eventually, the congregation dissolved, and the building once again became an empty shell.

After another glance at the ominous horizon, Dave concentrated on the two graves that lay side by side. While numerous tombstones along the south fence were crumbling with age, these remained unharmed by the elements. Amazingly, sixteen years had lapsed since Dave had stood beside the freshly dug graves, each with a casket suspended over it. He'd listened in shock as the minister spoke the final words over both his parents.

On one side of him stood Rick Wallace. On the other side, his brother George, only fifteen. He'd clung to Dave as if he were drowning. Dave now realized that George really had been going under.

I should have known! I should have known! he lambasted himself. He allowed his gaze to trail the guilt-ridden path to George's gravestone. While his parents' deaths had been devastating, George's death three years ago nearly took Dave to the brink of insanity.

Dave closed his eyes and held the memories at bay. He hadn't come here to brood over his losses, even though his heart throbbed for the family bond forever extinguished.

The longing to communicate with his parents and George had plagued Dave until three in the morning. Only after he decided to drive to the cemetery was he able to snatch a few hours of sleep. Now he pressed his work-roughened fingers between his brows. His forehead's dull ache didn't subside.

"I really don't know where to start or what to say," Dave finally said. He inserted his fingertips into his frayed jeans pockets and let his hands sag outward. "I guess I just wanted to tell you both about Eddi."

Dave kicked at the spindly grass and wondered if the cemetery's caretaker had quit and not been replaced. The row of weeds near the ancient plank fence nodded in the breeze as if in answer to his thoughts.

He bowed on one knee and traced his finger between clumps of grass. "I'd like to ask your advice on marrying her, I guess," he continued.

"This is crazy," he mumbled. "They can't answer. They don't even know I'm here…Why am I even here?"

Dave stared at his mother's tombstone. "Maybe I'm here mainly to get past the past," he answered himself and shifted his attention to his father's grave marker. "You two fought like cats and dogs in front of me the whole time I was growing up. I guess I never told you, but by the time I was seventeen, I decided I'd rather never get married than live like you did."

Phantoms of the past gyrated among the tombstones, rattling the rusty chains Dave had yet to shake. Chains that bound him in fear his whole life. Before he radically encountered Christ, Dave had insulated himself with his demanding career and short-term relationships. His brother's death had shaken him to the core because he partly blamed himself. One desperate morning Dave awoke with an empty bottle of bourbon on his chest. That day he sensed that if he didn't have a lifeline, he was going to drown—just like George. That lifeline proved to be Christ.

But even a renewed vow to the holy hadn't delivered him from his fear. Dave knew from the beginning of his awakened faith that the short-term relationships with women had to end— that if he ever became involved with another woman it would be about respect and honor and a lifetime commitment to love. That realization had sent him into a working frenzy, driven by a raw terror. In the past three years, Dave purposefully avoided the opposite sex by working like a maniac on his ranch. Until Aunt Maddy's play invaded his life, Dave had poured all his spare time into the building behind his house.

"Hello." The unexpected greeting sent a jolt through Dave. He jumped and pivoted to face a small boy behind him. The child looked to be no more than eight. He chewed on a wad of gum as if he were an overactive chipmunk. A dark mop of curls peeked from beneath a red baseball cap he wore backwards. His eyes were as dark as his hair, and a generous scattering of freckles covered his nose and cheeks. Torn cutoffs, mud-smeared shirt, and boy-worn sneakers attested to an adventure of Huck Finn proportions. Behind the boy a shiny blue bike was propped against the cemetery fence near the gate.

"I didn't hear you come up." Dave stood. As he extended his hand toward the child, he was stricken with how much he resembled his brother George when he was a kid. "My name's Dave Davidson," he said.

The child took Dave's hand, shook it, and nodded with the sage wisdom of an old timer. "Nice to meet you, Mr. Davidson," he said. "Name's Jeff Brown."

"Hello there, Jeff Brown," Dave responded as Jeff blew a gigantic bubble. When it popped, he resumed chomping as if the nation's safety depended upon his efforts.

"And what brings you out this morning?" Dave asked.

"I was just out ridin' my bike." He pointed toward the gate. "I live 'bout half a mile that way." He motioned to his left. "I come to the cemetery sometimes."

"Oh, really?" Dave asked.

"Yep." The child squinted up at Dave. "Funny, I've never seen you here."

"Well, this is my first time back in a few years." A blue jay swooped behind Jeff and soared to the limb of a nearby pine. The bird's raucous squawking mingled with Jeff's explanation.

"I come every week or so," the boy said. "When school's in, I come on Saturdays."

"I see," Dave answered and debated whether or not to pry into the reason for the child's visits. A white sedan purred along the country lane, stirring up a cloud of red dust. The wind swooshed behind the car and whipped the dust into a crazed billow.

"I come to visit my mom," Jeff finally said as if he'd read Dave's mind. His dark eyes stirred with pain-wrought insight that transcended his years. "She's over there." He pointed to a plot near the fence, about six feet from his bike.

"Really?" Dave questioned and felt a strange bond with this child he'd never met. "That's why I'm here, too." He looked toward the tombstones that marked his parents' graves and pitied Jeff's plight.

"I talk to my mom," Jeff said. "She died last year when I was just in second grade. Dad says her heart just quit. We don't know why. I guess she had problems with it, that's all. You talkin' to your mom, too?" He tilted his head and blew another bubble. The gum popped, and Jeff sucked it back into his mouth.

"Yes, as a matter of fact, I am," Dave responded and eyed the graves near the child's bike.

"What about?" Jeff studied the tombstones behind Dave.

"Well…" Dave hesitated as he searched for a way to avoid answering this unexpected interrogation. He observed Jeff Brown and recalled George's precocious childhood antics. Once, Dave's mother even caught him going from door to door selling worn out baseball cards for a dollar a piece. So many people in the neighborhood liked him, he had accumulated twenty-five dollars within a one-hour period.

Caught in pleasant memories, Dave hesitated and then decided to reveal the reason for his trip. "I'm telling my parents about a lady I've met," he said. "I'm thinking of asking her to marry me."

Jeff's bottom lip protruded as if he were in deep thought. "Do you love her?"

"I think so." Dave shook his head and marveled at the ease with which the admission fell from him. "Yes, I do."

"Does she love you?"

"I'm not sure, but…" He relived the spark of attraction in Eddi's eyes. "I think she might like me and maybe—maybe she could grow to love me."

"Well," Jeff responded, "then you should get married." He crossed his arms as if he were the replacement for Dear Abby. "My mother used to tell me that one day I'd grow up and fall in love and get married. If you're in love, then you should get married." He nodded as if he were sealing a major business deal.

"All men do, you know," Jeff added.

Dave smiled. "Yes, so I've heard," he answered. "So I've heard."

"Well, I guess my grandma's gonna be hollerin' for me for lunch. She moved in with us when Mom died."

"Okay," Dave began and hated to see the child leave so soon. "But first tell me," he said, "What were you talking to *your* mom about?"

"Oh, I'm trying to decide whether or not to buy a new baseball glove or a parakeet. I've been saving my money all summer. My dad says it's a big decision, and I just wanted to tell Mom about it."

"I'd go with the baseball glove," Dave advised and mimicked Jeff's arm crossing. "Parakeets have a way of getting eaten by cats. Do you have a cat?"

"Yep. Six of 'em," Jeff answered. "Our mamma cat had five kittens seven months ago. My grandma says we're going to have to make cat stew or something."

Dave snickered. "I've never heard of a cat eating a baseball glove," he said. Dave smiled as he remembered playing catch with George.

Jeff narrowed his eyes. "That's a good point."

"Yes. I figure your mom would agree, too. Baseball is a good thing for boys to spend their money on. All boys do, you know."

Jeff peered toward the horizon. "I think maybe you're right, mister."

As if responding to an unheard beckoning, Jeff dashed toward the gate like he was trying to steal home base. He hopped on his bike, jabbed at the kickstand with his heel, and pumped the pedals. "Bye," he hollered and waved toward his new acquaintance.

After waving back, Dave watched Jeff roll out of the church's driveway and onto the road. "Well, that was interesting," he mused, yet his heart insisted he'd been privileged with a visit from the past.

Dave walked one row over and stopped near a stone marked "George A. Davidson." A streak of dried mud marred the engraved name, and Dave tried to brush it off. Several stubborn clumps clung to his little brother's name. Dave dropped to his knees, unbuttoned his crumpled shirt, took it off, and frantically rubbed the surface of the tombstone as if trying to erase the guilt of three year's absence. The red dirt crumbled to the earth. The monument shone spotless in the midday sun.

He gripped the top of the grave marker and gazed after Jeff Brown. A thin trail of dust along the country road testified to the blue bike's progress. Jeff's red baseball cap bobbed up and down with his effort.

Dave closed his eyes and rested his head on his hand. Tears seeped between his lashes and plopped onto his fingers. And he prayed that Eddi heeded his warning about Rick Wallace.

Seventeen

Linda padded into Rick's unkempt kitchen and opened the refrigerator. A shaft of cold air sent a rash of gooseflesh along her bare legs as she shoved aside a gallon of milk. She examined the back of the refrigerator. A wide array of condiments and foil-wrapped leftovers cluttered the shelf, but no wine coolers. She frowned. Rick just told her he had a couple of wine coolers on the back of the top shelf. Accompanied by the smell of stale onions, she crouched in front of the refrigerator, squinted, and tried to peer past the maze of junk on the second shelf.

"Hey, babe," Rick called. "Having any luck?"

"No."

She glanced up. Rick stepped into the kitchen, pulling a T-shirt over his head. He shoved both arms through the sleeves and tugged the shirt down to the top of his gym shorts.

Linda smiled and toyed with the button of the uniform shirt she wore. The badge on the shoulder said Houston Police Force. Rick's nameplate was still attached, as it had been when Linda met him at the door an hour ago—except he had been wearing the shirt. The visit had been a surprise, but after a hard day Rick was thrilled to see her.

When they arrived from Eddi's Sunday night, Linda had dropped off André first. From there, she and Rick drove to his apartment in north Houston. By midnight Rick acted as if he'd never even met Eddi—just as Linda had predicted. Two days ago he'd given her the key to his apartment.

As he neared, Linda stood and leaned into him. He wrapped his arms around her from behind and nibbled her neck. Delicious tingles darted along her shoulders and she giggled.

"I can't find the coolers," she said.

"Ah man, don't tell me they're gone." Rick released Linda and bent in front of the refrigerator. After a round of mumbles and jar pushing, Rick straightened and shook his head. "Gone," he said and perused the kitchen.

"Ah ha!" Rick closed the door and stepped toward the sink full of soiled dishes. He reached near the faucet and retrieved two empty bottles. "I remember now. "André and I drank them Monday night when we were watching the baseball game."

"Oh well." He shrugged and tilted his head. "Want to go to Dolly's for a drink? It's just around the corner." He gazed past her as if trying to decide whether to make the next offer. "Or maybe you'd like to smoke some weed," he said with a silent dare.

"You mean marijuana?" Linda's eyes widened.

"Yeah. I've got a stash in my bedroom. Ever tried it?"

"Not really," Linda hedged. She hated to admit her lack of experience, but the idea scared her. So had getting drunk, until she'd done it a few times.

"You know what I'd really like." Linda stepped closer and pressed her body against his. "I'd like us to get high on *Hawaii*—together," she said with a pouty turn of her bottom lip that she hoped hid her misgivings about the marijuana.

"I already told you, babe," he crooned. "I don't have the money. I'm living on a policeman's salary."

"But you have money for marijuana," she whimpered.

"I get that for free every time I agree to turn my head the other way," he admitted. "If you want me to go to Hawaii, you'll have to pay my way."

Linda raised her head and examined his scrumptious brown eyes. She contemplated her anemic checking account and maxed charged cards and wished she hadn't indulged in the Neiman's shopping trip last week. Leave it to her friend Hallie to wait until a month before they go to plan such a trip. Hallie and her friends were all so rich that they didn't *have* to budget such luxuries.

"It's taking my whole allowance this month to make the trip," she said. "When I asked Dad for more money this morning, I thought he was going to have a heart attack. He told me if I couldn't make it to Hawaii and back on two thousand, I didn't need to go."

"Oh well." Rick shrugged, and his shoulders sagged. "I guess you'll have to go without me then."

"But you *want* to go, don't you?" Linda placed both hands on either side of his face.

"Well…" Rick hesitated as if he were trying to cover his desires. "I'd love to go anywhere with *you*, Linda," he admitted.

She lifted her lips into a tantalizing smile. "Then it's settled," she crooned. "I'll make it happen somehow. Hawaii just wouldn't be the same without you."

Rick pinched her bottom and Linda squealed. She dashed from the kitchen, through the cluttered living room, and into the hallway. With a growl, Rick followed. When Linda collapsed in the middle of the bed's tangled sheets, her cell phone began to blast forth a heavy metal tune.

Linda rolled to the end of the bed. She reached toward the floor and shoved her shorts and shirt off her purse. Rick collapsed beside her and lazily ran his fingers along her spine as she rummaged to the bottom of her cluttered purse. When she pulled out her phone, a flat, oval-shaped package plopped onto the floor.

Linda's fingers tightened around the noisy phone, and she looked at the pink pack of pills as if she'd never seen them before. A flutter of a thought irritated her mind. She tried to remember when she was supposed to start taking the birth control pills again this cycle. Rick began nibbling her neck, and a delightful giggle gurgled in her throat. Fully expecting her friend Hallie on the phone, Linda ignored the caller ID and continued to laugh all the way through her greeting.

"Hi, Linda," Jenny's voice floated over the line, and Linda grew rigid.

She sat up and began tugging at the neckline of her shirt as if Jenny could see her.

"Oh, hi," Linda said, and all traces of revelry disappeared.

"Who is it?" The bed jostled as Rick sat up beside her.

Linda covered the receiver and waved at Rick. "It's my sister, Jenny," she hissed. "Be quiet."

With a grimace, Rick got up and left the bedroom. An awkward pause seeped across the phone as Linda watched her lover disappear down the hallway. Her chest burned with an onslaught of anxiety. She hoped she hadn't irritated him so much that he lost interest in her.

"Linda? Are you there? Have I lost you?" Jenny prompted.

"Yes…I mean, no, you haven't lost me. I was just…" She stood and tugged on the end of Rick's shirt. "What's up?" she queried.

"I just wanted to let you know that Eddi's coming down this weekend. She's supposed to be here by six o'clock tonight. I was just on the phone with Mom. She said it would be great if we all could eat dinner there tonight. Dad even offered to grill hamburgers."

"Oh, sure," Linda said and checked her Rolex knockoff. She had four hours to play. Linda stepped down the hallway as Rick sauntered out of the bathroom. With a saucy grin, she wiggled her fingers at him. He responded with a wink that relieved Linda. "Do you think anyone will mind if I bring Rick with me?"

"Oh no," Jenny said. "Was that him I heard earlier?"

"Yes, it was. Uh, we're actually at the park. He asked me out for a walk." Linda repressed the telltale giggle while Rick released a sensual chuckle.

"Good," Jenny said as if she were relieved. "Eddi and I really liked Rick. I think Mom and Dad will be glad to see him again too. I'll call Mom and make sure they prepare enough food for an extra."

"Okay," Linda agreed. As soon as she disconnected the call, she inched the cell phone antenna down the side of Rick's jaw. "Want to go eat at my folks with me tonight?" she purred and dreaded a negative response.

"Sure." Rick's smile lines ended in dimples beside his mouth.

"Both my sisters will be there," Linda said and doubted the wisdom of trotting Rick out in front of Eddi again. What if he acted like their father and decided he preferred her?

"What we need to do is figure out a way to get one of your sisters to pay my way to Hawaii," Rick said.

Linda pulled the cell phone away from his face and looked at him. "Now *there's* an idea," she mumbled and began to brainstorm ways to manipulate Jenny or Eddi into forking over two grand.

"I was just kidding, Linda," Rick said.

"No." Linda held up her hand. "Jenny has already hinted that she doesn't think I need to go. She and Eddi are as thick as thieves. I bet Eddi already knows by now and is going to rat to Dad about how she thinks I shouldn't go."

"Well, if Jenny and Eddi don't think you need to go, then maybe she'd like it if you had a chaperone," Rick toyed with one of Linda's curls. "You know, somebody who is strong and brave and respectable and who will protect you." His lusty grin was matched by the unbridled desire in his eyes.

Eighteen

That evening Eddi settled into the lounge chair on her parents' patio, propped her head against the back, and relaxed. The sun warmed her legs, and she was glad she'd opted for walking shorts rather than slacks. Jenny had yet to arrive, and Linda was out with Rick. Eddi was left as her mother's sole helper. That meant she made the potato salad, baked the beans, and laid out the hamburger trimmings while her mom complained about her nerves.

Presently, Mary Boswick flitted from the food-laden table, to the gas grill, and back to the table. She rearranged the ketchup and mustard, scooted the plate of sliced cheese, and fretted over the dill slices.

"For Pete's sake, Mary," Edward Boswick groused, "go sit down. You're acting like you're as nervous as a cat on a hot tin roof." He mopped his temple with a paper napkin.

"Oh, it's just my nerves," she worried. The humid breeze whipped her oversized cotton dress around her ankles and sent a whiff of grilled meat to tantalize Eddi's taste buds. "I ran out of my nerve pills yesterday, and I forgot to get them filled today. I didn't think I was ready for a refill yet." Mary touched her temple. "But you know how I'm not good at keeping up with those sorts of things."

Eddi tuned out her mother's complaints and observed her father's huge greenhouse nestled in the yard's south corner. He spent hours a day cultivating his first love. Once at a Boswick family reunion, she overheard a distant cousin call her father a blooming idiot because he abandoned a career in oil for his plants. Little did that opinionated snob know her father had built a significant business shipping rare orchids all over the world. Some he'd even crossbred himself. Eddi planned a stroll through the greenhouse with her father this weekend and looked forward to the quiet time with him.

"Helloooo! Anybody home?" Linda's muffled call emanated from the kitchen.

"Out here!" Mary yelled. She lifted her dress and hurried toward the patio door. After a discreet peek through the window, she hissed over her shoulder, "Wonderful! She's got that yummy policeman with her!"

"Oh, goody," Edward said before flipping a patty. "We can have him for dessert." The gas grill sizzled.

"Oh, Dad." Eddi swung her feet to the patio. "I think this one's okay. I'm hoping he's going to be a wholesome influence for Linda." Her sandals scratched against the concrete as she stood.

"Really?" Edward appraised his daughter as if he had his doubts. "I guess we shall see."

Eddi didn't bother to tell her father that she had fleetingly harbored hopes about befriending Rick herself. But if he and Linda were hitting it off, she would graciously and gladly bow out.

The patio door slid open. Linda, dressed in a snug red T-shirt dress, burst into the family gathering with Rick close behind. He offered Eddi a brief handshake and a distracted smile before Linda insisted upon showing him her father's greenhouse. With a good-natured chuckle, Rick acquiesced. As they meandered toward the greenhouse, arm in arm, Eddi was left with the overpowering scent of Giorgio and the impression that Linda had chosen and made her conquest.

"Oh, he's *soooo* handsome," Mary chirped. She picked up a sliver of lettuce and munched it as she watched the couple walk across the oak-laden yard.

"The number-one requirement for a happy marriage," Edward drawled as Eddi neared him. She picked up the platter stacked with meat and extended it toward her father. He plopped the final patty on top. "If you're good-looking and have money, that guarantees you'll live happily ever after." He looked at Eddi, his gray eyes alight with sarcastic mirth. "Don't you agree, Eddi?" His tanned crow's feet stretched as he lifted his brows.

"Whatever you say, Dad," she said.

"Oh, would you stop it!" Mary dug her pudgy fingers into a burgeoning bowl of cherry tomatoes. Half a dozen tomatoes spilled onto the checked cloth as she hurled a tomato at her husband. The red missile landed on the side of his nose and exploded. A wet tomato seed slammed into Eddi's forehead and she flinched. A bit of tomato skin clung to the side of Edward's nose.

"You never have liked anything Linda does—no matter what it is!" Mary hissed. "For once, leave her alone!"

Eddi gasped. Her father's face darkened. He grabbed the platter of meat from Eddi and slammed it onto the table. The top patty teetered and then tumbled to the patio. His lips quivered until at last a guttural growl erupted into an edict, "Don't you ever—"

"Hi, everyone!" Jenny's greeting was accompanied by the sound of the sliding glass door opening. "The front door was unlocked, and I just let myself in. I hope that was okay," she said.

As Eddi stroked away the seed from her face, she turned widened eyes to her sister.

Before Jenny could utter another word, Edward stormed passed her and into the house. He hurled the patio door closed with so much force Eddi examined the glass to see if it had cracked. Jenny gaped and shot a silent question to Eddi.

A small white dome over the doorway lighted at the same time a pleasant chime echoed across the back yard.

"Good!" Mary exclaimed as if nothing were amiss. "That's probably Conner at the front door. I invited him to eat with us tonight."

"Conner?" Eddi questioned.

"Yes, Conner Boswick. He's your third cousin," Mary supplied. "Eddi, dear, go let him in," she ordered and shoved at her mop of wiry gray hair. "He's been *desperate* to meet you." Eddi's mom struck out for the greenhouse as if she never doubted her daughter's dutiful obedience.

Eddi's mind raced with each clue that had fallen from her mother's lips. The evidence suggested that Mary had embarked upon a matchmaking quest. The last time she'd attempted to get Eddi married off, the man had proven himself a groping, self-centered beast. Her mother had been furious when Eddi refused to pursue a relationship with him.

"But he's a doctor! He'll take care of you," Mary had wailed for a solid week as if Eddi didn't possess one skill to earn her own living.

The doorbell chimed anew as Eddi neared her sister.

"Do you think Mom would try to play matchmaker with a cousin?" Jenny asked.

"It's not illegal in the state of Texas for cousins to marry," Eddi said. "Even *first* cousins."

"Yuck!" The corners of Jenny's mouth turned down.

Eddi grabbed her sister's hand and tugged her into the breakfast nook. After the outdoor heat, a rash of gooseflesh erupted along the back of Eddi's arms. As always, her father kept the house as cold as the arctic. While the smell of baked beans stimulated her appetite, she snapped the sliding door into place and observed Jenny.

She noticed that Jenny's eyes were uncharacteristically red. Eddi's thoughts rushed to Calvin Barclay. During her five-hour drive to Houston, she'd concluded she disliked him even more than William Fitzgerald Davidson. At least Dave didn't misrepresent his feelings. If he didn't like a person, he didn't pretend otherwise.

Eddi made a mental note to discuss Calvin with Jenny later that night. Presently, she was faced with another problem.

"What's going on with Mom and Dad?" Jenny asked.

"The usual," Eddi rushed. "Dad made a caustic remark, and Mom threw a cherry tomato at him."

"That's usual?" Jenny's brow wrinkled.

"The tomato throwing isn't, of course." Eddi waved her hand. "But we'll have to talk about that later. First, what do you know about this Conner Boswick person?" she demanded.

"Nothing!" Jenny lifted both hands. "I'm innocent, counselor. Honest."

The doorbell wheezed out another announcement.

"Come on," Eddi said and pulled Jenny in her wake.

She rounded the corner, trekked through the kitchen, and marched across the living room. Like the rest of the house, this room looked like the showcase from Neiman's home decor section—right down to the claw-footed oak coffee table. The smell of the finest raspberry potpourri created the final christening touch to the room's appeal. Undoubtedly, Linda inherited her propensity for buying only the best from their mother.

Eddi shoved Jenny toward the front door.

"What are you doing?" she whispered and swatted at Eddi's hands.

"I'm not answering that door," Eddi hissed. "I'm not in charge of desperate cousins. That's *your* job. You're the oldest."

Jenny rolled her eyes. "Oh, get *off* it," she complained. "You've been trying to push yourself in front of me since the day you were born."

"Just open the door!" Eddi demanded.

"Okay, okay!"

Eddi held her breath as Jenny pulled on the door. She peered over her sister's shoulder and prepared to run. But the pleasant-looking man standing on the front porch proved much more promising than the psychotic doctor. He wore neat golfing shorts and shirt much like her father's wardrobe. His brown, straight hair hung just above his collar and was the exact color of his eyes. A ready smile nearly convinced Eddi she should relax... until the man spoke.

"You must be Jenny," he said in a high nasal tone that Eddi first thought was affected. He looked past Jenny to Eddi. "And you're Eddi!" The man tilted his head back and closed his eyes as if he were enraptured. "I've wanted to meet you for absolutely ages!"

"Oh, really?" Eddi asked and held on to Jenny.

"Yes, really." He brushed past Jenny as if she didn't matter and extended his hand to Eddi. "I'm Conner Boswick, your third cousin," he said. "Your mother has sent me photos of you and all sorts of information."

"She has?" Eddi croaked, feeling like a piece of furniture being auctioned off to the highest bidder.

"Oh, yes! I feel as if I already know you."

"You do?"

"Oh, yes!" Conner hovered over her as if he were a ravenous buzzard and she were the most delectable tidbit he'd ever seen. "You're as beautiful in real life as you are in your photos."

"I am?" Eddi didn't realize her fingernails were eating into Jenny's arm until her sister pried her stiff fingers from her arm.

"I think the hamburgers are ready," Jenny said.

"Good!" Conner rubbed his hands together and walked to the living room's center. He paused and turned toward the sisters. "There's nothing I love more than a good burger."

Jenny massaged her upper arm and darted Eddi a pain-filled glance.

"Sorry," Eddi whispered and nudged Jenny toward the newcomer. "You take him outside. I'm going upstairs to talk to Dad."

"And leave me to deal with him? What a good sister you are."

"He's not drooling over you. You're safe." Eddi bestowed a nervous smile toward her cousin who observed them as if he were trying to read their lips.

"Not only are you loyal, you're also complimentary."

"'Bye," Eddi hissed and hurried toward the stairway that led to her father's study.

"Oh, aren't you going out with us?" Conner called.

"Ummm…" Fully expecting the man to race after her, Eddi glanced over her shoulder and increased her pace. "I'll be out later."

"Come this way," Jenny urged. "Mom will want to see you."

"Well, okay," Conner whined. "As long as Eddi will be out soon."

Without an answer, Eddi took the stairs two at a time. When she reached the second floor, she hurried down the hallway and stepped into her father's study. The smell of aging books enveloped her, and she snapped the door shut and leaned against it.

Her father sat in his recliner near the picture window that overlooked the backyard. Surrounding him was a sea of library books, all in neat rows on bookcase shelves. The droop of his face suggested that he wished he were a million miles from his home.

"What brings you here?" Edward Boswick asked.

"Two things," Eddi answered. "I wanted to see if you were going to come back down and eat, and I'm also running from my third cousin." She turned around and inched the door open. Feeling like a spy, Eddi scanned the hallway for any sign that she'd been pursued.

Nineteen

❧ ❧

"Your third cousin?" Edward inquired.

"Yes." Satisfied that she had really escaped Conner, Eddi closed the door. She walked to the multipaned window and looked straight down. Below, Jenny and her mother stood at the food-laden table with Conner. He held a paper plate and appeared to be salivating over the food as much as he had Eddi.

"His name is Conner Boswick. Apparently, Mom has been shopping me around," Eddi complained. "He just arrived at the front door and said she'd sent my photos to him. She told me before he arrived that he'd been desperate to meet me." Eddi looked at her father. "Do you know anything about any of this?"

Edward grunted. "If I had known, I would have stopped her. Conner's father was that imbecile who called me a blooming idiot for not staying in the oil business.

"Your mother is worried sick that I'm going to die before her, and she'll have to find another place to live since this house goes back to the Boswick estate when I die." He propped his elbows on the chair's arms.

"But don't you have enough money invested for her to buy another home?" Eddi questioned.

"Of course," Edward agreed. "Problem is, she couldn't buy a house as nice as this one. Besides, she says she raised her kids in this house and worries sick about losing all those memories." His voice softened as if he were embarking upon a rare moment of understanding his wife.

"But," he continued, "if one of you girls were to marry a Boswick who stayed in the business, you could live here."

"Or we could arrange for her to live here," Eddi said.

"Exactly."

Eddi weighed the saved memories against marrying Conner Boswick. In a flash, she decided she'd rather slam dunk the memories into the Atlantic before marrying the likes of him.

"I guess this Conner person is worth a good bit—just like every other Boswick who's still in oil."

"Yep. Last I heard, his father has taken over the coveted position as king of the whole shebang." Edward lifted his head and gazed outside. "More power to them all, I say. I'm just glad I don't have to report to duty every day. It would drive me crazy."

"You made the right choice," Eddi agreed and reached for her father's hand. After an affectionate squeeze he released her.

"In career maybe," he said, "but…" Edward stood and paced across the room. His back to Eddi, he rested his arm upon the side of a bookcase and propped his forehead against his arm.

"Eddi, my dear," he began, "you're looking at a man who has allowed his passions to overrule his reason."

Intrigued by her father's admission, she moved from the window and leaned against the edge of his desk.

"Do you know why I married your mother, Eddi?" he continued.

"No why?" The tension mounted as Eddi caught an unusual glimpse of her dad's inner being.

"Because she was pretty. She looked so much like Jenny it's not even funny." When he turned around, his disillusioned eyes had taken on a frosty edge.

"She was the most beautiful woman in her whole college freshman class and was the life of the party on top of that," he admitted. "I became infatuated with her. I convinced myself I had to have her—even though my parents told me I was making a mistake." He rubbed his leathery face and moved to the desk. Edward picked up a pen and began tapping the back of his desk chair.

"Now, the infatuation is over, and I'm stuck with a wife who throws tomatoes at me." He tossed the pen across the desk. It slammed into the phone and spun across the desk calendar.

"I probably shouldn't be telling you all this," he admitted.

"It's okay," Eddi said, but didn't quite know how to handle such brutal honesty. She would far rather hear that her dad was still madly in love with her mother, even though she was difficult at times.

"Of course, your mother gave me three beautiful daughters," Edward said. "Especially you," he added. "I don't ever want you to think I regretted having you, Eddi. It's all so ironic, isn't it? I wouldn't trade having you for the option of rolling back the years and marrying someone else, but that still doesn't end the struggle."

"It's okay," she repeated for lack of anything else to say.

"All I can tell you, dear, is to marry for love. Don't let surface attraction make you settle for anything less."

"I fully intend to." Eddi shook her head. "I'd rather not get married ever than live in misery."

"That's my girl." Edward patted her on the back. "Would that we could hope the same for Linda and Jenny."

"Jenny maybe," Eddi acknowledged.

"All we can do is pray that Linda marries a man who will be committed to her no matter what."

Eddi thought of Rick and hoped he was the one. "Linda said she wants to go to Hawaii with some of her friends."

"Oh yes." Edward nodded. "Just what every fickle girl needs—a trip across the planet on her own. She'll probably come back with her hair dyed green or something."

"So you're going to let her go?" Eddi asked. Her father still seemed clueless about the serious nature of Linda's antics.

"What else can I do? She's twenty and has money of her own. It's not like she's thirteen anymore. Your mother is dying for her to go. I've about decided that Linda won't be happy until she's traveled the world." He looked down. "Maybe she'll find some man out there who'll take care of her."

"But, Dad—" Eddi began.

Edward held up his hand. "Please, Eddi," he said. "I know you don't approve, but there's nothing to be done. The way I feel tonight, I think I'd take one of your mother's famous nerve pills if she had any left. Let's just drop it, shall we?"

Eddi tried to flip her braid over her shoulder. She stroked the nap of her neck instead. "Okay," she agreed and wondered if there were any way to ensure Linda's safety to Hawaii and back.

"I'm going back downstairs, I guess," she said and moved toward the door. "If it weren't for Jenny needing moral support, I'd probably just leave right now."

"Oh? And what's up with her?" Edward settled back into his chair.

"To put it bluntly, she dumped Hal and the vet dumped her." Eddi opened the study's door.

"Bummer," Edward said. "Your mother won't get over that one for weeks. After our trip to your place last weekend, she was already shopping for a mother-of-the-bride dress for Jenny's wedding."

"Well, let her down easy, will ya?" Eddi asked.

"She'll take heart in still being able to shop for the darts." Edward's derisive smile did little to indicate his meaning.

"Darts?" Eddi asked.

"Yes. She was wanting to throw some at that Dave what's-his-face."

"Ah yes, Dave Davidson aka William Fitzgerald Davidson, former owner of USA Online, billionaire, and chief rude person around London, Texas. Is that who you're talking about?"

"Yeah," Edward said. "But I didn't know he was such a bigwig."

"He thinks he is anyway," Eddi groused.

"He seems to like you—if waltzing you across the stage in the middle of practice is anything to go by."

"Humph!" Eddi denied the memory of that pleasurable moment. "If he acts like he likes me, it's just bait to better insult me. Last weekend he accused me of being after him for his money."

"No way! You?"

"Yes, me."

"In that case, you could have Conner." Edward grimaced.

"I'll pass," Eddi said. "Speaking of him, are you going to join us for a burger? I need all the protection I can get."

"No," he said bluntly. "I'm going to steal a snack from the kitchen and read awhile. I've had all the party I can stand." He settled into his chair, propped his head against the back, closed his eyes, and stroked the side of his nose where the tomato had burst. "Hang on to Jenny. She's a good guard."

Eddi started to protest but stopped. She would find another time this weekend to be with her father. For now, she would hang out with Jenny and give her father his space.

She stepped toward him, brushed a light kiss atop his balding head, exited the office, and trotted down the stairs. As she neared the kitchen, Eddi rehearsed half a dozen tactics for keeping Conner at bay. The most effective one involved inhaling her hamburger and immediately taking Jenny to Baskin Robbins for dessert.

When she heard the patio door sliding open, she half expected Conner to round the corner. Eddi hovered by the kitchen counter and prepared to dash back upstairs. But the person who stepped into the kitchen was Rick Wallace.

"Oh, good," Eddi breathed. "It's you. I was expecting Conner."

"Who's Conner?" Rick mimicked Conner's high-pitched voice.

Eddi burst into laughter. "If I weren't so desperate to avoid him, this might be twice as funny," she admitted.

"Your mom's out there talking about you and him as if the two of you are already engaged," Rick said.

"Oh, puuuulllleeezzze." Eddi moved to the window over the kitchen sink, stood on her tiptoes, and looked onto the patio. She caught a glimpse of her mother and Conner huddled by the potato salad.

"I only just met him fifteen minutes ago, and Mom's probably already planning the wedding."

"Well, I hope the two of you enjoy a long and prosperous life together," Rick said as if he were reading a greeting card.

Eddi rolled her eyes and moved from the window.

"Linda told me there's a bathroom somewhere close." Rick rubbed his hand along the front of his navy shirt that read Houston Police Force.

"Yes. Just out the kitchen door and to your right." Eddi moved toward the breakfast bar and pointed out the doorway. "You can't miss it."

"Thanks," Rick said but didn't leave. Instead, he eyed Eddi as if there were something he wanted to say but didn't quite know how to form the words.

Eddi tilted her head and observed him. For some reason, Dave's e-mail warning bombarded her, but Eddi dismissed any probability that the admonition was valid. After all, Dave had unfairly insulted Eddi to Calvin and thus proven his opinions weren't always truth.

"Did you know Linda wants to go to Hawaii?" Rick finally asked.

"Yes. Jenny told me." Eddi picked up a paper napkin lying on the counter and began rolling the corner between her fingers.

"I'm worried," Rick said.

"Oh really?"

"Yes."

"So am I, actually," Eddi said.

"I'm not sure these rich friends of hers are all that, well, respectable." His kind brown eyes shone with concern.

"I wish I could get my father to see that," she said. "He said he hopes she doesn't come back with her hair dyed green." Eddi dropped the napkin to the counter. "I wish that was all we had to worry about.

"Really," Rick said.

A fresh option posed itself as a possible solution to the problem. "Why don't you go with her?" Eddi asked.

"Uh…" He looked down. "It's a little embarrassing to admit, but…"

"Don't tell me she hasn't invited you."

"Oh no, Linda has invited me. It's just that," he tugged on his ear lobe, "the truth is, I don't have the money," Rick admitted. "I live on a policeman's salary and—"

"If you'll agree to go, I'll pay your way," Eddi blurted as soon as the idea struck her.

"What?" He stepped back.

"No joke," she said. "It would be worth it for me to know that somebody was looking out for my sister." As the idea gained credence, Eddi's concern for Linda began to dissolve. She wondered why she hadn't considered this option before now.

"Well, I don't know," Rick said. "I'll have to think about it. I would rather *borrow* the money from you. And of course, it would have to be enough for me to have a separate room from Linda," he said with an honorable nuance to every word.

"Of course," Eddi acknowledged and decided that a little warm encouragement might be in order. *After all, we're discussing my little sister's safety!* "Just as long as you go. It's worth it to me to have someone protect my sister. Seriously," she stepped forward and grasped his arm, "I set aside some money for my move that I never had to use. I'd rather you just take it, Rick. I'll never miss it."

Twenty

By the time the weekend was over, Eddi wrote Rick a personal check for twenty-five-hundred dollars. Ecstatic, Linda actually hugged Eddi—something she hadn't done in over a year. With the excitement of a six-year-old on Christmas morning, Linda detailed their plans to fly to Hawaii in three weeks. The trip was scheduled to last two weeks.

Meanwhile, Conner had plagued Eddi until she was certain she would suffocate. Not only did he talk to her all Friday evening, but he also followed her to her vehicle upon her departure. The man seemed convinced that any woman would find him irresistible due to his six-figure income with Boswick Oil, which he mentioned at every turn.

Mary had given Conner Eddi's cell phone number. He called her all weekend, requesting a date until Eddi was so exhausted she nearly agreed just to stop the harrassment. By the time Sunday afternoon arrived, she was vowing to change her cell number and move to Botswana. Before leaving Houston, Eddi made her mother promise not to give Conner her home number.

All this plus her mother's incessant worrying about her nerves and her strained relationship with her husband confirmed Eddi had made the right choice when she moved four hours away. Never had she been so glad to see her townhouse, nestled in pines among a row of other homes just like it.

When Eddi walked through the front door Sunday evening, her telephone was ringing. Her pug bulldog greeted her by running in circles, yelping, and licking her legs as if he hadn't seen a person in months—even though Cheri had fed and walked him in Eddi's absence. Both her felines huddled on the striped sofa and watched the dog as if they were above such a show of emotions.

The phone's constant ringing scrambled her thoughts and demanded an answer.

"I see you Roddy," she cooed and stepped toward the oak end table.

Eddi looked at the phone and debated whether or not she should answer. She didn't want to talk to Conner Boswick for the forty-third time. While her mother often kept her promises, there were times when she was swept away by the moment and relayed private information. More than once, Eddi had thought of getting an unlisted number and not giving it to her mom. But no matter how exasperated she became with her mother, Eddi always stopped short of excommunication. After all, Mary was her mother, and Eddi was committed to honoring her, flaws and all.

As soon as the telephone released its last peal, the doorbell rang.

"Nothing like a little company before I even put down my suitcase," Eddi grumbled. She plopped her overnight bag on the striped love seat and slung her purse on top of it. Eddi retraced her steps to the front door. Before she turned the knob, she looked out the peephole. Eddi was certain Conner was on her trail at every turn.

The person standing outside was not Conner. She was none other than the illustrious grand dame of the theater, Mrs. Madelynne DeBloom. Eddi swung open the door, wondering what she had done to warrant the condescension of the lady's visit.

"Mrs. DeBloom!" she exclaimed. "I thought you had the flu!"

"I did, my dear," the matron admitted, her voice a bit raspy. "But I've stayed in bed most of the week, and I'm feeling better." Before Eddi could invite her in, Mrs. DeBloom brushed past her with a flourish and the smell of roses.

"Well," Eddi shut the door, "you just caught me. I've been away to visit my family this weekend." She scooped up Roddy and scratched his ears. The pug grunted and closed his eyes.

"Yes, I know." Mrs. DeBloom claimed a recliner—Eddi's favorite—and patted the straight-backed chair next to it. "Come sit awhile, dear."

Eddi, feeling as if she were the visitor, did what everyone did in Mrs. DeBloom's presence—she obeyed. "How did you know I was out of town?" she asked. If not for her offbeat sense of humor, Eddi would have been vexed by the matron's high-handed behavior. The ridiculous nature of Mrs. DeBloom's affectation left Eddi hiding a smile.

"When I was at her dress shop in town, Dina told me you left town." Mrs. DeBloom looked at Eddi's turquoise shorts set. "She said you bought that cute number. I was glad it went to someone young like you."

"Oh," Eddi answered and wondered if the whole town knew her underwear size by now. She was quickly realizing that Dina's Place, the combination coffee bar and dress shop, was certainly the store to go to if you wanted the scoop on London's citizenry.

Mrs. DeBloom tugged on her straight dress' lace collar and sniffed. "I'll get right to the point."

"If you wanted to stay awhile, I would be happy to make a pot of coffee for you," Eddi offered, fully expecting rejection.

"No thank you, dear." Mrs. DeBloom scurried through her leather purse. She retrieved a lacey handkerchief and covered her nose. She eyed the two felines as if they were rattlesnakes. "I have a horrible allergy to cats…and—and their odors," she added.

Roddy licked Eddi's hand. She stroked his head and wondered when Mrs. DeBloom would start complaining about him.

"The reason I came, dear, is because I wanted to have a heart-to-heart chat with you," Madelynne said while daintily lowering the handkerchief.

"Okay." Eddi scruntinized the gray-haired lady, who reminded her of Dave, especially the haughty tilt of her head. Eddi's fingers tightened around the chair's arm.

"You seem like a sensible young woman," she said.

"Well, I try," Eddi said dryly.

"Then you'll understand why I am…concerned about what I am hearing around town." Her blue gaze penetrated Eddi's calm resolve, and she floundered for some significance to Mrs. DeBloom's hint.

"You *are* aware of the gossip, aren't you?" Mrs. DeBloom leaned forward.

"It's been about a week since I was in Dina's Place," Eddi admitted. "So apparently I'm not up on the latest."

"Well," Mrs. DeBloom straightened her spine, "the latest is that my nephew is…smitten with you."

Eddi flopped back into her chair and laughed out loud. Every hint of irritation vanished in the face of the preposterous. "That's the craziest thing I've ever heard."

"Oh good!" Madelynne waved her handkerchief. "I am so relieved. I was afraid maybe you had started…" She paused. "That maybe you…"

"That maybe I'm getting too much into my part?" Eddi asked, growing suspicious of where this was heading.

"Exactly. I'm so glad to see that my assumptions were correct. You undoubtedly understand the difference in your and Dave's positions in life."

"Our positions?" Eddi enunciated each word. Roddy shifted in her lap.

"Yes, of course. When my nephew marries, it must be to someone who is as...who will understand the ins and outs of managing a sizeable estate and—"

"Dave seems to be doing that just fine on his own." Eddi crossed her arms. "Why would you assume that he would drop the whole of that responsibility into the lap of his wife?"

"Well, a *good* wife knows to do such things—especially if the wife has watched her mother take care of the same role for years. I speak from experience." She sniffed. I was married to a wealthy businessman myself. I understand these things all too well. A woman who marries an important man must fulfill her role. She mustn't be caught up in her own petty concerns."

Eddi made herself take three deep breaths before she spoke. When the words came out, she was rewarded by the even tenor of her voice. "For starters," Eddi stated, "a wife is a woman with value. She is *not* a role."

"Exactly." Mrs. DeBloom patted Eddi's hand. "Of course," she added with a patronizing lift of her chin that reminded Eddi of Dave all over again. She bit down on the tip of her tongue. Mrs. DeBloom continued, "I didn't mean to imply...It's just that—I'm sure you understand. We can't have Dave marrying someone who's not—"

"As valuable as he is because she's not as rich as he is?" Eddi finished. Mrs. DeBloom's face reddened. Eddi recalled all the demeaning things Dave had said on the Huntington House porch. Neither Dave nor his aunt minded throwing around insults when it suited them.

The flush in Mrs. DeBloom's face diminished. "You don't have to be so blunt about it," she finally admonished.

"Why not? That's what you meant, isn't it?" She arched her brows and didn't flinch from the matron's appaisal.

An obstinate flame flared in Madelynne's eyes. "I came for an answer to my question. I got what I wanted." Eddi waited for her to pull a gavel out of her purse and pound the coffee table. "Frankly, my nephew has been acting out of character the last few weeks."

"Maybe that's because he's playing the character of Darcy," Eddi said with a humorless grin.

Mrs. DeBloom found nothing to smile about. "I came in here, Miss Boswick, worried that maybe you read too much into that dance scene at our last practice. But I am beginning to see that you are not anything like your sister. You are far too brassy to entertain romantic fantasies, even for someone as rich and handsome as my nephew."

Eddi's grip tightened on Roddy. He squirmed and whimpered. She relaxed her fingers and gently scratched beneath his chin.

"Don't bring my sister into this," she ordered.

"And she's better off not in the mix, if you ask me. Dave was smart in warning Calvin off her."

"What did you just say?" Eddi demanded as she scooted to the edge of her chair.

Mrs. DeBloom looked as if she'd swallowed a golf ball and the thing was restricting air flow. "Oh dear," she whispered and jumped up.

Before Eddi could stand, Madelynne was grasping the doorknob. By the time Eddi deposited Roddy on the floor and scrambled to the door, Mrs. DeBloom slammed it in her face. Eddi snatched open the door. She rushed into the oppressive humidity, down the sidewalk, and around Mrs. DeBloom.

She targeted the sleek blue Cadillac parked near her Mustang and sprawled across the passenger door. The car's heat burned Eddi's arms and hands, but she didn't budge. Eddi glared up at

Mrs. DeBloom who hovered on the curb. Her purse dangling from her arm, she twisted the lace handkerchief as if she were no longer certain of a victorious battle.

"I'm not moving until you tell me every detail!" Eddi snarled.

"Oh no!" Mrs. DeBloom wailed as if Eddi were threatening to decapitate her. She touched her temple. "I just don't know if I can handle all this."

"You started it," Eddi barked. "Now handle it. I want to know what Dave did to break up my sister and Calvin. You can either tell all, or we'll stand here all night."

"But I don't know anything more than I've told you," Madelynne croaked. She drew herself up to her full height, yet her lips trembled. Usually, the lady's thin frame lent her a regal appeal. Now she looked like a terrified scarecrow. Under any other circumstances Eddi would have pitied the woman. But she had shown herself too brazen to warrant pity.

"Would you swear to that in court?" Eddi challenged.

"Y-yes." Madelynne shook her head. "All I know is that he broke them up." She clasped her hands as if she were praying. "That's all I know."

Eddi digested the admission and debated its veracity. After seconds of scrutinizing Mrs. DeBloom's desperate stance, she decided the woman was not lying.

"Fine then!" Eddi acquiesced and stood straight.

Her palms and arms continued to sting from contact with the sun-baked vehicle. An ice cream truck's jingling bell echoed from the street corner. Eddi wished for those carefree childhood days of creamy Fudgsicles and tart Bomb Pops. But childhood was long behind Eddi. Now she faced grown-up conflicts that threatened to rob her peace. *You know,* Eddi thought, *I don't need the upheaval this play is causing. Why don't I just bow out?*

After a decisive nod, she decided to tell Mrs. DeBloom she could find somebody else to play Elizabeth. With the words poised on her lips, Eddi stopped herself. The production of

Pride and Prejudice had turned into a county phenomenon. The *London Times* had already run a front page ad on the performance. According to Cheri Locaste, Mrs. DeBloom was already receiving ticket orders from people in surrounding towns.

Therefore, Eddi's role as Elizabeth had transcended a mere hobby. More people were involved besides Mrs. DeBloom and her overbearing nephew. Eddi had committed herself to the play and she would follow through if it killed her—and it just might!

Mrs. DeBloom clutched her purse handle and suspiciously appraised Eddi, her blue eyes as round as a cat's. Eddi suspected the aging woman had read her expression and fully understood that she had pushed her leading lady to the brink of quitting the play. With a touch of sarcastic mirth, Eddi watched the old woman watch her and enjoyed the moment of triumph.

The smell of hot concrete and pine needles hung in the air. Eddi's courage kicked in. "The only reason I'm not quitting the play at this point," Eddi supplied without preamble, "is because the rest of the community is looking forward to the play, and *I* keep my commitments, Mrs. DeBloom. Otherwise, I would tell you and your nephew that the two of you could find another Elizabeth."

"Well, dear…" While Mrs. DeBloom toyed with her strand of pearls, Eddi caustically wondered if the oyster they came out of was 24-karat gold. "I didn't mean to offend you so."

"Oh really?" Eddi challenged.

"Look, we're both church-going ladies. Let's don't say anything we'll regret later, shall we?"

"You're just worried that you've pushed me too far and that if I *do* resign you'll be forced to call off the play. This has nothing to do with going to church. If you and your money-conscious nephew ever got anything out of church, you'd have learned that money doesn't make a person valuable." Eddi stood to her full height and clenched her fists. "It never has and it never will."

Brushing past Mrs. DeBloom, Eddi stalked into her house. She slammed the door, locked it, and grabbed her overnight bag. She ran up the stairs with Roddy on her heels. After dropping her bag on the bathroom counter, she removed her clothes and stepped into a cold shower.

Eddi rested her hands against the tile as if she were trying to push the wall down. She shoved her head under the cold blast. But even the cool water couldn't extinguish the furious scream that burned her throat.

"Dave Davidson, you are the bane of my existence," she choked. "No sweeter woman ever lived than my sister. How could you be so ruthless?"

Rick Wallace's story erupted upon her mind. Eddi marveled at how similar his plight was to Jenny's. Dave prohibited Rick from pursuing the ministry. He prohibited Jenny from pursuing her heart. One thing proved constant. Dave Davidson enjoyed playing God.

Eddi shoved her hands into her hair, closed her eyes, and plowed her face into the stinging stream. *Don't you ever forget,* she thought. *You reap what you sow!*

Twenty-One

The weeks rocked on. The practices continued and the cast's performances grew more polished. In order to survive the weekly encounters with Dave, his aunt, and Calvin Barclay, Eddi adopted the same cool front she used when under fire in court. No matter how Mrs. DeBloom's demeaning assumptions haunted her, she remained calm. No matter how many times Dave tried to bait her, she refused to participate in his verbal battles. No matter how often she was tempted to confront Calvin, she restrained her words. Eddi remained solely focused upon her goal—to play her role, and play it well because the cast was counting on her.

By the first week of August, Eddi realized she was becoming a local celebrity. During an interview with the *London Times* general editor, Eddi learned that the editor once longed for a career as an actress and adored the theater. Therefore, the editor repeatedly gave the new dinner theater more than its share of press. At last, Eddi's face had been featured so many times in the paper that heads were turning no matter where she went. One morning Eddi stepped across the street for coffee at Dina's Place and a teenager asked for her autograph. As a result of the publicity, her name was gaining credence with the locals. Business at Boswick Law Firm was increasing. And Eddi thanked God she hadn't given in to the spiteful impulse to resign her part in the play.

Soon, the final touches were being given to Mrs. DeBloom's home, and the cast was enjoying the last practice at Dave's house. The next practice would be held at Huntington House. That balmy August evening, Eddi retraced the route to the country estate and thought of the first time she'd driven down the lane, lined in a thatch of woods. Jenny had been with her, and she was about to meet Calvin.

"So much for that," Eddi mumbled. She eased off the accelerator. The vehicle coasted down the final hill before Eddi caught sight of the sprawling home, replete with her dream porch and wooden swing.

Somehow, she had avoided all conversations with Calvin since he dumped Jenny. Eddi hadn't trusted herself to even the kindest of inquiries. She feared that if she ever spoke to Calvin she would demand a thorough explanation for his horrid behavior. At that point, Jenny would promptly die. Eddi could almost hear her sister saying, "I am going to die, Eddi!"

She pulled her vehicle into the broad parking area, turned off the air conditioner, and twisted the key in the ignition switch. "At least Linda seems to have found a good match," she mumbled as she considered her sister's reports the last few weeks. Eddi received an e-mail from her two nights ago before she and Rick departed for Hawaii. "I've never been happier," she'd written.

"Who'd have ever thought Linda would be the first one to find a good man?" Eddi glared at the home's front door, deceptively painted a welcoming shade of cranberry. While Dave might have been able to end all chances of Jenny's happiness, he hadn't succeeded with Linda. Eddi had finally come to the conclusion that he e-mailed that warning about Rick to spoil Linda's future as well.

Eddi got out of the vehicle, straightened her denim skirt, and trudged along the winding walkway toward the porch. After hoisting her bag on her shoulder, she darted a glance behind. *No Conner,* she thought and admonished herself for being so paranoid. *He won't follow you here,* she told herself.

But he would not stop calling her—no matter what. Two weeks ago when Eddi turned off her cell phone and left it off, he called information and got her home number. When she started screening her calls at home, Conner retrieved her business number off the internet. After Eddi pointedly told him to stop calling, he sent her two dozen red roses.

If he didn't seem like such a babbling nerd, Eddi would have feared he might stalk her. But she didn't think the man possessed the mental abilities to orchestrate a stalking. "Maybe he could do the Three Stooges…" she mumbled, "Larry, Curly, and Moe all at the same time." A laugh escaped her.

A time or two she debated how Conner ever was able to perform as one of six vice presidents at Boswick Oil. *Stranger things have happened,* she thought. While Conner might be a social buffoon, he very well could be exceptional at his job.

Shoving Conner out of her mind, Eddi trotted up the porch steps. The smell of hay and geraniums, coupled with the call of a bobwhite, slowed her gait. Before approaching the front door, she gripped the porch post and pivoted while absorbing the ambiance of the breathtaking estate. The verdant yard, stretching an acre to the woods, beckoned Eddi to slip off her sandals and run upon lush blades.

A movement near a distant oak snared her attention. Eddi leaned forward and scrutinized the area. At last, she discovered a buck grazing upon tender grass. The proud deer raised its head and looked toward Eddi as if he'd only just seen her. He stomped and watched her; again he stomped and watched.

Eddi didn't move as her fingers pressed against the post. She held her breath when a doe stepped from the woods, followed by a half-grown fawn. A crow's raucous call punctured the peace. Twenty feet from the deer, a covey of quail erupted into a flourish of wings and indignant shrieks. The three deer bolted. White tails twitching, they disappeared into the woods.

Relaxing her grip on the post, Eddi was tempted to covet the home. *But not if the man comes with it,* she thought and dismissed the deer, the lush grass, and the desire to take off her sandals.

She released the post and turned back toward the door, which had a white note taped to it. A balmy breeze whispered along the porch, lifting the corner of the note, and rocking the swing. The chain squeaked as the swing beckoned Eddi to enjoy its comfort.

She scowled at the swing and focused on the instructive note typed in bold letters: *Cast Members, Let yourselves in. We're in the pool room as usual. D.D.*

She turned the brass knob, nudged open the door, and stepped into the entryway. The smell of Mrs. DeBloom's gourmet cheese dip activated Eddi's taste buds. While the lady might be a domineering control freak, she did know how to spoil her cast.

As she closed the door, Eddi recalled the first time she'd walked into the home. She had nearly fallen to her knees in awe of the gorgeous house, replete with a winding staircase and gleaming maple bannister. All she said to Dave was, "Nice place." Now, she remembered his surprised expression with much satisfaction. Eddi figured he expected her to drool over his home and subsequently start drooling over him.

Not on your life, buddy, Eddi thought as she walked into the entryway. *I'd marry Conner Boswick before I'd marry you.*

Dave's voice floated from the dining room to her left. His part in the conversation involved a series of affirmatives that left no clue as to the subject. Eddi strained to detect any indication of what Dave might be involved in. As with numerous other phone conversations during their practices, Eddi figured this one must include that mysterious building behind his house.

Tonight's the last practice here, she thought, and then wondered if she might be able to sneak out back tonight and investigate. The growing urge to uncover his puzzling operation nearly sent her on an immediate detour to the backyard. But Eddi made herself wait. Subtlety was the ticket to not being detected. In her professional endeavors, Eddi had learned how to be subtle—and learned it well.

She tiptoed past the open door to the dining room. The last thing she wanted was a prepractice chat session with Dave. Discussing the weather with the man who destroyed her sister's happiness held no appeal. Despite Eddi's best efforts, her leather sandals clicked upon the hardwood floor. Once she stepped into the formal living room, Eddi relaxed. She upped her pace and maneuvered her way through the showcase room her mother would have swooned over.

When she'd just passed the grand piano and was within a foot of the hallway, Dave's call punctured her victory.

"Eddi!" he called.

She halted, cringed, and resisted a groan. Playing opposite him was strain enough without being forced to interact off stage.

"We haven't had a chance to talk lately," Dave continued.

Her face stiff, Eddi turned toward him. As usual, he wore the jeans and work shirt, both clean but badly faded. As usual, his hair was damp as if he'd just stepped from the shower. As usual, Eddi felt as if she were like a moth being lured toward a deadly flame. She despised herself for such a disgraceful reaction to so despicable a man.

For once in her life, she didn't know what to say. The only words that came to her involved a hot defense of Jenny and a command to know why he interfered with her and Calvin. So inept was Eddi to conjure an appropriate greeting that she chose to state the lines from the pending practice rather than risk her own words.

Eddi adopted her English accent and replicated her version of Elizabeth Bennet's voice. "'You mean to frighten me, Mr. Darcy, but I will not be alarmed.'" Coldly, she smiled into his speculative eyes.

"Ah, so we're playing that game again," Dave said with an impish twist of his lips. Eddi was reminded of the first cast gathering when Dave had silently responded to his aunt's reading the opening lines from *Pride and Prejudice*. He'd looked at Mrs. DeBloom the same way—as if he were daring the world to take him on.

"'There is a stubbornness about me that never can bear to be frightened at the will of others,'" Eddi continued and added an extra hint of steel to the words. "My courage always rises with every attempt to intimidate me."

Dave crossed his arms and lifted his chin in the manner that accented his long, straight nose. Mrs. DeBloom had used the same gesture when she insisted Eddi wasn't as valuable as Dave.

"'I shall not say that you are mistaken,'" Dave replied with such British finesse that Eddi would have vowed the man was a professional, "'because you could not really believe me to entertain any design of alarming you; and I have had the pleasure of your acquaintance long enough to know that you find great enjoyment in occasionally professing opinions which in fact are not your own,'" he finished as if he meant it.

"'Indeed, Mr. Darcy, it is very ungenerous in you to mention all that you knew to my disadvantage in Hertfordshire—and, give me leave to say, very impolitic too for it is provoking me to retaliate, and such things may come out as will shock your relations to hear.'"

"'I am not afraid of you,'" Dave enunciated the play's decree with taunting reality.

She had no idea what line came next, nor did she care. Eddi was too pressed with the weight of the moment. "I'm not afraid of you either," she snapped.

With hypnotic slowness, Dave leaned forward and stroked Eddi's chin. "I think that's one of the things I like the most about you, Eddi," he said as if he were divulging the most intimate of secrets.

His dark eyes danced as a trail of fire seeped down Eddi's neck. The ever-present magnetism sprang between them—a magnetism that promised Dave's kiss would be as unsettling as the storm they'd survived in each other's arms.

Eddi stood speechless and was sucked into that state of fantasy that had produced a plethora of ardent dreams…all about her and Dave. Despite everything Dave had done, despite her determination to despise him, Eddi couldn't stop her reaction to him. A slow burn started in her gut and swept to her head.

She twisted away from Dave and hurled herself into the hallway. Her agitated mind listed several possible plans for the evening. Each centered upon avoiding the man who now followed her. As she rushed toward the pool room's doorway, the sound of excited voices suggested something different might be underway. Eddi hoped that whatever it was meant she would get a miraculous reprieve from rehearsing her part. She studied the cream-colored carpet and doubted her ability to tolerate much more Dave-time without an outburst.

His footsteps grew nearer. She hunched her shoulders and concentrated on getting lost in the prepractice jumble. When she was a few feet from freedom, a man's leather loafers appeared in the pool room's doorway. Eddi recognized the expensive cut of the shoes and wondered who in London, Texas, had splurged on such a luxury. She slowed and lifted her attention to the man himself.

Eddi stopped. Her eyes bugged. She blinked hard and tried to convince herself she was hallucinating. But when Conner Boswick spoke, Eddi understood that her worst fear had come true.

"Hi, Eddi," he said in that high-pitched voice that raked her nerves.

If not for Dave mere inches behind, she would have run in the opposite direction. But Eddi couldn't indulge in such luxury. She was trapped between the two men who had made her summer miserable.

Twenty-Two

❧ ❧

"Conner!" Eddi exclaimed.

Dave stopped behind her and examined the man in the doorway. While he would never appear on the cover of *Gentleman's Quarterly*, Conner wasn't the ugliest guy Dave had ever seen. He recognized the cut of Conner's high-dollar clothing and glowered at the hole in the knee of his own jeans. He never remembered seeing Conner at any other practice. But apparently this was some guy Eddi already knew.

"Surprise!" Conner lifted his arms and smiled as if he were convinced she was thrilled to see him. A gold watch flashed with his arm's every move, and Dave recognized a Rolex. "I just couldn't stay away," Conner continued in a voice that suggested he sang tenor—really high tenor.

Probably the church choir star, Dave snarled to himself and wondered why he had resisted the choir director's plea for more members in July. He would have been able to claim a place in the bass section behind Eddi. The fact that he'd never sung bass seemed immaterial.

Frowning, Dave wished he could sneak a look at Eddi's face. He didn't like the idea that Conner was so thrilled to see her. Before getting thoroughly disturbed over this invasion, Dave wanted to read her reaction and determine if the knot in his stomach were validated.

"How did you find out where the practice was?" Eddi asked.

Dave eased to Eddi's side. She was so fixed upon Conner, she didn't even notice him. *Not good,* he thought.

"Remember, Jenny and you mentioned the play and Mrs. DeBloom when you were at your parents' house," Conner explained.

So, they met in Houston, Dave thought.

"I called Mrs. DeBloom yesterday and got the play practice schedule as well as directions," Conner continued with a satisfied smile that told the world he was *so* proud of himself.

Dave's fist curled. His blunt fingernails ate into his palm.

"How did you get her number?" Eddi held up her hand. "No, don't tell me—off the internet, right?"

"No, I just called information on this one," Conner said. "There was only one DeBloom in London. I'm a whiz at finding numbers," he bragged.

"Yes, how well I know," Eddi complained and gripped the back of her neck.

Daved sensed the first signs of Eddi's disinterest. His plummeting spirits soared.

"I understand you're the star," Conner said, as if he didn't even pick up on Eddi's reluctant vibes.

"That's probably debatable." She glanced toward Dave as if she'd just seen him.

Conner followed her lead and extended his hand toward Dave. "I'm Conner Boswick, by the way," he explained. "Vice president at Boswick Oil in Houston. You've probably heard of us," he added as if no one else in this hick town could match his position in life.

"Hi, Conner." With a tight grin, Dave wondered if Conner would be devastated to learn he wasn't the richest man present.

"He's my third cousin, actually," Eddi admitted with staid politeness.

"But it's not illegal for cousins to marry in the state of Texas." Conner winked at her, and Dave felt her hackles rising.

He chuckled under his breath and couldn't resist the next claim. "I'm playing the part of Darcy in the play. You know, Eddi's hero." Dave rested his hand on her shoulder.

For an expectant moment, he thought she wasn't going to step away. Dave was certain Eddi had been as stirred as he when he stroked her chin. No one could ever deny the electricity between them. Dave was beginning to think that very element was the reason for the play's growing allure and sparkle.

After a glare toward Dave, Conner grabbed Eddi's hand and tugged her into the pool room turned theater chamber. Dave was forced to follow close behind. They entered the festive atmosphere of an ecstatic cast being fitted by a leading New York designer.

"What's going on?" Eddi looked over her shoulder at Dave.

He started to answer but Conner interrupted. "I'll tell you what's going on," he crowed. "Your costumes are being designed by none other than Sean O'Reilly."

"Sean O'Reilly?" Eddi gawked at the makeshift stage where Calvin's sister, Carissa, was being measured by a gray-haired Chinese man who wielded his tape measure with a snap and flourish.

Anyone familiar with fashion knew that Sean O'Reilly was adopted by a Caucasian family when he was a baby. By the time he was thirty, the designer was wowing New York with talents that had ultimately ensured his place as a top international designer.

"When you told me this was a small town play, I thought of a performance about as entertaining as a junior high school drama." Conner tugged on the collar of his costly shirt as if he wanted to emphasize the worth of his opinion. "But it looks like *somebody* here has some connections and knows what they're doing!"

"Imagine that," Dave purred. A bitter bile seeped into his mind. He entertained images of tossing Conner into the deep end of his swimming pool and then drop-kicking him into the pasture with his meanest longhorn. Dave stepped beside Eddi and crossed his arms.

"Aunt Maddy's best friend in college married Sean O'Reilly way before he made it big. Her name is Mimi." Dave pointed toward an overly made-up blonde woman, as plump as his aunt was thin. She and Aunt Maddy stood in the far corner near trunks full of fabrics. The two examined cloth as if they were spies tracking down clues. For once, his aunt had broken her cardinal rule about dressing "properly" for practice and was actually wearing slacks.

"She contacted Mimi in June and asked if Sean would agree to create the costumes," Dave finished and didn't bother telling Eddi that his aunt dreamed of the day he married Sean and Mimi's daughter, Brittney. Brittney, twelve years his junior, proved too eager for his attention. When Dave got married, he preferred a mature woman—not a leech. Thankfully, the O'Reillys had miraculously arrived this weekend without her. Nevertheless, his aunt and Mimi had been dropping hints about Dave's visiting Brittney all evening.

"Why didn't she tell us about this before now?" Eddi asked. She continued staring at the stage as if she were seeing a mirage.

"Because she wasn't certain he could do it until last week. Then she decided to make it a big surprise."

Dave kept his attention upon Eddi and hoped Conner realized he was being ignored. He delighted in this rare moment of Eddi letting down her guard. During the last weeks, Dave had begun to despair that he'd ever reach her. Faced with actually being the one who pursued in this relationship, he had floundered with ways to let her know he cared. All summer Eddi stated her lines while her eyes remained as frosty as snow clouds. Dave had begun to doubt that Eddi would ever be his. But tonight when he stroked her chin, new confidence flared. And now she was actually relaxing with him. Maybe there really was hope.

"I wondered what we were going to do about costumes," Eddi admitted and shifted her purse on her shoulder. "Mrs. DeBloom never said anything about them, and we're only six weeks out on our first performance."

"Aunt Maddy says they've promised to have everything delivered within a month," Dave explained.

"And he can design everything just like that?" She snapped her fingers.

"He has some models from other costumes he's done for a Broadway play from the same time period," Dave admitted. "So he's not starting from scratch by any means."

"This must be costing a fortune." She surprised Dave with a calculating appraisal as if deducing who might be paying for this luxury.

While Dave was flattered that she immediately assumed he was generous enough to fund the project, he spoke the truth. "Nope," he declared. "Sean agreed to do it for the cost of the material and travel expenses."

"Who'd have thought it?" Eddi marveled and laughed. "Sean O'Reilly is our very own personal designer." She copied one of Sean's flamboyant moves with his tape measure.

"He's a generous man who loves his wife," Dave continued. "His wife asked a favor for an old friend."

"Come on, Eddi." Conner placed a possessive arm around her waist. "I think I heard somebody say you're next." Conner urged her away but eyed Dave with a possessive dare.

Dave delighted when Eddi purposefully removed Conner's arm from her waist. The octopus had no right to take such liberties with a lady who blatantly resisted him. Dave narrowed his right eye as Cheri Locaste approached Eddi from across the room. Holding a plate of chips and the luscious-smelling cheese dip, Cheri maneuvered through the crowd and stopped in front of Eddi. Excitement christened her cheeks in a rosy glow. Dave never remembered seeing Cheri looking so animated…and actually alive for once.

Dave wandered back to Eddi's side. If Conner Boswick thought Dave was going to leave Eddi in Conner's clutches, he was crazy.

"Can you believe this?" Cheri chirped. "Sean O'Reilly is doing our costumes!"

"I know!" Eddi said as Cheri's attention settled upon Conner. "It's the last thing I ever expected." Eddi's focus riveted to the stage once more. "I wonder what my costumes will look like?" she mused. "I hope he uses blue-gray fabric for one of mine. I think that's my best color." Her speculative smile reminded Dave of a little girl on Christmas morning, and it only made her more endearing.

Conner offered a distracted nod toward Cheri and looked at Dave as if he were a blight upon society.

"Hello." Cheri extended her hand toward Conner. "I don't believe we've met."

Eddi briefly introduced the two, and they shook hands. Then Eddi looked at Cheri as if she'd just discovered the cure for cancer. "We need to go to the restroom." Eddi grabbed her friend's arm.

"We do?" Cheri asked.

"Yes, we do," Eddi urged and pointed a meaningful stare straight at her.

"Oh, okay!" Cheri exclaimed as if receiving an ESP message only understood by females. "Yes, we do!"

Eddi grabbed Cheri's plate and shoved it into Dave's hands. The two women scurried toward the hallway and left Dave with the honor of Conner's presence. Tempted to kick the pompous intruder out of his home, Dave stalked away.

"What a good-looking guy," Cheri said as soon as Eddi locked the bathroom door.

Squinting, Eddi turned toward her friend. "Who are you talking about?" she asked and couldn't imagine that Cheri was referring to her cousin.

"Conner," Cheri answered. "Haven't you noticed?"

"You really think so?" Eddi squeaked.

"Well, yes. And didn't he say he was a vice president of some oil company?" She pointed at Eddi. "You should marry him before he gets away."

"He's my *third cousin,*" Eddi said as if announcing the biggest scandal of the century. "Didn't you notice we have the same last name?"

"Actually, I guess I missed that…and the name of the oil company," Cheri admitted.

"It's Boswick Oil out of Houston."

"Oh. That would make sense." Cheri nodded. "But the way he had his arm around you, I thought—"

"That's what he thinks too," Eddi wailed. She leaned against the bathroom counter and covered her face. The smell of room deodorizer agitated her taut nerves.

"I don't know how you do it, Eddi," Cheri sighed. "Not only do you have an oil tycoon chasing you, the most eligible bachelor in the county can't keep his eyes off you."

"Who are you talking about *now?*" Eddi lowered her hands and scrutinized Cheri.

"Dave, of course," Cheri supplied, her bland expression announcing the news was ancient. "The whole cast is betting the two of you will be married by Christmas."

"They're nuts!" Eddi exclaimed. Nevertheless, her chin tingled with the memory of his touch.

"Forget Dave!" Eddi continued. "Conner's the problem now. He's driving me crazy, Cheri." Eddi reached toward the brass rack and removed one of the thick hand towels. She twisted the towel as if it were Conner's neck. "I promise, if something doesn't change soon, I might file a harrassment suit against him." Eddi tossed the towel onto the counter. "Problem is, I'm not certain I could make it stick. His biggest crime so far is calling me and sending me flowers."

"I like flowers," Cheri said with a sly grin. "Want me to run interference?"

Eddi stared at her friend. "You'd do that?" she blurted.

"Of course." Cheri gripped Eddi's shoulder. "You're my friend. I'd do anything for you." Yet the determined gleam in her eyes suggested Cheri's motives were far from selfless.

Twenty-Three

Eddi was so busy watching Cheri talk to Conner, she barely remembered Sean O'Reilly measuring her. From the time she stepped on stage, Eddi was flabbergasted with Cheri. After their bathroom conversation, Cheri retrieved her purse and reentered the bathroom. Within fifteen minutes she strode back into the drama room. She had twisted her hair atop her head with a plastic clip and applied a light application of makeup. While Cheri still wouldn't win any beauty contest, she looked ten times better. At least, Conner appreciated the improvement. Somehow, Cheri had managed to monopolize him from the minute Eddi stepped onstage.

With her measurements finished, Eddi scurried toward the table where she deposited her purse. She noticed Calvin appraising her from across the room and realized he was about to approach her. Pretending she hadn't noticed, Eddi retrieved her bag and slipped toward the French doors.

Another glance over her shoulder validated that Calvin was no longer pursuing her. Instead, he was chatting with the master of the manor. Eddi twisted the knob, slipped into the backyard, and clicked the door behind her. The horizon had swallowed the sun. The velvet sky now sparkled with a myriad of stars. The faint whiff of chlorine verified the presence of Dave's pool, only twenty yards away.

In front of Eddi stood the building that nagged her since their first practice. She cast a cautious glance back into the house, but could no longer spot Dave or Calvin. While she exited the house with the intent to avoid Conner, her previous goal to investigate the building erected itself. Stepping into the home's shadow, Eddi rummaged through her purse and pulled out her keys. She fingered the cylindrical penlight, attached to her key ring. Feeling like a CIA agent, Eddi glanced around the yard. Shrieking crickets and a lonesome cow's moo were the only evidence of other life.

Eddi dashed forward and hoped the building remained unlocked. She paused at the door, looked over her shoulder, and then gripped the knob. Pinching her face into a expectant mask, she turned the knob. It offered no resistance. Eddi released her pent-up breath. She slipped into the room and closed the door. With the smell of paper and ink and stale coffee welcoming her, Eddi debated whether she should forgo the penlight and flip a switch.

She shook her head and clicked on her penlight. If Dave happened to look out and see the light glowing past the blinds, he would become suspicious. In her light's limited beam, the room appeared to be spacious. A computer, piled with clutter, claimed the right wall. Across the room, a large table sat beneath an expansive drawing. Eddi neared the table and directed her beam upon the wall. The drawing appeared to be the work of an architect and featured a sleek building that resembled a dormitory.

Frowning, Eddi allowed her light to trail across the table. A model of the drawing claimed the table's center. Various brochures and a scattering of paper cluttered the table's outer sphere. A royal blue brochure with a picturesque version of the dormatory grabbed her attention. Eddi picked it up, placed the penlight in her teeth, and prepared to peruse it.

The doorknob rattled. Eddi went rigid. She barely had time to click off her pen light and shove the brochure into her purse before the door opened. The light flickered on. Dave looked straight at Eddi as if he fully expected her.

"Hi, Eddi." he said with a knowing grin. "Curious about my little building?"

Eddi turned from the table and backed into it. She gripped the table's edge and lost all abilities to think. "I, uh…"

"I saw you duck out of the house." He closed the door. "By the time I was able to follow you out, I saw this door closing. If you'd told me you wanted to know about this, I would have given you the grand tour." He glanced around the room.

Now with the light on, Eddi soaked up the full ambiance of the building. The wall over the computer held several poster-sized pictures of a young man who favored Dave, all in different poses. For some reason, the black-and-white images dominated the whole room with a melancholic allure. Like a mouse trapped in a corner, her gaze darted around the room, taking in images she'd encountered in offices everywhere…file cabinets…a book-case…water cooler…a counter with a coffeemaker sitting on it.

An anticlimatic droop deflated the curiosity that had plagued Eddi for weeks. The building looked to be nothing but a normal office. There were no signs of money laundering or illegal weapons or drug trafficking. She eyed the computer. Even though such a machine could hold a wealth of incriminating files, Eddi sensed that whatever was happening in this building was far from illegal. Suddenly her suspicions seemed silly.

As the seconds passed, Eddi wished she could beam herself out of this awkward situation. The last thing she ever wanted to do was make Dave Davidson believe that anything he was involved in interested her.

"I...guess I should go," Eddi said. She walked toward the door, fully expecting Dave to step aside and let her pass. She stopped a few feet in front of him. Dave didn't move. Eddi fidgeted with her purse strap and mumbled, "Excuse me."

"Eddi," Dave started, "there's something I've been wanting to tell you for awhile now. I guess now is as good a time as any."

Her feminine warning system told Eddi not to make eye contact. She did anyway.

He lifted his chin in the way that made his nose look all the longer and made Eddi feel all the smaller. She was transported back to that day when Mrs. DeBloom arrived at her home and told her she wasn't valuable enough for her wealthy nephew. That reminded her that Dave didn't think Jenny was good enough for Calvin. Eddi's fingers tightened around the purse strap until it bit into her palm.

Dave stepped forward. Eddi retreated and bumped into the table. All sorts of possibilities bombarded her—including the fact that she was alone with a man who stirred her pulse, despite her better judgment. Eddi gulped.

"I've been silent all I can, Eddi," Dave began. "I think the time has come for me to tell you how much I...how much I've grown to admire you."

Eddi's eyes widened, and she couldn't catch her breath.

"The Lord knows I've fought it," he continued. Dave walked toward the computer. He stroked the top of the high-backed office chair. "I've told myself you weren't suited for me."

She began to relive that conversation with Mrs. DeBloom all over again. "Yes, I can imagine you have," she whispered and wondered if he heard her.

"I, I—I'm not really even sure your family would gel with mine." Dave turned to face her, his eyes a mask of guarded vulnerability.

In a breath Eddi was tempted to believe the man had really grown to care about her. Then she remembered his true character. His next words validated that memory.

"There are other reasons I won't get into as well." His voice held a cold edge.

Of course, Eddi thought. *You're smart enough not to mention your superiority to me. How kind!* Her pulse hammered in her temple.

"But the bottom line is, I'd like us to try to get to know each other better, and I don't mean a light flirtation." He inserted his thumb into his jeans pocket. "I mean something we'd both enter into, hoping to play for keeps."

"For keeps?" Eddi squeaked.

"Well, yes." Dave shrugged. "I think we're both a little old to be playing games here," he said as if he were reading a documentary.

"Are you proposing?" she asked incredulously.

"Not exactly," Dave admitted. "I think you'd agree it's a little soon for that, but—"

"There's never going to be a good time for that," Eddi blurted.

Dave's face tensed. "What are you saying?"

"I'm saying no!" Eddi hugged her purse as if it offered some protection. "Have you lost your mind?" she bleated.

His right eye narrowed.

"I'm the woman two months ago you said was too short, too prissy, and classless. Remember?"

"I thought you understood by now I didn't mean a word of that," he said, his words flat.

"Then why did you say it?" Eddi asked as if she were interrogating a witness in court.

He opened his mouth as if to defend himself.

"I'll tell you why you said it," she injected. "It's because you are just like your aunt! You are both about the rudest people I've ever met."

"Leave Aunt Maddy out of this, will you?" he barked.

"I'll leave her out of it when she leaves me out of it. She came over a month ago and told me there's no way you and I could ever marry because you're waaaay wealthier than I am and therefore waaaay better." Eddi lifted her arm in theatrical imitation of Mrs. DeBloom. Her fury from weeks ago exploded anew.

"What was Aunt Maddy thinking?" Dave gasped as a crease formed between his brows.

"Apparently, what you're thinking about me and my family."

"Not about you, Eddi!" He stepped toward her.

"Oh, but my family is a different matter! Is that it?"

"That's not what I—"

"Isn't that what you just said? Your family wouldn't gel with mine?" She lifted her chin at exactly the same angle he did and peered down her nose.

"It looks like I've misjudged the situation," he said. "I thought—" Dave shook his head. The vulnerability disappeared. Only a stony-faced stranger remained. "It doesn't matter. I think I've just made a fool of myself."

"Well, it's high time you made a fool of yourself," she snarled. "You've spent enough time making a fool of others."

"What are you talking about *now?*" Dave put his hands on his hips and looked like he was ready to charge.

Eddi, tempted to step back, held her ground. "What about what you did to Rick Wallace?" she demanded.

"I don't know what Rick has told you, but he's a—"

"And what about how you broke up Calvin and Jenny?"

"Who told you—"

"Your aunt let it slip the day she came over to tell me I wasn't good enough for you." Eddi declared. "She seems to think Jenny isn't quite good enough for Calvin, either!" She marched toward the door, placed her hand on the knob, and faced him. "I've lived in the big city my whole life," Eddi fumed. "Believe me I've met my share of materialistic snobs. But I don't think any of them compares to what I've found in *this* tiny town!"

A red veil crept beneath Dave's tan. "And I've never encountered such acid judgment," he snarled. "You haven't even *started* to get to know me. How could you—"

"Because I've got good instincts when it comes to people," she claimed. "My first impressions are usually right."

"Now who's arrogant?" he growled.

A primieval force urged her to hurl her purse at the jerk. *I should've put rocks in it,* she thought as a wicked chuckle tumbled forth.

"You can laugh all you want," he growled, "but—"

"You're absolutely right! I *can* laugh all I want. I don't have to ask your *or* your aunt's permission. Believe it or not, there are some people in this town the two of you can't manipulate!" She slung open the door and stomped into the balmy night.

"Eddi!" Dave yelled before the door's slam ricocheted across the yard.

His breathing rapid, Dave strode to the door. A second before he swung it open and chased Eddi down, he stopped and forced himself to count to twenty aloud. For some situations, counting to ten wasn't sufficient. By the time Dave reached twelve, his pulse slowed. When he hit eighteen, his breathing was less intensive. When he said twenty, Dave propped his head against the door.

"So let's say I chase her down and let her have it. What good will it do?" he reasoned. "It would just turn into a screaming contest."

Dave pounded his forehead against the door until he could no longer bear the pain. Calvin's prediction that he would be begging Eddi's attention by summer's end taunted him. He thought of the women in his past whom he'd either brushed off or ignored…of those years when he assumed every single female was his if he expressed an interest.

The memories mocked him, and Dave wondered if this was divine recompense for his own youthful heartlessness. Eddi had certainly given him more than a dose of his own medicine.

Right now all Dave wanted was to crawl into a hole and lick his wounds in solitude. He wondered if Aunt Maddy might be missing him and switched off the lights.

As the darkness wrapped around him, Dave reflected upon his aunt's part in Eddi's anger. If Aunt Maddy had insinuated the things Eddi mentioned, no wonder she was incensed. Sometimes his doting aunt could be a royal pain.

The moonbeams and yard lights provided enough illumination for him to find the computer desk again. Dave collapsed into the chair and blankly stared into the darkness streaked with slashes of pale gold light. He placed his elbows on the chair's arms, made a tent of his fingers, and rested his chin on them.

The last few months gyrated through his mind, and Dave thought of all that had passed between him and Eddi. Not only had Dave insulted her to Calvin, he'd told her not to get her hopes up about a relationship. At their first practice, Dave tried to bully her into resigning her part as Elizabeth. In the dugout, he insinuated Eddi might chase him for his money.

"Okay, so Aunt Maddy isn't the only one who can be a pain." Dave tapped the computer keyboard with his index finger and slumped lower into the chair. *It's no wonder she believed whatever Rick Wallace told her.*

Dave eyed the computer. The only thing he didn't regret was warning Calvin off of Jenny. The longer he stewed about an engaged woman teasing his friend, the more convinced he was of his stance. Eddi seemed like such a logical person. He couldn't understand why she wouldn't agree that an engaged woman had no business flirting with another man—even if that woman *was* her sister.

At last, the need to defend himself wouldn't be denied. A rousing case of renewed irritation overtook the gloom. Eddi

Boswick had done what she would never allow to happen to a client in court. She hurled accusations at him and stormed out before giving him the chance to state his side.

He rolled the chair forward. The wheels squeaked to a stop as Dave booted up his computer. The log-on page announced the project that consumed his heart and much of his money. He signed into his computer, accessed his e-mail, inserted Eddi's address, and began a systematic self-defense.

Twenty-Four

The next morning Eddi arrived at her office by seven. While that time wasn't unusual for a weekday, she had yet to match it on a Saturday morning. Yawning, she closed the door and locked it. This wasn't about business. She needed a change of scenery that would enable her to logically assess the last twelve hours. Her home had offered no inspiration. Eddi finally drifted off to sleep, but around six in the morning Roddy awoke her by barking as if a whole army of burglars were invading the townhouse. Eddi found him in the kitchen. Both cats had him cornered. They were hissing and clawing as if they'd like to take out the dog's eyes.

After an almost sleepless night, Eddi hadn't possessed the patience to deal with the war. She placed the cats in the laundry room and headed for the office.

As with last night, Eddi was again bombarded with everything from anger with Dave for being so pompous to anxiety over having broken Jenny's confidence. If her sister ever found out that Eddi had spoken with Dave about Calvin, she would not be happy. But presently, Jenny didn't even know that Dave was to blame for Calvin's dumping her. So maybe the whole horrid secret would remain that way.

Eddi turned on the light over her desk and rubbed her eyes. A stack of paperwork in the to-do cache reminded her she had yet to finish the details on the latest real estate closing.

"Oh joy," she mumbled and dropped her purse on the desk.

She turned her back to the paperwork and trudged down the hall to the kitchenette. Like a zombie, Eddi went through the steps of brewing a pot of coffee. After filling her cup with the steaming liquid, she trudged back toward her desk and dropped into the chair. With a sigh, Eddi sipped the bitter liquid and grimaced. Not only did it taste twice the strength of her normal brew, she'd forgotten to put in cream and sugar. Eddi gulped the coffee anyway and wished it would somehow blot out last night.

"That was about as close to a proposal as you could get without actually being one," Eddi mumbled and wondered what had possessed Dave. *Maybe he's hitting his midlife crisis a decade early and is going insane,* she mused and then thought of what Cheri said about how the whole cast presumed they'd be married by Christmas. Last night, Eddi thought the cast was hallucinating. Now, she wondered if they all saw something she'd missed.

Eddi considered the play…the weeks left of practice and performance…the scenes where she had to calmly interact with Dave. "How in the world am I going to do it?" she moaned and thanked the Lord there were no kissing scenes.

With a groan she rested her forehead in her hand. Her cell phone emitted an upbeat tune, and Eddi glared at her purse. Thinking a funeral dirge would be more appropriate, she recalled turning the phone on yesterday when she called Jenny. At the time Eddi felt as if even turning on the phone for a few minutes opened her up to a call from Conner.

"I must have forgotten to turn it back off," she mumbled. "How brain dead can I be?"

Eddi retrieved her phone and winced before checking the screen. After ducking out on Conner last night, Eddi hadn't given the guy another thought. She examined the number. Her suspicions were well founded. She started to toss the phone back into her purse but decided the time had come to move from being firm to being blunt. She pressed the talk button and spoke her greeting.

"Eddi! What happened to you last night?" Conner's high-pitched voice took on an accusatory edge.

"I just needed to get away," Eddi said and then reminded herself such an evasive answer would accomplish nothing. She gulped a generous swallow of the acerbic coffee, grimaced, and plunged forward.

"Actually, Conner, we need to have a heart-to-heart talk here."

"Really?" he said with a positive lilt.

"What I mean is," Eddi said in a no-nonsense tone, "I'm going to tell you exactly how I feel, and I'm certain you are *not* going to like it."

"Oh."

"Yes. It's been very clear to me that, from our first meeting, you have been…interested in a lasting relationship. I've tried to be nice, and I thought you'd get the hint. But apparently you need a more direct approach." She snatched a breath and continued before he could interrupt.

"Conner, this is a hopeless case. In the first place, I—I think it's really weird to date or marry your own cousin," her words took on a desperate shrill as she mashed a button on her sleeveless shirt. "I know people have done this for centuries, but it's just not for me, okay?" Eddi didn't add that Conner was not and never could be her type, even if he *weren't* her cousin. Being blunt was one thing. Being cruel was another.

"But in the state of Texas—"

"Yes, I'm aware of the laws," she snapped. "I'm a lawyer, remember?"

"I know," he confirmed. "But your mother told me you were interested in meeting me."

Eddi closed her eyes. Nothing Conner could say about her mother would surprise her. "My mother has a tendency to create scenarios that fit her plans," she said.

"You know, Edwardia," he began with a condescending tone.

Eddi plopped her cup on the desk and stood straight up. "Don't call me Edwardia!" she demanded as a slosh of hot liquid burned her fingers. She shook her hand and reached for the tissue box.

"Okay, sorry," he said, and Eddi imagined Conner rolling his eyes. "Whatever…I was just going to say that you need to be aware that if you pass up this opportunity, there are many other women who'd be thrilled to grab it."

"I imagine there are." As Eddi mopped up the spilled coffee, she thought of Cheri. "If there's someone else who's interested, by all means I urge you to encourage her. Frankly, you are wasting your time with me."

"I know what's going on," he huffed. "Do you think I don't have eyes?"

She tossed the tissue into the wastebasket. "What are you talking about?" Eddi shook her head.

"You've got a thing for that Dave person, don't you?"

Eddi's mouth fell open, and she stared at the corner ficus tree as if *it* had spoken the words. Everyone from Mrs. DeBloom to Conner seemed bent upon projecting romantic motives upon her.

"I'm right, aren't I?"

"You have never been further from the truth," she blurted.

"I know what I saw!" Conner insisted. "And I think you must be losing your sense of judgment or something."

"Why would you say that?"

"It's beyond me why you would go after a half-baked cowboy type when you could have the vice president of an international oil company."

Eddi couldn't stop the laugh. "That half-baked cowboy owned the home you were in last night and is listed in—" She stopped herself before blurting the Forbes 500 secret. Eddi had promised Dave in the dugout she wouldn't share that information with a soul.

"We'll just say he could probably *buy* Boswick Oil," she said.

"Humph. Could have fooled me," Conner said resentfully. "He looked like he didn't have a dime to his name."

"Looks can be deceiving," Eddi said.

"So, that's it then?" Conner accused. "You're dumping me for somebody who has more money!"

"I'm not after Dave, and I'm not dumping you," Eddi insisted and picked up her coffee mug. "We never were an item, Conner." She sipped the hot liquid and wondered if she should have made it double the strength.

"Maybe we weren't an item as far as *you* were concerned, but—"

"I had no intention of hurting you," Eddi soothed and sensed that the man had finally gotten the message. Even though he wasn't her type and had driven her nuts, she still hated hurting him. After all, Conner Boswick was as valuable a person as she.

"I hope you never thought I was leading you on," Eddi continued.

"Not in the least."

"Good. As a matter of fact, last night when Cheri Locaste—"

"Cheri is a very nice lady," Conner admitted.

"She thought you were really nice too," Eddi said. "I think the two of you might have a lot in common."

"I think you might be right," he said with a hint of bitterness.

"Good then." Eddi turned toward her computer and floundered for something else to say.

"Well, I guess I'll delete your numbers off my cell phone then," Conner continued.

Eddi imagined his mouth settling into a pout.

"That's fine," she said and booted up her computer. As the machine began a series of hums and clicks, a faint tick floated over the phone line. Eddi looked at the phone screen and read, "Call Ended."

With a long sigh she dropped the phone into the top of her purse and didn't bother to turn it off. For the first time in weeks, Eddi no longer felt the need to look over her shoulder for Conner.

"What a relief," she mumbled and turned on her computer screen. Within a few minutes, she was receiving her e-mails. Eddi chuckled as the computer finished screening her messages. "I guess I came to the office just to drink coffee and check e-mail." *Oh well*, she thought, *it beats sitting around the house playing animal referee.*

Her first message was from Jenny. Even though Jenny was far from an e-mail enthusiast, the few messages Eddi received from her the last several weeks mentioned Calvin. This one was no different. "I know it's crazy because we were barely getting to know each other, but I miss him, Eddi."

"Of course you do," Eddi wrote back, her brow furrowed. "He treated you like a queen." *And then heartlessly dropped you*, she added to herself. "What woman wouldn't miss that?" She added a few more chatty details and hit the send button. As soon as the message was on its way, Eddi scanned the list of other messages in her box. Her gaze riveted on the last one, labeled Dave Davidson. Eddi clicked her mouse once on the message line and stared at it for thirty seconds. Her rigid index finger hovered over the mouse as Eddi debated whether to delete the message unread or actually open the thing.

I'm not interested in anything he has to say, she thought and detected Conner's petty tone in her own words.

"Okay," Eddi relented, "everyone has a right to a fair trial. Maybe all testimonies aren't in yet."

Twenty-Five

She double-clicked the message line, and his single spaced e-mail filled the screen. *As usual, some witnesses aren't short on words,* she thought. She hadn't expected Dave to be the long-winded variety. Eddi rubbed her left palm against her walking shorts and told herself she still didn't have to read the message. She began reading anyway.

> Eddi,
>
> I'm not going to bore you with unnecessary details, so I'll just get to the point. First, I wanted to clear up some stuff about what you said about your sister and Calvin. The night we were all at Huntington House, I overheard your mother tell your father that Jenny was engaged. After that, she said something to the effect that she was thrilled Jenny was encouraging Calvin because Calvin had way more money than Jenny's fiancé. Frankly, that alone would have made me inform Calvin that he

should back off. But the fact is, despite what your mother said, I couldn't agree that Jenny was actually encouraging Calvin. The whole time they were together, she acted as if Calvin were her brother and nothing more.

I care a lot for Calvin. He's like a brother to me. A few years back he caught his fiancée with another man a week before the wedding. After seeing him get two-timed like that, I didn't want to see the whole process repeated. Honestly, Eddi, after watching your youngest sister arrive with two men and watching the way she acted with them, I wasn't convinced that Jenny wasn't perhaps more inclined toward Linda's values than your own. If I have been wrong in this matter, please let me know. Was I in error to assume that your mother would be an authority on your sister's engagement?

"Yes, you were," Eddi stiffly asserted. "Why didn't you ask Jenny or even me? We would have gladly told you Jenny has never been engaged and that our mother jumps to conclusions!"

She glared at the screen. "And how dare you belittle Linda like this? No, she might not be the most mature person on the planet, but she's my sister! The least you could have done is had the decency to—"

Twisting her lips, Eddi hit the delete button with the message only partially read. She wanted no more of Dave Davidson's opinions.

"Anybody who'd blindly take the word of somebody without verifying the evidence doesn't deserve any more of my time," she stormed.

Eddi strode back to the kitchenette, dumped the coffee down the drain, and flung open the door of the tiny refrigerator. She pulled out a Diet Dr Pepper and a jelly roll, left over from last week. Eddi popped the top on the soda, unwrapped the jelly roll, and eyed the thing. Speckles of green verified that the treat was not safe to eat. She dropped it on the counter and guzzled the soda, welcoming the sting that banished the bitter coffee taste.

She eyed the half-dead ivy sitting on the window's ledge. Eddi grabbed the clay pot, shoved it under the water spout, and turned on the hydrant. All the while, one question hammered at her, *What's in the rest of that e-mail?* When the water overflowed the pot, she blurted, "It doesn't matter!"

Eddi deposited the plant back in its place, scooped up the jelly roll and dumped it into the trash can under the sink. She drummed her blunt fingernails on the countertop and considered finishing the real estate closing. Still, the e-mail plagued her. Her fingertips rested atop the cool counter.

Despite her best efforts to stop herself, Eddi hurried back to the computer. All the while, Dave's logic chipped away at her initial exasperation. *If I had never met Linda and saw her show up with a man on each arm, what would I think?* Eddi didn't bother to answer.

Neither did she deny that Jenny wasn't the most demonstrative woman when it came to men. She was, in fact, the exact opposite of Linda. *Cheri even commented on that the first night we practiced at Huntington House,* Eddi admitted as she slipped back into the chair.

And what would I have done if I overheard Calvin's mother mention that he was engaged? Eddi downed another swallow of the soda. "I'd probably have told Jenny she needed to back off," she admitted with brutal honesty.

"Okay," she whispered, "maybe he's got a point or two."

Eddi plopped the Dr Pepper on her desk. She made a series of clicks that accessed her deleted files and found Dave's e-mail. Eddi skimmed to the place where she'd left off and continued reading.

Concerning your comments about Rick Wallace, I think it's time for me to tell you what I have resisted repeating to a living soul. I will admit that part of my reason for remaining silent has involved my own pride. But another issue involves family honor and what I know would have been the wishes of my grandfather. From my earliest memory he drilled me to protect our family name. Nonetheless, I believe for my own peace of mind as well as defending myself, the time has come for me to tell you the whole story.

Eddi snatched the soda and downed a fourth of the can. She rubbed her fingers along the desktop and eyed the e-mail. Some unexplainable precognition warned her that she was about to encounter information that might alter her life, and maybe the life of her younger sister.

Already, she was wondering if she had been blinded by her own prejudices against Dave. *Maybe, I was too ready to believe anything Rick Wallace told me because I was looking for more reasons to dislike Dave.* She guzzled the rest of the Dr Pepper and gripped the empty can. With a mixture of dread and anticipation, Eddi dared encounter the next lines.

I don't know if Rick has told you, but he is my foster cousin. My uncle and aunt—my father's brother and his wife—took Rick to raise when he was only 10. He never went back to his biological parents, but he was also never adopted by my aunt and uncle because his parents refused to release their rights. My whole family, including me (I was 11 at the time), welcomed Rick into the family with open arms. My father encouraged my grandfather to treat Rick the same as he treated me and my brother. We even had a family meeting, where the four of us—my mother, father, my younger brother, and I—agreed to make an extra effort to show God's love to Rick.

Things rocked on that way for years. Ironically, my younger brother and Rick hit it off better than Rick and I. I say it was ironic because Rick was a full three years older than my brother and only one year younger than I. Rick and I were together a lot at school, although he kept to himself somewhat.

The end of my senior year of high school, I learned that Rick had been playing around with drugs and alcohol. Specifically, I received word from a friend that Rick was at a party where he got drunk and disappeared into a room with a girl who, we'll just say, wasn't known for her virtue. Frankly, I refused to believe the story and defended Rick. He had just made a profession of faith at church and was saying he thought he should go into the ministry. But the negative reports came more and more often until finally I couldn't ignore them.

One night, the year after I graduated from high school, Rick came by the house for awhile—we lived just down the road from each other—and he told me he was going to the library to study. I decided to follow him. What I witnessed was Rick buying marijuana and then picking up a woman who was much older and far from being a lady.

Strangely, he had just begun to send out applications to seminary and was saying God had called him to be a pastor. See, our grandfather had died and left money for Rick to attend seminary. I guess Rick figured it was his free ticket to college, I don't know. Anyway, when I found out about Rick's true character, I did the only thing I knew to do. I told my father, who did the only thing he knew to do. He made the seminaries Rick had applied to aware of the issues. Needless to say, Rick wasn't able to get into the seminaries, and I believe the ministry at large was saved a scandal.

Eddi squeezed the soda can until it crackled. Her breathing was unsteady, and her heart pounded in her chest. She scrolled toward the end of the message and assessed the wealth of information waiting to be digested. Eddi didn't question the veracity of Dave's story. While the man might not be the most socially agreeable, her gut instinct insisted he was not a liar.

Which makes him a man of integrity, Eddi thought with a conviction she could not shake. *And that makes Rick a liar. And it would mean I have misjudged people.* Eddi compressed the can until it collapsed. She looked at the smashed aluminum as if she'd never seen it. She dropped the can in the trash basket near her desk and reminded herself she had yet to absorb all of Dave's e-mail.

"No jury makes a decision until its heard the whole story," she begrudgingly admitted.

Eddi hated the idea that she might have been wrong. Her whole career was based on her abilities to ascertain evidence and defend the innocent. She wrestled with how to acknowledge Dave's honesty while maintaining her grudge against him.

After resting her elbow on the desk, she pressed her fingers between her brows. Engulfed in a fountain of confusion, Eddi decided to finish reading the e-mail. If the last section weren't as convincing as the first, she would be able to maintain her negative opinions of Dave. If the last section were as credible as the first, then Dave would prove himself unworthy of many of last night's insults. While a part of Eddi hoped the final section validated her, a rebel voice rooted for Dave. Consumed by conflict, she peered at the rest of the e-mail.

> Soon after this happened, my parents were killed in a car wreck when they were on a mission trip to Mexico. I was nineteen. My little brother, George, was fifteen. Rick was eighteen, and just out of high school. By this time, he realized he wasn't going to seminary and why. He verbally attacked me at my parents' funeral. It didn't matter to Rick that I was facing both my parents' deaths and wondering how I was going to console my brother. Really, I think Rick was drunk. When we were alone in the church, Rick swore he would get even. Little did I know he would stoop to such low levels to do it.

> My brother moved in with Aunt Maddy, and she gave me a place to come home to during college breaks—that was my freshman year. I didn't finish that year, of course, as you well know. When I moved from Aunt Maddy's and pursued a career in computers, George begged me not to leave. I was convinced I needed to try my wings, and I have regretted that decision in ways you will not understand until you get to the end of this e-mail.

> As things turned out, George and my aunt didn't get along. I think Aunt Maddy meant well, but she smothered him. One night they had an awful argument, and George ran away. After a week of us pulling our hair out with worry, George called me. He was at Rick's apartment. Believe it or not, I was relieved. Even though I knew Rick hadn't been a model citizen, I was glad George was with

somebody I knew and that he was alive. I tried to get George to move in with me, but he wouldn't. I think he was still mad at me for leaving him, actually. Rick even smooth-talked me into believing he was in church and would be a good influence on George. I knew he was thinking about going to the police academy, so I was gullible enough and stupid enough to believe he had taken a turn for the better.

To make a long story short, Eddi, the next time I saw my brother he was high on drugs. I won't bore you with the details, but essentially Rick Wallace proved that he hadn't changed a bit. I eventually suspected that he was the one who taught George the "glories" of marijuana, and I'll go to my grave believing he did it just to spite me. George liked it so much, he started doing harder drugs.

Eventually, George moved out on his own, and I suspect he was even dealing drugs. No matter how hard I tried to pull him back, George wouldn't budge. Three years ago, Rick called one day to say a fellow police officer found George in a hotel room in Houston. He overdosed on cocaine and was dead.

"Oh my word," Eddi whispered. She pushed away from the computer, rested her head on the back of the chair, and gazed at the ceiling.

The gold specks blurred together as she recalled taunting Dave about his brother the night Mrs. DeBloom assigned roles. Eddi asked him if his brother jumped to Mrs. DeBloom's every command as he did. Dave had simply replied, "No, never." He had also told her his brother *was* outside Dallas, not the he *lived* outside Dallas. Eddi remembered Dave acting a little awkward. At the time, she had assumed he was just being distant and difficult.

A queasy knot formed in her stomach. The Dr Pepper and coffee no longer proved a good mix.

"How could I have been so cold?" she asked. *But I didn't know,* Eddi reasoned. *I would have never said what I did if I'd known.*

A new realization dashed aside her mortification. Eddi sat straight up. She gripped the chair's arms and stared ahead. Feeling as if she'd seen a grotesque specter, Eddi remained rigid. One thought rotated through her mind: *I paid for Rick to go to Hawaii with my sister!*

Eddi imagined her little sister high…or worse…dead. A slow fire started in her belly. Eddi glared at the wall holding her framed degrees. Not only had she been fooled, she had been manipulated.

Her head began to ache, and she wondered if Linda were a vital part of the whole manipulation. "Probably," Eddi decided and mused that Rick might have met his match.

She glanced at the computer. The rest of the letter still remained unread. Propelled by an unquenchable urge, Eddi leaned forward, found the last line she'd read, and started digesting the rest of Dave's story.

> Frankly, I wasn't the most gracious recipient when Rick called about George's death. I screamed at Rick and told him he was partly to blame because he introduced George to drugs. Rick denied everything and said I didn't have proof. Really, I don't have physical proof, but there are things in life you just know. Rick didn't even bother to show up at George's funeral. At the time, it made me furious. Now, I think he was probably too scared to be there.

For a full year, I blamed Rick for George's death. Now that I've moved past some of the hard grieving, I can admit that George made his own choices. However, I cannot deny that Rick aided in his initial corruption.

Frankly, I have been tempted these last few years to hire a private eye to see if I couldn't take Rick down. I don't believe for one second that he's straight just because he's now a police officer. I wouldn't be surprised if he were dealing drugs himself. But part of me has wanted peace and wanted to put an end to the whole mess. Now that I've seen Rick again, I'm not certain I can live with myself if I don't somehow make him take some responsibility for his actions. I'll stop ranting on that subject here.

My parents always said that God brings something good out of every tragedy. Well, He used George's death to get my attention and draw me back to Him. From there, I have developed the ministry you were so curious to investigate. I imagine you were in my little building long enough to discover my secret. If nothing else validates my character, I believe my efforts in the last three years will.

Dave

Ministry? Eddi thought. She had been so distracted by Dave's borderline proposal and her own anger that she had forgotten about the brochure. "I never forget stuff like that," she mumbled. "I must be losing it."

She reached for her purse and scratched past the cell phone. The blue brochure had slipped to the side, between her billfold and pocket computer. Eddi grabbed the dog-eared brochure and read the caption: "Valley of Hope: Mentoring Troubled Boys to Manhood." A photo of the dormlike structure on the table claimed the center of the front page. It stood at the base of a hill, surrounded by rolling pastures that suspiciously resembled an area near Dave's home. The bottom read: "Demo brochure, #3."

The attractive promo piece highlighted future plans to build a dorm on Dave's ranch. It also detailed Dave's past outreach efforts—including sponsoring teens through drug rehab programs and creating a fund for families in search of lost teens. The last lines on the brochure's back secured Eddi's full remorse: "In loving memory of George A. Davidson."

She laid the brochure on the desk and accepted a belittling truth. Minutes ago when reading Dave's e-mail she had accused him of blindly believing her mother about Jenny's engagement without asking for verification from her or Jenny. Yet she had done the same thing. Eddi blindly believed Rick Wallace without consulting Dave. She had suspected Dave of foul play in his little building, only to discover he was running a national ministry. She had believed he was heartless, only to learn he was dedicating his life to charity. She had accused him of being arrogant, only to realize he had dealt with more pain than Eddi could ever imagine. She had prided herself on respecting the poor as much as the wealthy, only to disrespect Dave because he was wealthy.

"Oh, God, forgive me!" she breathed.

Eddi propped her elbow on the chair's arm and pressed her index finger and thumb against her eyes. She contemplated her uneventful life. Aside from having a less-than-functional family, Eddi could say that she was truly blessed. She had endured no tragic losses. Even all four of her grandparents were still living. Although she wasn't her mother's favorite child, her father doted on her. Her parents had paid her way through law school. She was realizing her dream now in building her own practice.

If I had gone through half what Dave has gone through, I might be a little hard to get along with myself, she thought.

She picked up the brochure and reexamined the back. Dave's photo claimed the upper right corner. Eddi scrutinized his clean-cut image and recalled the picture of him with Laura Schock on the *People* magazine website. With a frown, she tried to blot that pink-sequined siren from her mind. The harder Eddi tried, the more troubled she became. There was no way she could ever make herself as drop-dead gorgeous as Laura.

She stroked Dave's photo and relived the day of the tornado. She remembered what it felt like to be sheltered in his arms. And his gentle touch when he had wiped away her tears....

With sinking spirits, Eddi doubted Dave would ever extend his offer again—especially not after last night's insults. *Oh well,* she told herself, *we probably wouldn't have made it in a relationship anyway.* But the words lacked conviction.

Presently, all Eddi could hope was that maybe Jenny and Calvin's situation could be repaired. She dropped the brochure back on the desk and turned to her computer. Eddi hit the reply button to Dave's e-mail and debated for several seconds how to respond. Finally, the cryptic words came:

> Dave,
>
> Thanks for taking the time for your explanation. Just so you and Calvin know, Jenny is not, nor has she ever been, engaged—or married, for that matter. My mother can be presumptuous at times, for lack of a better word. My sister had been seeing a man named Hal Gomez for about a year. While Hal was hinting about marriage, Jenny had never committed. She recently broke up with him because of Calvin. There's an old saying, "Quiet water runs deep." I think that best describes Jenny's feelings for Calvin. I think most decent

people would also agree that if a woman errs, it's better to err on the side of being cautious in her behavior rather than too compulsive. Oh, and if my mother mentioned money, those are her thoughts, not Jenny's.

Eddi's fingers hovered near the keys. She mulled over other possible commentary, including an apology for her eruption last night. *But will he think I'm chasing him?* she wondered. Dave had blatantly admitted that he wasn't fond of women pursuing him. With a decisive nod, Eddi chose to never give Dave reason to add her name to the "Women Who Have Chased Me" list. She signed the e-mail and hit the send button.

Twenty-Six

Linda had never been so nauseated. Her forehead clammy, she collapsed by the toilet and wished for relief. None came. Her low moan floated along the marble-covered walls, the color of gunmetal. Her friends had insisted the group stay at the Hilton, right on the beach. Their balcony hovered over a turquoise sea surrounded by white sand. While the room was expensive, she and Rick had pooled their money and were managing to keep up the pace of her wealthy acquaintances…until yesterday.

Yesterday morning, Linda awoke with a disturbing case of nausea. While everyone else lazed on the beach, she stayed in the hotel room. Rick insisted upon remaining with her. At first Linda had been so moved by Rick's consideration she was certain he must be falling in love with her. By noon, she questioned her assumptions. Despite her weakened state, Rick pressed her for physical favors until Linda relinquished.

After a sound nap, she was vastly improved that evening and even enjoyed a night out with the gang. They'd taken a sunset cruise around the island and arrived back by midnight. Everyone else wanted to go to a club. Linda, feeling spent, had declined. Rick protested and told her she was welcome to go back to the room without him. Linda did exactly that. The last glimpse she had of him, he was laughing at something Hallie said. Hallie's boyfriend looked as disgruntled as Linda felt. She had no idea what time Rick arrived back in the room.

"I'm going to die," Linda groaned. She stood up and grabbed a washcloth from the overhead rack, knelt, and crawled toward the bathtub. Linda twisted the faucet and dampened the cloth with cool water. She sponged her face and then rested her forehead against the cold tub. The smell of deodorant soap only increased her nausea.

"Are you sick again?" Rick's drowsy voice held an edge of accusation.

Linda jumped. She looked up at him and didn't try to hide her misery. "I feel like I'm going to barf."

"That's what you said yesterday morning," he complained while rubbing his bare chest. "I hope you aren't going to give me a virus."

"Thanks for being so concerned," she moaned.

"Whatever," Rick said. "Look, we're in Hawaii. This is a gorgeous day. Last night after you left, everyone decided we'd go snorkeling today." He leaned against the door frame and crossed his arms. "I really don't want to spend another day in the room."

"Of course not," Linda snapped. "Why would you want to be cooped up with me when you could go snorkeling with Hallie?" Her stomach rolled, and Linda scrambled back to the toilet.

She sensed Rick's appraisal as she endured a dry heave. He didn't offer a hint of consolation.

"You look awful," Rick finally said. "What is the matter with you, anyway? I thought you were going to be somebody fun on this trip. But now—"

"I *am* somebody fun!" Linda defended with a wobbly voice. She wadded the tail of her satin nightshirt and looked up at him. With her on the floor, his lean physique appeared seven feet tall.

"I got you a free trip to Hawaii, didn't I?" she asked.

"No, I got *myself* a free trip to Hawaii," he claimed. "I was the one who talked to Eddi."

"And I was the one who told you what to say!" she wailed.

Rick released an oath and stomped from the bathroom. While silent tears trickled down Linda's cheeks, she dabbed at them with the cloth. She hoped Rick didn't remain with her the rest of today. Even though she hated the idea of his ogling Hallie, she didn't want a repeat of yesterday either.

Silently, she arose, closed the door, and locked it. Linda lowered the toilet lid and sat atop it. She didn't have to look at her appearance to see she was gray. She now understood what it meant to *feel* gray. Never had she endured a virus that made her so wretched.

What if it's not a virus? The thought invaded her mind and nearly made her collapse back to her knees. A moist flash of heat washed her face, and Linda stumbled toward her toiletry bag on the counter. She fumbled through the paraphernalia until she found the flat, pink disk. Linda examined the pills and counted six she'd missed this month. Frantically, she calculated the days since her last cycle and realized she was a week late.

Slowly, she raised her gaze until she examined her reflection in the wall-to-wall mirror. Linda's blue eyes, marred by dark circles, lacked sparkle. Her complexion had indeed faded to a sick gray hue. And her hair hung against her red nightshirt like a limp, matted mop.

A light tap sounded from the door. "I'm going down for breakfast," Rick said.

"Fine," Linda acknowledged and expected an offer for him to bring her something. A 7 UP would have been nice. But all she heard was the sound of the room's door opening and then clapping shut.

"Thanks a lot," she muttered but dismissed him as quickly as the door had closed.

One of the good things about staying in expensive hotels was they offered shops for visitors. This particular Hilton even featured a small drugstore. Linda had purchased a tube of toothpaste yesterday and noticed they had a wide array of toiletry essentials.

Maybe they have a pregnancy test, she thought.

Linda rinsed her face and ran a brush through her hair. She dragged herself from the bathroom and donned the shorts set she'd taken off last night. After slipping on her sandals, she got a bottle of ice water from the refrigerator. The cold liquid sliced into her stomach like a spike of ice through a heaving sea. She moaned again.

Slipping from the room, Linda took the back elevator. The last thing she wanted was any of her friends to see her looking so bad. Linda hurried across plush carpet, through brass-trimmed doors, and around an indoor water fountain before slinking into the store. A quick perusal of the shelves proved the manager had thought of everything. Within five minutes, Linda was back in the hotel room, tearing into the test box.

After getting a urine sample, she dipped the wand into the liquid, held her breath, and waited. The instructions said one pink line meant she was not pregnant. Two pink lines indicated she was. Linda watched in horror as two pink lines appeared in the test window.

Her stomach churned anew. She dropped the test wand in the garbage and hung her head over the toilet. This time, the heave wasn't dry. With a whimper, Linda cleaned up her mess. She downed more water, crept to the room's window, and grasped the curtain rod. The palm trees, azure waters, and snow-white beach beckoned her to lose herself in their beauty. Linda closed the curtains.

Welcoming the darkness, she collapsed onto the bed, curled into the fetal position, and closed her eyes. The smell of her perfume on the sheets sent a nauseous threat through her empty stomach.

What am I going to do? she wailed to herself. *I don't want to be pregnant!* Silent tears seeped through her lashes and plopped onto the sheets. With each drop, her dismay grew tenfold.

Dad is going to be furious! she thought as if she were a fourteen-year-old. All her life, Linda had somehow managed to shift circumstances to her advantage—especially with her mother on her side. Now she had never felt so alone, so without options. Linda grappled for a simple way out of this situation. Only one choice offered a discreet end to the predicament.

Linda opened her eyes and peered into the shadows. While she never imagined needing an abortion, the possibility proved inviting. *No one would ever know,* she mused.

No one but God. The haunting thought wouldn't be denied. Linda tugged her knees closer to her chest and tried to erase the years she'd been taught the sanctity of human life. Even though she hadn't attended church services for months, Linda couldn't erase the guilt that plagued her soul with the very thought of ending a baby's life.

Another idea posed itself. Linda sat up and stacked a trio of pillows against the headboard. She leaned back and gazed across the darkened room cluttered with clothing.

The notion involved Rick and her doing the honorable thing and getting married while they were away. At first, no one would suspect that Linda had gotten pregnant out of wedlock. Eventually, the child's birthdate would indicate Rick and Linda's sin. But since she would be married and on her own, no one would probably mention the discrepancy. She wagered that her family would be too excited over the new baby to unveil dissatisfaction with the child's parents. Her nausea subsiding, Linda pulled the covers to her chin.

By the time Rick entered the hotel room, Linda had convinced herself that he would feel the same way. When the door closed behind him, she turned on the lamp. He stepped into the room, looked toward the curtains, and eyed Linda with a familiar leer.

"Are you feeling worse or just waiting on me to come back to the room?" he asked and crawled onto the bed. Lustfully appraising her, he stroked her arm.

Linda eyed the brown eyes and dark hair she thought were so yummy mere days ago. Now, his looks did little to move her. Instead, she stiffened and resented Rick's wanting physical favors after his earlier behavior.

"I've been waiting for you," Linda said.

"Good!" His hand moved to her thigh. "I'm sorry about earlier," he purred. "I guess I was a little grouchy, that's all." Rick reached to pull her closer, but Linda placed a flattened hand against his chest.

"No!" she asserted. "I—I need to tell you something."

He backed away. "Okay, what is it?" he asked as if her words were of no consequence.

Linda looked down and struggled with how to break the news. The air conditioner's steady hum took on the dark roar of dread. She gnawed on her lower lip and didn't dare look at Rick.

"I'm pregnant," she finally blurted.

"What?" Rick sat up.

She looked at him, only to have her worst fears confirmed. His derisive glare sent a chill through her soul. "Why did you let that happen?" he demanded. "I thought you were on the pill. I've seen you take them!"

"I *have* been on the pill," Linda claimed. "But I forgot to take it some days, so…" Linda shrugged.

"Oh, for crying out loud!" Rick spit out. He stood up, walked to the end of the bed, and placed his hands on his hips.

"It's not like I did this on purpose," Linda squeaked.

He paced to the window and tugged on the curtain rods. The Pacific sunshine danced into the room as if life were perfect. Linda braced herself for a full-blown explosion.

"Are you sure you're pregnant?" Rick asked, his voice now void of irritation.

Linda picked at the comforter and relaxed. "Yes. I went down to the drugstore while you were eating and bought a pregnancy test. It showed positive."

"Are you sure the baby's mine?" He toyed with the balcony door's latch.

"Yes," she answered and was too distraught to contemplate the insult.

"Oh, well." Rick turned to face her and shrugged. "We'll just arrange for you to have an abortion. It's not that big a deal," he said as if this wouldn't be his first time.

"Not that big a deal?" she panted. "It might not be for *you!* But we're talking about my body here!" Linda tugged at a clump of her hair and considered the logistics of such a procedure. She had never even experienced an operation. After a desperate hiccough, she teetered on the brink of uncontrollable emotions.

"Look," Rick crooned as he knelt beside her. He gazed into her eyes, held her hand, and Linda was reminded of the first days of their relationship. Rick had been unbelievably charming—miles removed from the rogue who left for breakfast an hour ago.

"It's really not all that bad," he said. "You'll be fine, and we won't have to deal with having a baby. It's the easiest solution to the whole problem."

"But I don't have the money for an abortion," she despaired. "And I know my father won't fund it. No way am I even telling him!" Linda adamantly shook her head as if she were a toddler.

"I'll take care of it," Rick offered and kissed the back of her hand.

"But you didn't have the money for this trip even. How can you—"

He broke eye contact. "I *do* have an account I can access. I'll have to pay a penalty to get the money out, but I'll do it...for you." He stroked the length of her nose and brushed her cheek with a kiss.

"Okay," Linda haltingly agreed. "But I thought we might also discuss maybe, uh…"

"Oh, honey," he said over a laugh, "I hope you're not going to mention the 'm' word. You're not ready to get married any more than I am. Let's just deal with this little problem and move on. We'll finish our vacation and then when we get back to Houston, we'll take care of it all. You can even stay at my place a night or two if you don't want your parents to suspect anything. Just tell them you're with Hallie, all right?"

Linda nodded and clung to Rick's hand as if she were being tugged into the great dark unknown with only him as her guide.

Twenty-Seven

~ ~

Eddi pulled into the church parking lot and cruised until she found a place to park. Normally, she arrived at church on Sunday morning in time for Sunday school. Then she met for prayer with the choir and was in the choir loft by now. But today, Eddi overslept. Actually, she had been so worried about Linda and so distracted over Dave, she had barely slept all week. Even after oversleeping this morning, Eddi covered a yawn before switching off the ignition.

All week long, when the phone rang, she thought it might be Dave. Every time she checked her e-mail, she wondered if he had sent her a message. By Friday, Eddi was even skimming her mail for some sign of Dave's distinctive scrawl. All her expectations remained unfulfilled. Dave never even responded to Eddi's e-mail about Jenny.

She scratched through her purse, extracted a mint, and popped it into her mouth. An explosion of peppermint filling her mouth, she gathered her purse and Bible, opened the Mustang's door, and got out into the mid-August heat. Eddi scanned the parking lot in search of Dave's truck and thought she spotted it near the road. She hadn't even noticed him at church last Sunday. He'd also been mysteriously absent from play practice at Huntington House all week. Mrs. DeBloom just vaguely mentioned that he wasn't feeling well. Eddi wondered if he were purposefully avoiding her.

Most likely, she thought. *After everything I said, he probably can't stand the sight of me.*

Eddi pressed the lock button on her key chain at the same time her cell phone began a cheerful tune. With a grimace, she looked at her watch and calculated she had five minutes until church started. She pulled her phone from her purse and noted the caller was Jenny.

That's odd, she thought, *Jenny's normally in church at this time.* She leaned against the car and pressed the answer button.

"What's up?" she asked without a greeting.

"Eddi," Jenny's voice was low and urgent, "I've just been on the phone with Linda."

"Really?" Eddi's back straightened. "She and Rick were supposed to be back from Hawaii Friday, weren't they?" All week, Eddi had fretted over Linda and prayed for her protection. She even called her twice to make sure everything was okay. Both times, Linda sounded a bit distant but insisted she was having a great time in Hawaii.

"I've got some really bad news," Jenny continued.

"Oh, no." Eddi gazed toward a clump of clouds hanging over a pine-covered hill. A mockingbird's cheerful song belied Jenny's anguished tones.

"It looks like what Dave told you is right about Rick," Jenny continued.

Eddi's fingers bit into the phone. "What's happened?"

"Linda's pregnant," Jenny explained, "and she's decided to get an abortion."

Jenny's words affirmed that Rick was playing her for a fool when he mentioned getting separate rooms for him and Linda on the trip. Eddi speculated that the two had probably been sleeping together for weeks. She felt as if her soul sank to her knees. Thoughts of her niece or nephew discarded like a scrap of garbage made her want to bellow in protest.

"If she doesn't want the baby, I'll take it, for pity's sake," Eddi croaked. "Why does she think she's got to have an abortion?"

"I have no idea," Jenny said. "I've been on the phone with her this morning. She called me and said she just wanted to talk."

"That doesn't surprise me. She's always been closer to you than me," Eddi said.

"I think it's because Dad favors you, and she resents it," Jenny said.

Sighing, Eddi gazed upward. "But Mom favors her."

"I know, I know."

"So what about the pregnancy?" Eddi asked.

"When she called, I promise, Eddi, it was almost as if she was telling me about the abortion so I'd tell her not to do it. I'm not kidding."

"Is the procedure scheduled yet?" Eddi asked.

"No. They're going to a clinic tomorrow to take care of the details."

"Who's paying for it? Surely not Dad—"

"No way! He doesn't know. Linda said Rick is paying."

"Rick?" Eddi shrieked and covered her mouth. Guiltily, she peered at the stain-glassed building thirty yards away. "I just paid his way to Hawaii because he said he couldn't afford it. And now he's paying for an abortion?"

"Yep."

"Everything Dave said about him is true, Jenny!" Eddi's face grew hot as she repeated Jenny's claim. "Everything! I knew it as well the day I forwarded Dave's e-mail to you as I do now!"

"That e-mail was nothing but the truth," Jenny agreed. "You could feel truth just oozing out of the computer screen."

"What are we going to do?" Eddi asked and eyed a family of three entering the church. The young mother held a baby girl, dressed in frilly pink. Eddi was almost certain she smelled baby powder. "We've got to somehow stop her," she urged.

"We can start praying now that she'll change her mind," Jenny said.

"You said she sounded like she wanted you to talk her out of it."

"She did. The weird part is that when I started trying to talk her out of it, she started arguing with me."

"She probably doesn't know *what* she wants!" Eddi stated.

"You just said a mouthful. But I have a hunch Rick knows exactly what *he* wants, and it's not a child-support lawsuit."

"So, the quicker he can get rid of the baby, the freer he remains." Eddi narrowed her eyes.

"Bingo," Jenny said.

Eddi's first impulse was to hop into her vehicle, drive straight to Houston, and convince Linda not to go through with the abortion. A still, small voice insisted her best defense lay in walking through the church doors and laying her petition in the hands of the Father.

"I'm standing in the church parking lot," Eddi explained. She pulled on the front of her red suit jacket and wished she'd worn a sleeveless blouse beneath. "The service is going to start in about one minute. They always have open altar time early in the service. I think I need to be there for this one."

"You better believe you do," Jenny said. "I was going to church this morning too, but Linda's call ended all that."

"And you said Mom and Dad don't know?"

"Are you kidding? Linda made me promise not to tell."

"I'm surprised she wanted you to tell me."

Jenny remained silent.

"Oh, I see." Eddi shook her head and chewed the last bit of her mint as if it were the enemy.

"I didn't promise her I wouldn't tell you," Jenny explained. "But I think she'd rather I kept the whole thing to myself. If she calls, please act like you don't know."

"I seriously doubt she's going to call," Eddi said.

"Honestly, so do I. You need to get into church," Jenny continued. "I'll be praying the next hour. Maybe together, we can make a difference in this baby's life."

"I hope so," Eddi said.

"Oh my goodness," Jenny exclaimed. "I got so upset over this, I almost forgot to tell you that Calvin e-mailed me. I got it this morning."

"No way!" Eddi exclaimed.

"Yes! He asked if I minded if he called."

"And do you?"

"Are you kidding? I called information and got his number. *I'm* thinking about calling *him.*"

"Really, Jenny, I don't think it would hurt at this point."

"You sound like you know something I don't," Jenny said.

Eddi debated whether to tell Jenny Dave's e-mail had been edited. She'd cut the part about Jenny and Calvin before forwarding it to her sister. But if Eddi told Jenny that, she would incriminate herself in breaking her sister's confidence.

"I do, uh, know a few things I'm not telling you," she admitted. "It's a long story that involves a misunderstanding." Eddi glanced toward the church and felt the pull of the open altar time. "Would you be okay with my calling you back this afternoon and explaining everything?"

Jenny hesitated. "So, I guess I get to chew my fingernails off with curiosity between now and then, right? And I just got a French manicure. Come on, Eddi!"

"Oh, okay." Eddi briefed Jenny on the details of the proposal scene she had discreetly avoided. "I haven't told you before now because I didn't want you to know I discussed the breakup with Dave after promising you I wouldn't. It wasn't on purpose, Jenny—*really*. I was just so mad at Dave that the whole thing popped out."

"I understand," Jenny said. "Don't feel bad. If your telling Dave has cleared up the misunderstanding, then I'm *glad* you told him."

"Well, good," Eddi said. "You're probably the most understanding person in the world, Jenny."

"And you're the best," Jenny affirmed.

"Let's just hope between the two of us we can stop Linda from something she'll regret the rest of her life," Eddi said before the sisters ended the call.

The longer Eddi thought about Linda's abortion, the more her eyes threatened to sting. But she'd never been the crying sort and was determined not to start now. Her heels tapped against the sidewalk as she hurried toward the church doors. She stepped into the foyer and welcomed the blast of cold air that chilled the sweat along her hairline.

The sound of an upbeat chorus floated from the sanctuary as the usher handed Eddi a church bulletin. With an absent smile, she looked past the suit-clad gentleman and stepped toward the sanctuary full of worshipers. She noticed an empty pew by the door and slipped into the spot nearest the aisle. The smell of hymnals and a whiff of a woman's perfume brought back a lifetime of memories, all centered upon her family in church. Eddi marveled that Linda had drifted so far from the principles their parents taught them.

Eddi settled in the pew and focused upon the choir dressed in blue-and-white robes. While missing participating with her friends, she caught Calvin Barclay's eye. He usually sat in the tenor section, far removed from Eddi. She had managed to avoid him every practice since he dropped Jenny. Then she realized two weeks ago he was avoiding her.

This morning Calvin didn't look away. Instead, he smiled as if they were the best of friends. Eddi figured he would have waved if he weren't in the front of the church. A tight knot unraveled within Eddi. The misunderstanding was truly at an end.

The minister of music hailed the congregation to stand. Eddi retrieved her hymnal and checked the bulletin for the next song number. As she was rising to her feet, she glanced across the aisle...into the eyes of Dave Davidson. Eddi's eyes widened a fraction as he offered a faint nod. She glanced down and couldn't remember the song number.

Mrs. DeBloom had vaguely mentioned Dave wasn't feeling well when he missed practice last week. *For someone who isn't feeling well, he looks really good,* she thought and sneaked a peek at his polished black shoes. He even wore a suit today. Eddi wondered if that was a first around London.

Wagering that Dave was no longer looking at her, Eddi allowed her gaze to trail up the dark suit. Her heart thudded harder. She was reminded of those early days of summer when she erroneously assumed Dave was nothing more than a back-woods ruffian.

Oh, how wrong I was, she thought. Her attention settled upon his profile...the shaven square jaw...the prominent nose... the heavy brows. His full hair attested that he had been avoiding the barbershop again. While Eddi enjoyed the appeal of the meticulously groomed gentleman, a side of her missed the dare-devil persona that originally attracted her.

As Dave sang in sequence with congregational worship, Eddi's initial attraction flamed anew. But this time the magnetic pull involved more than the chemistry between the opposite sex. It included Eddi's respect for the man's character. While she would admit that he wasn't perfect, Eddi couldn't deny that Dave was a man of integrity...a man who extended himself to make the world better for others.

As she absorbed every angle of his features, Eddi marveled that she could have been the mistress of his home—her dream home. *If only I hadn't been so blind*, she thought. Fleetingly, she imagined a chorus of single women in the choir singing "Eddi Boswick, the Craziest Woman in the County." A perverse chuckle wouldn't be denied.

Dave slowly turned to appraise Eddi again. She smothered her smile. Her hands flexed against the hymnal. And she didn't look away this time. Neither did Dave.

Twenty-Eight

If ever a woman was issuing the "come closer" look it was Eddi Boswick. Dave nearly collapsed with the impact of her femininity. She was wearing that classy red suit she had on the first time he saw her. Eddi's cropped hair lent her a sharp professional appearance while emphasizing her wide set eyes and the angle of her slender face. After Dave got over the disappointment of never seeing her long hair unbound, he decided he liked the short style. At this point Eddi Boswick could shave her head and he would love it.

Dave wondered if she possessed any idea the effect she had on him. He'd spent all week at his ranch and purposefully stayed out of her path. The fact that he had been nauseated gave him a great excuse to avoid play practice and church. By Thursday Dave realized his queasy stomach had nothing to do with a virus and everything to do with his heart being tied in knots.

When he got Eddi's e-mail a week ago, Dave read it thirty times. He hoped to discover some hidden meaning that indicated a change of her heart. Dave finally decided he was looking for something that didn't exist. There were no hidden meanings whatsoever.

While Dave had spent the last few years sidestepping women who chased him, he prayed all week that Eddi would make some move to indicate her interest. In the wee hours of the morning, Dave finally decided to stop altering his life to avoid her. While he still held no plans of romantically approaching her, Dave had to live. So he got up this morning, dressed in his best suit, and chose a pew near the back.

As Dave continued to appraise her, a dozen scenarios cavorted through his mind. The final one involved his slipping across the aisle, placing his arm around Eddi, and tugging her as close as propriety allowed. The longer he looked into her kitten-soft eyes, the more logical the plan became. They were both in the back pews. The standing congregation was focused upon the minister of music. No one would probably even notice.

Before acting out the impulse, Dave looked down and reverted to a reasonable thought pattern. *Eddi would probably slap me if I tried such a move.* This wasn't the first time she'd given him the "come closer" look. Every time they touched, Eddi's eyes stirred with a warmth that couldn't be ignored. That's why Dave had convinced himself she would respond favorably to his suggestion that they become better acquainted.

Boy, was I wrong, he thought and resisted another glance toward the red-suited lady. *Just because Eddi's attracted to me doesn't mean she wants a relationship.* The last thing Dave needed was her turning him down again. He didn't think his pride could take two venomous rejections in just over a week. Dave refocused on his song book, held his ground, and decided that Eddi would have to make a move before he risked another rebuff.

Somewhere in all his thinking, Dave lost track of what song number they were on. After the hymn finished, he closed his eyes and concentrated on the lyrics of "Open Our Eyes, Lord," a prayer chorus they often sang before the open altar time. Try as he might, he couldn't concentrate on one spiritual matter. All he could think about was the alluring woman across the aisle. Keeping his head down, he strained to catch a glimpse of her from the corners of his eyes.

During the chorus' closing bars, the minister of music spoke the familiar words, "The altar is open for anyone who has a special prayer request or burden this morning."

A movement from Eddi's pew indicated that she was stepping into the aisle. Dave watched her red shoes until she was halfway to the altar. Then he lifted his attention to the lady who had captured his heart. Dave couldn't remember Eddi going to the altar during prayer time before. While she always struck him as reverent, she was not the most demonstrative church member. Eddi knelt with her back to Dave. She reached for a tissue, dabbed at her cheeks, and lowered her head. In all the months he'd known Eddi, he never recalled seeing her cry.

Dave shifted and placed his hymnal on the pew. *Something must be terribly wrong.* His mind began to churn with various possibilities from issues with her health to an unexpected death. When her shoulders began shaking, Dave could take no more.

He stepped into the aisle. *I'm going to regret this if she rejects me,* he thought as he walked toward the altar.

After kneeling beside Eddi, Dave detected her light floral fragrance—the scent he smelled the day he buried his face against her hair. He reached to touch her shoulder, hesitated, and then lightly brushed her hand with his fingertips.

"Eddi?" His faint whisper mingled with the organist's rendition of "Amazing Grace."

She opened tear-drenched eyes and mopped at her cheeks.

"Is everything okay?" Dave questioned and felt like an idiot. If everything were okay, she wouldn't be bawling her eyes out. He waited for an answer. When none came, he began to wonder if his worst fears about rejection were being realized.

"N—no," she finally whispered as the pastor began to pray. "It's Linda," she continued. Eddi tucked her chin next to her chest. "You were right about Rick Wallace."

Dave's jaw clenched. "What has he done?" he rapped out. Dave cast a cautious glance over his shoulder and thanked God the organist had crescendoed during his question.

"I feel like such a fool," Eddi continued. "I don't even deserve for God to hear my prayers. I—I believed Rick would—would be a good influence on Linda." She sniffled. "I worry about her so much. I might not always agree with what she does, but she'll al—always be my little sister."

"Yes, I know the feeling," Dave said.

Eddi reached under the altar, tugged up a fresh wad of tissue, and sponged her eyes. She looked up. The agony stirring her soul bade Dave to wrap his arm around her. His hurting pride insisted he resist.

"She was planning a trip to Hawaii with a bunch of her friends who have more money than good sense. I really thought Rick would help keep her out of trouble. So…I paid his way on the trip." She looked down as if the shame were too great. "He claimed they would be staying in separate rooms."

Dave could only imagine where this story was leading. The further Eddi progressed, the more disgusted he became. Rick Wallace's schemes never ceased to astound him.

"What an idiot I was to believe him." Eddi balled her fist upon the padded altar. "Jenny just called on my cell—right before I walked into the church. She said Linda called her this morning. She's pregnant. Rick is the father. And he's going to pay for an abortion—and after telling me he couldn't afford a trip to Hawaii." Eddi glanced behind her.

Dave followed suit. The whole congregation remained standing with heads bowed. Dave's pulse began a hard thud in his temple. "Does Linda want an abortion?"

"Jenny doesn't seem to think Linda really knows *what* she wants. We wondered if this was something Rick has talked her into to get out of the responsibility of a child." Eddi rested her forehead on the altar's edge.

"That sounds about right," Dave rumbled.

"I'm wondering if he's done this sort of thing before," Eddi's distraught words were barely discernible.

"It wouldn't surprise me," Dave growled. He hadn't cursed in years. While he held no plans of reverting to the old habit—especially not while at the altar—the temptation was nearly too much. He was as disgusted with himself as he was with Rick.

I should have told Eddi everything the first time Rick showed up with Linda, he thought. Dave closed his eyes, clamped his teeth, and began a slow count to twenty. When he reached fifteen, the pastor pronounced a firm amen. While others at the altar began to stir, Dave grappled for something to say. At last, he realized there were no appropriate words. This situation required action.

As Eddi moved to her feet, Dave stood. Without another glance her way, he marched up the aisle, past his pew, and into the foyer. One mission drove him into the unforgiving heat—a mission that would be in full swing by five that evening.

Two years ago, he successfully assisted distraught grandparents in saving their twin grandsons from the gang scene in Houston. Both their parents had skipped out on them, and Mr. and Mrs. Howell were left with raising two angry teenagers who were more interested in partying than academics. With Dave's influence and full-paid scholarships, both men left street life, attended community college, and succeeded on the basketball team. They each stood six-six and tipped the scale at 280. While empowering their team to win third place in state, their teammates had dubbed them the Deadly Duo. Even though Dave expected both of them to positively impact society, he couldn't deny that they were a formidable-looking pair. If he were in a dark alley, they were the last type Dave wanted to meet.

He received a letter last week from their grandmother. She reported that Larnell and Klynell were each expressing an interest in doing something in Dave's ministry to help repay what he'd done for them.

"Do I have an assignment for you," Dave mumbled as he rushed across the parking lot. When he reached his Chevy truck, Dave whipped off the suit coat and loosened his tie. He tossed the coat into the passenger seat and retrieved his cell phone from his belt holster. By the time he steered out of the parking lot, Dave was making an appointment with the Deadly Duo for that very evening.

After the benediction Eddi accepted that Dave was not coming back into the church service. She debated the reason for his abrupt departure after their conversation at the altar. One of the reasons he gave for fighting his attraction for her had been that he doubted their families would gel. An unexpected onslaught of insecurity suggested that Dave was so disgusted with Eddi's family problems he could endure her presence no longer.

With sinking spirits, she stepped into the aisle and joined the after-service bustle. As usual, the post-service mix resulted in several conversations, smiles, hugs, and pats on the back. With Eddi's increasing popularity around town, escaping the church grounds was becoming more and more difficult. After answering a myriad of questions about the coming play, Eddi decided she would never again have to wish to be a part of the community.

Just as she prepared to step through the foyer doors, Calvin Barclay approached from around the corner. "Eddi!" he called and hurried toward her.

Her hand on the glass door's bar, she stopped. As he neared, Eddi struggled with her feelings. After a pleasant friendship, she and Calvin had been sidestepping each other for weeks—all because he had believed Dave's assumptions about Jenny. An unexpected tide of exasperation nearly sucked Eddi under.

Then she remembered her own error in judgment…her own refusal to consult Dave about Rick's story. The exasperation disappeared.

She observed Calvin with a welcoming smile. "Hi, Calvin. How are you these days?"

"Great!" he said with wary enthusiasm. He stopped mere feet away and awkwardly shifted his weight. "And how's Jenny?"

"Jenny's…" Eddi debated her options and then decided the time had come for transparency. "Jenny is missing you, actually."

Calvin looked down and nudged at the carpet with the toe of his leather shoe. Eddi wondered if the socks he wore today had a hole in the toe. "I, uh, guess there's no reason to pretend here," he finally said. "I feel so foolish."

"You know, Calvin," Eddi laid her hand on his arm, "we've all made mistakes. I think you should just chalk this one up to experience and move on. I'll do the same."

He looked up and appraised Eddi. Speculation soon turned to relief. "Thanks," he breathed. "I never expected you to be so gracious."

"I'm not sure what that says about my reputation," Eddi said with a wry smile. For the first time since her crying jag at the altar, she concluded that she probably looked a mess. Thankfully, Calvin seemed too distracted to notice.

"Do you think Jenny would mind if I call her?" He toyed with the flap on his suit jacket's pocket.

"I was actually just on the phone with her," she said. "She mentioned you e-mailed."

"Yes, I—I finally got up the courage this morning." His ginger-colored eyes reminded Eddi of a basset hound with an anxiety disorder.

"I think you're worrying too much, Calvin." Eddi looped her arms through his and the two walked toward the door. Calvin opened it, and Eddi stepped from cool air into unbearable heat. "She'll be thrilled to hear from you."

"So you don't think she's angry?"

Eddi laughed and released his arm. "I learned how to be gracious from her," she claimed. "Jenny is the queen of mercy."

"Yes, and she deserved better treatment than I dished out." The two slowed as they neared the parking lot.

She's not the only one who deserved better treatment, Eddi thought and scanned the parking lot for Dave's vehicle.

"Why don't you just plan to move forward from here?" she asked as they stopped by her Mustang. "Who knows where it will lead?" She gently punched his upper arm and moved away.

Eddi hesitated and debated whether to say more. Finally, she decided enough had been left unsaid. The time for complete honesty was upon them. "My sister isn't the most demonstrative woman on the planet," she continued. "But I have it on good authority that she thinks you're a special guy."

A relaxed smile chased all vestiges of distress from Calvin's features. "Thanks," he said.

"No problem." A group of chattering teens rambled around them, and Eddi glanced toward her vehicle. All she could think of now was getting out of this hot suit and calling Jenny again. She had delivered some pointed prayers in that church service, and Eddi fully expected positive results.

"I'm ready to go home and change now." Calvin slipped his suit jacket off.

"Me, too," Eddi said and moved to her vehicle's door. "I can't wait until fall. This heat is killing me."

"Oh my word!" Calvin slapped his forehead with the heel of his hand. "I can't believe I almost forgot!"

"What?" Eddi pulled her keys out of her purse and was thinking toward her car's air conditioner being on maximum.

"Have you heard the latest?" Calvin questioned.

She hadn't been to Dina's for coffee in five days. Eddi figured she was behind on tons of gossip. "No, what's happened now?" She pressed the unlock button on her key chain and the car door produced a muffled click.

"You are *never* going to believe this one!" Calvin shook his head. "The whole choir nearly fainted this morning when we heard."

"What?" Eddi asked and leaned forward. "I wasn't in choir today because I overslept."

"Well…" Calvin observed Eddi with an anticlimactic droop of his features. "Oh, I just realized, you probably already know since it involves your cousin."

"My cousin?"

"Conner Boswick," Calvin supplied. "Oh well, maybe you *don't* know. He and Cheri Locaste have eloped!"

Eddi's mouth dropped open.

"I was thinking you probably already knew since he's your cousin."

"N–no, I hadn't heard," she stuttered. "For pity's sake, Calvin! They've only known each other a week!"

"That's what Dina said in choir practice this morning." Calvin shook his head as if confirming the town authority's opinion.

"Has Cheri lost her marbles?" Eddi squeaked.

"Who's to say?" Calvin said. "I sure wouldn't get married after only knowing someone a week."

"Me, neither." Eddi eyed the church's stained-glass windows. The sounds of car doors slamming and engines revving attested to the departing congregation.

Eddi focused on a young mother chasing a toddler toward the parking lot. "I never suspected Cheri would be so...so..."

"Impulsive?" Calvin inserted.

"Yes, I guess." Eddi dropped her purse on the top of her car and slipped out of her jacket. "Maybe rash would be a better word..." she added. "I once worked on a divorce case when I was in England that involved a lady who married a guy after she'd only known him for two weeks," Eddi said. "She met him on a cruise, and he swept her off her feet. I'm not a proponent of divorce—not in the least. But when I saw the horrible abuse photos and gathered evidence of the man's adultery, I think that woman was wise to take legal action. But it could have been avoided if she hadn't rushed into marriage with a total stranger."

"But this is your cousin, right?" Calvin questioned.

"My *third* cousin," Eddi said. "And he was trying to get me to marry him the day he met Cheri."

"Oh," Calvin said, and his lips remained puckered. Then he grimaced. "Are you saying you think he's abusive?" he asked.

Eddi laughed and shrugged. "Oh, I guess I insinuated that, didn't I? No, I don't think he's abusive. I'd say he's a bigger wimp than anything else."

"That's kinda what I thought," Calvin agreed.

"I just think it's dangerous when people haul off and get married so soon. One in a million might work, but for the most part, I think it's like playing Russian roulette."

A blast of hot wind did little to ease Eddi's perspiration. "He's got money, though," she said. "I guess that's what Cheri wanted."

"I guess a lot of women feel that way." Calvin looked passed Eddi as if he were afraid to make eye contact.

"Not me," she said with an assuring grin, "and not Jenny."

He peered at her. For the first time, Eddi was reminded of what so attracted Jenny to Calvin. While his fair good looks didn't hurt his appeal, the man's heart was in his eyes, and his heart was good.

"I already knew you weren't a fortune hunter," he affirmed. "But…"

"You needed affirmation about Jenny?"

"Well…" He shrugged and leaned against Eddi's Mustang.

"Believe me, if Jenny wanted to marry for money, she could have done that a long time ago." Eddi didn't detail the suitors whom Jenny had spurned.

"And I guess you probably could have too, right?" Calvin asked.

Eddi crossed her arms, tilted her head back, and laughed outright. "You don't see a line of waiting men, do you? I've about decided I'm too ornery to have a man chase me for long."

"Some men like their women a little ornery," Calvin teased. "Frankly, I think the fact that you *aren't* chasing Dave is driving him crazy."

Her shoulders stiffened. "Oh, and did he tell you that?" she asked with all the nonchalance she could muster.

"No," Calvin admitted. "But I know what I see. Ever since he moved to London nearly every available woman in town has made a play for him. I honestly think he thought you'd do the same thing. When you didn't, you got his attention. Now that you've hooked him, you still won't give him the time of day. I think the whole thing is hilarious." His genuine smile brightened his face.

"Maybe you just have a weird sense of humor," Eddi chided and tried to hide the fact that she cared more than Calvin ever suspected.

"Maybe, but I'll have to admit the show has been fun to watch this summer." Calvin straightened and stepped away from her car. "In case you don't know, the whole cast is waiting on the two of you to get married."

"So I've heard," Eddi drawled. "They might have a long wait."

"Maybe." Calvin's shoes tapped along the pavement as he moved toward his ebony Jeep, parked three cars away. "And maybe one day Dave and I will be in-laws. Who knows!" he said with far more certainty than Eddi felt.

Twenty-Nine

After all the arrangements had been made, Dave tread up the flight of steps to the apartment building's second landing. Klynell and Larnell Howell were close behind. He rang the doorbell and jutted his thumb to the left. "You guys stay away from the peep hole, okay?"

"Yes, sir," the pair said in unison as they stepped aside.

He looked up at the twins—identical except Klynell had green eyes. Larnell's were nearly black as night. Both men were every bit as intimidating as Dave remembered. They were also every bit as respectful. Funny thing, they always insisted on calling him sir—even before he hired them. They could have squashed Dave with a flick of their wrists. Instead, they chose to venerate him as the benefactor who helped them get an education.

While Dave stood six feet, the hulking men towered over him by half a foot. Their dark-skinned arms rippled with enough brawn to take down half a dozen men each. Dave had been thrilled when the two of them walked out of their house, dressed in tank tops and gym shorts. Not one muscle was hidden.

He smiled at the Deadly Duo and gave them the thumbs-up sign. "Remember, we aren't here to be polite," he said.

Klynell nodded. Larnell's white teeth flashed against his shiny skin, the color of rich coffee. "We'll take care of everything, just like you said, Mr. Davidson," he said, his thick lips firm.

"Just call me Dave, okay?" He doubled his fists and held them up. Both young men knocked their fists against his as if they were beginning a championship game. Dave pressed the bell again.

The doorknob rattled, and Dave prepared hiumself for the confrontation. The door swung inward. Eddi's sister, dressed in a policeman's shirt and a pair of leggings, stood on the other side. She looked at Dave as if she recognized him but couldn't quite remember where she'd seen him.

"Linda!" Dave said. "I wasn't expecting you." *But it might be for the best,* he thought. "Is Rick here?"

"Yes, he's—"

"Who is it, babe?" Rick's drowsy voice floated from close behind. He appeared in the doorway, his eyes droopy and blood-shot.

He stiffened and glared at Dave. "What are you doing here?" Rick demanded.

Dave crooked his finger toward the Deadly Duo and pushed against the door. "Excuse me, Linda," he said.

She gasped and scooted back.

"Hey, you can't just barge in like—" Rick looked behind Dave. His eyes widened. "What's going on here?" he asked.

Larnell and Klynell, their faces impassive, moved to either side of Rick. Dave closed the door and turned the deadbolt with an ominous click. Offering a humorless smile, he observed Rick, who glanced from one hulk to the other and back again.

This couldn't be better if we'd rehearsed it, Dave thought.

He eyed the apartment and was glad to note no signs of extra money, no hint of opulence gained from drug dealing. The place appeared to be a typical bachelor flat, replete with worn plaid sofa and love seat along with a big screen TV, blaring the latest pre-season football game. A bowl of popcorn and the smell of butter rounded off the whole cozy scene.

"What do you think you're doing, Dave Davidson?" Rick's voice wobbled out in a pathetic quake.

"Well," Dave purred, "I came to chat with you. But since Linda's here, I believe I'd like to chat with *her* first." He offered a reassuring smile toward Eddi's sister.

She licked her lips and backed toward the kitchen.

"No need to be afraid," Dave said. "I'm here to help." He tilted his head. "You can think of me as your…summer Santa, if you will."

Klynell and Larnell both laughed. The rhythm of their mirth took on a nefarious nuance as they each laid a hand on Rick's shoulders.

"Call the police, Linda." Rick commanded.

She lunged for the kitchen, and Dave grabbed her arm. "I don't think that would be a good idea, Rick," Dave said, "not unless you want me to inform them about the marijuana you probably have." He narrowed his eyes and watched Rick, whose face drained of all color. Dave smiled again. His hunch had proven correct. Linda struggled against his hold and began to whimper.

"Let go of her!" Rick demanded and jumped forward.

Dave looked at the Deadly Duo. "I think your new friend needs a trip to the little boy's room," he said and pointed toward the room's far doorway. "It's probably that way. Keep him in there until I come for him. Okay?"

"Right boss," Klynell said.

"Rick!" Linda cried. She stumbled back and bumped into the wall. Her eyes fillled with tears, and she looked at Dave as if she expected the worst.

"I'm pregnant," she pleaded. "Please don't—"

"Linda!" Rick hollered again as the twins dragged him into the hallway. "Dave, if you hurt her, I'll—"

"When have I ever hurt anybody, Rick?" Dave mocked. "I believe that's *your* usual role, isn't it?"

He turned back to Linda, released her arm, and held up his hands, palms facing her. "Linda, I'm not here to hurt you, honey," he crooned. "I'm good friends with your sister, Eddi. I already knew you were pregnant. That's the reason I'm here."

"You know Eddi?" Linda asked and her agitated breathing slowed.

"Yes. You and I briefly met at a play practice in London, remember? I'm the guy who's playing Darcy." Dave infused his words with a British accent.

"Oh!" Linda nodded. "I remember you." She appeared to wilt against the wall. "What are you doing here?" she asked and glanced toward the hallway.

"I came because Eddi went to the altar this morning in church."

"Oh," Linda answered, her blue eyes blank.

"She was crying," Dave explained. "I figure you know as well as I do that Eddi's not the crying sort."

"Uh huh," Linda agreed.

"I went down and knelt beside her. She was praying for *you*, Linda," Dave explained.

"For me?"

"Yes. She said you were pregnant and planning an abortion."

Linda looked down. A Gatorade advertisement burst from the television. She walked toward the large TV and pressed a button. The screen went black. Silence claimed the room—a silence broken only by the refrigerator's faint hum. Linda moved toward the sofa, pushed aside a woven throw, and settled onto the couch's edge.

"I guess Jenny told Eddi," she mumbled.

Dave nodded. "She said Jenny called on her cell right before she walked into church this morning."

"She didn't waste any time, did she?" Linda's lower lip protruded in that barracuda line Eddi often displayed. "I must have just hung up with Jenny when she called Eddi. I told her not to tell anyone." Linda pressed her fist against the couch's arm.

A series of rumbles and bumps echoed from the hallway. Rick's muffled holler followed, "Linda!"

"She's fine!" Dave bellowed, never taking his attention from Linda.

"Everything's okay," Linda called.

"I think you should count yourself lucky." Dave walked toward the love seat and sat down. "You have two sisters who care enough about you to agree to pray for you."

"It's my life and my choice." Linda lifted her chin. Dave would have vowed she was closer to fifteen than twenty.

"I can't say I agree with abortion," Dave said, "but I've got enough sense to know I can't stop you…if that's what you really want."

"It is," she defended, yet her lips trembled.

"Is it what *you* want or what Rick has talked you into?" Dave asked.

Linda averted her face and picked at the throw.

"What do *you* really want, Linda?" Dave asked. "Just tell me. I'll even help you find a home for the baby if you'd like to place it for adoption. I've got contacts all over the U.S. I'm sure we could find—"

"No!" Linda riveted her attention on Dave. "If I have it, I'm keeping it. I couldn't stand to release it for adoption."

"But you can bear to end its life?" Dave asked and felt as if he might be winning this battle much easier than he'd anticipated.

"That's different," Linda said. "I won't ever get to see the baby that way. But if I ever saw it—"

"God sees it," Dave said.

She looked down and kneaded the throw. "I know." The words were barely audible.

"So...let's just pretend I really *am* your summer Santa..." Dave said, infusing every word with kindness and hope, "...what would be your very first choice in all this?"

Linda observed Dave as if he were a fairy she'd stopped believing in years ago, and now she'd discovered he really did exist. "Are you saying you'll make it happen?" she asked.

"I'm saying I'll make it happen," Dave affirmed.

"Okay, then." Linda looked into Dave's soul. "If you really think you could make it happen then...what I wanted to do at first was, well," she shrugged, "you know, get married."

"That's exactly what I figured," Dave asserted.

"Rick says that's old-fashioned," Linda said with a sad smile.

Dave stood. "It's called doing the decent thing," he growled. "Back in the good ol' days there was a thing called a shotgun wedding. Ever heard of it?" he asked.

"Uh, no," Jenny said.

"It's where the father of the bride makes sure his daughter's honor is defended when the cad who got her pregnant takes responsibility for what he's done and marries her!" Dave stomped toward the hallway. "In case you're wondering about those two black, beautiful hulks I brought in with me..." he paused at the doorway and turned back toward Linda, "they're my shotguns."

Linda looked at Dave as if he really were her fairy. "You mean you're going to—"

"I'm going to make Rick Wallace do what's right, and I'm going to make sure he treats you like a queen."

"But wh—why?" Linda gasped. "You don't even know me."

"Because I know your sister," Dave said and marched down the short hallway. *And I love your sister,* he added to himself.

Dave paused outside the closed door he assumed was the bathroom. He tapped on the wooden panel. "It's me," he said.

The door opened and Klynell smiled down at him. "We kept him here, just like you said, boss," he said.

"Good." With a villainous grin, Dave entered the cramped bathroom and closed the door.

Larnell towered over Rick who huddled in the corner by the shower stall as if he feared decapitation. *Too bad that's illegal,* Dave thought. He crossed his arms.

"From what I understand, Mr. Wallace," he began in a deceptively calm voice, "you have a child on the way."

"Who told you—"

"Doesn't matter," Dave interrupted. "The thing that matters is that I care." He stepped toward Rick and motioned for the Deadly Duo to move in as well. "I'm tired of watching you refuse to take responsibility for your actions. And," Dave examined his fingernails, "I've decided it's time for you to grow up."

"Listen you!" Rick lunged forward.

Klynell barred him with one beefy arm.

"You have a choice here," Dave said and never blinked. "You can either marry the woman who's carrying your child, stop the marijuana smoking, and start going to church like you promised our grandfather you would, or I'm going to hire a private eye and find out stuff about you you'd rather your police chief didn't know." Dave grabbed Rick's collar and leaned within inches of his face. As he calculated, Rick's breath was laced with alcohol. "Take your choice," he snarled.

Rick looked at Dave as if he were a monster he'd stopped believing in years ago—and now discovered the monster really did exist.

"I…I…" he hedged.

Dave released his shirt.

"I guess we—we *could* get married," Rick stuttered. "It's not like I don't have any feelings for her. It's just that—"

"Now you're talking." Dave stroked the side of Rick's face. "Somehow, I knew you and I would come to an agreement." He backed away. "To make sure you do what you've promised, I've arranged for my friends here…" he slowly appraised the Deadly Duo, "…to keep an eye on you. They'll be sleeping in your living room for a few days. Then they're moving into the apartment across the hall from you."

"But that place isn't empty," Rick argued.

"It will be as of Wednesday." Dave assured. "I offered a financial incentive to the manager and the current tenants for them to move to another apartment in the complex. Congratulations," he cooed, "for the next few years, you won't be able to sneeze without my knowing about it." He patted Rick's face again.

"B–but this is like prison!" Rick croaked.

"Oh no," Dave said, "this is a piece of cake compared to prison. Believe me, Klynell and Larnell are perfect gentlemen… when they want to be."

The twins smiled on cue. Dave reminded himself to reward them with a bonus.

"Guys," he continued, "your first assignment is to go through every drawer and crevice in this apartment. Any drugs you come across—flush them."

Rick released an oath.

"If you find any hard drugs, I want to know about it." Dave jabbed his index finger against his chest.

Rick's face contorted, and a vein bulged in his neck. "I tried to tell you when George died," he hollered, "I don't do hard drugs, and I never have."

"If there's any sign of drug dealing," Dave continued as if Rick had never spoken, "let me know."

"I don't deal drugs!" Rick screamed, his dark eyes emphatic and desperately honest.

For the first time in years, Dave believed him. "Okay," he said.

"Why won't you believe me?" Rick demanded. "I told you when George died I didn't have anything to do with his going off into hard drugs. I've never done anything but smoke some pot— that's it!" Rick lifted his hands. "I did give some pot to George! I'll admit it. There!" He flipped his wrist as if he were tossing information between them. "When he started wanting the harder stuff, I told him he'd have to get it elsewhere. All I ever gave him was marijuana because that's all I've ever done."

"It's still illegal," Dave insisted and felt as if a chunk of ice in the center of his soul was beginning to thaw.

"Do you think I don't know that?" Rick said.

Dave narrowed his right eye as a supposition turned to certainty. "Could you quit if you wanted to?" he asked.

Rick's gaze faltered. "I don't know. I've gone stretches without it before—long enough for my urine to be clean for drug screening tests at work."

"Maybe you need some help quitting altogether then," Dave offered, and for the first time since George's corruption he experienced compassion for Rick Wallace.

"What are you suggesting?" Rick asked.

"There are all sorts of drug rehab programs," Dave said. "If you're addicted to marijuana, I could arrange for you to get involved in a program. My ministry would take care of expenses."

"Why would you do that?" Rick asked.

"Because you're going to be a daddy soon. You need to be straight."

"But what about my job?" Rick asked.

"Nobody on your job needs to know," Dave responded. "We can keep it all as discreet as possible."

Rick produced a barely discernible nod. About the time Dave thought he was going to fully cooperate, he lifted his chin with a little too much cocky assurance to suit Dave.

"I'll think about it," Rick said as if the choice were his.

Dave's fists clenched. Even though he might be working through some of his attitudes toward Rick, that didn't mean the guy had completed any form of metamorphosis. Until he did, Rick still needed to understand he'd never be allowed to con Dave again.

"Put him in the shower, guys," he ordered.

Rick sputtered and struggled against Klynell and Larnell as they stuffed him into the stall. A shampoo bottle toppled off the ledge and rattled to a stop against the fiberglass tub.

"One thing you'll learn about these fellows," Dave said as he leaned into the stall, "is that they don't take 'no' or 'I'll think about it' for an answer. The four of us will get along *sooo* much better if you understand that from the start of this little operation."

Dave hesitated before following the impulse to turn on the cold water. Rick's rebellious glare provided the catalyst for him to act out the urge. "Time to cool off, lover boy," he drawled and then twisted the water knob. Dave slammed the shower door in unison with Rick's howling protest.

Thirty

Eddi stood outside her townhouse, watering her potted plants that hung from an iron holder. Her parents and Jenny were scheduled to arrive in an hour, and Eddi wanted every element of this visit to shine—especially for Jenny. She had invited Calvin over for dinner so he could get better acquainted with her parents.

According to Jenny, she and Calvin had been on the phone every day since he e-mailed her, asking for permission to call. Eddi and he had repeatedly chatted during play practices about the progress of his relationship with Jenny. Given his comments and Jenny's, Eddi was beginning to suspect that Calvin would be her brother-in-law by this time next year.

She moved the water hose to the next hanging fern and waited while the basket filled with water. The smells of soil and running water accompanied the swish and whir of traffic along London's main highway.

Eddi's mind wandered to Dave, as it had been so apt to do the last few days. After their hurried conversation at the altar two weeks ago, he and Eddi had exchanged only the words necessary for the furtherance of the play. Dave had arrived at the last few play practices without so much as a glance her way. When he didn't even inquire about Linda, she convinced herself he was determined not to associate with the likes of her family. She was at last certain that her family issues plus the tongue-lashing to which she subjected him had annihilated all hopes of their ever developing a relationship. From that understanding, Eddi purposed to never give Dave reason to suspect her growing feelings for him. She didn't think she could endure his categorizing her as just another woman who'd chased him.

Her shoulders slumped, and she tugged a dead stem from a hanging ivy. At least there was some light in their lives. God answered their prayers, and Linda decided not to get an abortion. According to the latest, though, Eddi's parents still didn't know about the pregnancy.

Eddi aimlessly gazed around the rows of townhouses. A green sports car pulled into the parking lot a hundred yards away. At first Eddi speculated that the vehicle might be Jenny's Toyota. The last she heard from her parents, they were all driving down together in their minivan. But plans had a way of changing at the last minute.

She squinted against the sun. As the vehicle neared, she deduced that the car was a Mercedes, not a Toyota. The trickling of water announced that the fern pot was overflowing. Eddi moved the hose to a pot of geraniums and continued to observe the vehicle.

Someone in the passenger seat began to wave. At first Eddi politely returned the gesture and assumed the person would soon realize the mistake. When the vehicle whipped into the spot beside Eddi's Mustang, she recognized the person waving.

"Cheri Locaste!" Eddi whispered and the water hose slipped from her hand. Eddi had received a postcard from Cheri last week. The front of the card featured the mountains of Switzerland. A hurried note from Cheri announced her marriage and declared she and Conner were having the time of their lives. Other than that, Eddi hadn't heard a word from Cheri since the week before she and Conner eloped. At last night's practice, Mrs. DeBloom mentioned that Cheri would be back soon. Eddi had wondered then if she and Conner planned to live in London, although the prospect seemed highly unlikely. She couldn't imagine that London, Texas, population 6,352, would ever be sufficient for Conner's elite taste.

Her friend opened the car door and jumped out. "Eddi!" she squealed with more vivacity than Eddi imagined Cheri had ever possessed.

"Cheri!" Eddi returned. She stepped over the running water and hurried forward.

Cheri met her halfway and enveloped her in a warm embrace. The whiff of Chanel No. 5 bespoke Cheri's change in fortune. When Eddi pulled away from her, she realized Cheri also wore a light application of makeup that looked far more refined than the over-the-counter variety. She also sported a wispy haircut that did wonders for her oval face.

"Can you believe it?" Cheri exclaimed. "Conner and I got married!" The groom's car door slammed.

"No, I can't believe it!" Eddi responded and tried to make herself sound far more enthused than she actually was.

Conner stepped to Cheri's side and slid his arm around his bride. "Good to see you, Eddi," he said with an aloof nod.

"It's good to see you, too, Conner," Eddi returned and couldn't miss the resentful glint in his eyes.

"So this is your little home?" he questioned as if he couldn't believe Eddi would turn down his riches to continue in her present status.

"Yes, this is it!" Eddi motioned toward her townhouse and hesitated a second before extending an invitation to enter. At last, she decided that Cheri was still her friend. Even if Conner wasn't her most cherished acquaintance she still wanted to be hospitable. "Would you guys like to come in?"

"Sure," Cheri agreed and moved beside Eddi. "Oh, you should see our home," Cheri oozed. "It sits on a small lake with a vaulted great room and a huge picture window that overlooks the lake. We even have deer."

"Sounds like every woman's dream," Eddi said as she walked toward the water faucet. She bent and twisted the handle to the off position. The water's telltale hiss ceased.

"Absolutely!" Cheri agreed.

"You'll have to come visit us sometime," Conner said as Eddi walked to her front door.

"Of course, I'd love to," Eddi agreed. When she opened her home and stepped inside, the aroma of roasting brisket enveloped them. Roddy pranced from his spot near the window and offered a welcoming yap.

"This is so quaint," Conner said. He tugged on the edge of his collar as Eddi had seen him do a hundred times.

She figured his and Cheri's less-is-more shorts and polo shirts cost as much as half her wardrobe. Eddi glanced down at her simple capri pants and cotton shirt. She started to tell Conner about last year's job offer from a major Boston law firm, but she stopped herself. By now, she could have been making leagues more money than the small town would ever supply her. But she had purposefully chosen a simple life in a town where the new dinner theater was the center of culture. Eddi doubted her affluent cousin would ever understand her lack of interest in the fast lane.

"Oh, Conner!" Cheri exclaimed. "I left my pictures out in my suitcase. I wanted to show Eddi some shots of our honeymoon. Would you go out—"

"Sure, dear," he said and bestowed a kiss on Cheri's forehead.

The second the door closed, Cheri turned to her friend, clasped her hands, and said, "I know you well enough by now, Eddi—you think I shouldn't have married so quickly, don't you?"

"Well..." Eddi hedged.

"It's best for us to just get it all out in the open," Cheri continued with candid certainty.

"Who am I to..." Eddi began and then stopped herself. "Okay, Cheri," she said and toyed with the fringe of her short hair. "You've made your choices, I just hope it all works out. I just hope..." Eddi shook her head. "I hope you don't rock along a few years and meet the man you could have fallen madly in love with. I would die a thousand deaths if I married for convenience and then someone like—like—" *Dave Davidson came along,* she thought. Her heart twisted into a knot of despair, and she restated her comment. "If someone came along who knocked my socks off so much I could never be happy with my husband again because I never loved him in the first place."

"Who's to say I won't fall madly in love with Conner?" Cheri asked, her hazel eyes sure of the possibility.

"Who's to say you will?" Eddi countered and couldn't imagine herself ever falling in love with her cousin.

"Just because Conner isn't your cup of tea, doesn't mean he isn't another woman's," Cheri claimed with pragmatic conviction.

"Of course. I can understand that," Eddi concurred.

"I could have gone my whole life and not had another opportunity like this one." Cheri raised her chin. "The way I see it, I don't have to worry about growing old and being penniless and childless now. Conner has already shown me a richer life experience than I've ever known. My mother says I've done the right thing."

My mother would have said the same thing if I'd married him, Eddi thought and couldn't imagine being the wife of a man who had been chasing another woman mere days before. She wanted to ask Cheri how she could ever trust Conner's vow of loyalty. Roddy scratched at her leg, and Eddi bent to pick him up. She thought of her father and his heart-wrenching honesty about his marriage. In that second Eddi decided she would rather be an old maid before settling for a marriage without earthshaking love.

Eddi shifted Roddy into the crook of her left arm and gripped her friend's hand. "Cheri, we all have these choices to make in life. I want you to know that even though I wouldn't have made your choice, I will always respect your decision. Besides all that," she paused for a spontaneous hug, "we're third cousins now."

With delightful glee, Cheri clung to Eddi and graced her with another whiff of expensive perfume. "I know. Isn't it great? Once I move to Houston with Conner, I'll have you over, okay?"

"Sure," Eddi said. "So, you're going to stay here awhile then?"

"Yes. I've talked to the school, and they've asked me to stay until Christmas break. I'm actually contracted through the whole school year. They're graciously releasing me six months early. Conner and I will take turns commuting on the weekend. And this way, I get to finish my part in the play."

Soon, Conner stepped back into the house with the honey-moon photos in hand. While Eddi and Cheri settled onto the couch and enjoyed a fulfilling conversation about Switzerland, Conner strolled around the modest living room. Eddi figured the man was taking inventory of all her inferior furnishings so he could make a point of mentioning them later to his wife. On a testy urge, she almost told him her couch came from the "nearly new" shop next to her law office. Finally, she decided that might be a little too spiteful for the well-being of future relationships.

The only comment Conner made involved his satisfaction that Eddi had never been to Switzerland. She didn't tell him that she'd spent time in England as an intern or that she'd lived in the Amazon jungle six weeks or that she'd been to Cambodia,

Romania, and Mexico on mission trips. Instead, Eddi endured Conner's remarks with a grace Jenny would have applauded.

Within an hour, Eddi's patience was rewarded. Cheri ended the visit with vows of sisterly devotion before speeding away in Conner's Mercedes. As Eddi stood in her doorway and watched them leave, she could only hope that her friend didn't one day call, lamenting her rash choice.

She was about to close her front door when she caught sight of her parents' van turning into the townhouse parking lot. Eddi hurried onto her sidewalk and waved with as much gusto as Cheri had upon her first arrival. Only when her father had parked the van did Eddi notice the blue Chevrolet truck pulling into the place beside her parents' van. Her full attention riveted upon Dave Davidson in the driver's seat while her family clambered from the minivan.

Only when Linda hurried in front of her, squealing, "Dave, whatever are *you* doing here?" did Eddi realize her younger sister had joined her parents for the visit.

Calvin stepped from the truck's passenger side and said, "Thanks for the ride, Dave," before slamming the door. He looked at Eddi. "My Jeep's in the shop," he explained. "Dave offered to give me a lift, and I took him up on it. Do you mind giving me a ride home tonight?"

"No, not in the least," Eddi answered, but her focus remained upon Dave, who slid from the truck to welcome her younger sibling.

Thirty-One

Linda flung her arms around Dave's neck, and he returned the gesture as if she were his own little sister. To her left, Mr. Boswick's polite greeting mingled with Eddi's mother's giddy exclamation over meeting Calvin again. Eddi moved near their circle to give the appearance of being a part of their conversation. But, she tuned them out and strained to detect every nuance of Dave and Linda's exchange.

"I hear everything is going well with you," Dave said.

"Yes! Oh, yes, it is!" Linda giggled and held up her left hand. "We're married now." She wiggled her fingers, and Eddi caught sight of a modest diamond twinkling in the evening sun. "We kept it a secret until we tied the knot yesterday. I didn't even tell my parents until this morning."

Eddi gasped. Nobody had informed her of Linda's marriage.

"Great!" Dave said enthusiastically and acted as if the news were really no news at all.

"That wonderful minister you suggested married us in his home, just like you said. It was perfect," she continued with rapture.

"Is Rick here, then?" Dave glanced toward the van.

"No, not this time." Linda shook her head. "He had to work a double shift this weekend, and I decided I needed to get away."

"So, how is everything with…" Dave glanced up as if he sensed Eddi's scrutiny, "…with your new neighbors?" he continued but remained focused upon Eddi.

Eddi's insides warmed past the comfort zone, and she eyed her red toenails ensconced in her open-toed sandals. She slipped her hands into her capri pants pockets and feigned nonchalance. Nonetheless, she labored to detect every word of Linda and Dave's conversation.

"You mean Larnell and Klynell?" Linda asked.

Who? Eddi thought.

"Yes," Dave answered.

"Those two are absolute jewels!" Linda exclaimed, and Eddi sneaked another peek toward the conversation. "They are so helpful and so respectful and so full of kindness. I'm just so thrilled you arranged for them to help us." Her head bobbed with every word, her reddish-blonde ringlets jostling with every move.

"I'm sure Rick couldn't agree more." Dave's calculating undertone only heightened Eddi's curiosity.

"Are you going to stay and join us for dinner? Please say you will!" Linda tugged on Dave's hand.

"No, no, I'm sorry. I can't. I promised I'd have dinner with my Aunt Maddy." Again Dave looked at Eddi, who at once became aware that her family and Calvin were no longer nearby. She picked up the echo of her mom's voice and the word "bathroom" from near her front door. Eddi stood alone by the van, a prime spectacle of the nosy elder sister. She debated half a dozen ways to retract herself from the awkward situation—all of which included running into her townhouse.

"How are you, Eddi?" Dave asked.

"Fine," she responded and was proud of how cool her voice sounded. "And you?" she asked, her heart beating for even a hint of softness in his eyes.

"Okay," he said as if her interest were of little consequence to him. He'd acted much the same during the last several practices.

And how did you get to be so cozy with Linda? Eddi wanted to ask but didn't. She suddenly suspected that there was much more to Linda's not getting an abortion and marrying Rick than she'd ever imagined.

"You are welcome to stay if you like," Eddi offered, but her words sounded more stilted than genuine.

"No, that's okay." Dave averted his eyes. "Aunt Maddy is waiting."

"Sure, I understand." After an awkward silence, Eddi pointed toward her home. "Well, I guess I'll, I'll, just, uh, go on inside with the rest of the family," she muttered and sauntered into her townhouse. Before closing the door, Eddi spied Linda in animated conversation with Dave. The smell of roasting brisket reminded her she needed to check on the evening's entree. Instead, she moved to the narrow window beside the door and tugged aside the curtain.

"Interesting, isn't it?" Jenny's whisper sent a jolt though Eddi, and she jumped.

"You scared me," she said and turned to her sister.

"If you haven't figure it out," Jenny continued, "there's a lot you don't know."

"No joke." Eddi placed her hands on her hips. "Why am I always the last one to find out?" she asked.

Jenny glanced over her shoulder. Eddi noted her father, amiably chatting with Calvin near the television. She assumed her mom had found the restroom.

"Let's sneak upstairs for a minute." Jenny jerked her head toward the spiral stairway.

"Let's do," Eddi agreed and led the way to her bedroom.

As soon as Jenny walked into the room, Eddi closed the door and passed her brass bed. The window facing the parking lot was her targeted destination. She inserted her index finger between the blinds and separated them enough for a peephole. Sure enough, Linda and Dave were still locked in conversation. Eddi's assumption that Dave detested her family began to waver.

"What is going on?" Eddi asked.

"You want the long version or the short?" Jenny asked.

"You know me, give me the long," she said over her shoulder.

"It would appear that the reason Linda didn't get an abortion was a direct result of Dave's intervention," Jenny began.

Eddi knitted her brows, turned from the window, and listened as her sister detailed the facts. When she finished, Jenny said, "All Dad and Mom know is that Linda is married and is expecting and that Dave helped her make arrangements because he's Rick's cousin. They don't know the extent to which Dave was involved. And, well, when Linda called last night she asked me not to tell them."

"Or me either, for that matter. Am I right?" Eddi quizzed.

"Right." Jenny slumped onto Eddi's bed, her head tilted like a weighted iris. "I don't know why I can't keep secrets from you," she complained and pinched at the pleat in her linen slacks. "I feel like such a snitch right now."

Eddi lowered herself beside her sister. "If it's any consolation, I'm grateful that you're such a big snitch."

"Thanks a lot," Jenny said with a sarcastic twist to her lips. "You really know how to encourage me, don't you?"

Staring at the plush carpet, Eddi considered the implications of everything Dave had orchestrated. "I just hope it all works out for Linda. I mean, Rick isn't the most reliable person. I hope he doesn't abuse her, or—"

"All we can do is keep praying for God to work a miracle, Eddi. Rick might surprise us. We just never know."

"Right," Eddi said, "Linda got married yesterday and today she's coming here for the weekend. What is wrong with this picture?" Eddi placed her finger on her chin and lifted her gaze to the ceiling.

"They've been living together for weeks," Jenny said. "They've already been to Hawaii together, too. It's like they had their honeymoon and now they're getting married."

"You're such an eternal optimist." Eddi smiled at her sister and then sobered. "I guess if he winds up abandoning her and the baby, at least I can nail him on child support for her."

"Sounds like you've got all the worst bases covered, as usual," Jenny said.

Eddi flopped back and stared at the ceiling. "I guess it goes with my territory, Jenny," she admitted. "I see so much that I've learned to at least prepare for the worst."

"But there are times when the best happens," Jenny encouraged, her blue eyes as positive as always.

"I guess you're right," Eddi said. She sat up, pulled a pillow from near her headboard, gathered it to her chest, and rested her chin on the soft folds. "Remember in Dave's e-mail he said he wanted to make Rick take responsibility for his actions?" Eddi asked.

"Yes, I do."

"I guess he's finally done it."

"Do you think that's the only reason he did this?" Jenny asked.

"Why else?"

"Beats me." Jenny's eyes indicated another motive that involved Eddi.

"Don't even go there," Eddi challenged. Nevertheless, she wondered if when Dave left her crying at the altar he'd gone straight to Houston. "I don't ever expect anything to come of Dave and me. While I might be in—" Eddi stopped herself and looked past Jenny, toward the oak armoire. She'd been about to admit what she had barely acknowledged to herself.

"You might be in what?" Jenny prodded while a grin overtook her features.

"I was just going to say that if Dave had any feelings for me when he asked for us to get to know each other better, I think he's fully recovered. The man acts like he doesn't care whether he ever sees me again."

"That's not what you started out saying," Jenny said.

"Okay, then," Eddi blurted. "I'm in love with him. There! Are you happy now?"

Eddi tossed the pillow at her sister.

"I knew it!" Jenny crowed in a singsong voice that echoed childhood laughter.

"You're such a glory hog," Eddi teased but soon sobered. She moved toward her dresser and toyed with a silver-plated hair brush she never used. "I've come to the conclusion that I…I was wrong about Dave." She avoided looking at herself in the dresser mirror. Admitting she was wrong went against every grain of her professional training. "He isn't a jerk after all, is he?"

"No joke," Jenny said. "I never really agreed with you on that one anyway. I think this whole thing with Linda proves that."

"Yes, and he's developing a ministry to help people get off drugs." Eddi raised her gaze to the mirror's lower half and examined the reflection of her bed's patchwork comforter.

"I guess it's time for me to tell my secret now," Jenny admitted. "I knew you had a thing for him the first time we saw his house. That's why I was laughing," she claimed. "I could see it written all over your face, but you wouldn't dare admit it."

"Well…" Eddi walked back to the bed. She sat beside her sister and rested her weight on her elbow. "He said all those horrible things about me and made me mad."

"But I don't think for one minute he meant a word of it."

"That's what he said when he sort of proposed—or whatever you want to call what happened in his ministry building."

"Eddi, if you want the absolute truth from me, I still can't believe you turned him down flat," Jenny said. "I know you were mad about what happened with Calvin and me and all that business about those lies Rick Wallace told you, but still, William Fitzgerald Davidson—one of the most eligible bachelors in America—asked you to possibly marry him and you didn't even consider it." Jenny rested her hand on her short hair and scrubbed her fingers through her bangs.

"I know, I know," Eddi relented. "It all seems so ridiculous now. The way I feel tonight," she sighed, "I can't believe I turned him down either."

"Jenny?" Calvin's muffled call floated from the hallway.

"Ooo, that's Calvin." Jenny stood. "I guess I need to get to him."

"Sure thing. By all means, don't keep him waiting," Eddi teased.

"Believe me, I won't," Jenny said over her shoulder.

Eddi rose to her feet. "The brisket needs to be taken from the oven anyway." As Jenny stepped into the hallway, Eddi moved toward the window and parted the blinds with her fingertips. Dave's truck cruised across the parking lot toward the exit. Wishing she were in the vehicle with him, Eddi began to pray for one of Jenny's miracles…for a second chance with Dave Davidson.

Dave steered from the parking lot and kept sight of his rearview mirror. He longed for Eddi to run out of her home and call him back. He was only rewarded by the sight of a pair of striped felines trotting across her yard.

He propped his elbow on the door's ledge and pinched his bottom lip. *I should go back,* he thought. *This is crazy. I'm keeping my distance, waiting on her to make a move. She's making no moves. What if she never does?*

"Do I stay walled up like this for the rest of my life?" he questioned. "I could grow old, get gray, and die without ever getting married at this rate!"

He pressed the brake and decided to go back and tell Eddi exactly how he felt. *But remember the last time you tried that?* he reminded himself. *She slashed you to strips with her tongue.*

Dave contemplated the nuance of her every expression tonight. Not once had she observed him with anything more than detached interest when he was talking to Linda. Even during recent play practices, Eddi had restrained from the "come closer" look she'd offered at church that Sunday morning he had followed her to the altar. Dave finally concluded that since Eddi had been so cold after that day, she really hadn't wanted him to talk to her at the altar. So she was taking every measure not to encourage him toward more conversation.

Dave winced and pressed the accelerator. The engine revved. The truck rolled forward. He couldn't take the chance—not tonight. The stakes were still too high; his heart was still too sore. His aching pride was no more ready to risk her rejection today than it had been two weeks ago.

Thirty-Two

The night of the first performance finally arrived. The cast huddled backstage and discreetly watched as the room gradually filled with guests. Mrs. DeBloom had space to seat 104 people. According to her report, the first night was sold out. So were the next three weekends.

The smells of catered roast beef and peach candles trailed Eddi as she lifted her skirt and took the back stairway leading to the second floor. She desperately needed some quiet time to calm her nerves. Playing the leading lady was proving more stressful than she'd ever imagined—especially with a county full of people clamoring for a brilliant performance. The *London Times* had raved about everything from the cast to the costumes to the dinner theater until the whole community buzzed with expectation. Sean O'Reilly, his wife, and daughter were even on the guest list for this evening; and so were Eddi's family and London's mayor.

"No pressure here, right?" Eddi mumbled as she entered the large hallway onto which all the bedrooms and library opened.

The ceiling towered nine feet overhead and featured a relief design painted in shades of cream.

Eddi squinted against the chandelier decorated in crystal droplets and eyed the ceiling's artwork. The sounds of tinkling silverware, the front door opening and closing, and the faint hum of voices diminished as Eddi discovered the solace needed to gain her composure.

She adjusted the demure English bonnet tied under her chin and admired the princess design of her costume—created blue-gray, exactly as she had requested. Since her dress covered her shoes she had been able to purchase a pair of flats that went with the dress at the local department store. She was thankful they were as comfortable as the costume.

Eddi slowed her pace and gazed up at the long row of portraits gracing the hallway wall. The best she could guess by the fashions, some of the portraits dated back a couple hundred years. A recurring family resemblance reminded her of the life-sized portrait downstairs—the dark hair and eyes, the stern face, angular and tawny, the mysterious smile that hinted of both good humor and intelligence. From there, her mind drifted to the man who resembled so many of the men in the portraits.

She had watched for Dave ever since she arrived half an hour ago. So far, she hadn't spotted him. Although he hadn't said much at last night's dress rehearsal, Eddi detected a change in him. She couldn't define the reason, but she sensed that Dave had made a decision he didn't plan to negate. Until the closing lines of the play, she had hoped the decision might involve her. Then, Dave's cell phone rang and he abruptly dismissed himself. Eddi assumed he was heading for the building behind his house.

After weeks of embarrassed silence, Eddi finally came to the conclusion that she must thank him for intervening on her sister's behalf. She loathed giving the man any reason to suspect she was pining for his affection or chasing him. Nevertheless,

Eddi concluded a mere thank-you wouldn't indicate her love. She simply could not open herself to his potential scorn.

With a sigh, she wandered toward the library. Double sliding doors eight-feet tall afforded passage to the room about which so many of the cast had raved. Eddie pushed against the handles. The panels grudgingly parted with a coarse groan. When she stepped through, the smell of leather and old paper hung in the air. Eddi closed the doors and absorbed the room's ambiance. Four broad windows filled with amber glass reached from floor to ceiling and produced an odd, golden glow. The sun wouldn't be setting for an hour. Its amber rays, heightened by the colored glass, mellowed the richness of the mahogany bookcases lining the walls.

Eddie circled the room and didn't bother to penetrate the aisles of bookcases. Nevertheless, her attention rested on titles from Plato to photography. Many were old and worn. Some looked new. A plain writing desk done in oak had been placed between an eighteenth-century piano and a large globe in a metal frame. Imagining herself as a classical author, she pulled out the chair and sat down. Eddi posed as if she were about to pen a brilliant line that would reverberate through the ages.

She reached for the plumed pen resting near a dry ink well at the back edge. The instrument warmed in her palm. As she held it, lines of poetry from Shakespeare and Bradstreet and Frost coursed through her mind. All vestiges of tension drained from her body, and Eddi no longer felt the need to rehearse her lines. The fear of forgetting them evaporated.

Eddi relaxed and gazed upward at one of several portraits hanging around the library. After scrutinizing the ones in the hallway, Eddi paid little attention to the paintings in the library. But this portrait spoke to her as none other; for it was of the man she'd grown to love. She held her breath and felt as if the keen brown eyes were peering into her very soul. Dave, dressed in the finest of business suits, stood with his arm on a rest, his mouth lifted in an intriguing smile that suggested he wouldn't dare reveal his secret.

Her pulse responded to the image just as it did to the man. Earlier in the summer, Eddi couldn't wait until the play was over so she could distance herself from Dave. Now, with only a mere six weeks of performances, she wondered how she would live without interacting with him.

The library's door slid open and broke her reverie. Eddi jumped. She pivoted toward the doorway and encountered the gentleman whose portrait she'd been absorbing.

"Dave!" she blurted.

He looked at Eddi as if she were the last person he expected to see. "Eddi!" he exclaimed.

"What are you doing here?" the two said together.

Eddi laughed, and Dave followed suit. "I came up here to escape, actually," she said.

"Me, too." Dave stepped into the room, closed the door, and watched Eddi as if he were gauging her level of acceptance.

A voice within encouraged Eddi to graciously welcome Dave into her quiet time. She decided that as long as his behavior suggested no hint of scorn she would set aside her reserve, if only for a few minutes. Once again, she darted a heavenward plea for the miracle of another chance with this remarkable man.

"I told Aunt Maddy I was going upstairs, and I'd be back five minutes before curtain time," he explained and moved toward her. "I made the mistake of walking through the audience on my way backstage. Believe it or not, a teenager stopped me for my autograph. Before it was over, we'll just say I had a small group of admirers." His smile held a hint of shyness Eddi had never noticed.

I can imagine you did, she thought. His hair was long again, and he had brushed it back in the style characteristic of the early nineteenth century. The waves hung just below the collar of his black suit, whose coat touched his knees. During the last two weeks Dave had grown short sideburns. He appeared to be every bit an English gentleman from ages past.

"You're certainly looking your part, Mizz Boswick," Dave claimed as he stepped closer, pausing when he was six feet away.

"And you, dear sir." Eddi mimicked a British accent, bowed her head, and curtsied.

"Would that those were our only lines," he grumbled and hung his head.

"Humph. I can't believe *you're* worried about your part!" Eddi said. "You had your lines virtually memorized after our first practice, didn't you?"

"Well," he hedged, "I guess I was close. I'm just hoping my part doesn't escape me the minute the curtains go up. I've never done anything like this before, you know." His inviting smile suggested he had no intent but to charm.

"And you're doing a remarkable job." Eddi ran her fingertips atop the writing desk and decided now was as good a time as any to thank him for his intervention with Linda.

"And it would appear you've likewise done a wonderful job with Linda and Rick," she added.

Dave lowered his gaze for a second and then observed her. The amber sunshine intensified the sparkle in his dark eyes…eyes that bespoke a man who had endured hardship but refused to be defeated, a man whose intelligence ran as deeply as his feelings.

"So my secret is out," he admitted.

"Yes. Jenny told me the night you dropped Calvin off at my place. You should know you can't keep anything a secret around the Boswicks."

"Let me guess," Dave placed his fingers near his temple. "Linda broke her promise to me not to tell and told Jenny anyway. But Linda made Jenny promise not to tell. She, in turn, made you promise not to tell."

Eddi rocked back on her heels and smiled. "Something like that," she admitted, "except Jenny wound up telling my parents as well. We know about everything, by the way, the summer Santa business and the whole nine yards. Some things have to be shared."

"Ah, the summer Santa." Dave inserted his hand into his jacket pocket and gazed toward the window. "I thought that was kind of clever, even if I have to say so myself."

And really appealing, Eddi thought. She didn't mention she would relish his being her Santa any season he chose. Then, she imagined Dave in a Santa suit, white beard, and snowy eyebrows. A giggle tottered out.

"Now you're laughing at me," Dave accused with a lazy drawl.

"No, honestly." Eddi shook her head. "It's not you. It's not even the red suit—just the white beard and eyebrows you'd have to wear."

Dave joined her laughter.

"All I can hope," Eddi said, "is that Rick honors his vows and treats Linda right. I'd hate to think she married him only to have him abandon her or—"

"I think he'll do fine," Dave assured. "I've got a couple of guys on it."

"Ah, yes," Eddi said. "That would be Larnell and Klynell Howell."

Dave nodded. "They're making sure he even goes to church. It's not that I have so much faith in *him,*" Dave admitted. "But I *do* have faith in the power of God and the influence of godly people." He extended his arms. "Hey, it worked with me! I could have been every bit as bad as Rick, but for God's grace."

Eddi thought of that picture of Laura Schock. She started to ask him about the woman but stopped herself. If Dave and she ever got close, she was certain he would answer any questions she might pose.

As Dave's gaze lazed across her features and settled upon her lips, Eddi leaned against the desk.

"We really need to talk," Dave began. "I…I'm afraid we got off on the wrong foot earlier this summer." He offered a guilt-ridden smile. "I said some things about you and to you that I've wished a million times I could take back. And the way I acted in the dugout at the picnic…" he shook his head, "…it was uncalled for."

Eddi's knees began to quiver. "I guess I should say the same thing," she admitted. "I can think of a few times I was less than, well, kind." Her pulse thudded at her throat, and Eddi could only pray this was leading up to her miracle.

Dave walked forward and reached for her hand. Never breaking eye contact, he lifted her hand to his mouth, pressed his lips against her skin, and closed his eyes as if in rapture. "Mmm, you smell *so good,*" he murmured against her knuckles.

Consumed by a delicious shiver, Eddi swallowed and fought against collapsing.

Dave lowered her hand and rubbed her palm with his thumb. "Eddi, I've got a confession to make…" he started.

"Oh?" she whispered as her lids drooped.

"Yes. When I got backstage, I asked Calvin if he'd seen you. He said he saw you heading upstairs, so I followed you up."

"You did?"

"Yes. I did. It took me a few minutes to figure out which room you were in, but I did find you."

"Yes…yes, you found me," Eddi babbled.

"I wanted to tell you I haven't said anything much to you these past few weeks because I've been afraid."

"Afraid?"

His lips wobbled with a hint of vulnerability. "Yes. I didn't want to set myself up for another rejection." He searched her eyes, begging for some sign that would destroy every scrap of apprehension.

Eddi allowed the veil to drop from her heart and silently revealed her undying love.

"But finally," Dave continued with more confidence, "I came to the conclusion that we weren't getting anywhere like that. I decided before last night's practice that I was going to put myself out of my misery and tell you how I really feel. If you wouldn't have me, then so let it be. Then," he shook his head, "wouldn't you know it? I got a call and was tied up until after midnight."

"One of the kids you're trying to help?" Eddi prompted.

"Yes." He lowered his gaze.

The last scraps of Eddi's reservations melted. She no longer worried about whether or not Dave would think she was chasing him. All that mattered was that they finally spoke their hearts.

"I guess I should tell you that I was afraid, too," she admitted.

"You were?"

"Yes. I haven't really communicated with you since that night in your little building because I...I convinced myself that I didn't want you to think I was chasing you."

Dave chuckled. "If ever I wanted a woman chasing me, it was you, counselor. I guess I've had so many women, well," he cleared his throat, "to put it bluntly, so many women throw themselves at me because of my money I just expected you to do the same. The minute I felt the sparks fly, I went into my repelling mode. When you didn't come after me, I was shocked. I finally figured out you didn't give one flip about my money."

Shaking his head, he shifted away from her. "It really dealt my ego some grief when I realized you didn't give a hoot about me, either." His final words held a hint of uncertainty.

Eddi's focus lowered to the gentleman's scarf under his shirt collar. "Well, I didn't care about your money anyway," she admitted and dared make eye contact again.

His gaze warmed. "But you still made me eat my own conceit."

"I, I…" Eddi looked down. "You aren't the only one who ate conceit. I was so sure I could trust my first impressions. I was so wrong and so judgmental."

"Well, don't feel like the Lone Ranger," Dave comforted. "The last few weeks, I've repented of my arrogance a hundred times."

"Sounds like we've kept God busy between the two of us."

Dave stroked the side of her face, and Eddi leaned into his touch.

"I woke up one day and realized I'd give everything I owned for you to chase me—and you were the one woman determined not to. Oh, Eddi…" he breathed.

"You once told me not to get my hopes up about a relationship between us," she whispered. "Even then, I was hoping."

"Hope all you want," Dave encouraged, "because I want to fulfill all your hopes and then some."

His warm hand slid to the base of her neck as his attention again settled upon her lips. Eddi lifted her chin and closed her eyes, fully expecting a kiss that would tilt the library.

Thirty-Three

❧ ❧

The library doors scraped open. Eddi and Dave jumped back as if they were teenagers caught in a secret tryst. Mrs. DeBloom invaded the room. She peered over the top of her steel-rimmed glasses, and the pearl chain swung wildly on either side of her face as if she had been leading a frantic race.

"What are you two thinking?" she exclaimed as if they were preschool escapees. "The curtain is supposed to go up in two minutes!"

The words hurled Eddi and Dave into action. Eddi lifted her skirt to her knees and ran toward the hallway with Dave in her wake. By the time she took the stairs two at a time and claimed her position on stage, she barely remembered the harried trip from the library. Mrs. DeBloom, as stern-faced as ever, hadn't uttered a word of rebuke or praise upon Eddi. But she could only imagine the lady's disapproval at finding her prized nephew in the company of the very woman she didn't want him to marry.

Act by act, scene by scene the play unfolded into the work of art the cast had anticipated. Eddi, committed to a professional performance, spoke her designated lines with Dave in such a manner that no one would have guessed the two had been involved in a library rendezvous minutes before the curtain rose. By the time they neared the end of the famous dance line, Eddi recalled the evening Dave twirled her across stage in a waltz that left her reeling.

The second Dave spoke his final words from that scene, he bestowed a discreet wink upon Eddi and whispered, "Meet me in the library later. We can finish our waltz there."

Eddi, swept along by the play's choreography, moved away from Dave. Although she never answered him verbally, her heart answered without hesitation. Eddi possessed no doubt that Dave held full intentions of reissuing his offer of potential matrimony. This time, Eddi longed for the opportunity to better acquaint herself with the man who had stolen her heart.

By the final scene, her exhaustion was overcome with a giddy high. The cast had miraculously enthralled the audience. After every scene, the crowd clapped and cheered so profusely that Eddi was certain a Broadway scout would soon whisk them all to full-blown acting careers. Even Carissa Barclay, as undedicated as she had been to the play, shone as Jane Bennet, Elizabeth's supporting character.

At last, the play's closing scene was upon them. Carissa and Calvin, posing as Jane and Bingley, had announced their engagement and were strolling through the countryside with Eddi lagging behind just as she perceived Elizabeth would have done. Her hands clasped behind her, Eddi walked alone and appeared to be in deep thought, although her every fiber was honed into the audience. She strode in front of the lush greenery that had transformed the stage into a grand outdoor set.

Soon Eddi was on stage alone. On cue, she paused near a Styrofoam boulder that appeared to be hard as granite. Out of the corner of her eye, Eddi glimpsed the cast, back stage right, as enraptured with the scene as the audience. She saw no signs of Dave for he was backstage left. Mrs. DeBloom had written a section of script that involved Eddi speaking Elizabeth Bennet's thoughts. Eddi knew the exact syllable when Dave would enter the set. She now anticipated his arrival with as much excitement as Elizabeth might anticipate Darcy's.

"'All afternoon I have watched Darcy,'" she mused aloud. "'When he walked away to another part of the room, I followed him with my eyes. I envied everyone to whom he spoke and scarcely had patience enough to help anyone with coffee.'" She moved in front of the boulder and settled upon a bench disguised as a pile of rocks.

Eddi looked up, as if gazing at the sky, and continued her monologue. "'A man who has once been refused! How could I ever be foolish enough to expect a renewal of his love?'" She fretted with her bonnet's tie. "'Is there one among the sex who would not protest against such a weakness as a second proposal to the same woman? There is no indignity so abhorrent to their feelings!'"

She sensed Dave's presence as he entered from stage right. The faint tap of his shoes upon the wooden floor announced his nearing. Eddi turned toward him. As if surprised, she stood and laid her hand over her heart.

"'Mr. Darcy,'" she said, purposefully infusing her words with breathless amazement, "'you gave me a fright.'"

"'Miss Bennet.'" Dave stopped within two feet of her and bowed with all the reverence of a nineteenth-century romantic. "'Your mother told me you had joined Bingley and Jane for a stroll.'"

"'Yes, yes, I did,'" Eddi answered.

"'I hope I have not ended your necessary reverie with my presence,'" Dave continued.

Eddi held his gaze and could barely speak her lines for the memory of his lips on the back of her hand two hours before. "'No, I assure you, dear sir. You have not.'" Eddi began the slow stroll back in the direction she had come. Dave fell in beside her.

"'I have spent most of my day reflecting upon a matter of utmost importance,'" Eddi said.

"'Oh?'" Dave asked. "'Does the lady care to share her thoughts?'"

Eddi stopped in front of the thickest silk tree, her dress whispering with every move. "'Mr. Darcy, I am a very selfish creature; and for the sake of giving relief to my own feelings, care not how much I may be wounding yours. I can no longer help thanking you for your unexampled kindness to my poor sister. Ever since I have known it, I have been most anxious to acknowledge to you how gratefully I feel it. Were it known to the rest of the family I should not have merely my own gratitude to express.'"

"'If you *will* thank me,'" he replied, "'let it be for yourself alone.'" Eddi was nearly overtaken with the finesse and grace that Dave portrayed in his black suit and hat. "'That the wish of giving happiness to you might add force to the other induce-ments which led me on, I shall not attempt to deny. But your *family* owe me nothing. Much as I respect them, I believe I thought only of *you.*'"

Eddi looked down and feigned embarrassment exactly as Mrs. DeBloom had dictated.

"'You are too generous to trifle with me.'" Dave touched her arm, gazed directly into her eyes, and posed his question as if he wanted Eddi's—not Elizabeth's—answer. "'If your feelings are still what they were last April, tell me so at once. My affections and wishes are unchanged; but one word from you will silence me on this subject forever.'"

Again, Eddi moved toward the boulder. Keeping her back to Dave, she looked over the audience and enunciated every word with the earnestness of a woman in love. "'My sentiments have undergone so material a change since the period to which you alluded, as to make me receive with gratitude and pleasure your present assurances.'" The lines held a conviction that Eddi had transcended her role.

Dave neared and rested his hands on her shoulders. Eddi tensed. That move had never been a part of any practice. She stole a glance backstage to see Mrs. DeBloom standing at the curtain's edge, her eyes bugged, her reading glasses shoved atop her head. Some of the cast huddled behind her, as if expecting the play to take an unexpected turn.

"'When my aunt told me you refused to deny our engagement, it taught me to hope as I had scarcely ever allowed myself to hope before. I knew enough of your disposition to be certain, that had you been absolutely, irrevocably decided against me, you would have acknowledged it frankly and openly.'"

Eddi turned toward Dave. He gripped her hands and caressed her palms with his thumbs. She had no idea what gesture was planned for the coming lines. Dave had altered the whole scheme of things. Eddi stood captured by his nearness and babbled forth the lines engraved upon her memory.

"'Yes, you know enough of my frankness to believe me capable of that. After abusing you so abominably to your face, I could have no scruple in abusing you to all your relations.'"

"'My dearest Elizabeth,'" Dave continued, the stage lights reflecting the ardor of his inky eyes, "'what did you say of me that I did not deserve? For, though your accusations were ill-founded, formed on mistaken premises, my behavior to you at the time had merited the severest reproof. It was impardonable. I cannot think of it without abhorrence.'

"The only thing that brings me relief," Dave continued with a mischievous turn of his lips, "'is your present willingness to be my wife. Have I mistaken your affections in any form?'"

"That's not in the script!" Eddi hissed out of the corner of her mouth.

"Now it is," Dave whispered. His eyes danced as she floundered for the appropriate line. Never taking his gaze from Eddi, he slowly lifted her hand to his lips and repeated the kiss from the library. Once again, Eddi was engulfed in a tide of tingles that heightened her bafflement.

"What's he doing?" Mrs. DeBloom's aghast question from stage left barely brushed Eddi's ears.

"I think he's proposing—*for real,*" Calvin's whisper floated from stage right.

As the realization penetrated Eddi, she sensed the audience's tension…as if they suspected something was amiss but had yet to decipher the clues.

"Must you keep me in suspense another minute before answering my appeal?" Dave prompted, and Eddi marveled at his ability to produce language so fitted to the play yet so spontaneous.

"Mr. Darcy, you have taken me by such surprise." She laid her hand on her chest and her heart thudded against her palm.

"And you, my dear, have captured my heart," he breathed and wrapped his arms around her. "Please assure me you will be my wife." Dave bestowed a kiss on her forehead and pulled her closer.

"Ah, Eddi," he breathed into her ear. "I can't stop. I love you. I don't know when it happened or how it happened. But there it is. I love you. I'm not suggesting we get married next week, but can't we give us a try?"

Eddi closed her eyes and drank in his nearness. Her hand inched across the front of his suit. His heart hammered as wildly as her own. She moved back and slid her fingers into the hair at his neck. The waves proved as soft and inviting as Eddi imagined they ever would. She leaned closer and begged to be kissed.

"I have been certain of my sentiments for you for so long, Mr. Darcy," she said, "that I dare not keep you in suspense a moment more. Presently, I must assure you that I dream of nothing more than our eventual matrimonial felicity."

When the last syllable left her mouth, Dave pressed his lips against hers.

The audience erupted into applause. As Eddi clung to her hero, a series of wolf whistles floated from backstage. She assumed the matchmaking cast was gratified at last.

When Dave released her, the whole stage felt as if it were spinning. A script fluttered from behind the curtain, and Eddi caught sight of Mrs. DeBloom's rigid back as she retreated from the curtain's edge. A light flashed from the front row, and Eddi caught sight of the *London Times* editor behind the camera. She could only imagine the society page's next headline.

Epilogue

One year later, Eddi stood in front of a full-length mirror and fretted over the short veil atop her head. "It's crooked!" she snapped and tugged at the ecru-colored mesh with shaking fingers.

"Here, let me help." Jenny moved to her side just as their mom and Linda stepped into the bedroom—one of six in Dave's sprawling home. The poster bed was piled with the clothing Eddi, her sisters, and mother had changed out of. The mother of the bride and Eddi's sisters were all dressed in satin the color of sage. The muted color complemented Eddi's tea-length bridal gown and created an appealing fashion scheme for a wedding that had been the talk of the summer.

"I promise, I am a nervous wreck," Mary worried.

A harpist's mellifluous notes floated from downstairs as Linda swung the door closed.

Mary perched on the edge of a settee covered in striped polished cotton. "I've never seen so much finger food in my whole life!" Her fingers twittered with nothing as she rocked back and forth. "And the caterers are refusing to change the groom's cake to German chocolate. We had German chocolate at Jenny's wedding. Has spring been so long gone that they forgot our preferences?"

"Calm down, Mom," Linda said as she jostled her baby, a rosy-cheeked, four-month-old girl who looked exactly like her mother, except for Rick's brown eyes.

"Dave requested milk chocolate frosting because he hates coconut," Jenny explained for the sixth time.

Eddi tugged a strip of bangs back into place as Jenny removed the veil's comb and reinserted it into her hair.

"Whoever heard of a groom who doesn't like coconut?" Mary stood. She paced to the end of the cherry-wood bed, toward the matching dresser, and back again. "If it weren't for the fact that Dave somehow got those stingy Boswicks to sell us our house, and everything he did for Linda, and that national ministry he has, I would say he was too odd for you to marry, Eddi!" She paused behind her daughter and peered around her into the mirror.

The bride focused on her veil and tried not to let her mother's nerves get on *her* nerves. Mary Boswick had yet to completely recover from her first impression of Dave.

"Oh, I almost can't stand this!" Mary exclaimed. "My third daughter to get married in a year! It's too much for my poor nerves."

"There!" Jenny said as she put the final touch to Eddi's veil. "You're set now."

Eddi gazed at her image in the mirror. The lace-trimmed dress and simple pearls made her skin and hair come alive. She hoped Dave appreciated all the work. With a smile, she turned and gazed at herself from a side angle. Upon Dave's insistent determination to shower her in chocolates and fine dining, she had gained ten pounds in the last year. The last time Eddi fussed over the pounds, Dave proclaimed he liked a size twelve much better than a ten.

Mrs. Boswick rested her hands on Eddi's shoulders and sniffled. "You look nearly as pretty as Jenny and Linda," she quivered out.

"Thanks, Mom," Eddi said with a wry grin.

"I just don't know how you got so grown up like this," Mary continued.

In a rare moment of mother-daughter bonding, Eddi wrapped her arms around her mom and held her close. The smell of her Youth Dew perfume reminded Eddi of a childhood laced with the same fragrance.

"It's all going to be okay," Eddi whispered as the two parted. "The wedding will be over before you know it."

"I just don't know how to act. Jenny's wedding was in a church. Who ever heard of having a wedding way out in the boondocks like this?" Mary complained. She waved her hand as if Dave's estate was a shack.

Eddi released her mother and was exasperated at having to explain her and Dave's choice all over again. After their encore performance the play's first night, Eddi and Dave had become the town's hot item. Never did Eddi expect the community to take such ownership in their romance. For weeks, everyone from Dina to the corner grocer had insisted upon a wedding invitation. Finally, she and Dave decided to limit the guests to their family and the theater's cast, along with a few close friends. Otherwise, they would have had five thousand guests with no church in town big enough to hold them.

"Mom," Eddi said, "Dave and I decided we'd be better off here because everyone would assume it was a small wedding, and we wouldn't have to invite the whole town."

"A small wedding!" Mary exclaimed. "There are a hundred people out there!" She pointed toward the door. "I don't see what it would have hurt to open up a church and add a few more guests to the list."

Baby Nicole whimpered. Mary turned to Linda who scrounged through her diaper bag for a bottle with one hand while clutching Nicole with the other. "Oh, are you hungry, baby?" Mary crooned and stroked the infant's cheeks. "Well, we're *all* hungry, and there won't be any German chocolate for any of us."

"She's driving me crazy," Eddi mumbled under her breath.

"Okay, okay," Jenny responded. "I'll take her down so she can drive Dad crazy."

"Just don't let her throw any tomatoes at him, okay?" Eddi whispered.

Jenny winked and looped her index finger and thumb into an okay sign. Her one-carat solitaire sparkled on her ring finger. Eddi was certain her mother would proclaim the superiority of Jenny's engagement and wedding for the rest of her life. Eddi eyed the modest ruby on her own ring finger. The ring had been Dave's mother's. When he quietly asked if Eddi would like to wear it for her engagement ring, she had been thrilled. She understood the ring meant far more to Dave than the four-carat rock her mother had suggested.

Mary had detested the ruby from the very first time Eddi showed it to her. She had ungraciously asked, "If he's so rich, why can't he buy you something better than that dinky ol' thing?"

Eddi sighed and glanced at Jenny, who tugged on her mother's arm. "Mom," she said, "Eddi's ready. You and I should go on down and wait in the recreation room with Calvin and Dad and the minister."

The doorknob rattled and Edward Boswick's voice floated through a hairline opening. "Is it safe to come in?" he asked.

"Yes, Dad!" Eddi called.

Edward, dressed in a dark suit, stepped inside and glanced around the room. "All the Boswick women together in one place. What a lucky man am I," he teased and closed the door behind him.

"Oh, stop it!" Mary slapped at his arm.

He ignored her and stepped toward his daughter. Without a word, he pulled Eddi close for a tight hug. "I'm so proud of you," Edward rumbled, and Eddi thought she detected an unexpected dash of emotion in his voice.

When they parted, Eddi blinked against her stinging eyes. "Oh, Dad," she said, "thanks."

"You've chosen a man better for yourself than I ever could have." He lowered his voice and continued, "If you weren't my daughter, I'd envy what the two of you have." Edward touched her veil. "How did you get to be all grown up?" he asked.

Eddi gripped his arm. "Go on with Mom," she squeaked. "You're going to make me cry and that won't do."

"Okay, okay." Edward dabbed at his eyes with his handkerchief and raised his voice. "I'll go with your mother and her nerves. They and I have become such good friends through the years, you know."

"Oh, stop it!" Mary demanded from the door. "Come on now. Calvin's waiting on us!"

After patting Eddi's back, Edward followed his wife and eldest daughter from the room. Before closing the door, he gave Eddi the thumbs-up sign. She returned the gesture as her mother's voice seeped back through the doorway. "I believe I love Calvin almost as much as you, Edward. I declare…" The closing door cut off the rest of her words.

The favorite son-in-law, Eddi thought. *At least* Mom's *favorite,* she added and recalled the summer trout fishing expedition that had bonded her father and Dave.

Baby Nicole released a shriek that demanded something be done about her empty stomach. "Oh no!" Linda bleated as she tried to convince Nicole to take the bottle. "She won't have it. I was afraid of this." She lifted the bottle from the baby's face. "This is what I get for breast feeding."

"Here, let me have her," Eddi offered.

"You can't help her!" Linda huffed.

"I know, I know," Eddi agreed and reached for the baby. "But I can keep her occupied while you get ready for her."

"Okay, thanks." Linda released her baby to Eddi's arms and began to wrestle with her dress zipper. "I'm just glad this is happening now and not in thirty minutes—in the middle of your wedding vows."

Eddi half listened to her sister, who had turned into "mother superior" once Nicole arrived. The whole family had watched in amazement as motherhood blossomed Linda into a level of maturity she hadn't demonstrated before. Eddi cooed at the baby and ran her index finger across her cheek. For the thousandth time, she thanked God that her soon-to-be-husband had interfered in Linda and Rick's lives. While Rick wasn't the perfect husband, he, too, had undergone a metamorphosis once Nicole arrived. The diminutive creature in Eddi's arms had somehow done what no other female could. She had wrapped Rick Wallace around her tiny fingers, and there he remained tightly affixed. Much to Eddi's surprise, there were no signs of Rick's committing adultery or abusing Linda. According to Dave, he had even stopped smoking pot for good and was attending church of his own free will.

A firm knock sounded on the door. "Linda!" Rick's concerned call mingled with Nicole's new cry.

Eddi strode to the door, bent, and twisted the knob while holding tight to her bundle. "She's in here."

"I was in the hall and heard Nicole cry," Rick said, his brown eyes full of fatherly concern. "Is everything okay?"

"Yes, she's just hungry." Linda stopped struggling with her dress. "Could you help me here?"

"Sure," he said before reaching for his daughter.

Eddi extended the child to Rick. "Here you are," she said. "I'm ready to go down anyway. I'll just leave you two with your problems," she said through a smile.

"Don't laugh at me, Eddi," Linda demanded. "You'll be doing this sooner than you know."

"Who's laughing?" Eddi blew a kiss to Linda. "I think it's all great." She reached for her bouquet in the wing-backed chair beside the door, stepped into the hallway, and clicked the door closed.

When she looked up, Eddi stared straight into the eyes of her fiancé. Compulsively, she raised the bouquet in front of her face and gasped. "What are you doing here? You aren't supposed to see me before the wedding!"

Dave laughed. "It's my house, remember? You aren't supposed to be out here in the hallway."

Eddi lowered the bouquet and peered at Dave over fresh roses whose fragrance reminded her of Mrs. DeBloom.

"Did your aunt come?" Eddi asked and glanced toward the stairway. As of last month, Mrs. DeBloom was still praying that Dave would repent and marry Brittney O'Reilly.

"Yep. She's here," Dave said with a proud nod. "I told you she'd come around."

With a sigh, Eddi relaxed. "I'm so glad. I don't like her disapproving of me."

"She's got a heart of gold, really, Eddi," Dave claimed. "She just doesn't always show it."

You got that right! Eddi thought but held her tongue.

"Brittney is here, too," Dave said, "with her parents. She brought a friend of the masculine variety." He wiggled his eyebrows.

"Oh, good," Eddi breathed. "I was wondering how I was going to stand her hanging all over my new husband at the reception."

"I wouldn't have allowed it," Dave growled and wrapped his arm around Eddi's waist. "You're the only woman I want hanging on to me."

Eddi's heart warmed. Dave looked better than ever, all dressed up in his black tuxedo and cream-colored shirt.

"You look *so good,*" she breathed.

"Hmmm." Dave adored her with his eyes. "And you look scrumptious, Mrs. Davidson," he said.

"I'm not a Mrs. yet," she said over a giggle.

"No, but we're really close," Dave purred into her ear. "So close I can almost taste it." He playfully nipped her ear, and Eddi released a faint squeal.

"Stop it!" She shoved at his chest. "You're going to mess up my hair and tilt my veil!"

"That's the whole point," he teased.

Breathless, Eddi gazed into his eyes as the harpist's music crescendoed into a classic love ballad.

"You're so beautiful," Dave whispered. "I can't believe you're almost mine."

"Oh, Dave," Eddi complained, "I'm not half as beautiful as some of the women you could have had."

"Like who?" he challenged. "Name one."

"Laura Schock," Eddi pronounced the name without one trace of affection.

"Ah, but my dear," Dave crooned, "you've got something no other woman has ever had—not even Laura Schock."

"And what might that be?" Eddi asked.

"Me," he said and pressed his lips against hers in a promise of things to come.

About the Author

Debra White Smith continues to impact and entertain readers with her life-changing books, including *Romancing Your Husband, 101 Ways to Romance Your Marriage, Friends for Keeps, More than Rubies: Becoming a Woman of Godly Influence,* and the popular Seven Sisters fiction series. She has nearly 40 book sales to her credit and close to a million books in print.

The founder of Real Life Ministries, Debra touches lives through the written and spoken word by presenting real truth for real life and ministering to people where they are. Debra speaks at events across the nation and sings with her husband and children. She has been featured on a variety of media spots, including "The 700 Club," "At Home Live," "Getting Together," "Focus on the Family," "John Maxwell's Thrive Ministry," "Moody Broadcasting Network," and "Midday Connection."

Debra holds an M.A. in English. She is pursuing a second Master's Degree through Trinity Seminary. She lives in small-town America with her husband of 21 years, two children, and a herd of cats.

To write Debra or contact her for speaking engagements, check out her website:

www.debrawhitesmith.com

or send mail to

Real Life Ministries
Debra White Smith
P.O. Box 1482
Jacksonville, TX 75766

Seven Sisters

Second Chances

Marilyn's happy life as a minister's wife ends when her husband leaves. Marilyn begins to piece together a new life that doesn't include a husband or God. When she meets her charming new neighbor, Joshua, her heart begins to awaken. But when she learns that he is a pastor, she decides to cut off all contact. She will not risk her heart again. Joshua is also trying to make a new life of his own, one free from his sinful past. But when a former acquaintance sends him mysterious letters, Joshua realizes that his secret (and his life) are in danger. *Second Chances* is a tender story of redemption, forgiveness, and the healing power of God's love.

The Awakening

Supermodel Kim Lan has beauty, wealth, an engagement to heart-throb Ted Curry, close friends, and a budding faith that seldom interferes with her plans. When a secret admirer sends flowers and notes, Kim is flattered. But as the letters become more possessive, warning signals flash. To escape the mysterious gift-giver, Kim joins a mission outreach to Asia. But coordinator Mick O-Donnel's vision for a quiet, sincere offer of aid is threatened by Kim's celebrity. Sparks fly as their lifestyles clash, their values collide, and they battle an undercurrent of passion. When Kim's "secret admirer" reveals he's close by, Kim desperately turns to the only person in Vietnam she can trust...or can she?

A Shelter in the Storm

*An old southern mansion. A deadly game of cat and mouse. Love that won't surrender....*When Sonsee realized she loved Taylor, discouragement gripped her. He'd made it clear that romance wasn't for him. Struggling to find peace, Sonsee relinquishes her heart to the Lord. But when her father is shot and Taylor is identified as the killer, Sonsee must choose between the "facts" and her heart. Entering a maze of betrayal to search for the murderer, Sonsee and Taylor find a hidden chamber and a family secret. They rediscover their friendship and the freedom to love.

To Rome with Love

Melissa gazed into velvet brown eyes. Kinkaide hadn't changed much in six years. His expressive eyes and vibrant smile brought back memories and images of a time filled with promise and love…a time she thought would last forever. Melissa stepped back. Nothing could break through the barriers surrounding her heart…nothing. And now Kinkaide was standing before her, believing she had accepted his invitation for a Mediterranean excursion. He held out a note signed with her name…a note she had never seen before. Shock slowly softened to interest. Despite his broken promises hope stirred. What if…

For Your Heart Only

Come with me. Come with me. We'll fly to the stars. Lawton's soft invitation lingers in Jacquelyn's mind as she grapples with his abrupt disappearance, his desperate phone call, and the dread filling her heart. Drawing on her detective skills, Jac Lightfoot locates her secret love. But when another attempt is made on his life, Jac and Lawton spring into action. Uncovering a 35-year-old mystery, they plunge into a dark tangle of greed and vengeance. Drawn together for survival, they wrestle with their feelings for each other—and the past that keeps them apart.

This Time Around

After the death of her abusive husband, Sammie, and her young son, Brett, try to begin a new life insulated from the painful past…and protected from future betrayals. When her high school sweetheart takes over day-to-day operations of *Romantic Living* magazine, Sammie intends for their relationship to remain strictly professional…but R.J. has romance on his mind as he becomes aware of an ever-deepening love for Sammie. Will Sammie risk her heart once more and accept R.J.'s promise to love her and her son?

Let's Begin Again

From her beautifully decorated house to the set of her television show, everything Victoria does exudes talent, confidence, and organization. In her tidy world, only one problem stands out—her husband, Tony. Why doesn't he make their marriage a top priority? Tony is frustrated. If he can't measure up to Victoria's standards now, what will happen when she discovers his past? Bogged down in "what ifs," he can't get past the shame in his heart. Until he is shot at. Until he is plunged into a deadly game. Until circumstances strip away the lies. Torn apart by dark secrets and conditional love, can Victoria and Tony find the strength to meet the deadly challenge and face the past together?

Romancing Your Husband

Early days in a relationship are exhilarating, but they can't touch the thrilling love affair you can have now! Cutting through traditional misconceptions and exploring every facet of the Bible's message on marriage, *Romancing Your Husband* reveals how you can create a union others only dream about. From making Jesus an active part of your marriage to arranging fantastic romantic interludes, you'll discover how to—

- make romance a reality
- "knock your husband's socks off"
- become a lover-wife, not a mother-wife
- find freedom in forgiving
- cultivate a sacred romance with God

Experience fulfillment through romancing your husband...and don't be surprised when he romances you back!

101 Ways to Romance Your Marriage

Everyday romance, special nights out, and intimate interludes. These are what true, lasting love is made of. Debra White Smith, author of *Romancing Your Husband* (more than 50,000 copies sold), offers you insightful suggestions, "I love you because" ideas and "wow your spouse" dates, and romantic poems to spice up their relationships.

101 Ways to Romance Your Marriage helps you and your spouse create special moments that will keep your hearts entwined. From simple gestures, such as a lipstick-kissed napkin sprayed with perfume, to romantic weekends that start with a limo ride to a favorite restaurant, the fun and easy applications will add zest to your love life!

Marriage can be the exciting, satisfying experience God intended